PRAISE FOR *KAFKA'S SON* PUBL

"By following a labyrinthian circuit—under the sign of Calvino and Perec—Curt Leviant takes us along the trail of Kafka. Breathtaking! In the dark alleys, we see the ghosts of the past, with a parade of characters so Protean they could have stepped right of 'The Metamorphosis.' Curt Leviant blends fantasy and literary detection, while constructing a stunning maze. His magic lantern superbly recreates Kafka's now-forgotten Prague, a city that resembles a shadow play theater where everything is possible. As to whether or not Kafka had an heir, the answer is obvious. His name is Curt Leviant."

—*LIRE Magazine*

"Halfway between Carol Reed's *The Third Man* and Orson Welles's *Mr. Arkadin,* the wizard Leviant recreates a mythical and fascinating Kafkaslovakia, in a wild baroque style which brings to mind the mirrors scene in *The Lady from Shanghai.* To the delight of the reader, Curt Leviant will not stop at anything improbable. *Kafka's Son* is a thrilling novel." —*Nouvel Observateur*

"Leviant likes to captivate his readers, to dazzle them, to shake them off as he leads them deep into the recesses of his labyrinth, only to find them again unexpectedly." —*Le Monde*

"The most impressive achievement of *Kafka's Son* is the way in which Curt Leviant, after opening up a truly awesome number of different trails, manages to bring them all together to give us the overall picture, just like the pieces of a jigsaw puzzle which suddenly seem to fall into place as if by magic. *Kafka's Son* is a realistic fantasy, a captivating maze, a detective novel, a love story, with multiple layers that never ceases to delight." —*Magazine Litteraire*

"A true literary success. Here Prague reveals itself as a magical, bewitching, mysterious, perplexing city. *Kafka's Son* is fascinating novel that, once finished, tempts you to take the first plane to Prague carrying a pile of Kafka's books." —*Art Press*

"With the genius of a Salman Rushdie, Leviant takes his readers into a kind of cinematic journey. He grabs the reader's attention and keeps him in suspense until the final page." —*Soundbeat Magazine*

Praise for *Diary of an Adulterous Woman*

"Astute character studies drive this sexy, witty, philosophically complex novel. Without sacrificing humor or character development, Leviant manages to write an ingenious romantic farce in the tradition of Vargas Llosa's *Notebooks of Don Rigoberto.*"

—*Publishers Weekly*

"If Milan Kundera lived on Long Island, he might have written this novel, a meditation on love and intimacy. Like David Foster Wallace's *Infinite Jest* or Martin Amis's *The Information*, Leviant has put a post-modernist strategy in service of a character-driven novel with good results." —*Library Journal*

"Lots of fun. Leviant wanders into Harold Pinter's dressing room and ends up hanging out with James Joyce.... A comedy of errors as well as a bedroom farce—and much more." —*Kirkus Reviews*

"Curt Leviant is a leading candidate for the title of best unknown American novelist. *Diary of an Adulterous Woman* is the novel that Tolstoy might have written instead of *Anna Karenina* had he been a modern American writer with an essentially comic sensibility. Compulsively readable and entertaining." —*Sun-Sentinel*

Praise for *Partita in Venice*

"A comic literary narrative with a dash of magical realism and a tone of beguiling romanticism. Leviant has infused the tale with an impressive degree of suspense." —*Sun-Sentinel*

"A madcap adventure…magical telling…told with such infectious delight that it becomes a real joy to read." —*Kirkus Reviews*

"Curt Leviant's *Partita in Venice,* like his previous novels, is a delight."
—Elie Wiesel, Nobel Prize–winning author of *Night*

Praise for *The Yemenite Girl*

"I read straight through without a stop. I don't often read so quickly and with so much interest. I enjoyed every turn of the story.… Shultish is a man with a life of his own…and the celebrity [the Israel Nobel Laureate, one of the heroes of the novel] too is marvelously drawn. *The Yemenite Girl* is done with great tact, feeling, and skill."
—Saul Bellow, Nobel Prize–winning author of *Humboldt's Gift* and *Herzog*

"A passionate story…a true fiction.… The tension between the charm of the text and the intensity of the subtext is what keeps the pages turning." —*New York Times Book Review*

"The best novel I've had the luck to review this year and it may be the best novel many people will have the luck to read. In his first book, Curt Leviant has put together depth, delicacy, full-fleshed characters and gloriana—literature.… The writing is rich and luxurious."
—*Boston Globe*

KAFKA'S SON

Other Fiction by Curt Leviant

The Yemenite Girl
Passion in the Desert
The Man Who Thought He Was Messiah
Partita in Venice
Diary of an Adulterous Woman
Ladies and Gentlemen, the Original Music of the Hebrew Alphabet and *Weekend in Mustara* (two novellas)
A Novel of Klass
Zix Zexy Ztories
King of Yiddish

KAFKA'S SON

Including selections from the

newly discovered Journals of K

Curt Leviant

5220 Dexter Ann Arbor Rd.
Ann Arbor, MI 48103
www.dzancbooks.org

The characters and events in this book are fictitious. Any similarity to real persons, living or dead, is coincidental and not intended by the author.

Designed by Steven Seighman

Library of Congress Cataloging-in-Publication Data

Leviant, Curt.
Kafka's son / by Curt Leviant.—First U.S. edition.
pages ; cm
"Including selections from the newly discovered Journals of K."
ISBN 978-1-938103-38-4 (softcover)
1. Jewish fiction. I. Title. PS3562.E8883K34 2016
813'.54—dc23
2015022768

ISBN: 978-1-938103-38-4

First U.S. Edition: February 2016

Printed in the United States of America

10 9 8 7 6 5 4 3 2 1

For
Dalya and Harry
Dvora and David
Shuly and Alon

CONTENTS

PART ONE

Seven Beginnings 3
At Dinner 56

PART TWO

-1. On the Plane 71
1. Back in Prague 76
2. At the K Museum 82
3. Again the Girl in the Blue Beret 93
4. First Visit to Altneushul 98
5. Looking for Karoly Graf 116
6. Going to the Concert 123
7. Everyone Disappears 133
8. To Eva Langbrot 136
9. To Mr. Klein's Room 144
10. The Dream 160
11. Graf. Filming Hruska. Miss Malaprop on Old Town Square. 164
12. With Marionettes 175
13. Calling Mr. Klein 179
14. Hero to the Rescue 181
14a. Second Version 185
15. Looking for Katya. Filming the Shamesh. Actor Returns. 189
16. Dream, Again 204
17. Visit to Mr. Klein 206

18. In a Dream State 215
19. Back to Altneu 218
20. The Chase 224
21. The Transformation 229
22. The Extra Kroner 241
23. A Message from the Shamesh 250
24. How He Got Better 253
25. A Thirty-Minute Trip 261
26. The Life-and-Death Favor 268
27. An Old Document 271
28. The Eulogy 275
29. In the Altneu Again 283
30. Quandary 293
31. The Letter 296
32. The Old Man Is Out. Guess Who's In? 301
33. In the Mystery Shul 317
34. Resolve and Dissolve 324
35. Exchanging the Secret 327
36. Why the Old Man Fled 334
37. Calling Luongo 341
38. Filming in Restaurant 346
39. About Dora 351
40. Filming, Continued 360
41. Listening to the Tape 364
42. With Her 369
43. Finally, Michele 380

PART THREE

Seven Endings 385
The Journals of K, a Selection 409

I am memory come alive.
—Franz K

Oh, to ride on the borderline of Fable and Truth.
—Based on a remark of Lord Francis Napier of Scotland, 1857

To me this world is all one continued vision of fancy and imagination.
—William Blake

PART ONE:
SEVEN BEGINNINGS

SEVEN BEGINNINGS

1. Call me Amschl 5
2. This is a true story 6
3. Two letters shaped my early years 9
4. Call me Franz 15
5. Summary of beginnings 16
6. Literary infinity 17
7. Eldridge Street Shul meetings 18

BEGINNING 1

Call me Amschl.

All right, so don't call me Amschl.* Nobody does anyway. Except when I'm called up to the Torah by my Hebrew name: Amschl ben Moshe.

---

* pronounced AHM-shl

BEGINNING 2

This is a true story.

True story!?*

Humbug.

I'm sorry I yoked these two words that invariably begin late medieval Jewish folktales, even though I like the phrase "true story" for its literary ring, its trisyllabic succinctness, a kind of rite de passage into a make-believe world where beneficent ghosts—what else?, they're Jewish—often play a part.

But back to true story.

True story, let's face it, is a contradiction in terms, an oxymoron like weather forecaster (the only people in the workforce who, like presidential advisors, are paid for constantly being wrong).

True story, indeed. You have to be either an ox or a moron to hold credible that coupling. True story belongs in the same oxymoronic oxcart with dark light, sweet lemon, military intelligence.

Either a narrative is true or it's a story.

It cannot be both.

Period.

End of story.

* Or: True story?!

But you know what?

Come to think of it—

I changed my mind. I just said a narrative is either true or it's a story; it cannot be both.

On second thought, mine can.

And is.

A true story.

BEGINNING 3

Two letters shaped my early years. Isn't it strange to have part of the alphabet influence your life? Here's where true becomes story and story becomes true.

The letter was "K."

But that's only one letter, you say. What's the other? The other was also "K." One "K" for Danny; the other, Franz.*

Now one doesn't readily draw a line or connect the dots between Danny K and Franz K. But with me they are inextricably linked. Here's how:

In my teens and up through my first year or so in college, people said I looked like the first K. They said I moved like him, had his gestures, his ease of mimicry, his comic timing. Who knows? Perhaps in admiring—even adoring—him so much from childhood, something rubbed off. For a while I could actually get away with saying I was Danny K's son. Truth is, I loved his films and personal

---

* Curiously, in Hebrew, the K sound can be two letters, *kaf* and *coof.* (There's also a third K, but no one knows about it because, like a cat tracking on padded feet, it makes no sound; like a lost chord, the history of this third K sound hasn't been chronicled yet.)

Even curiouser, in English there are more letters and combinations thereof for the K sound than for any other: k, c, ch, ck, cq, q, x.

appearances long before people (usually girls) told me of the resemblance. I danced well, had a good sense of humor, sang, and eventually learned to imitate his double-talk and to lip-sync his greased lightning presto Russian composer's song, which I would perform at college parties. When I was a youngster, my beloved Uncle Monia, a lifelong bachelor like the other K, would take me to see Danny K in person in New York. We would arrive at the theater in time to see the stage show—even now as I write this, the excitement of seeing Danny come out slowly from the wings as if teasing the audience, a smile on his face, his quirky, little boy's giggle, and a wave of laughter and applause fills the theater, even now I feel the thrill and anticipation overwhelm me—and then we see the feature film, and then—rapture!—stay for another stage show, which with Danny K was entirely different from the first show. (In those days, they didn't clear the movie theater after each show like they do now. Also, in those days, we had more time on our hands. We were able to stretch time, expand time, save time.) Oh, the joy of seeing Danny K twice.

Years later, when I was grown, I saw him in person, when he had a show on Broadway. How did I get to see him, me, a guy whom Danny K had never heard of? First, I wrote to his publicist in Hollywood, but she turned me down. Then I called the New York theater house manager, said I'd spoken to someone at the studio and they said to contact him, that it'd be okay since I was a filmmaker. The house manager, a decent chap, told me to address the envelope to him and he would see that Danny gets it. I wrote Danny c/o the theater manager and included an ad for my documentary film about Sholom Aleichem's children. I figured: one Jewish humorist to another, and wrote that I want to present him with a video of my first documentary, which I had made last year.

To my good fortune, the manager wrote back inviting me to visit Danny after one of his Wednesday matinees—to just come to the stage door with this letter.

Danny K welcomed me in a light blue robe, as if he'd just taken a shower after the show. I was surprised how tall he was.

For in his films one never got a handle on his height. Maybe because he never stood still. I thought I was tall and lanky but Danny, at six foot two, towered over me. He was very cordial, asked me to be seated, and expressed an interest in how a very young filmmaker had made the Sholom Aleichem documentary. We chatted a few minutes more and then, realizing how exhausted he must be after a performance, I thanked him and said goodbye. Only after I left did a flood of questions I should have asked him inundate me.

The moments I had with him slipped away like a trout in water. I wanted to relive, replay my time with Danny, but all I was left with was a fading, vacuous aura and a vague hunger for more. Even as I shut the door behind me I already felt a strange sense of loss, palpable as pain.

Like Danny K, I had a long aquiline nose, light brown wavy hair combed straight back, although his hair had a more reddish tinge. During my second or third year in college, my hair darkened and my features sharpened. With shorter hair my ears protruded somewhat. Even my humor became more serious.

I became more interested in books and literature than patter songs and imitating Danny K. People (different people from the aforementioned) began saying I resembled the other K. My God, you could be K's son, they told me. Well, I am, I would joke, parlaying my old other K routine with just a change of first name. Actually, my beloved Uncle Monia looked more like Franz K than I did. *He* could have passed for K's son, for his resemblance to K was far stronger than mine.

If character is fate, as Paracelsus—or is it Heraclitus?—once wrote, then looks is not a distant second. What, or whom, you look like can also direct, or at least influence, your path in life.

In fact, the affinity to the other K seemed so strong (in other people's eyes, not mine) that a wonderful gym teacher I had in college, Mr. Schuman was his name, once spoke to me about it.

One September, in the beginning of my junior year, he told me:

"Boy, have you grown over the summer! And you've changed too. You look like—" and he stopped. "Have you read anything by Franz K?"

Now *there's* an oxymoron: a gym teacher who likes literature.

"Sure."

"Ever see a picture of him?" Mr. Schuman asked me.

"No."

"Well, find one and you'll see you look like him. Tall. On the thin side. High cheekbones. Serious demeanor. Even, no offense meant, slightly protruding ears."

I looked through biographies and found a photograph of K as a young man. I wondered if I too should sport a derby and an old-fashioned, rounded high-collar white shirt to enhance the resemblance.

A few years later I bumped into Mr. Schuman at the Brooklyn Academy of Music, which was presenting the Czech National Theater's staging of *The Trial.* We met in the lobby during intermission.

I introduced myself and asked if he remembered me.

"Of course. How are you? What are you doing now?"

I told him I was taking a Master's in film at NYU and asked good-humoredly if I still looked like K.

Mr. Schuman studied my face.

"Even more than ever. Now you could really pass as his son."

"If he had one."

"Of course, if he had one. How could you pass as K's son if he didn't have children?"

I didn't answer right away, for I was stuck on a little word. If. I could write—*if* I were to write, *if* I could write—a complete dissertation on that word. That tiny word, I thought, is the engine for all of imaginative literature. *If* I were a mouse called Josephine. *If* I were a gigantic insect. *If* I were an animal in the synagogue. *If* K had a son.

"On the other hand," Mr. Schuman continued, "in a K-esque world anything is possible."

"Except skipping generations. I'm too young to be K's son."

"All right," he conceded. "Then grandson."

"If… But it defies logic."

"You're too logical, my boy. We're not in the gym, where parallel bars are always parallel. In space, Einstein said, parallel bars meet… Stretch your imagination."

I laughed. I closed my eyes. I tried to stretch.

Then I said:

"I suppose you won't find it hard to swallow the news that, despite the nearly three decades that separate my alleged daddy's death in 1924 and my birth in 1951, K sent some of his genes to a lab which my parents then bought and had implanted in my mother's placenta."

"Now that's what I call a good stretch," Mr. Schuman said. "Now you're ready for parallel bars that meet in space."

So much for letters.

Let's now turn to sounds.

Can sounds determine a person's course for—or in—life?

Listen.

I was a good baby, a pleasant child. How do I know? My parents said I was obedient. Even the first sounds I made pointed to agreement, acquiescence.

Where other babies' first sounds are "M…m…m…" for "Mama," *my* first sound sounded like "OK." The initial vowel was a truncated non-sound, compressed and sort of swallowed, something like an African click, followed by the robust "k."

"Want your botty now?"

" —k."

"Want to go beddy-bye?"

" —k."

"Come help me clean up, sweetie."

" —k."

When I was two, I learned the alphabet ditty, sung to the tune of "Twinkle, Twinkle, Little Star," stolen from Haydn's Surprise

Symphony No. 94, which in turn was swiped from Mozart's "*Ah, vous dirai-je, Maman*," or vice versa. When I got to "k," I invariably let out a sound that some called a giggle, others a squeal. I loved that letter, loved that sound. Now that I think of it and try to recreate the sound I might have uttered years ago, it was probably more like a nasalized "N-kay." Even then I was already showcasing the importance of that letter later in my life.

Years after, people said of me: "He knew even back then, that prescient little *mamzer*."

BEGINNING 4

"Call me Franz,"

was one of the ways I wanted to begin. To tease you. Alert you. Mystify you. Entice you. But it was just a thought. Not a serious one. A fleeting thought. Because why give things away? So this opening is just a hint of what might have been. A thought that bobbed up like a cork but was at once suppressed by my heavy authorial palm.

For that imagined opening was really a trifle. Only a lure. As false as the swaggly little faux fish near the hook. Which isn't a fish at all but a sidekick of the hook, silent partner to the hook. Not fish important here but hook. Not décor but bite. And you are the fish and by that false beginning I wanted to lure you into these pages, into a magic world of gold dust and rainbows, orchids and light.

BEGINNING 5

There are so many ways to begin a book. I could begin to tell this story with:

"Call me Amschl."

Or:

"Call me Franz."

Or:

"This is a true story."

Or:

I don't know where to begin.

OK, how about?

Prague was open, the communists gone, the spires in the city coruscating with the magic of rainbow colors they sucked in with the onset of freedom, colors hidden during the decades over which communism greyed the city, made it slower and somber, obdurate as a concrete wall.

Or this one:

One Sabbath morning early in October, I sat in the recently renovated Eldridge Street Synagogue, one of New York's historic Lower East Side shuls…

BEGINNING 6

I could keep on going forever with beginnings and never get to the middle or end, trying for a kind of literary infinity. As long as you keep commencing, you see, there are no fears for ending. For ending is what all of us fear.

BEGINNING 7

So how did I get to Prague in the first place? What was the revolving wheel that cast me over there to that gorgeous city, so real to me that even now I can grasp its spires and mold the fog that drapes the city at dawn to any building silhouette I wish? Why Prague and not anywhere else? It wasn't chance, like the little steel ball that is rolled down into the roulette wheel, suddenly thrust into the vortex of a spinning mass, and cast quickly out until chance has it land on one number or another.

Or maybe it was chance. If destiny is chance.

But to get to Prague, my Prague, that magical city, you can't just go to Prague. There are steps you have to go through, steps you must ascend. Imagine a batter at home plate. He has to reach home—but he's home already. But no, in order to reach home he has to go to certain places, round certain bases, and only then, if he's lucky, can he come home home.

My Prague began in New York City (to be precise, it actually began years ago in Prague), and I didn't reach home until I had ascended steps and rounded bases.

First step, Jiri.

But I'm getting ahead of myself.

It all began in one of New York's historic Lower East Side synagogues, the Eldridge Street Shul, which, after years of work, had recently been restored to its late-nineteenth-century splendor. The *New York Times* ran a feature story with several photos that drew me there for Sabbath services.

One shabbes morning early in October I sat in the shul. The sun through the old stained-glass windows created a warm, rosy ambience amid the red oak pews and the wooden bimah. I was surprised to see about twenty older men scattered around the men's section. I had assumed few Jews still lived in the area.

I didn't pay much attention to the man one row before me, whose black yarmulke and head of grey hair were in my peripheral vision, until it came to the Torah reading. I had been too busy looking at the shul's interior space, the lamps and old brass chandeliers, the women's gallery upstairs, and the grand, hand-carved Holy Ark.

But then I heard his sunny voice lovingly explaining a verse from Noah to an older man next to him. I closed my eyes to concentrate. Suddenly, I was a little boy, enchanted by the words of a beloved teacher; I floated in a green meadow, craggy peaks before me, unafraid of the winding *wanderweg* that led down deep into the valley because I knew an older brother was watching over me, and I basked in a happiness that comes only in childhood.

The man's gentle comments on Noah and the dove mesmerized me; his sweet words washed over me. I hadn't heard a voice like that before. The music and intonations of his European-accented English sounded familiar but I couldn't place it. Then I opened my eyes to look at him. He was probably in his mid-to-late sixties, with an aristocratic face, a self-prepossessed but not smug look. His round glasses added a touch of élan. Such faces, proclaiming their social status, tend to fence themselves in, if not thrust you away. Not his. His had an openness, a warmth, especially his brown, deepset Jewish eyes.

I have a simpatico for these old European Jewish men, whose numbers, sadly, dwindle from year to year. One look and I know the outline of these Holocaust survivors' histories. But I want to know details, for they could have been my uncles, grandfathers, had not the enemy murdered them. Perhaps I am drawn to them because of the grandparents I never knew, since both my father and mother were survivors too.

Noticing a newcomer in the congregation, the gabbai approached to give me an aliya. Just then the man in front of me—the man with the sunny voice and aristocratic face—rose and went to the entrance door. I wanted to talk to him. I imagined myself splitting in two. One me went up to the bimah; the other followed him, even though it's disrespectful to run the other way when one is summoned to the Torah.

"Your name?" said the gabbai.

"Amschl ben Moshe."

All during the Torah reading I could barely concentrate on the unfolding Noah and the Flood narrative. I wondered if the man with the sunny voice would return, like the dove with an olive leaf, or if he had gone home. Happily, just as I was making my way to my seat, I saw him coming back too.

At the end of the service, he bent forward to the next row and from the little book holders behind the pews pulled out some candy wrappers and crumpled napkins that others had inconsiderately stuffed in there. It wasn't fitting, he seemed to say, for refuse to share space with the holy books.

As the worshippers were streaming out of the shul, we stood in the Indian summer warmth outside and spoke. By now he had exchanged his yarmulke for a dark blue beret. A few of the congregants wished him, "Gut shabbes, doctor." I introduced myself and he told me his name: Jiri—Yirmiyahu in Hebrew, after the prophet Jeremiah—Krupka-Weisz.

"When I heard you explaining the Torah verses to that older man next to you with such patience and love, I said to myself: I must speak to him. I must get to know him. Your remarks about Noah and the dove sounded like a loving lullaby, and I felt myself transported to Eden-like, flower-filled fields."

"You put it very nicely, even poetically, but you're making a, how shall I express it colloquially, a big deal out of it."

But I wasn't making a big deal. I wasn't exaggerating. He spoke with an *edelkeyt* one doesn't encounter very often.

"You must be a wonderful teacher because I remember what you said. The Torah's verses are eternal truths. What the Torah says, for instance, about the dove and the olive leaf is not something that happened only once. It can happen again. Like the pots of olive oil the prophet Elisha gave the poor woman, as we read in the Bible. These verses, you told the old man, are just models for what happened and can, and did, happen again."

Jiri looked uncomfortable with my praise.

"I just did what anyone who knows the Torah would do," he said softly. "Plus a bit of my own insights."

What impressed me was that Jiri hadn't made the other man feel inadequate. Ingeniously, he made him feel as if *he* were teaching *Jiri*. For after Jiri had asked him to retell in his own words what he had learned, Jiri said: "With your explanation the verses are even clearer to me than ever before."

He had a magical voice, I told him. "There was a Greek Jewish philosopher, I think it was Aristopholus, who said that a man's voice is a mirror of his soul."

Jiri looked down, then back up at me shyly. "If you'll excuse me, but I think you're conflating two names: Aristophanes and Aristobulus."

"Yes, Dr. Krupka-Weisz, you're right."

"Still, it's remarkable you remembered that quote."

"Well, it's the only quote of his I know. Not that I read his work. I had read that line somewhere, maybe in a novel, and I was taken by the thought. It's so right on the mark."

"There were several kings and their sons during the first two centuries BCE named Aristobulus," Jiri said. "But you're probably referring to the Jewish Hellenistic philosopher Aristobulus of Paneas."

"If you say so." And I smiled.

He smiled too, then we both broke into a merry laugh.

"I'm trying to place your accent but can't seem to do it."

"I'm from Prague."

"Really? I've never met anyone from Prague before. Jews with accents here are either from Poland, Russia, or Germany."

"It's my hometown. Why so excited?"

"Because that's where I was born."

Now Jiri's face lit up. "I knew you looked familiar," he joked. I could have sworn a flush came over his cheeks. He took a step closer to me. "But I hear no accent in *your* English."

"Because my parents of blessed memory brought me here as a baby."

"Did they survive in Prague?"

"Not quite. It's a long story, which I'll tell you some other time. But after the war their work brought them for a period of time to Prague… And you, Dr. Krupka-Weisz, how did you survive?"

"Please call me Jiri… My story too is a long one. But I ended up in Theresienstadt, or Terezin."

"I know an older Czech writer, a filmmaker like me, who also survived in Terezin."

"Who?"

"Arnošt Lustig. Do you know him?"

Jiri laughed. "What a question. Of course I know Arnošt. But he's from Prague too."

"Oh, my goodness. Of course. I just blanked out on that…I knew your accent had a familiar melody."

"Little Arnošt!" And Jiri's laughter rolled on. "I remember his mama pushing him in his pram when he was a baby, in 1926 or '27. I must have been thirteen or fourteen then, but I can still see the scene, even describe the fancy shiny dark blue pram he was in, as though it were happening now."

"I'll have to tell him that next time I see him…"

"Well, when you do, give him my regards, and ask him if he's stopped crying when his mama puts his bonnet on." And Jiri laughed again. "He was such an adorable baby with big blue eyes… Interestingly enough, we were both in Terezin at the same time and we both ran away from Prague at the height of our professions. But Arnošt left in 1968, many years before me."

"Excuse me, Jiri, but you said you were thirteen or fourteen in the late 1920s. How is that possible, when you look sixty-four or sixty-five?"

"I'm eighty, my boy. Born in 1913."

"That's amazing."

"Perhaps it's good genes. Members of our family, if they survived the Germans, live long lives and look younger than their years."

I looked at him. By no means did he look eighty. There was a vigor in him, even a youthfulness. He had a head of greying hair; he stood erect; his eyes sparkled. Should I now bid him "gut shabbes," tell him it was a joy to meet him, and say I hope we'll meet again? For indeed I had decided to come back here next Saturday. I meant what I said. I wanted to get to know him. Something ineffable drew me to him. Meanwhile, as these thoughts tumbled, we looked at each other as though we were conversing. I wondered what he was thinking. Was he too wondering what thoughts ran through my mind? But I realized I didn't want to leave him just yet, so I asked:

"Why did you stay in Czechoslovakia after the war?"

Jiri looked down at the sidewalk. The sun shone on the little stone fragments embedded in the concrete. They glittered in the light like tiny gems. The little clusters of people who had gathered to chat after services had gone. We were now alone in front of the shul. The street was as quiet as a country lane.

"My wife and son were killed…"

I felt a tweak in my heart. "I'm so sorry."

He nodded pensively. "But I still had some family in Prague. You see, Polish survivors couldn't go home, and if they did, couldn't stay. The Poles threatened them, made life miserable for them, even killed them a year after the war. But the people of Prague, the Czechs in general, are more humane. They hated the Germans too. Remember Lidice?"

"I certainly do. The Germans killed every man in that town in revenge for the killing of the SS leader Heydrich."

"And what's more, I had a profession to return to."

"Doctor?"

"Doctor yes, physician no. I have a PhD in Jewish history."

"A professor at the university?"

Jiri shook his head. "No, but a researcher and archivist at the Jewish Museum. My specialty was the history of Prague Jewry."

"The famous Jewish Museum?"

"The one."

"Did you have a good career there?"

He looked over my head, as if seeing Prague, the Jewish Museum, maybe even his office.

"For a while. Eventually, I became the director. But after the 1968 Soviet invasion, it became more difficult. The Czechs wanted to out-Soviet the Russians. I muddled through, as one of Dickens' characters says, another twelve years until 1980 and then, while on a business trip to London, I decided not to return. Later, I came to the USA and got a part-time position here in New York's Jewish Museum."

"And now?"

"Retired for five years, with some occasional consulting. And you? You said something about films."

"Yes. I make documentaries. Videos are my specialty."

"Do you have your own studio? A big staff?"

"Oh no. I basically do all the work myself. I'm the photographer, editor, director, writer, idea man. A solo artist."

"And has it gone well for you?"

"I think so. A couple of my films were shown in Cannes. One, about Sholom Aleichem's family, on the Public Television Network and another one on NPR."

"National Public Radio? How do they manage to show a film on radio?"

I laughed. "Good question. It was on *All Things Considered*. They played some excerpts from the audio of my film on Dutch Jews hidden as children on farms during World War II, and then they did an interview with me."

"How wonderful! And Prague, have you ever been back to Prague?"

"No. I didn't want to visit under communism. People told me it was a depressing place. In fact, it was Arnošt Lustig who said the people are grey, the buildings are grey, the sky is grey."

"Very true, but now," Jiri said, "for the past three years..."

"I know. I heard the change is striking since the fall of communism. In fact, I'm thinking about going soon. I have an idea for a film."

"About whom, if I may ask?"

"How can one make a film in Prague without reference to Jews, to the Altneu Synagogue, to the golem, to K?"

"Good. Excellent." Jiri actually clapped his hands in approval. "Go now. Now is the time. The country is free. No one will follow you. You won't have to look over your shoulder. And I'll send you to someone who will introduce you to interesting people."

"That's so kind of you. I can't wait to start that documentary. I feel that's where the real world is. In films. And you, have you been back?"

"Yes. Just once. Two years ago. But I didn't feel comfortable there anymore..." Jiri looked back at the synagogue, as if he didn't want to elaborate on his visit. "Seems to me this is your first time here, right? Any special occasion that brings you to the Eldridge Street Shul?"

"Let me put it this way," I explained. "I'm not a regular shul-goer, but when I'm in a foreign city, or, like today, have the opportunity of seeing a historic synagogue, especially after the *New York Times* feature, I make it my business to go."

After bidding goodbye to Jiri, I took the yarmulke off my head, put it into my pocket, and made my way home.

A week later I returned to the shul—to see Jiri again. Once more we chatted outside after services, but this time he said:

"How about coming up to my apartment for Kiddush? It's only a few blocks from here." And in fatherly fashion he took me by the arm.

In the book-filled living room of his small apartment, he introduced me to Betty. I had expected to see an equally aristocratic woman. Instead, I saw a small, stocky, rather coarse-looking hausfrau. As European as Jiri looked, so Betty looked American. Traces of her Lower East Side background dotted her speech. What a mismatched pair, I thought. A professorial type with a working-class woman. How did this happen? Her Sabbath garb astonished me too. She wore a short-sleeved blue sweater and dark brown slacks, not the dress or skirt one would expect on a woman whose husband had just attended an Orthodox shul. Contrasting the warm, good-natured expression in Jiri's eyes was the furrowed-brow look of suspicion she gave us as we walked in and wished her "gut shabbes."

"Imagine. He was also born in Prague," a smiling Jiri told her with a bounce in his voice.

"Your parents are Czech?" she asked.

"No."

"Then why were you born in Prague?"

I saw Jiri put both hands out, palms facing her, as if telling her to slow the pace of her inquisition.

"You see," I answered her, "my parents were both survivors, my mother Polish, my father French of Polish descent. They met in Italy after the war. Then they got a job with a Jewish relief agency and were transferred to Prague. And that's where I was born."

"What year?"

"Betty!"

"That's okay. The young man is not a woman who has to hide her age. If he has something to hide he'll tell me and I'll shut up. Do you have something to hide?"

"That's not the point," the exasperated Jiri said. "He hardly came through the door and already you're asking him so many personal questions."

"It's all right," I said, uncomfortable with marital discord. "I was born in 1951."

Betty thought a minute. "So you're forty-two. You look much younger, mister. You seem more like thirty."

"That's what everyone says. I always looked thirty, even when I was fourteen."

Jiri laughed gaily, but no smile cracked Betty's stolid countenance.

"Are you…" she started to say, but Jiri interrupted:

"Now I see it…" he said suddenly, loudly too, as if to override Betty's as yet unsaid words.

At this, perhaps piqued that Jiri had cut her off, Betty marched back to the kitchen. I heard dish closet doors opening and closing and the clatter of crockery.

"Now I see it," Jiri said softly as he inspected my face. He leaned back like an artist viewing his model. "I've been thinking about it ever since I saw you last shabbes and now I see it. Do you know who you resemble?"

Of course I knew it. I've always known it, but I wanted him to say it. Surely Jiri didn't know Danny K. But he did know his hometown hero, the other K.

"Who?" I said innocently, all guile.

"K as a young man. The resemblance is quite remarkable. Especially when you laugh."

When could he have seen K laugh? I wondered.

"Some people say that after a while husband and wife start to resemble each other," was my response. Oops, I shouldn't have said that. What a comedown for Jiri if he would start to look like Betty. But if he caught the slip he was too gracious to react. "When I was younger people would say I looked like Danny K, you know, the comedian and film star. But ever since my later years in college my well-read friends say I look like the other K. Which leads me to conclude that if you read a lot of a writer's work you begin to look like him. As if reader and book are husband and wife."

"Have you read much of K?"

"Every word he's written."

"Bravo! So few Americans read him. In that case, I have a treat for you. Come here." And he led me to a shelf filled with K's books in the original German.

"Look." Jiri pointed at a book. "You'll appreciate this." He pulled out *Meditation.* "You know this one?"

"Sure. His first book. 1911."

"Open to the title page."

"I don't believe it… My God, little shivers are running across my face." I looked at Jiri. "An autographed copy of K's first book?" I stared at K's signature. "What a historic document! What a collector's item! How did they let you out with a treasure like this?" I gave the book back to him.

"As head of the Jewish Museum in 1980, I had a diplomatic passport. They wouldn't, didn't, touch my luggage."

"Please let me see it again." I carefully opened to the title page and absorbed—drank in—K's handwritten name.

"Poor K," I said as I held the book that K had once held in his hands. I thrilled to the touch as if I'd shaken hands with him. "Poor K. Why couldn't a wonderful man like him have married and had children? I always felt so sorry for him and for that romance that could not be with Dora Diamant. For her too I always had a special simpatico. A lost love is always so sad. Poor Dora. Poor K. Poor us."

Jiri opened his mouth as if to say something. I saw him inhale prior to speaking. But he held back.

Then he said, "Right. Poor us. Poor us is right."

I was sorry I spoke. Jiri had lost his wife and child and I was bemoaning a lost love.

"How did you get this book, if I may ask?"

In reply Jiri just ticked his head up in Middle Eastern fashion, raised eyebrows and eyes, as if to say: Only Allah knows. I should have known better than to ask.

As I reverently replaced the book on the shelf, I noticed a little framed snapshot. A sad photo of a woman and a five- or six-year-old boy, both unsmiling in the European fashion. Obviously, Jiri's murdered wife and young son. She had a demure 1930s hairdo and wore a dark dress with a white collar. Her right hand was around the boy. His head was tilted and his right index finger pressed his cheek.

Now Betty reappeared, drying her hands on a dishcloth.

"Are you married?" she asked, finishing the sentence she had started some minutes earlier.

"Enough, Betty. Please. You're asking too many personal questions."

"Let him tell me." Betty faced me. "You. You tell me, mister. Am I asking you too many personal questions?"

Then, surprising me, she quickly told Jiri something in a language I didn't understand. How could she possibly know Czech if I couldn't imagine her speaking anything but English? But before I had a chance to tell her I didn't mind her questions, she turned and left the room again, sulking.

"It's all right. It's okay," I said loudly so she could hear me in the kitchen. "I'm not married now."

She stood in the doorway.

"But you were?"

I nodded.

"And you're not looking, a nice young man like you?"

"I can't say I'm looking, but I do keep my eyes open, if you know what I mean."

"Then—"

"Let's make Kiddush," Jiri sang out. He asked me to follow him into the tiny kitchen. Here Betty had prepared wine, three glasses, and several small salads.

I listened to Jiri's beautiful chant, a blend of the typical East European melody with a touch of a Western mode.

"Help yourself," Jiri said.

"Thank you. Is there any meat in any of them?"

"You don't eat meat, mister? What are you, some kind of vegetarian or something?"

"Yes."

"Me too," said Jiri. "So please help yourself, my boy."

As we ate we spoke about the shul, the neighborhood, its relative tranquility. Betty remained silent. She slowly ate egg salad and hardly looked at us. Then Jiri invited me to lunch. I caught the astonished look on Betty's face, just like the one I had noticed when Jiri brought me, the surprise guest, into the apartment.

"Sorry, I can't make it today."

"Then some other time," was Jiri's quick response.

I addressed my "Thank you" to both of them. But before I had a chance to say goodbye, Jiri said he'd accompany me downstairs. My tendency is to run down—even up—flights of stairs, but in deference to Jiri I slowed my pace.

"Since I got to know you," I told him on the steps, "I'm even more excited about my trip to Prague."

"When you get there, be sure to seek out Yossi, an old family friend, almost a relative. He's always in the rear corner of the Altneushul weekday mornings, at seven. A tall man with a big face. You can't miss him. Tell him I sent you and give him my regards."

Outside, Jiri put his hand on my shoulder. I thought he would begin to apologize for his wife's behavior—if indeed they were husband and wife, for I had my doubts. Not once did I hear Jiri say the words "my wife"; in fact, he didn't even introduce Betty that way. And Betty neither called Jiri by name nor referred to him as "my husband." Between them nothing meshed, nothing matched. Intellectually, they were acres apart. He, Mitteleuropa intelligentsia; she, Bronx fishwife, now in the Lower East Side Diaspora. He, of refined, noble features; she, a graceless face, which didn't stop her from looking at herself in the mirror each time she came from the kitchen to the living room. His, a softly modulated voice; hers, rather strident.

"I'm so glad we met," Jiri said, his eyes misting.

"I feel the same."

Then, like brothers meeting after a long separation, we spontaneously embraced. Like in trick photography, we blended for a moment, maybe even exchanged places. It seemed I had become diaphanous, amorphous, felt myself cloud thin, boneless. I had the mass of a ghost, felt my rib cage swathing through his and sensed him moving through me like a wind with a soul. For a moment I didn't even know how, when, I was.

I returned to the Eldridge Street shul the following Saturday too—but Jiri wasn't there. The gabbai told me why.

"Dr. Krupka-Weisz called yesterday from Beth Israel."

"The hospital? My goodness, what happened?"

"He didn't tell me. But if you want to see him, he's in Room 233."

"Have you seen his wife?"

"Wife? I didn't know Dr. Krupka-Weisz was married. Are you a personal friend?"

"I just became acquainted with him here a couple of weeks ago. Remember, you gave me an aliya?"

"Of course. Amschl ben Moshe."

I marveled at his memory.

"That's a gabbai's job. To have memory."

"Room 233? I'll go see him soon. Probably tomorrow."

"I will too," the gabbai said.

That night I dreamt of Jiri, even though I usually dream only of abstract people or close family. I'm in a subway car, locale unknown, and I see him sitting opposite me. He gives me an OK sign. He opens a book by K and from it flies a dove. It flutters around the car until it spots a man holding a bouquet from which the dove pulls a tiny leaf. The dove brings the green leaf to me. Again Jiri gives me the OK sign. Then I notice Betty, stolid Betty, sitting there too, and she, even she, allows me a small smile.

It was a shock to see Jiri in bed. His head was uncovered and his round glasses were on the nightstand. He was pale but wasn't attached to an IV. I didn't know if that was a good or a bad sign. Some kind of monitor that looked like a stereo receiver intermittently flashed thin red lines on a small screen.

"Oh," he said, a happy smile crinkling his wan features. "How did you know I was here?"

"Easy. I saw the gabbai in shul yesterday. How are you feeling?"

"So-so." And he spread his hands in a gesture of resignation. "Maybe my good genes are getting tired."

Above Jiri's head a framed print hung on the wall. It was a happy Miro design full of swirling colors, starbursts of yellow and chartreuse and burnt orange, and, if you stared long enough, the seeming outline of a smiling face.

I almost didn't notice Betty in the easy chair. Her dark blue sweater and slacks melted into the blue chair and only her swarthy face was seen.

"I'm so glad you came," Jiri said. "I was thinking about you."

"And I missed you in shul yesterday, and so did the old man you helped last time."

"Ay, ay, *bruderl, der mentch tracht un Gott lacht,*" he quoted the Yiddish apothegm. "Man makes plans but God laughs; or, man proposes but God disposes."

I liked that Yiddish word, *bruderl.* It meant, literally, "little brother," but was used to signify "pal," "buddy," "good friend."

To change the mood, I said enthusiastically, "Well, I'm going..."

Up piped Betty. "But you just came, mister. Stay another few minutes."

"I didn't finish. I wanted to say that I'm starting to work on plans for my trip to Prague."

"Wonderful," said Jiri. "Don't forget Yossi at the Altneu. He'll be a good *shadchen,* a good matchmaker, for you," here he took a deep breath and sighed slowly, "to meet interesting people. When I go back home, I'll give you more names and addresses. But Yossi is the key."

In response, as a gesture of friendship, I was about to share with Jiri a fascinating bit of personal information that few people knew, but just then Betty began speaking that language she had used briefly in their apartment last week. This time Jiri responded.

The language was so unfamiliar I couldn't even place it. Betty spoke more than Jiri. I picked up the shards of her words, tried to reconstruct them, but they fell apart like dry clods. It was like working with a jigsaw puzzle not only on the verso side but with the little rounded tentacles snipped off. What I was able to dredge up fit no language, no syntax, I knew. I had a hunch it wasn't Czech. In fact, I was sure it wasn't.

Then two phrases surfaced. Each was two words and the first was the same in both phrases. Again and again I heard Betty exclaim "tara pilus" and "tara glos." Jiri repeated the phrases but preceded them with "nepa"—"nepa tara pilus," "nepa tara glos." After a while, among the jibble jabble, bibble babble, I gathered that the phrases meant "too young" and "too old," and that "nepa" was a negative—with Jiri arguing "not too young" and "not too old."

How did I penetrate those phrases? I'll tell you how. Why did they use them? I'll tell you why. The how is fact, the why speculation. I kept hearing the word "tara" before "pilus" and before "glos." So I assumed it was a modifier. Then, once or twice, when Betty said "tara pilus," she stretched her hand, palm down flat, and lowered it to the floor, as if indicating a child or young person; one other time, when she said "tara glos," she ran her thumb and forefinger over her chin, as if stroking the hairs of an imaginary beard. It then dawned on me that "tara pilus" meant "too young" and "tara glos" too old. That's the how.

The why is guesswork. Perhaps they wanted me to get the hint and when—and if—the time (whatever time it was) came, to act accordingly. Then again, even if I was right on those phrases, what did they have to do with me? If it had *any*thing to do with me. And, anyway, what was I too young or too old for?

Then, suddenly—as if in mid-phrase—Betty said:

"So you were born in Prague, right, mister?"

I nodded, amazed that at last I was understanding their language. It took a moment for me to realize that she had spoken English. Betty and Jiri exchanged glances; then, without so much as a pause, or shift in gears, they resumed speaking.

Nevertheless, despite my frustration, their language fascinated me. I almost didn't want them to stop. I felt I had landed in an undiscovered bourne, was hearing something no one had heard before. Did they speak in etymons or glyphs, metaphors or metonyms? I don't know. I was hypnotized, paid scant attention to the hum of the hospital, Jiri's shifting positions in bed, Betty's rocking motion as she spoke, the coming and going of nurses, the stereo broadcasting its zigzag thin red lines. All I know is I didn't understand a word. No, that's not quite so. I *could* understand a word, about one in seventy. I understood but couldn't grasp its meaning. The words came to me in spurts. As if a radio was on and every few seconds the volume knob was suddenly turned left and right, erratically, maliciously. It sounded like waves rushing, as if someone had clapped palms over my ears, then opened and shut them, oo-wah, oo-wah, oo-wah, the rush, the arrhythmic swoosh of words, then silence. Maybe they were using reverse phonemes, or perhaps articulating logographic symbols.

But there were moments—like in a fleeting daydream or in an exhaustion-induced, sleep-deprived hallucination, the sort of one-second waking dream that seems to last for minutes—when I thought I understood them, and I imagined myself in Prague (I knew they were speaking of Prague even though they didn't mention Prague; how could they *not* be speaking of Prague?), in some exotic, surprising locale, discovering people and sites no one knew of, like perhaps a secret entrance to the Altneu synagogue attic or a magical shul no one knew about. Perhaps rescue a damsel in distress or become a hero of my own film. And my video camera is capturing every moment.

Imagine this contradiction. They spoke slowly. I heard quickly. Words and sentences compressed by locomotives huffing at both ends. Adding to the verbal traps were the glottal stops in Jiri's remarks, the !clicks in Betty's chatter. They spoke in sonorants and yeks, they alternated voiced and unvoiced aspirants. I wish I could have recorded them. I couldn't tell if the arcane phrases, spoken in what I now presumed was High Double Dutch, were purposeful or spontaneous. Who knows, perhaps all of it was amphigoric speech.

Or maybe phonic mesmerization. Maybe even aphonic.

One thing was obvious. They were talking about me. About me? Yes, about me. I don't know how doubt is shredded, but the phrase "without a shred of doubt" is applicable here. For once in a while Jiri's eyes slid in my direction—I who was standing at the foot of his bed, while Betty, who sat in an easy chair almost blending into it, now bent close to him, her chin over the edge of his blanket—even though he looked at, faced, Betty. She didn't look at me either, but occasionally nodded or tilted her head to the left where I was standing, to the tune of—yes, again—"tara glos," too old. But after a while that phrase disappeared. By the shifts in tone, the up-and-down decibels of their private lingo, small gestures in body language, I gathered they were arguing, negotiating whether or not to reveal something to me.

This wasn't the first time this happened to me, but it never lasted long. I seem to be a magnet for secretive speech. Here's number two, the third will come soon. Once, in Jerusalem, where I had been filming a documentary about the Western Wall, I had to see a dentist. As I sat in his waiting room, two sixteen-year-olds entered. They had long curly *payess* and wore the typical black hats, tieless white shirts, and black suits of the ultra-Orthodox community. They sat down next to me on the small red plastic-covered bench and immediately began to chatter in Yiddish. But it was a Yiddish that would have been Greek even to Sholom Aleichem. They spoke in quick gushes, swallowing without even a blessing most of the syllables, then slowed down and feigned an accent, perhaps Warsaw Yiddish, that distorted and stretched some of the vowels and shortcutted others. They obviously used this private cant in public—a kind of kosher Yiddish Pig Latin—to bamboozle all eavesdroppers. Like me.

During Jiri's and Betty's argument, displeasure pulsed in Betty's pursed lips and longer nose. Why was she the Cerberus of whatever information Jiri wanted to share with me? When she finished, she leaned back in her chair, her face set in stone, a tamped fire in her hazel eyes.

"Don't forget, in Prague..." Jiri said softly.

At this, Betty was propelled forward again. From her erect position she moved toward Jiri's bed, chin out, eyebrows up. Aggressive she looked despite her silence. Her hand was up, all five fingers outspread, as if signaling Stop!

"...go see Yossi in back of the Altneu..."

"You told him that already."

I interjected quickly, "You said he's almost a relative. Is it something like your father's father's second cousin by marriage?"

Again Betty moved, hands out, as if to block, intercept, Jiri's words.

"Who's asking personal questions now?" she muttered. "It's only no good when Betty does it."

Jiri didn't even turn to her.

"No, *bruderl,* it's more complicated that that. Call him a family friend."

For a moment they fell silent. Maybe they were catching their breath, ready for the next volley of vowels, consonants, and Danny K double talk.

Again I looked up at the framed Miro above Jiri's head. Out of the apparently inchoate dots and lines, curlicues and orbs, a map of the Old Town of Prague materialized, and in the squiggles of the print I saw a path that led to the Altneushul from the Old Town Square. It seemed my unconscious was already attempting to take still vague plans and make them real. I navigated through starbursts and pastels—mauves and velvet greys—and splashes of primary colors from point A to point B. But when I looked again the map was gone and other configurations, algebraic unknowns, surfaced.

Then again began their Ubangi. Its rhythm, klippetop, klippetap, klippetop, klippetap, reminded me of words on horseback. I saw John Wayne galloping, klippetop, klippetap, across a field; the Lone Ranger klippeting toward the sunset. But when Jiri spoke alone, the horses were stabled, returned that sweet gentle tone I first heard when he sat before me in the Eldridge Street shul.

I listened to them. Had Jiri said aloud in English, Let's not talk over his head, behind his back, I would have jumped up—well, I was standing already—and exclaimed, No, no, please continue, I love listening to you. Their words transported me to some distant civilization; the sentences like a tape running backward, full of !clicks from African languages. As if conversations were stretched out on tape, then cut up and pieces arbitrarily spliced together; as if that recently discovered defective gene for language were suddenly blossoming in their words, giving them the timbre of connected speech, but which upon closer examination was partial Gibberish, spoken—as everyone knows—in the tiny equatorial principality, formerly a Dutch protectorate, now known as Gibber.

A nurse floated into the room. To the three of us a fourth was suddenly added.

"Time for your blood pressure, Doctor, and a little sponge bath too, hon."

She swooshed the curtain bunched up by the wall until it surrounded Jiri's bed. Although the nurse didn't ask me to move, I stepped into the hallway. A man passed me in a wheelchair. A hefty woman aide pushed a tall aluminum food cart slowly down the hall. Although there were other noises in the hospital, I still heard the rush of sounds that Jiri and Betty had created.

"Okay," the nurse told me a few minutes later. "You can go back now."

Jiri looked refreshed.

"I'm going, Jiri. I hope you feel better soon."

"Wait, please don't go yet."

Truth is, I didn't want to go, but I didn't appreciate just standing there, a mute, even dumb listener to their two-way conversation.

I went back to my place by the wall, near the foot of Jiri's bed.

"You have brothers or sisters?" Betty asked suddenly.

"No. I'm the only child."

At once they continued their chant, interrupted only by a brief intermission. Again Danny K sounds bobbed in, nonsense words from his presto patter like "garip kasay" and "hatip katay." But if it was Danny's lingo I should be able to understand it. I had mouthed those words often enough. Nevertheless, they eluded me.

Still, I was entranced by the music of their words. I tried to come up with something to compare it to. You write all the letters of the alphabet on one-inch square cards and carefully arrange them from A to Z. Then someone puts the cards in a metal capsule, like the ones used for dice, shakes them up, and pours the letters out all ajumble, which is the way the letters of the alphabet existed originally, when they were modified from the Hebrew. Then, in 433 BCE, along came the Greek poet, Alphabeticus, the first person to put a Western alphabet into alphabetical order, a brilliant stroke no one had ever thought of before. A well-deserved homage it was to name the alphabet after that great poet from Ionina.

Shaken-up letters, that's what it felt like listening to them.

Note how much time I spend describing their speech, detailing my confusion, my fascination too. Angry as I was that they were hoodwinking me, I still admired that language, if language it was. The swinging trapeze inventiveness of it. Its Stravinsky rhythms and James Joyce sounds. A fine pretense they made at conversation. Spoke it they did, yes. But did they understand it? Perhaps neither knew what the other was saying. Putting on a show. Sheer bluff. The entire charade for my (dis)benefit. Perhaps they had even reached the outer limits of non-communication. Two people speaking a concocted Greek to each other, Greek to me and maybe to them too. Going even further than the dying language I had once read about, high in the Uzbek mountains, where the last living speaker lived alone, speaking to himself a language he only barely understood. We know that languages are constantly dying, while new ones are not being born. Except the one this couple invented for the sole purpose of excluding me. Soon, at the newly rebuilt Tower of Babel, we will all speak one tongue. Not Betty's, I hope.

Oh, if I could break their code. If only I could break their code. If only, what wonders would ensue. For code it was. I knew in my guts it was code. Or a private language only the two of them shared. Maybe only one of them, for once in a while Betty turned away from Jiri's drawn face and gave me a look of complicity, softer than the hard edge she had presented when I appeared, unannounced, with Jiri that Saturday in their apartment. A look that seemed to say, I too don't understand a word of this. But maybe that too was part of the game, for if she didn't understand a word, how come she spoke in that arcane, concocted language so fluently? Or was it like that man in the famous 1940 survey of Yiddish speakers—the only one in that incredible category—who said he spoke Yiddish but didn't understand a word?

But, yet, but, still, if this indeed were so, why did their conversation sound so two-way, with the normal rises, dips and waves, the beat and strophes of quotidian exchanges? Watching them was like watching a film with the sound turned off. You know dialogue is taking place but you can't understand it. Or better yet: a foreign-language film sans subtitles. Betty was putting me on, she was, making believe she didn't know what was flying in that language, but yet so adamantly advocating her views.

Then an idea crossed, it actually flew through my mind. As director of the Jewish Museum of Prague, Jiri had had access to all kinds of books. My guess was that he had studied and mastered an ancient Incan dialect. For all kinds of strange, exotic sounds emanated from that soft-spoken verbal volley. I said I heard !clicks and glottal stops. Did I mention insucks? A palette of sounds from the world's language bin coruscated in their talk. Missing only were double-hung mytes and tashraq lixiviates. It could be that they used one or two and they passed me by. Could also be they knew about them but chose, for obscure grammatical or syntactical reasons, not to incorporate them into their language.

I put up my hand just like Betty had done before. They stopped and looked at me.

"I want to wish you well, Jiri. *A refu'eh shleymeh,*" I said in Yiddish, wishing he'd have a complete cure. "Get well and I'll see you soon."

"Goodbye," said Betty.

But Jiri waved an index finger.

"No no. Not yet, *bruderl.* It's not yet time for you to go. Just a few minutes more."

I stood rooted. As if preplanned, as if programmed, as if he couldn't help himself, Jiri again began speaking and Betty answered.

Back and forth went the words until it was difficult to discern who was asking and who replying.

Again I tried to make out words but got only sounds. Yes, I concluded, they were making it up, improvising as they went along. That was their goal, to keep me in the dark. Even if by so doing they kept themselves in the dark too. But that didn't seem to mesh with Jiri's beneficent character. Something was wrong here. Maybe Betty was bewitching him and once he got caught up in the flow of words his day-to-day *mentchlikh* personality was swallowed up by their language. Many words sounded like voodoo, a cross between Cymric and Wendish with a dash of Ural-Altaic. In short, like no language under the sun. Even under the moon.

Once, in Canada—here comes secretive speech anecdote number three—while making a film about Jewish life in the western provinces, I was invited to a rabbi's house in Manitoba for the Sabbath. This rabbi had had a harem of wives, serially of course. He hadn't yet converted to Mormonism, but given his libido it wasn't out of the question. Rabbi Menashe Buchsenbaum-Vardi went around, like a United Nations ambassador, from one land to another, choosing wives: Chinese, Italian, Swedish, French, Korean (one from each), converting each new goyish bride to Judaism, then abandoning her for another country. Increase mitzvas was his religious credo. The more Jews the merrier. Meet a girl, make her, then make her Jewish. His current one, Deidre, was a cute and spunky Irish woman with big eyes and a freckled face about twenty-five years the rabbi's junior, he with grey and white crowding his beard, she a sexy, slender thirty. During supper they also spoke a language I didn't understand. This obviously pre-planned little scenario lasted only a few minutes during the Friday night meal and was probably a bunch of nonsense syllables they had made up for their own amusement and for the consternation of their house guest.

Insulted, I wanted to get up and leave—but something had happened about an hour earlier that rooted me to the house. Their language too fascinated me. By no means was it equal in sound, complexity, or variety of tones to Jiri's. And even though I understood neither of these outlandish tongues, I can say definitively that I didn't understand Jiri's better than I didn't understand the Canadian rabbi's.

Rabbi Buchsenbaum-Vardi may have wanted to be mysterious, but the wordless message his live-wire, attractive, pert-nosed wife sent me was quite clear. Before the meal, when a few other people were present, Menashe announced that they had a custom of holding hands and dancing in a circle while singing *Sholom aleichem,* the song that welcomes the Sabbath. All of us joined hands for the dance. I found myself next to Deidre and, in the course of the dance, she squeezed my hand a few times, press and release, press and release, while innocently looking straight ahead, a shy and somewhat enigmatic smile on her face. What I was supposed to do about that obvious come-on, which needed no words, no language, no syntax, I still can't figure out. Did she expect me to press back as a signal that she should/could slip into my bed in the guest room that night?

But back to Jiri and Betty.

Listening to their language was a challenge. Maybe they even enjoyed my puzzlement. Focusing on the words, I thought one of them said "gra"—the first word of the two-word morning greeting ("gra dnasta") that I had heard so often on the streets of Mustara. I had spent a few days there on that island nation off southern Europe, formerly under authoritarian rule, but now—free of the Soviet yoke—a model ex-communist dictatorship.

"Have you been to Mustara?" I asked into the air, addressing one, both, of them.

They looked at me blankly but did not stop the interchange of puzzling words. For a while they even spoke at the same time, at each other, over each other, and it sounded like a duet to me, full of rich, complex tropes.

I bet, I thought, if I had the text of their words and studied it long enough, I could break the code. One word, however, that I did not hear was "Prague" or "Europe." Maybe they used words like "city," or even "there" to avoid giving me any hints.

Another thing: I usually ask people to identify a language I don't understand. But now, for some strange reason, I did not. Perhaps because they spoke it around me, trying to bind me with the bonds of their unfathomable words.

Then Betty jumped up, walked quickly, with an oddly stiff gait, between me and Jiri's bed and rushed into the bathroom. She probably had held back all along from going, not wanting to leave Jiri and me alone. Now she could no longer contain herself.

Jiri spoke quickly. "Tell Yossi I sent you. Very important. He'll introduce you to some interesting people. Also, you'll be pleased to meet, it will be important for you to…my…he will send you to a man named… An old man who will sh…"

But he did not complete his thought. Instead, he pointed to an old-fashioned pen on the night table, an item I hadn't noticed before, or, if noticed, hadn't paid attention to.

"Write down the following."

I pulled out a notepad from my pocket and took the pen.

In the bathroom, Betty flushed, and I prayed she would stay there a while longer, perhaps affected by a stomach cramp or two. She was washing her hands. I leaned forward.

Jiri turned his head toward the bathroom.

"Quickly," he said. "I want you to see…" Then his eyes fluttered shut.

Now it was too late to write. And in an unconscious gesture—a move I did not analyze until later—I slipped the pen into my inside jacket pocket, out of sight.

Jiri opened his eyes again, looked at me with his mild glance, and whispered, "Amschl, Amschl."

"Yes," I said.

How did he know my Hebrew name? He had stepped out of the sanctuary that Sabbath two weeks or so ago when I gave the gabbai my name before my aliya to the Torah.

But once more Jiri closed his eyes and fell silent, a morose, frustrated silence—perhaps I should even say angry silence—etched on to his face.

Betty came out of the bathroom, looked at Jiri, and put an index finger to her lips.

"He's asleep," she said in a low voice. "Please, mister, don't sap the little bit of strength he has. He's not a well man. Can't you see that? Can't you?"

"Seems to me you're talking to him much more than me."

Jiri opened his eyes. He turned to Betty.

"Please." And he made a drinking motion with his cupped hand.

Betty looked at the night table. "Where's the water? The nurse forgot to fill the pitcher. What's the matter with those nurses? All they do is hang around the nurses' station and jabber."

Then she rushed to the bathroom again.

"Come tomorrow, *bruderl*," Jiri said softly. "Early. She doesn't come until..."

"I can't, Jiri. I teach a film course on Monday mornings... What about the old...?"

But all Jiri said was, "I hope you weren't hurt by our language. But I hope you'll understand someday."

Which sense of understand did he mean? That I would someday understand that language, or that I'd understand why they used it today?

"It's all right...absolutely fascinating... Please tell me about the old man."

Betty returned with the water but Jiri's eyes were shut again.

"You're not very considerate," she said bitterly.

Through still-closed eyes Jiri countered with, "Leave him alone."

His remarks during Betty's brief absence made me feel a bit better. Still, I couldn't shake off my annoyance. Why did such a courtly, decent man use that private lingo right in front of me, shamelessly violating all standards of social politesse? It didn't add up. Once again, I was about to share with him something about my Prague past but held back. A childish bit of getting even. Maybe next time, I consoled myself. When he clarifies that business with the old man.

I prayed Jiri would recuperate and return home soon. He was special. He was special from the moment I first saw him—tall, dignified, of princely demeanor—and heard his wise, gentle voice. Looking at him, kinships tumbled within me: father, zayde, uncle, brother.

Like other children of Holocaust survivors who had no grandparents, I missed the older people who surrounded my American-born friends, their faces beaming with love when they visited, crouching down, arms spread wide, waiting for their little grandchildren to dash into their embrace. Maybe for me Jiri was the zayde I never had.

Sad to say, I didn't feel that way about his wife, or whatever she was. She was American, Lower East Side, crass, lowborn, simple, uncultivated. No match for him, despite her fluency in that Togo-flavored, Tagalog-spiced Ubangi Gibberish they wove like fine silken threads around me. From her I felt distant. I sensed her chill. Maybe she resented his warmth toward me. They didn't seem to have any children and he treated me like a son or young brother—remember that sweet *bruderl* word?—like family. Maybe she wanted him all to herself, even though there didn't seem to be any affection between them. To be fair, but, she devotedly cared for the much older man. And, somehow, I felt sorry for her. Yet, still, each time she left us alone, a distinct sense of relief waved through me.

"I'm going," I said. I thought she'd say: to Prague?

"Go."

I watched her lips. Was it my overwrought fantasy, or did I really see her mouth the words: Go to Prague, mister, go?

Still stood room the. Jiri, Betty, me in a frame freeze. Even the thin jagged jumping red lines of the monitor stopped. Into the instant video replay of my mind came all the words of that Babel tongue. All the words of that Babel tongue that comprised all sounds. All the words of that Babel tongue that comprised all sounds of all languages returned. All at once the words returned, not as hammer blows but as a massive pressure on my soul, soft walls squeezing me from all sides. And from the chrestomathy of unfathomable words, one phrase—that signature phrase—surfaced. Which then bubbled, blurted, out of me.

"*Nepa tara glos*," I hissed at Betty. "I understood every word."

It hit her like a bolt of lightning, a sudden storm wind—for her head snapped back like a dead branch on the easy chair and her eyes fluttered shut, the whites rolling as consciousness fades.

I said I understood everything. And a second later I did. What started out as bluff ended up as truth. Soon as I said those words I broke the code. I felt a surge. A flow. A current. A Rosetta Stone clicked into place in my head and at once it all made sense. The words lined up swiftly with their translations. What I read overwhelmed me. It was astonishing. Headline-grabbing. Page-one news. What a film this will make, I thought. But no one will believe it. It was too incredible. I couldn't wait to get to Prague, and here I was still in Jiri's hospital room, full of the secret language, its dense secret content—its dense secret content revealed.

I leaped up from my chair; better yet, the phenomenal revelation catapulted me from it. Wait a minute! What am I talking about? Was I in la-la land? There was no chair. I wasn't sitting on a chair. I had been standing all along. Everything understood I now. No wonder they wanted to keep all this from me. I understood the language and I understood why they used it, meshing, as Jiri wished, both senses of understand. Anyone with information like that surely wouldn't have shared it with outsiders. I would have done the same, I confess. Now I didn't blame them for their secret language, that lingua polynuanced magnificent, that brilliantly orchestrated transcultural code.

Everything was clear now. Oh, how clear it was. Sunshine flooded my head. The clouds gone. I must get to Prague quickly. Before it's too late. But the knowledge I now bore within me was like a forty-minute symphony, the molecules of whose notes are pressed together—to make it graphic, imagine a huge hot-air balloon compressed to golf ball size—to form a piece no longer than four seconds. Music of unbearable intensity. No sooner do you sense the first movement than the second is finishing. The tones as thick as smoke. The replay of their conversation, the torrent of words repeating in my mind overflowed like an open faucet pouring water upon water into a little cup without stop. What I held back from telling Jiri before fused seamlessly with what they didn't want to tell me now. These two unsaids clicked together like pieces in a jigsaw puzzle.

Now I had the entire picture. I couldn't wait to get to Prague. Oh, if only I were in Prague right now! But, alas, my torrent of understanding lasted only the four strides from the chair I wasn't sitting on to the door. Only four seconds, as long as that supercompressed symphony. For as soon as I got to the door it all vanished, was vacuumed—whhsht—out of me. There, at the door, on the threshold, I promptly forgot everything. I didn't even know what it was I forgot. It was as if I woke from a dream, knew I had a dream—was groping for words to describe the scenes and people I had just seen, but ended up clutching air, a passing shadow, grasping the edges of clouds—but remembered absolutely nothing of the dream.

Like the Italians say: I was kissing fog.

Later, when I walked out of the hospital, I thought I heard a woman's voice. I turned but saw no one. Again, over the din and through the thicket of noise, I heard the insistent female voice, which now seemed to come from above me.

I looked up. It was Betty, way up on the fifth floor, shouting some words that were subsumed, absorbed, drowned out by automobile traffic, ambulance sirens, heavy trucks rumbling, an occasional motorcycle that revved up like a 747 taking off, mouthing something—how she was able to open a window which in hospitals never open I'll never know—words that sounded like: "...take the pen."

I waved my thanks to her and even cupped my hands around my mouth as I shouted, "Thank you" in appreciation of her astonishing generosity. Don't feel bad you took the pen, she seemed to say. It's my gift to you. Perhaps she was unwittingly—or maybe even unconsciously—reprising the famous Talmudic anecdote of a sage who witnessed thieves running off with items from his house. A goodhearted man, the rabbi did not want the thieves to bear the sin of theft, so he shouted, "*Hefker!*"—abandoned property.

Then, a moment later, my mind played with Betty's words and spun them in a different dimension. I heard other words that turned her beneficent phrase upside down. Instead of "Take the pen," she might have said, "Why did you take the pen?" And with the city swallowing the first three words, I heard the last three to my own rhythm. Rather than offering me the pen, perhaps Betty was complaining about my inadvertent act of taking it. No wonder she looked like she was ready to leap out of the window and swoop down on me like a predator bird, a hawk, an eagle, maybe even a pterodactyl. But if it was indeed her pen, and she was calling for it from the window, it was too late now to return it, for I had an appointment uptown. I figured I'd give it back at my next visit.

A couple of days later, unable to go back to the hospital, I called Patient Information.

"Beth Israel, how may I assist you?" came the voice of a female operator.

"I'd like to know how Jiri Weisz-Krupka is doing?"

"It's Krupka-Weisz."

"That's what I meant. How is he?"

I knew they'd say Fine. They always say Fine, even if a patient is clinging to life. Even if he already unclung it.

"How do you spell the name?"

I spelled it, last name first, first name last. She repeated the spelling.

"That's right," I said.

"Gone."

"Gone?"

"Gone."

"Gone where?"

"Gone gone."

I barely choked out the word, "Dead?"

"I'm sorry," she said, "but the new privacy laws do not permit me to give out any personal information."

"Then why did you correct his name and ask me to spell it?"

"So as not to disappoint you right away."

"Then why did you say, 'Gone'?"

"Three reasons. But I'll give you only the fourth. We don't give out personal information."

"But I don't want personal information. I just want to know if he's alive, at least if he's still in Beth Israel."

"That's personal and I cannot give it."

"May I speak to your supervisor?"

"Of course."

After a brief delay a woman with a raspy smoker's voice answered.

"This is the supervisor. The lady at the other end was right. We cannot give out personal information without the patient's consent."

"All right. But if, let's say, he's—I'm not saying he is, but for argument's sake, suppose he is. How can he give his consent?"

The supervisor seemed to take a sip of something, then cleared her throat and said:

"So if you know that already, not that it's necessarily so, which I can neither confirm nor deny, why ask me?"

"I *don't* know it. I just used it as an example. But I would *like* to know."

"That is personal information."

"Can't you contact him to see if he will authorize information to be given to a relative?"

"Not without his permission. Sorry."

"Can I speak to *your* supervisor?"

"Certainly."

A moment later I heard, "Supervisor speaking."

"Wait a minute, I recognize your voice. I just spoke to you."

"I know. I am the supervisor's supervisor. I supervise myself. I'm very sorry."

"You don't sound sorry."

"But I am. Very, very sorry."

"We're talking in circles, lady. I'm a relative—" I figured since Jiri affectionately called me *bruderl*, little brother, I could honest say: "Actually, I'm his younger brother." And I gave her my name.

"But that's not the same name."

"I know. We come from one different father and two of the same mothers and the one who is my mother changed her name when she remarried my uncle for the second time to avoid confusion. You see, she had the same name."

"As who?"

"My uncle."

"Then why did she have to change her name?"

"You see, that's just the point. So as not to get it mixed up with my other father, who fathered Jiri, who also had the same name after he changed it after my adoption papers were misplaced. You follow?"

"Even Napoleon couldn't follow what you're saying." The she sniffed. "And anyway, a supervisor never follows. Always leads. Now let's see if you're on the list.… How do you spell your name?"

"If you tell me how he is, I'll spell it for you. I'm at the airport, madam, about to take off for Prague…"

"How do you spell *that*?"

"…and I desperately need this information for his other brother in Prague who cannot contact him."

"I am not permitted to give out that information, I regret."

Indeed, now the dark timbre of regret sounded in her voice.

"Okay, I'll spell my name for you."

"It's not on the list," she said.

"Then what *can* you do for me?"

"Connect you to Billing."

"Wait! If you can't give me any information, what is Patient Information?"

"In our department, my dear sir, Patient Information is not a compound noun. People always make that mistake. Patient is an adjective. That means I am extremely patient when I give or withhold information," she said softly.

"One last attempt. I don't want personal information. What illness he has. What medications he's on. If he has Medicaid or Medicare. What his account number is. If he's contagious. If he has a disease that's spelled only with all caps. If he has one of the dozen sicknesses or syndromes with other people's names. Or even better, if he has a hyphen with a doctor's name tagged on either end, like Creutzfeld-Jakob. I just want to know if the poor man is alive."

"According to the new federal guidelines on privacy, that is precisely the kind of personal information we're not allowed to give out."

I could swear I heard a catch in her throat.

"Telling me if a person is a patient at your hospital is also patient information."

"That is correct."

"But your colleague confirmed that by asking me how Dr. Krupka-Weisz spells his name."

"That wasn't confirming. That was curiosity. And we do slip up once in a while, for this is a very emotional job."

"Okay, I'm curious too. I'm curious if he's alive."

"Curiosity killed the cat. Him too." Gloom inundated her voice.

"So he is dead."

"You still didn't spell Prague."

"P…r…a…g…u…e…"

The supervisor burst into tears. "He was such a special man. Everyone in the hospital loved him. One of the most unusual patients I ever met. There was something otherworldly, even saintly, about him… Do you know, when he came into the emergency room with a heart attack there was a child crying next to him and he told the doctor to take care of the little one first? Did you ever hear such a thing? But you didn't hear the news from me. It's not official. And probably wrong."

I couldn't talk. I couldn't thank her. I was touched by her sudden weeping.

I wanted to call Jiri's apartment but his phone was unlisted.

Or maybe it happened this way:

I called the gabbai at the Eldridge Street Shul.

"Hello. This is Amschl. Do you by any chance know where Dr. Krupka-Weisz is?"

"Isn't he at the hospital?"

"I called them and they won't tell me. Privacy laws. And I'm not on their 'give information to' list. Are you?"

"No, I'm not."

"If he died would you be notified?"

"Not necessarily."

"Do you know where he lives?"

"No. He wasn't a member of the shul, so he's not registered with us, even though he davenned here quite regularly. I just saw him once at the hospital last week. He was a very private person, you know. He never invited anyone to his house."

All the more reason not to tell the gabbai that I had walked home with him but failed to note his address.

I tried Patient Information again. This time it was a man.

"I'm sorry, I can't give out personal information without the patient's consent. This call is being recorded for quality control or training purposes."

"Can you contact him if he will allow it?"

"Who am I speaking to?"

I gave him my name and said I was Jiri Krupka-Weisz's half kid brother.

"How can you be his kid brother if he's eighty and you sound like you're thirty?"

"My mother was very attractive. And I always sounded thirty, even when I was fourteen."

"Physiologically impossible, a fifty-year birth span. I used to be a doctor… And how come you have two different names?"

"Because in our society first and last names are always different. Yours are too, I'm sure, though I won't ask because it's personal information. I have two different names because I'm not Chinese, where you have people named Chin Chin, Ling Ling, and Ping Pong."

"I mean your family name and your so-called brother's family... are different."

"Oh. That's because we come from two different mothers and two different fathers. But because both of us were twins we're actually half-brothers on either side."

"If he's really your half-brother, why aren't you here watching over him?"

"Am I my half-brother's keeper?"

He didn't answer me.

"All right. Let's try it this way. If you had a patient named Jiri Weisz-Krupka..."

"It's Krupka-Weisz, but I can neither confirm nor deny that."

"Okay. But if you *did* have a patient by that name, how would he be doing?"

"If I had a patient by that name—and mind you, this is all suppositionally speaking—he wouldn't be doing."

"Which means he's been discharged."

"That would be a gross exaggeration."

"Then how is he doing?"

He remained silent. I tried another approach.

"All right, if he hasn't been discharged and he's not here, then should I assume...?"

"You certainly should... He took an alternative route out."

"Then he's..." I couldn't bring myself to say it.

"Logical conclusions," said the man stiffly, "are the sole responsibility of the interlocutor. At the risk of losing my job, we cannot, dare not, give out personal information about Dr. Jiri Krupka-Weisz, God rest his soul."

"When did he die?"

"Who said he died?" the man shrieked.

"You did."

"I did not. I could lose my job."

"But you just..."

"And what's more, now I *know* you're not his brother. Dr. Krupka-Weisz spoke with an accent. You don't. And what's even more more, he doesn't even have a brother. I'm sorry, but I can't help you."

"You're driving me crazy," I burst out.

"Just a moment, please, and I'll connect you."

The phone buzzed.

"Psychiatric counseling, how may we help you?"

I drove to the shul, parked, and tried to retrace the way to Jiri's house. After several wrong turns I found it. At the apartment house entrance hallway I looked for Krupka-Weisz on the bell list. Not under Krupka, not under Weisz. I rang the super and spoke my question into the intercom.

"Mr. Weisz-Krupka? No longer live here."

"Not Weisz-Krupka. Krupka-Weisz."

"He gone too. Both of them."

"The wife too? I wanted to speak to his wife."

"He dead, you know. Shame."

"But is his wife still here? I must see her."

"What you say? Speak into microphone."

"Where's the lady?"

"What lady?"

"His wife."

"Wha choo talking mabout? He got no wife."

"No wife? Impossible. What about lady?"

"Lady he with no wife."

"Then where is she?"

"Who?"

"The lady who no wife."

"No lady here, I said," he said.

"She move?"

"Who?"

"The lady. The wife."

"All four move. Weisz-Krupka. Krupka-Weisz. Wife. Lady."

"Where?"

"Where what?"

"Don't you understand English?"

"No. If I understand English, I be outside where you is and you be here inside listening to me asking question that Eisenstein hisself can't answer."

"Okay, me talk slow. Where lady move?"

"There never no lady here."

"Impossible. I saw her. You say she move. Her name be Betty."

"You seeing things, mister. Need glasses."

"I'm wearing glasses."

"Then take off glasses. No lady here."

"No lady here? Ever? Named Betty?"

"No. She move. Jump into moving van with other four. Weisz-Krupka. Krupka-Weisz. Lady. Wife. And Betty. Crowded plenty. Boy. Tight. All five. Almost each other's laps on. Need stretch limo."

"Then where she go?"

"Who?"

"She."

"Oh, she? She gone too."

"Gone?"

"How gone?" I probed. "Where gone?"

"Gone gone."

"Gone gone?"

"Gone gone. With others. Hitch ride. On roof."

"Apartment empty?"

"Rented. One two three. Hard to get apartment here. Big Apple. Big waiting line. Sorry. Much regrets. You like your name on list? I put."

"No. Me no want apartment. Me want speak to lady."

"Wha choo talking mabout, mister? I tell you no lady ever be here. She move. With three girlfriends. All going. Going. Gone. No lady. No wife. No Betty. No she. No here."

No intercom.

NOTE: Beginnings #8, 10, and 9—in that order—have been deleted from this text. Deleted but not purged. Readers curious about the above-referenced beginnings may send a self-addressed, stamped envelope to the publisher and request the three deleted beginnings to *Kafka's Son.*

AT DINNER

About a month before my planned six-week trip to Prague for my film project, a delicious surprise awaited me. One of those memorable moments in life that you never even dreamt would occur. That morning, while shaving, I looked in the mirror and fantasized: If I were to fly to Venice for a brief getaway from my work in Prague (very nice, I reprimanded myself, you haven't even started filming and you're already planning a vacation), and be invited to one of those masked balls that people give in Venice, who should I go as—K or Danny K? Just then a call came from a documentary film buddy inviting me three days hence to a dinner party. His wife couldn't make it, he said, and he thought I might enjoy the evening with some other filmmakers, about eight or ten people in all. I can still see my face, full of soap, as I hesitated. Colleagues would ask me the usual question in the arts world, What are you working on?, and I didn't want to discuss a project that hadn't even begun. But my friend said a producer would come and a distributor too. These get-togethers, he added, always yield some contacts. You never know. Holding the phone with one hand, wiping the soap off with the other, I said yes. Thank God I didn't refuse, for I would have kicked myself after finding out who was there and whom I had missed by stupidly staying at home.

Guess who sat opposite me at that dinner? He was brought as a surprise guest by a successful producer I won't name. He came late, after all of us were already seated. He wore a wide, dark brown Australian slouch hat and—it was quite chilly that night—a long suede coat. A white-capped maid helped him out of the coat and took his hat.

One would have expected cries of "Danny, Danny," when he entered. Instead, a stunned silence hummed in the room. He was pale to his ears, the pallor enhanced by his dark blue cashmere turtleneck sweater that covered the loose skin on his neck. I began applauding and all the other guests joined me. Danny gave a little smile; he raised his hand a bit and waved. The hostess led him and his friend to the two empty seats opposite me.

Why the stunned silence? I'll tell in a moment. I looked at my hero, unable to believe my eyes. Danny K and me, the erstwhile pretend Danny K, in the same room. Finally. As if fated. He was only in his early seventies but looked like an old man. Old and, unfortunately, seemingly out of it. He still had a full head of hair, but at the roots white was edging into the familiar reddish blond color. But what was worse, and I felt so bad for him, shocked, even embarrassed, was that he was heavily made up. Which everyone noticed, of course, and it took their breath away. Had he just come from a performance and hadn't had time to remove the makeup? Hardly likely, for I would have known of a Danny K appearance in New York. Was the cake makeup a cover for a skin eruption, an ailing face? Who knows? Except for his lips, the flesh-colored stuff was all over his face, chin, cheeks, around his nose, and especially heavy at the corners of his eyes. But still the pallor showed through. It reminded me of the last scene of Thomas Mann's *Death in Venice*, where the ailing, aging Aschenbach is persuaded by a barber to restore to his face "what was naturally his."

A picture on the wall behind Danny's head caught my eye. It looked familiar. Wait a minute. Where had I seen that lithograph? In a gallery recently? At MOMA or the Gug? Perhaps a *New York Times* ad for a Miro show at the Pierre Matisse Gallery? The same blaze of primary colors and velvety pastels, happy swirls, hint of a man smiling. Then it came to me; it slid on a sliding door into my mind. Jiri in the hospital, the cheap, commercial-print version of the Miro image above his bed. And here was the much larger—perhaps 14" x 36"—original lithograph, signed and numbered by Miro, an enormously valuable work of art.

At once memories of Jiri flooded me. I missed him. I wanted to ask him about Terezin. I wanted to ask him about his job as director of Prague's Jewish Museum. I wanted to ask him about his family, his father, his mother. There were so many questions I wanted to ask him. I had known him so briefly yet befriended him so quickly. I was the middle link between him and his friend in Prague, whom I would find in the Altneushul. A tenuous link was I. Jiri was gone and his friend in Prague was still a shadow in my mind. Busy with plans for Prague, I hadn't realized how much I missed Jiri until that Miro floated into view behind Danny K's head.

Was this picture another secret message being sent to me, like the arcane language that Jiri and Betty spoke whose messages I could not penetrate, except for "nepa tara glos" and "nepa tara pilus"? If you remove the "K" that has accompanied me all my life, what link, what possible connection could there be between the "K" of Krupka-Weisz and the "K" of Danny K?

Never mind. No time now. There was Danny to look at—and so I fixed my gaze on him. Except for a few whispered exchanges with his friend, Danny hardly spoke. He sat quietly and ate slowly from the platter the producer had brought him from the buffet table. I noticed Danny's fork trembling as he brought it to his mouth. Seeing others watching him, he switched to his left hand. When he turned he moved his head slowly. Had he had a stroke?

My heart fell. I felt I was seeing my childhood idol, one of my two spiritual K fathers, shattered, defeated, broken. As if a rock cast at a windshield caused a spiderweb of shattered glass—and I'm seeing my beloved Danny through those glass spiderwebs. Could it be that he already had dementia and was reliving his early days in show business when greasepaint was applied to his mobile face? But why would anyone bring him to a party if he was unwell?

Conversations swirled near him, to his left and to his right, leaving him powerfully alone. I longed to rescue him, to become a hero of one of his films, like *The Secret Life of Walter Mitty,* where he wins all battles, rights all wrongs. Were people afraid to talk to him, afraid of disturbing or annoying him? Or were they avoiding him like people avoid the deformed and the incurably ill? But Danny did not seem to mind. No sign of petulance, disdain, or impatience was on his face. While others went to the buffet, he didn't move. He looked down at his plate or up at empty space as he chewed. Once in a while, his left index finger absently traced a little line on his left cheek.

The hostess had placed one extra linen napkin next to every goblet. Danny took one stiff napkin, opened it, made some folds, and shaped a little boat. He did the same with a neighbor's napkin. Then he reached for another and another and did the same. Soon he had a small armada. Others watched Danny as they ate, but they did not use this odd game of his to open a conversation.

An idea suddenly flowered. I took my napkin and made a large boat. Then, from a glass vase filled with red roses on the buffet, I took one rose. I broke off most of the stem, placed the flower in my linen boat and sent it sailing with my gift, my homage, to Danny. He looked up, saw my ship approaching his fleet, and made room for my rose-bearing craft by moving two boats. He smiled delightedly as with thumb and forefinger he pulled in my rose boat to shore. For a moment I fancied he'd pick up the rose, place it between his teeth, and break into a little dance.

Instead, he picked it up, sniffed it, and said softly, "Thank you," in his nuanced, high-pitched, and rather nasal voice. Then he gave out his famous charming little giggle that I remembered from his films and stage shows. Just then the producer sitting next to him was called into the living room. I too rose and pounced. I moved around the table and slid into the vacated seat.

"Hi," he said. "I'm Danny K."

My heart thumped. All my memories of Danny K coalesced at that moment. Sitting next to him, it was as if a waterfall of photos and scenes had come cascading into my head and they were about to pour out.

I smiled. "Don't I know it!" I introduced myself. We shook hands.

"Thanks for the rose. Very imaginative."

"No less than the armada you created as if you wanted to sail away from here."

Danny looked me in the eye. In his warm glance pain and sadness mingled, but he didn't respond to my comment.

"Can I ask you a question?" I said.

"Sure."

Danny K studied my face as if wondering where he knew me from. From my resemblance to you, I thought. But I wasn't going to tell him that. Or maybe he remembered me from that backstage visit years ago.

"What's your question?"

"I hope this won't sound strange. But for years I've had two heroes. The two K's. You and K. I'm just wondering if you've ever read anything by him."

He perked up from his seeming slumber. He smiled, shook his head in wonder.

"I can't believe someone is talking to me about something other than show business."

"Do you mind?"

"Mind? I'm delighted… Of course I've read him."

"Which is your favorite work?"

"'The Metamorphosis.'"

I said, "Mine too."

Now his face lit up. He shifted in his seat as if to drive away the immobility, the almost sculpted freeze position he had had for half an hour. He stood. He was still as tall as I remembered him from years ago.

"Come, let's sit here on the sofa."

Now he became animated, the old Danny K. He was plucked out of his somnolence. His chalky complexion vanished. Natural oils overtook his pores. The mask of makeup dissolved. All the other guests stared at us, wondering who was this guy who had pulled Danny K out of his torpor.

"I love that story," he said. "I'll tell you something few people know. Once I even proposed to a producer to make a film version in which I would play the lead."

"A comedy?"

"Yes. Of course."

"Good." I wanted to hug him. "No one thinks of that story as a comedy. Everyone considers it a tragedy. But K himself thought of it as a comedy. When he read it aloud to Max Brod and his other friends, they all laughed, including K. Same thing happened when he read selections from the *The Castle*."

"Are you a K scholar?"

"Yes. A Danny K scholar."

He laughed his delightful high-pitched giggle.

"And what happened to your film proposal?"

"What do you think? They turned it down, of course. It wouldn't make money. I even proposed that for the scene where the three lodgers see Gregor creeping into the room where his sister is playing the violin, I suggested that for that hilarious scene they get the Marx Brothers for a cameo appearance—but it didn't come to pass."

"Too bad."

"That's Hollywood… I understand you're all filmmakers here. Why don't you make it?"

"Well, I do documentaries."

"Then focus on K."

"You read my mind. I'm leaving for Prague in less than a month…"

"Go for it. I'm sure you'll do well."

"You know, this is the second time I've seen you one on one."

"I thought you looked familiar," Danny K was kind enough to say.

"When I was a kid, my beloved Uncle Monia used to take me to see your stage shows in New York. We'd see two of your shows with a film sandwiched in between. And years later, in the Mann Auditorium in Tel Aviv, at a concert by the Israel Philharmonic Orchestra. Just before the intermission, a man onstage announced in Hebrew and in English: We have a surprise guest from America with us tonight. I'm sitting in the balcony and I see someone I think I know, someone who looks so familiar, whizzing past me up the steps of the balcony, probably from row one, and the audience is susurrating, bubbling, whispering, then applause breaks out from the people sitting down in the orchestra as the man dashes to the front, applause mingled with laughter and happy sounds, and then the chant 'Denny Denny Denny' fills the air as you leap onstage, snatch the baton from the conductor, and the audience is now on its feet and applauding and still shouting, 'Denny, Denny, Denny' and you turn to the audience, raise your baton as a sign for silence, and say to them, 'Shalom, Yidn. Sholom aleichem. Shalom al Yisrael,' and then you begin to conduct the IPO."

"Yes, I remember that. What a thrill! It was the *Barber of Seville Overture*. My specialty... But when did we meet?"

"On Broadway. I came to see you once after a matinee and gave you a copy of my first documentary, the one I did on Sholom Aleichem's children."

"Oh yes, of course. Forgive me for not contacting you and thanking you. Then I saw it at least one more time on Public Television. And it surely deserved all the praise it got."

"Boy, am I glad I came tonight. I almost didn't accept the invitation."

"That would have been too bad. To whom would I have told my K story?"

My mind was racing. My idol sitting before me. If I didn't make a move now, I would never have the opportunity. Should I engage him with more K talk? I wanted to ask him if—it was on the tip of my tongue to ask him if I could make a documentary about him. But it would be pretentious. And untrue. Poor Danny was fading. How would he look in a film that would obviously have to focus on him? One of my two K heroes. And here he was chatting with me, no longer the lonely, lost soul at a dinner party, trying to sail away on ships of his own creation, like that jailed Roman philosopher, or was it a poet, whose name escapes me at the moment, drawing ships on his prison wall that would take him to freedom.

"When you whizzed past me on the balcony at the Mann Auditorium, I didn't know who it was. The man on stage said, We have a surprise for you. But in my skin I felt it was you. It was as if the corner of my eye had a vision that the rest of me couldn't quite grasp. And then, when from downstairs comes the adoring cry, Denny, Denny, Denny, my joy was complete. I'm seeing my hero again. And the delight was all the greater because it came in a totally unexpected place. Who would have dreamt that you'd be in Israel, in Tel Aviv, in the Mann Auditorium, and in the *balcony* just rows away from me the very same night I was there?"

"Yes, I remember that evening. It was very special. And you describe it so nicely I wish I could have been there."

Was he joking? There was no twinkle in his eye as he said this.

Then he burst into his merry laugh.

Again that feeling at the tip of my tongue. Go for it, like Danny said. So what if he's old. It could add poignancy. As far as I know, no one has done a documentary on him. From a personal angle. With him reminiscing. With him showing photos, posters, memorabilia. Go for it. Now. He's in the mood. He'll agree. You'll get access to stills, to clips from films from his private collection. Perhaps even precious outtakes. He'll secure permissions for you.

Instead, I said:

"Do you know people used to tell me when I was in high school, and even the first year or two in college, that I looked like you?"

He examined my face. Would he agree or would he say, No way? He nodded slowly. Maybe out of politeness. Maybe so as not to contradict the fellow who sent him a rose, who snapped him out of his sleepwalker's malaise.

"Yes, I can see that. You even have that Jewish bend in your nose like mine."

Which led me to say, "I even learned some of your double talk, quick patter routines, was able to mouth, to lip-sync your Russian composers' song."

"How nice." For a moment he looked distant; he seemed to remove himself and sail far away. Then he looked back at me and said: "Do you want to hear a sad joke?"

I didn't want to hear a sad joke.

"Danny K is here," he said softly, "and there is no laughter."

"No no no. Not so, Danny. May I call you Danny? I'm dying to call you Danny. All my life I've been calling you Danny..."

He was smiling now and nodding. "Yes, of course." But through the smile, behind the smile, behind the pallor, Danny K looked like a little boy humiliated in class, fallen, hurt, alone.

"You don't understand," I said. "Danny K is here and there's joy."

"Really?"

"Really. Really really. Wherever Danny is there is joy...joy is what laughter brings. Can I get you something? A glass of water, some juice, tea?"

"No, thanks, I'm fine. I was thinking back to my early days in Hollywood. Those Jewish moguls, the big shots, wanted me to get a nose job...imagine! They thought I looked too Jewish. Not enough Kaminsky became K, they wanted a mohel to circumcise my nose."

And again he gave his famous high-pitched giggle.

I laughed with him.

"You see? Laughter and joy."

"But I put my foot down," he continued. "Refused flat out. Did you know that my hair was naturally dark? It was the Hollywood studio that made me reddish blond. To make me look more goyish. That was the compromise on their part, those anti-Semitic, self-hating heads of Hollywood studios, developed and run and owned by Jews. And that's how we solved the Danny K Jewish problem."

"Danny, we're talking showbiz and we weren't supposed to."

"Such is the nature of the beast. It's in our blood, pores, genes."

I looked into Danny's eyes, those beautiful blue eyes, a bit duller than years back, the laugh lines filled with cake makeup.

"Danny, I want to ask you another question."

"Sure."

And before I had a chance to censor my gall the words were already out.

"Danny, would you be amenable to me making a documentary about you? A very personal one. I don't think such a film has ever been made. You see, though I majored in literature, after seeing your films I decided I wanted to be a filmmaker."

I felt I was on a precipice. Which way would it go? He could say no outright or say he was too busy now with other projects. He could say he'd think about it. He could say a hundred things that meant no.

Danny K looked at me, his eyes blank. For a moment I looked over at the fleet of ships Danny had created. My ship still had the red rose on it.

Danny nodded, once, twice, then many times slowly before saying a word.

"After all," he said with an upbeat tone, "if you looked like me and imitated me, if I'm your hero, what more can a documentary subject want?"

What's next? I wondered. Did he say yes? Should I give him my phone number, ask for his?

We both were standing now.

"And for my Prague film I'd like you to retell that 'Metamorphosis' film project story. It would make a marvelous addition to the film."

"Excellent. I want you to call me. Will you call me?"

I just gazed at him. I'm sure my jaw had dropped open. Will I call him? Will the day dawn tomorrow and wane at dusk?

"Of course. Even without a phone number I'd shout to you from my rooftop."

Danny smiled. "Then, here, let me give you my number." And he patted his pockets, looking for a pen.

I took Jiri's pen from my shirt pocket.

Danny K took it. "What an elegant pen, or, as they say in the carriage trade"—and here he gave his trademark giggle—"writing instrument."

Then he did something unusual, something I had never seen before. He brought the pen to his nose and sniffed it.

"Mmm. Smells good. I had a pen just like this when I was a little boy. And I still remember the smell." He took a little piece of paper out of his wallet, wrote his name and phone number on it, and handed it and the pen back to me.

"Here's my number."

I looked at it. "Is that a zero or a six?"

"A zero. Sorry. My hand shakes."

"That's okay. Sometimes mine does too."

"I'm leaving for India for ten days the day after tomorrow on a UNICEF tour. So call me in two weeks. We'll get together when I come back."

Where are the words—are they in the heart or the brain—that can describe that surge of soul, that cerulean sensation of happiness?

"Thanks, Danny."

He mimed the next thought in response to my gratitude. He placed his palm tenderly on his heart and then pointed to me. And then, with a suddenness that surprised me, he embraced me and pressed his face to mine. I smelled his aromatic makeup. Some of it must have rubbed off on my face.

"I have a confession to make," I said.

"Yes?" And he scanned my face like a newspaper, line by line.

"After I would do one of my imitations of you, girls would come up to me and say I looked so much like Danny K I could pass for Danny K's son. Sometimes I couldn't resist saying I *am* his son."

"Well," Danny said. "One never knows…did your mama ever go up to the Borscht Belt?"

And we both laughed.

But Danny never went to India. Within days it was reported that he had fallen seriously ill, some sort of rare blood disease, perhaps contracted from a previous visit to either Africa or India. Two weeks later, just a fortnight before I was about to leave for Prague, Danny K, the man I thought would live forever, Danny, my early lookalike, Danny, my hero, Danny, one of my two spiritual K fathers, Danny K was dead.

PART TWO

-1

On the Plane

On the evening of my flight, at the airport waiting lounge, I had Jiri's pen in my inside jacket pocket, same place exactly as on the day I took it from Jiri's hospital night table. It was a fine pen, and I mean pen, not one of those cheap, ubiquitous ballpoint or gel flow pens, but an old-fashioned fountain pen that uses real ink, with a fine golden nib, that beautiful, almost hourglass-shaped and curved golden tip that I remembered seeing in upscale stationery stores. With just the right sort of thickness, it gave an elegant cursive flow to my letters and actually made my calligraphy look more handsome than it was when I wrote with a ballpoint pen. Yes, the pen pleased me; I liked it. Using it, of course, I thought of Jiri—and Betty too (re the latter a wave of anxiety always ran through me like a little pain), but at the same time, I also felt the pen had belonged to me for ages. That's what happens when you possess something for a while. Even though you aren't the original owner, the mere fact of possession gives you the feeling not only of ownership but absolute ownership. The item wasn't just yours; it had never belonged to anyone else.

Waiting to board, I jotted down on a pad a list of things to do in Prague. As I wrote, the list kept growing. Each item grew and I was writing comments and kept expanding on phrases until I was scribbling miniscule letters in the margins and in between lines, even writing in tiny script at the edges around the corners of the pages so that the words snaked around and about and created an upside-down border to the pages.

If I believed in automatic writing, which I don't, I might even say that once I began writing with Jiri's pen the thoughts seemed to flow on their own with that beautiful golden-nibbed pen in my hand. For instance, it turned out that I had written down the entire Danny K dinner episode and the entire conversation word for word without even realizing I had written it.

When I finished, I took the top of the pen and pressed it to the body until it clicked shut.

"Don't forget the shul in Prague."

I turned to the people sitting next to me. Who had said that?

Then came the call; my flight was boarding. I stood, looked about. A face flashed. No! Impossible. Could that be Betty in a crowd of people back there? And if so, what was she doing here? Then my wild imagination began ticking out a chain of telegraphed messages: No wonder I couldn't find Jiri and Betty. They had gone off somewhere and were now flying to Prague. But if so, where was Jiri? And how come they were on the very same flight as mine? That whole death scene (for Jiri) and departure (for Betty) was an elaborate ruse staged by the hospital telephone operator and the apartment super.

It was Jiri's voice telling me not to forget the Altneushul and now, if I wasn't mistaken, they (at least Betty) would maybe, possibly, be on the same plane. I pressed my hand to my chest to make sure the pen was there, instinctively protecting what belonged to me.

And then again, a moment or two later, in the pen, from the pen, around the periphery of the pen, Jiri's voice: Someone near and dear to me gave me this pen. That's why, *bruderl*, I could not give it to you. Unlike a flame which can be given, transferred, without diminishing its essence, a pen can only be given once. But I am glad you took it. Absently. Inadvertantly. Automatically. Without thinkingly. It was *bashert*, destined, fated, that it end up with you. Once you land in Prague I will tell you who to see.

As I boarded I looked about but couldn't spot the face I had momentarily glimpsed before. Once we were airborne and the seat-belt sign was off, I walked up and down the aisles of the plane to see if I could find Betty or Jiri. But no one on board looked like either of them. Perhaps they were in business or first class. But no, I reconsidered, given their modest means, that was hardly likely.

The lights dimmed; the stewardesses sat down in the back of the plane. Time to sleep. But before closing my eyes I made a few more jottings. As I clicked the pen shut again I heard—and this time it seemed to come from the pen itself, "And Yossi in back of the shul.... But most important is to..."

I put the pen to my ear. Was this some kind of high-tech pen qua taperecorder that Jiri had given me—rather, had somehow arranged for me to take? But no more words came. I put the pen back into my pocket, turned off the overhead light, stretched my legs, and closed my eyes. The drone of the plane and my fatigue made me drift off into a pleasant sleep.

Then as if out of a dream, a mystery novel, a suspense film, I feel a hand on my chest and I immediately, instinctively, grab—

The same thing had happened to me once on a night train to Trieste. The train pulled into Milan at 2 a.m. and the predators were waiting to spring. Thinking I was asleep, one dashed into my sleeper to see what he could nab. He was already by my window when I—a light sleeper (my valuables were under my pillow)—bolted up and roared. The surprised thief reeled back and hit his head at the edge of the steel doorframe. I turned him around, grabbed him by the neck, and kicked him out of the doorway which was almost opposite my compartment. He went flying the six-foot drop and sprawled on the concrete pavement face down.

—that hand before it gets into my pocket and I press hard. I sense it's a woman's hand and I hear a soft, muted, suppressed cry of pain and I squeeze and twist ever more, and in the dark I do not know who my antagonist is, but I suspect at once, and then, relenting, I let go and let the grey apparition escape back into the darkness. I felt I was like Jacob, wrestling with a creature of the night. And like my forebear, I too prevailed. But like Jacob, I also had my thigh wound, a wound in the hollow of my thigh, which metaphor will be made clear below. Half asleep, perhaps half adream, to protect it from further incursions I put the pen into my shirt pocket.

It was the pen she no doubt wanted. And in wanting it so desperately (maybe not wanting it so much as wanting desperately that *I* not have it), I reconstructed the words she sent down at me from five stories up through the noise of trucks, din of traffic, cacophony of ambulances. Now I was sure she did not say, "Take my pen"—rather, "Why did you take my pen?"—the uptick of the question and the first three words swallowed up by the traffic.

It goes without saying that I couldn't find Betty when I got off the plane.

What was it about that pen that drove her to follow me to retrieve it? What secrets did it contain? What mysteries did it possess? Did it have more than the two brief messages I had already heard?

But now the pen was silent, its previous seeming magic muted.

It was only when I discovered to my annoyance and surprise a nickel-sized blob of navy blue just above the pocket of my white shirt—my metaphoric thigh wound—that I realized in the dark of the plane, with me floating in a semi-dream in the drone of the plane, that the grey apparition (although I did not touch it, it seemed to me made of gauzy grey flannel) had absconded with the top of my pen.

My pen was now stripped of its cover, deprived of its top. Although I was able to write with it, when I rubbed my finger on the brand name imprinted on the body I heard only half of Jiri's voice. Rather, all of Jiri's voice, but only half his words. It was intelligible discourse, graspable by the senses but not by the mind. Trouble was, my senses were askew. A good thinking cap would have helped, but I had on but a half. The other half was neatly slithered away from me by a swift, unseen, horizontally moving scythe. Jiri's message, cleaved in two. Jagged were his remarks, truncated the words, and I was left with only the top, or bottom, of the letters.

Imagine a zipper on a seamstress's work table. Pull the zipper to the end and you have two pieces of cloth, each with a thin line of tiny teeth, of absolutely no use to each other unless they are attached. That's what my magic pen now resembled. For though I heard the sounds, the letters were detached, unzippered, exactly half of what was whole. The alphabet of speech shorn. Half the letters mown away.

Now that I think of it, the jagged music of this sawed-off language was similar to the sounds of Jiri's and Betty's private cant. If only I could provide, or reconstruct, the tops (or bottoms) of the aborted language, I would be able to understand what was being said.

Later, in Prague, whenever I saw a pen in someone's pocket, my first thought was: there's the top of my pen, and I had to clench my fists behind my back not to grab the pen, and clench my teeth to avoid asking the stupid question that bubbled in the back of my mouth.

1

Back in Prague

All right, I'm back in Prague, I tell myself as the plane lands, although the words "back in" can be misleading; it gives the impression I've just returned after a short absence. Nevertheless, I *am* back in Prague, and an accurate remark it is, even though—as I informed Betty not too long ago—I left the city forty-two years ago when I was just a few months old.

I could have gone to a thousand different places, but I chose to go to the city I was born in. Chose? Rather chosen. I didn't choose; someone chose me. Up in space someone held a magnet, waved it once or twice—maybe three times like in fairy tales—until it found my wavelength and drew me to the city. We fool ourselves into thinking we have free will, don't we? But we are like a rescued swimmer holding on to the robe, "robe" I type by mistake, perhaps unconsciously thinking of King Saul holding on to the prophet Samuel's robe for safety, to save his life, to save his kingdom, but it's "rope" I mean, saying we are like a rescued swimmer holding on to the rope tossed from a lifeboat pulling the nearly drowned man to shore. Does he have free will to let go? Thin strands connected to God knows where pull us. We click with unseen magnets.

In short, I was summoned to Prague.

And with Dr. Jiri Krupka-Weisz's unwritten recommendation in all caps fluttering like a banner in my mind, I'm looking forward to meeting a man named—oh my God, what's his name? I know Jiri told me. Of course he told me, and now I've forgotten it. I should have written it down. I think and strain but a bag of sand stands guard and blocks the rectangle in my mind's eye where the man's name is supposed to be.

I know he's tall; I know he stands in back of the Altneushul near the far corner. I know weekday services begin at 7 a.m. He's the key, Jiri said. I'll recognize him even though I've never seen him. He has a big face, I remember. Also that he's a family friend. I remember all that completely without having written it down. But his name, for the life of me, I have no clue to his name. It slipped away from me. In vain I go through all the letters of the alphabet. If only Jiri had given me his full name, first and last, I would have more readily remembered it. (Or maybe forgotten both, snickers a demon within me.)

But there is a way out. When I find him and introduce myself, in the European fashion he'll obviously state his name, surely with a slight bow or inclined nod of his head, last name first, first name last, again in the central European manner, and that's how I'll get to recall the name of the man whose name I forgot.

Then I know what will happen next. The tall man with the big face, narrowing one eye suspiciously, will ask me a question. Maybe to test me. Test my authenticity. To see if I'm the man I claim to be. Now that I think of it, maybe it is better that I forgot his name, because if I went up to him and said, Hi, are you (for instance) Ricardo?, anyone could easily say, Yes, I am, on the chance that I had something of value to give him. But this way, once he tells me his name, I'll recall it, and I can be sure that he's Jiri's friend. Or maybe I should even quote "nepa tara glos" at him, to show him I'm a bona fide member of the club. And if he asks me about Jiri, what am I going to say? That I know little about him? In fact, next to nothing? That he showed me K's first book, *Meditation*, with K's signature in it? And if he asks me, What about a letter? Do you have a letter from

Jiri? I'll mumble, What?, to stall for time. And he'll repeat slowly, as if speaking to a golem: A letter. Then with exaggerated clarity he'll enunciate, "Do...you...have...a... letter?"

Indeed, that's what I should have gotten from Jiri. Plus that promised list of names and addresses. But he left us—and Betty, friend, wife, ad hoc housekeeper, keeper of secrets, whatever, vanished. Maybe still hidden on the plane; maybe somewhere in Prague. At least I'll bring the man with the big face regards from Jiri. That's all I can bring is regards. And if he asks a third time, "Do you have a letter?" I'll point to the *aleph* on my forehead.

As I checked into the apartment hotel at 11:15 that pleasant, star-filled end of October night, I knew I wouldn't be at the Altneushul the next morning at 7, even if it was only a short walk. At the same time, I wanted to be there. But my knowing was more powerful than my will. Even though on the plane, thinking of Jiri and his old friend, I had decided—never mind jet lag, which I don't recognize, for I consider it a matter of willpower—to get up early and meet his friend at the Altneu.

The girl at the front desk, thin, slight, and with swarthy skin, perhaps part gypsy from Slovakia, mistaking me for a businessman, asked if I wished to be awakened at a certain hour.

"No, thanks," I said. "I'll get up on my own."

As soon as my head sank into the soft pillow—so good to rest, that warm featherbed over me—I fell into a deep, anesthesized sleep. The last thought that flitted through me was, I know I won't get up at six thirty. Not only wouldn't I be able to, I had no desire to.

I woke late. I knew it was late but didn't realize how late it was until I look at my little portable square clock, which I turned several ways to make sure I was reading the numbers correctly. It was eleven; I had even missed the buffet breakfast. I was so drugged with sleep and exhaustion, a potent chemical mix, that at first I didn't know where I was and why I was wherever I was. Then, slowly, like mixed letters of words reassembling, ym eadh yslowl cleared. 11:05 a.m. I still couldn't believe it. I usually get up at 6:30 every day. Well, I guess it wasn't in the script that I be in the synagogue at seven my first morning in Prague.

A quick, cool shower woke me. I'll go to the Altneushul tomorrow. First, a walk to the huge Old Town Square—the essence of Prague, like the Eiffel Tower to Paris or Piazza San Marco to Venice—which was just a few minutes away from the quiet, cobblestoned street my hotel was on.

I took a deep breath, breathing in light and air. Finally, in Prague. The spacious square opened before me like a flower. At one side was the famous clock tower, and nearby—according to my map—in the same building where the K family had once lived at the end of the nineteenth century, the K Museum.

I looked around, at the throngs of people, at the buildings. Prague had its arms outspread. The communists gone. The city, one of the most beautiful—if not the most beautiful—in Europe was magically back to its former glory. Under the communists, as I told Jiri in New York, greyness covered the city like a mold. But now sunshine was everywhere. Lambent in the darkest corners. At night; in shadows; inside houses; within clouds. On people's faces. Light.

Books always had Prague as a center of intrigue, filled with double and triple agents who had so many presumed loyalties that when they woke in the morning they didn't know whose side they were on. I had my own intrigue. I was supposed to meet a man whose name I forgot, who would recommend me to other people whose names I didn't know. All of a sudden, perhaps because of my febrile imagination and the sense of the fantastic inspired by the great writer of Prague, perhaps because of the pen that spoke in guillotined words, I thought of myself as an agent bringing secret messages, phrases in a language I didn't know, an innocent pawn in a three-dimensional chessboard bringing word to the king in his castle.

I saw conspiracies, hidden messages, everywhere, as if all of Prague was a CIA outpost or a set for a spy movie, which was strange, for I didn't watch spy movies. Jiri and Betty were part of this too, and the secret message I had intercepted was "nepa tara glos"—not too old. Intercepted, yes. Even deciphered. But to whom do I bring my prize? And what if "nepa tara glos" were not the secret password, but "nepa tara pilus"? For I remember Betty in the hospital room throwing me a significant glance when she said either "nepa tara glos" or "nepa tara pilus." But which was the right phrase? Maybe both together were the magic combination.

On the square, I saw at least a score of college-age youngsters and a few older people walking around carrying placards on their chests and backs advertising the many concerts offered daily in Prague. They reminded me of the men who hang around New York's Eighth Avenue and Fifth Avenue touting bargain leather jackets or bargain diamond rings.

One girl in particular attracted my attention. As I told Betty, I'm not looking, but I do keep my eyes open. When I saw that girl's face my eyes were open. She had a classically oval face, dark eyes, impeccable skin, and black hair covered by a navy-blue beret worn at a fetching angle. I imagined her at the mirror, tilting the beret this way—no, that way—until she had the proper slant. That lovely blue beret, the crowning touch, set her apart, made her look like a cover girl. Does the hat make the face, or does the face add allure to the hat?

But look down and see the poster she carries for tomorrow night's Dvořák concert, featuring his Piano Quintet in A major, at the great Dvořák Hall. Perhaps a hidden message to me. A major. A major something awaited me. If only I could find it. First morning on the square. Or maybe it was a message to meet someone at a major location. The box office perhaps. Another poster told of an all-Vivaldi concert. The RV number of the Vivaldi composition might be the first three digits of a phone number I was to call. But what if it was my own hotel? And what if I answered?

I ate lunch at a vegetarian restaurant at the edge of the square, then wandered around in the square itself, delighted with the little men moving up in the huge clock as the hour struck. I made my way through the press of people and again I saw the girl in the blue beret. Aside from that little fantasy I was concocting about secret messages—I don't believe in omens and oppose superstition—seeing such a lovely girl a second time my first day in Prague made me happy. I considered it a blessing. She must have recognized me, for she smiled at me. I noted the place and time of the concert.

Suddenly, another guy wearing a placard for a competing concert for tomorrow night approached her. I thought they would bump into each other—but no, they joined forces and marched toward me as if a mini parade were staged just for me. I looked at the fellow's sign. It read: MAJOR DISCOVERY: HITHERTO UNKNOWN SYMPHONY BY REICHA.

The two stopped. He stood to the left of the girl in the blue beret. The message was clear. From left to right I read the message directed at me. Now I could no longer doubt it, or think it was chance, coincidence. A chill rolled down my back. The words flashed in black and white, but they could very well have been in color too: A Major, Major Discovery.

Then, their mission accomplished, the two turned, took two steps forward, and parted ways.

I stopped for a moment to absorb what was happening. I took a deep breath. The fresh air of that mild, sunny morning entered my lungs. Next stop, the K Museum. No, I hadn't forgotten the Altneushul. First of all, it was too late. And anyway, K, you should know by now, was at the top of my list.

First things first. Which you can read any way you like. Forward, backward, or upside down.

2

At the K Museum

I went into the little K Museum, saw what I saw (more on that later), and stepped out of the K Museum. An encounter outside the door was to have more meaning for me than what I had just seen inside.

An elderly gentleman, tall and thin, with slightly hollowed cheeks and a prominent Adam's apple approached me. He too had just emerged from the museum. At first I thought it might be a beggar. The hair on his unshaven cheeks was two days old. I couldn't tell an old man's neglect from a growing beard. On the other hand, his jacket and tie were surely not a beggar's garb.

"Excuse me," he said in heavily accented English. "I just saw you upstairs on the second floor, is that not correct?"

I felt my cheeks, my lips, stiffen, the normal reaction when a beggar or other person you want to avoid approaches you. Before I had a chance to speak, he added:

"It is nice to see someone so enamored of K. I was listening to you speaking to your friend—"

"Actually, not really a friend. Just a chance encounter with a fellow American."

"—is all right, and every other word out of your mouth is K."

"Well, this is a K museum. It would be odd if we talked about Picasso here."

I thought he'd laugh. But he did smile. It surprised me that his teeth were straight.

Then I said: "The fact is, I might almost say: Every other word I read is by K."

The smile he smiled wasn't just a smile. It was a glow, an aureole of ecstasy that suffused his entire face, as if he were the director of the tiny museum and my remark validated his, and the museum's, existence.

"You can't imagine how I am delighted to hear that. Visitors to this museum are not familiar usually with K's works. They come because in Prague they have to see two things: K and the golem. They come from curiosity and not—" He seemed to search for a word.

"Homage?"

"Precisely. Yes. Exactly. That's the right word. Not from homage."

"And I come out of homage."

He bowed his head. As if acknowledging shyly the compliment directed at him.

"I can see that..." He put out his hand. "With your permission, may I introduce myself? My name is Graf, Karoly."

I shook his hand.

"I have the honor of informing you that"—and here he looked me straight in the eye, and if not straight then at least at the bridge of my nose, which gives the impression of looking one straight in the eye—"that I am K's son."

At first I thought I didn't hear him. I didn't exclaim, "What?" or ask him to please repeat what he had just said. I re-heard the echo of his words. No. I had not misheard. The words were the same. He said, "I am K's son," and I heard, "I am K's son." The words he said were the words I heard. Then little bells tinkled in my brain. A swirl of colors shaped like butterflies flitted before my eyes. Was that a shiver than ran down the bumps of my vertebrae? Music I had not heard in a long while played in my ears, whether folk tunes or gypsy violins or the *Slavonic Dances* I could not say. But something was happening in me. Then the girl in the blue beret and her fellow marcher appeared before me. I read their message—came again that stream of bubbles—and wondered if this is what they were hinting at. Was this the A Major Major Discovery that awaited me here in Prague?

I had read that some K scholars held that K may have fathered a son. On that there was no unanimity in the scholarly community. And, as usual, one camp belittled, denigrated, even insulted the other. Depending on which side of the controversy you stood, you were either a fool, a scandalmonger, a liar, a naïf, or a cover-up artist.

But that that myth should be standing before me seemed like a rather farfetched possibility. You don't even look like him, I wanted to say. I wondered if he was looking at me and seeing any resemblance to K, the way others saw it in the USA. You know, I wanted to tell him, if we're dealing with outré possibilities, I'm probably a better candidate to be K's son than you.

On the other hand, Prague was a city wrapped in mysticism, even miracles. It was the only major city in Europe that had escaped destruction by the Germans, the Russians, the Allies. So there *was* a chance, however slim, that the man's assertion might be true.

"No, *I* am honored," I said. "Thank you for coming up to me. Are you the director here—?"

He began shaking his head even before I finished.

"—or affiliated in any way with the museum?"

"No no no. I just come here often to look and remember, remember and recall, and occasionally greet true K lovers like you." He narrowed his eyes, tilted his head with a questioning look, gazed at me, and nodded slowly. "You know, you look more like him than I do."

"Who?"

"K."

"I'm honored. Thank you. But which one?"

He scratched his chin. "Which one what? What do you mean which one?"

"There is another K. It could also be Danny."

"Who is this Danny?"

"An American comedian and film star."

"I do not know him… That is so strange. 'But which one?'"

"Mr. Graf, may I… I'm staying in Prague for several weeks. May I invite you to lunch one day and we can talk some more?"

"I will be so happy." He put his hand into his jacket pocket and withdrew a raggedy-edged business card. He said, "Here is my vee-zeet kart," as they do in most European countries.

"Thank you," I said. I noted that Graf was his family name, but I wasn't going to question him now on that.

Karoly Graf stepped back into the doorway. "And now, if you will excuse me, I will proceed upstairs again."

"Before you go, one quick question, for which I hope you will pardon me, but I come from the Show-Me State…"

"Where is exact geographic locale of this Shawmee state?"

I thought he was pulling my leg or being sarcastic. But he wasn't. I regretted using such a thoroughgoing Americanism with a man who had no doubt learned English here from books.

"It's just an expression that means, prove it. Show me. You see, *you* know you are K's son. *I* know you're K's son. But how will you prove it to others?"

And I immediately regretted my crass remark. But once words are uttered it is impossible to withdraw them.

He looked hurt, the old man. I felt bad I had insulted him. As if I had violated his essence, gone into his very being and extracted a dime-sized gland that comprised who he was in this world. He was pale. Perhaps no one had ever confronted him in this manner before.

"Do you…" he said in a voice that trembled, "…do you have to prove to others that you are your father's son?"

I wanted to be nice. I wanted to be kind. I did feel sorry. I had the urge to be sympathetic to this tall, thin man with hollow cheeks, stubble on his face, and a prominent Adam's apple, but nevertheless there was no holding back the words rising on my tongue and begging to let loose.

"No. But, then again, I don't go around saying I'm K's son. Or Jaroslav Hašek's son. Or Schweik's son. Or Masaryk's son. Claims like that have to be proven."

He leaned back as if repulsed, weakened, by the force of my words.

"I invited you already to come see me tomorrow. All the more reason now to come. Come tomorrow and I shall show you. Thank you. I now bid you au revoir."

Tomorrow? I don't remember him saying tomorrow. But tomorrow was fine with me. As proof, I imagined he would show me a letter from his father, in K's unique, slanty handwriting which I would recognize. And I would apologize for my lack of trust and tell him I had a leading, nay, a starring role for him in my Prague film.

A wave of excitement akin to an erotic surge rose in me as I considered a surprise addition to the film. Not only an addition but a major—here's that "A Major" phrase again—shift in focus. Thinking this, those little bubbles ran across my skin for a third time. I was tingling. There was a shift in me that made my previous outline for the film melt like an overheated negative. Yes, no matter what, Karoly Graf would be featured. I might even have him in the opening segment.

As if by magnetic force, or by the energy created by the astounding news I had just heard, I too was drawn back into the doorway. Graf went upstairs again. I stood near the entrance desk. An officious-looking man, about sixty, bald, hair greying at the temples, was looking at a ledger with the receptionist. By her expression, it seemed he was castigating her. Yes, I thought, he must be the director. The smaller the facility, I've noticed, the more self-important are the directors.

"Excuse me, sir," I addressed him. "Do you speak English?"

"Why of course I do." He straightened up. "For an educated person to be un-Englished nowadays is the equivalent of being without a tongue."

I liked his formulation but wondered if he realized his apt pun.

"I want to compliment you on your beautiful museum." I don't know why I said that. I was being obsequious, condescending, and a liar too. Aside from some enlarged photographs and a romanticized thirteen-minute video that showed more of Prague than of K, there wasn't much in this so-called museum. No manuscripts, no memorabilia. The museum coasted along on its K name. This pathetic little space didn't even deserve the name museum; it was more a tourist diversion, a well-meaning but very minor showcase.

"I am so pleased. We try to keep the name and legacy of our great writer alive here. I am Doctor Hruska."

I decided to cloak the important question bubbling on my lips in the guise of a compliment.

"And the fact that the legendary K's legendary son also occasionally graces your museum is surely a plus for you."

The director's face fell. He beckoned me away from the receptionist to the rear wall where no one was standing. Dr. Hruska glanced up the stairs. Was anyone descending? Like in a spy movie, he checked left and right, surveying if the son or "son" was anywhere about before he spoke. I imagined the director would share some fantastic news with me, a true lover of K. Today was my lucky day. The A Major Major Discovery message that was sent to me—and by my pretty girl in the blue beret too—had seemingly come true. And now I would hear from him more amazing news, something like: Many of K's children are here in Prague. Most of them survived the war. If you wish, I will introduce you to some of them. Did Dr. Hruska realize he was again shifting the focus of my film, perhaps even creating a new one for me? *K's Children.*

At once my eyes became lenses, my ears microphones. I was already—heart racing in anticipation for the second time in minutes—filming, recording, interviewing these legendary people, already living these precious, nonpareil moments. Modesty aside, I was making, rather, going to make, history.

But yet. And even. And but. But still. Even so. In that blank, neutral, empty, even gloomy moment before Dr. Hruska began to speak, my excitement abated. My prophetic heart. Even as he opened his lips, even before the words came out, I sensed no stars glittering, no music rising within me, saw no spiral of colors exploding before the credits: *K's Son(s)—The Living Children of the Legendary Master of Prague*, a documentary film by…

The director said:

"You asked me before if I understand English. Now I shall ask *you* if you understand international sign language?"

But before I had a chance to ask him what he meant came another twist in the falling-leaf, turning-page scenario in which I was a participant, an actor, a golem.

To understand what happened next—and something did happen next, and it had nothing to do with K or his son—and how it happened, the museum's ground-floor layout must be described. From where I stood with Dr. Hruska at the rear wall near the staircase, I had a grand view of the Old Town Square through the large front window. Perhaps the big plate glass, which cut down enormously on display space, was important for the museum, since people passing by outside—and there were multitudes—could look in and possibly choose to enter. In any case, as the director spoke, I was gazing out the window, watching the endless movement of people on the vast square.

Just then the girl in the blue beret came by again, rubbing her elbow on the window. She walked so close to the huge plate glass the back of her sign scraped the window. Like in trick photography, it penetrated the glass and a corner of her placard was on this side of the fluid, penetrable window.

As Dr. Hruska spoke, I made up my mind quickly—my movement actually preceding my thoughts—and broke off the conversation.

"Sorry, Dr. Hruska, I'll...I'm...I have to..." And I shouted over my shoulder, "Be right back."

The K Museum. The Altneushul. The girl in the blue beret. Sometimes I put third things first. Straight out the door I ran, not even turning to see the expression on the director's face. With balletic agility—I'm a good dancer, remember?—I pirouetted and turned a quick right. Crowds of tourists, a group of Italian high school students singing and walking ten in a row, their arms around each other, a panoply of strollers block my view. The cascade of people so thick and swift it was like a horizontal waterfall. But I charged forward like a linebacker through the rush-hour crowd, stepping to the right here, veering and weaving to the left there, holding that imaginary football, racing to the one-yard line, one hand out stiffly, ready to thrust aside all tacklers who stood in my way, seeking the moving ad for the concert.

Aside from talking to the girl in the blue beret, I wanted to thank her for the message she and the unnamed fellow next to her brought me, bringing me closer to K. Even if Karoly Graf was not K's son, it still would make an exciting addition to the film. And I would include the museum too, without commentary. Let the viewer make his own decision on that insignificant little space.

I caught up to her, pretended to be deeply interested in the details of tomorrow night's concert printed on her placard. She smiled again. It wasn't the smile of a hostess at an outdoor café luring customers with a smile that started and stopped with her teeth. From within came the smile of the girl in the blue beret. That smile affected me. Yes, I admit, it did. I held that smile in the palm of my hand and later glanced at it from time to time.

"Hi, do you speak English?"

"Yes."

"How much are tickets for tomorrow night's concert?"

She pointed to the fifteen kroner price.

"But if you buy now, it's only twelve kroner. At the door, fifteen."

I looked at her face, noted a little wave of black hair peeking out from under the beret.

"You have an interesting accent. Where are you from?" I asked.

"Georgia."

"Atlanta?"

She smiled, chin down, looking at me over glasses that weren't there. "No."

"Macon?"

"No."

"If y'all come from Joe-ja, how come ah doan heah a Suthen accent?"

"'Cause I come from northern Georgia." And now she laughed.

"Ah, then you must be from Augusta."

She gave a happy laugh.

At once I had the entire scenario. She had migrated from some European country to America and was now studying in Prague because tuition was much cheaper and was working to pay for her college costs.

I looked around at the other placard holders. No one else looked quite like her. Nobody wore a beret. The others had Slavic faces, either from here or Slovakia, high cheekbones, flat noses, wideset eyes. But she looked different. Maybe she wanted to call attention to herself with that navy-blue beret. Then again, maybe she just wanted to keep her head warm.

"You're a college student, right?"

"Okay," she said noncommittally. "So would you like to buy a ticket?"

Why didn't she ask me where I came from, what accent I had, what I was doing in Prague? I wanted to tell her that she and her coworker had been instrumental in giving me a positive message. But I decided to hold back. If she was all business, I would keep still too. For a moment I also thought of sharing with her whom I had just met outside the K Museum. But just because Karoly Graf blurted out sensational info to me didn't mean that I had to do the same. That's how rumors spread.

True, I liked talking to her, but since I had impolitely left Dr. Hruska practically in mid-sentence, I thought it would only be decent to return.

"Maybe I'll buy one later," I told her. "I have to rush back to the K Museum. Will you be here in fifteen, twenty minutes?"

"In the vicinity, yes."

"Okay, I'll look for you."

I don't know why my heart was racing as I entered the museum. Was it delayed excitement from speaking to the girl or guilt that I had rudely broken off talking with Dr. Hruska just as he was answering my question about K's son?

The receptionist sent me upstairs to his little office.

"Ah, you're back. Good," the director said. "I thought I had insulted you when I asked you if you understood international sign language."

"No, not at all. Please forgive me. I saw someone I knew…if I didn't catch…"

"It's okay, it's okay."

"Forgive me for running out so abruptly."

"Quite all right. So, kindly have a seat, make yourself comfortable, and we shall continue. In response to your declaration that the visits by the so-called or self-styled son of K to our museum are a plus for us, I asked you if you understand international sign language."

"To which I was going to ask: What do you mean?"

Dr. Hruska tapped his right temple three times, then circled his right index finger clockwise around his ear a few times. I nodded, I understood. Then I took out Karoly Graf's visit card and showed it to the director. He took it and looked at it. He waved the card several times as he spoke, brought it to his chest, teasingly close to his pocket as though he would take it from me for bringing an illegal or false document into the museum. Perhaps he had worked for the previous regime—lots of people continued in posts they had had under the communists—before the political turnaround and was used to doing just this, confiscating false documents. For a moment I feared he would do just that, for it's hard to shake off old bureaucratic ways. Lips pressed, Dr. Hruska nodded knowingly.

"Now do you understand?"

"I see," I said, my heart sinking. "Oh, my. He's…"

"Yes, absolutely, I regret to say. The poor man, otherwise a decent, knowledgeable fellow, is deluded with this ridiculous idée fixe… He comes here often, and because of his age we give him complimentary admission. I'm sorry to disappoint you…but I must tell you"—here he returned Graf's visit card—"don't waste your time."

"Is he Jewish?"

Dr. Hruska, who very likely was not a Jew, looked at me. I thought he would say, What difference does it make? But he said:

"He claims he is, but I cannot confirm that."

I saw the director looking quickly at his wrist. He was too polite to lift his hand up and openly glance at his watch. But I got the hint. I shook his hand, thanked him, and said I had to be on my way.

"Come back soon," Dr. Hruska said.

3

Again the Girl in the Blue Beret

Maybe I will buy a ticket from the girl in the blue beret, I thought as I walked out of the museum. Then I'll ask her if she wants to join me, and if she says yes, I'll buy another ticket. Again I made my way through crowds in the Old Town Square looking for her. The girl in the blue beret was right. She wasn't in the same spot she was in before.

When she saw me she raised her eyebrows in a gesture I thought was welcoming. As if to say, Ah, hello, you *are* back. You said you'd come back and you did come back.

"So, then, which part of Georgia," I said as if there had been no break in our conversation, "do you call home?"

Again she laughed, closed her eyes for a moment, and shook her head.

"Actually, I'm from Gruzinye, the other, the real, Georgia. From Tbilisi."

As soon as she said she was from Georgia, I had a rush, a high, call it inspiration. That's what pretty girls can do—in the Middle Ages inspire feats of knightly valor; today, feats of wit in middle age.

I had gone several times to a Georgian restaurant in New York and tasted their vegetarian specialties. I was ready to show off my Russian too. True, she said she was Georgian. But I figured Russian,

Georgian, it was all the same. Stalin, a Georgian, spoke Russian. Hitler, an Austrian, spoke German. Dictators' language was interchangeable. They all spoke the same tongue.

I asked her in Russian, How are you, my dear? "*Kak pozhevyitese, moi dorogoi*?"

"I don't understand Russian."

"But you don't understand enough of it to realize it's Russian."

"True. But I still don't understand it."

"Neither do I."

"Then how do you speak it?"

"I speak it but I don't understand it."

I thought she would laugh. Even I laughed at my own joke. But she only made a face.

"Do you know Georgian?" she asked.

"No, but"—and this was what I was waiting for—"but I love simiki with willy-nilly takashvilli."

The girl in the blue beret looked at me blankly. I thought the mention of local Tbilisi delicacies like cottage cheese and raisin latkes would make her smile with joy. I thought she'd be overcome by a wave of nostalgia, her mouth watering. And pleased and impressed by my knowledge.

"Don't you just love," I pressed on, "zakuski and khachapouri?"

Now her blank stare had an overlay of concern. Her confusion matched my clarity. I closed my right eye slightly and looked at her.

"You're not from Georgia, are you?" I said with a smile to take the edge off my accusation. "For if you were, you would melt with happiness, hearing a stranger recite your national dishes."

But the girl in the blue beret, the girl from alleged Georgia, was not to be outdone. For she came back with:

"Really? Hot dogs. Coke. Big Mac. Rice Krispies," she said. "I don't see you melting with tears of joy."

"Your point," I conceded, marveling at her riposte. "Do you know the difference, Miss Atlanta, between blini and blinchki, between *Petrouchka* and petrushka?"

Now she smiled. But it wasn't a loving smile. It wasn't the welcoming smile I had seen before. It was the smile that preceded a sharp verbal thrust. I imagined her taking off her placard, grabbing a foil, stepping back and saying, *En garde!*

"If I were from Kabul, would you recite Afghani national dishes and try to trip me up in your pseudo-Swahili as to the difference between Stravinsky's ballet and the Russian word for parsley, which we willy-nilly also use in Georgian. My mother tongue, you know, is part of the Slavic family of languages."

That remark clinched it for me. Now I knew she was fibbing. Georgian is not part of the Slavic family. It is not related to any other family of languages.

I looked her in the eye. "You're still not from Georgia."

And she, instead of answering, looked over my shoulder and said through tight lips:

"My boss is coming toward me. Quick, buy a ticket or he'll think I'm offing goof."

Suppressing a bellow of laughter, I bought a ticket from her, even though I assumed it was a ruse.

"Is he still headed this way?" I also said through tight lips.

"No. Soon as he saw me making a sale, he turned."

I examined tomorrow night's ticket.

"Will you be there?"

"No. The tickets cost too much."

"The management doesn't give you guys free tickets?"

"No. There are too many of us advertising. That's their policy."

"Here," I said in a sudden gesture that wasn't planned. "Take it. You go. I can't make it tomorrow anyway. I bought it just to save you a problem."

"You did?" she said with regret in her voice. "I'm so sorry I made you buy a ticket. Here. Back your money take."

"No no, it's okay. Go. Enjoy."

"Thank you so much."

The girl in the blue beret looked at me admiringly. It's not ego speaking. I can tell by that certain look in the eye, the tilt of the head. I was about to ask her what I really wanted to ask her but remained silent. Why? Why did I remain silent? Maybe I wouldn't see her again. Why should I lose this opportunity when it was now within my grasp? Nevertheless, I sort of waved to her and turned to go.

"No one has ever given me a ticket before."

Not even a traffic cop? I thought of saying but didn't know if the word "ticket" was used here in that sense. But her words seemed like an opening. I considered them a gift.

Now I was about to say what I wanted to say before but some stupid masochism masquerading as a sense of propriety still paralyzed my will.

"Next time, we'll…" I said, but she cut me off before I had a chance to add, *go together to a concert.*

"Now I really have to move about. The boss, he's still somewhere on the square. He will let me go if he sees me talking too much to one customer."

"I'll let you go," I said, letting go slowly, not wanting to go at all. I went around the bend and joined the crowd of tourists looking up at the clock tower.

About ten minutes later I bumped into her again in a different part of the square.

She saw me and said something that sounded like, "Kay."

"What?"

"You look like Danny K."

It had been years, and I mean years and years, since I had heard a girl say that.

And I couldn't resist saying, "I knew him."

"What?" Her eyes widened. "You did? Really?"

"Yes, I did. In fact, I saw him about a month ago, just two weeks before he died."

She put her hand under the placard to her heart. "Oh no! He died? Danny K, dead? Oh my God! When?"

"A couple of weeks ago. Wasn't it on the news here?"

"No. What's the matter with this country?"

"It was front-page news all over America."

"I'm so sorry. I loved his films. And you saw Danny K? In person?" She looked at me skeptically. "You really really knew him?"

"I sat right next him at a dinner party in New York. I was heartbroken when he died. It came so suddenly. He hadn't even been ill. One morning I open the *New York Times* and there on page one is the sad news of his sudden passing." I put my hand on my heart too. "I've been in love with Danny K since I was a kid."

"He was my hero too," said the girl in the blue beret. "He ran all over the world raising money to help poor children."

I looked over my shoulder surreptiously. "Is your boss coming? Is this chat costing me another ticket?"

Came now a fetching smile, her eyes almost closed. With the opening she'd given me, I almost said I'll buy another ticket. But I held back. I wanted to, but I couldn't seem to crash through that barrier. A few minutes earlier I had started to say, Next time we'll go together, before she interrupted me. Now I could have spoken but restraint—down, away with, false politesse—held my tongue. Although it needed only a few motions of lip and tongue to turn dream into reality, and just as she had given me that A Major Major Discovery message before, now she gave me another message. But I still couldn't leap the gap from here to there.

Why?

Why why why?

I suppose I wanted to secure my reputation with her. Figured I'd go slow. I didn't want her to think I was like every other male tourist on the square.

I walked away from the great plaza, frustration orbiting me like a quick moon. The missed opportunity gnawed at me. An empty feeling swirled in my stomach like a vague pain. I'll see her again on the square, I consoled myself. Next time, I swore to myself, I will, I will, I will articulate what I wanted to say and drive that cavernous emptiness away.

4

First Visit to Altneushul

I had a fantasy that my first day in Prague would be K-esque. But as it turned out it was my second.

At 6:45, per Jiri Krupka-Weisz's instructions, I walked up to the Altneushul. How out of place this nearly one-thousand-year-old structure with its peaked roof looked among the modern office buildings and fashionable shops on Parizska Street. The street was deserted. I was the only person in sight. I walked into the narrow lane where the Jewish Town Hall meets the entrance to the synagogue. I looked up to the top of the Jewish Town Hall, at the famous reverse-running clock with its polished brass Hebrew letters that serve as numbers. Then I noticed the policeman patrolling.

"What time do services begin?" I asked in English.

He stared at me with his simple, Schweik-like face.

I pointed to my watch. Well, actually, I didn't have a watch. To the place where the watch would have been. And then I pointed to the door of the synagogue and mimed opening it.

The cop waved his hands, crisscrossing one over the other like an umpire signalling "safe." But here it meant the opposite. No. Closed. Then he turned his fingers and fist as if to lock a door.

"Sinagoga geshpert," he said in pidgin German.

"How is that possible?" I exploded. "The booklet said the shul is open every day. Offen, offen!" I said, miming an open door.

"Turistika," he said, pointed to his watch and held out ten fingers.

I didn't want to join a 10 a.m. tour with hundreds of people traipsing through the shul. I wanted to see the shul as a shul should be seen, when it breathes with worshippers—not when it holds its breath. Of course, I also wanted to meet my contact whose name I had forgotten.

I had risen at six, dead tired, ordered breakfast, and made sure to be here at least ten minutes early. And now the policeman tells me the Altncushul is closed.

Then, out of the corner of my eye, I spotted a man in motion. He moved in what I call the shul walk, slightly bent forward, in a rush, using a stride that is reserved just for synagogue services. He wouldn't walk that way to catch a train. He wouldn't walk that way for exercise. He walked that way to shul because that's the way he saw his father and grandfather walking to shul. And then under his arm I noticed the telltale tallis bag.

I thought I'd try the international language, Yiddish.

"Sholem aleichem. When does davenning begin?"

"Aleichem sholem. Soon. At seven."

"The cop told me the shul is closed."

The man made a disparaging motion with his hand. "What does he know? His job is to protect the shul. So he does it by keeping people he doesn't know away, the idiot." The man pulled a rather large, old-fashioned key from his pocket and unlocked the ancient door. He looked at his watch and didn't relock the door.

I followed him down three stone steps. A thrill ran through me as I entered the fabled shul, where the Maharal, the creator of the golem, had prayed four hundred years ago. I wondered if the people here were similarly in awe of this holy space. Two men were already inside. One, to the right front, was putting on tefillin. The other, on the bimah, was shifting books. So few Jews for the morning service in the oldest synagogue in the world, one of Jewry's treasured sites? But as my eyes grew accustomed to the chiaroscuro light, other figures appeared. Two men way in front near the Holy Ark. Three to the side of the door in pews perpendicular to the bimah. Three in the back. Exactly ten, a minyan. Wait, I was there too, which made it eleven.

Jiri had told me that his old family friend always prayed by the rear wall in the corner. I looked at the three men standing there and thought I knew which one it was. He stood there in the corner by himself, the tallest of the three. Since he didn't move, I imagined for a moment he was a statue, something that George Segal might have made, akin to the outdoor statue of Schweik sitting at a café I would see later. But actually the man was just meditating before putting on tefillin. Unlike the others, who were chatting before the start of the service, he spoke to no one. He was about six-two or six-three, vigorous-looking, in his mid-fifties, with a big head and a round, reddish face.

I saw the man in profile. His right eye seemed lifeless. He looked a little slow, like a golem. But what wasn't golemic in Prague? Even the uncooperative policeman looked like a golem. As the man took four steps forward to get a Siddur, I noticed his deliberate, awkward movements. His dull, expressionless eye and lumbering gait made him seem retarded. I immediately nicknamed him golem. The phlegmatic way he wound the tefillin straps around his arm and the largo recitation of blessings confirmed my judgment. Was this the man Jiri had sent me to? The man who supposedly would be so helpful to me? He, the key? Still, I couldn't take my eyes off him. Why did I stare at him so incessantly? Did I think this would help reveal his name to me?

His big face and slow movements somehow indicated strength. I imagined how powerful he must be, the golem. I fantasized that if the ceiling were to collapse, he would lift his powerful arms like the golem did in the silent film classic, *The Golem*, when the ceiling of the emperor's palace began to crumble. The

Rabbi of Prague, the Maharal, had warned the courtiers not to laugh when he magically showed them scenes from the Exodus from Egypt or there would be serious consequences. But laugh they did, and the vaulted stone ceiling began to descend and the golem stretched his hands up and the ceiling bent around his arms and you can see the striated lines in the stone straining, lines like wrinkles in an old woman's face. And I imagined from my stone seat by the doorway, about twenty-five or thirty feet from the modern golem, that with his powerful arms he could enact the same feat.

Then I rose and walked toward him.

"Shalom," I said. "I have regards for you from—"

He turned slightly.

Just then, without excusing himself, another man interrupted. He stood in front of the golem and began to speak. I was about to protest this rudeness, as I would usually do when peeved, but I restrained myself. I was a visitor. I had just arrived. I wouldn't want to alienate anyone here.

Their lively conversation in Czech made me realize the man I had nicknamed Golem wasn't dimwitted at all. Not with that crackling, assertive burst of Czech.

The other man went back to his seat.

I introduced myself. "Do you speak English?"

"Yes. Welcome to the Al-tnigh-shul." He used the alternative pronunciation.

We shook hands. I was surprised by the gentleness of his handclasp, rather soft and meek.

Just like with Jiri, I couldn't quite make out where his accent came from.

"I bring you regards from a family friend, Dr. Jiri Krupka-Weisz."

Now I saw the golem full face. No wonder I thought his face was expressionless. His right eye was glass. His right cheek seemed stiffer than the left, as if the nerves had been damaged. But the left side was quite animated.

"I didn't know dead men can send regards," he said drily.

It was too late for foreboding. At once the pain of sadness swept over me. Oh, my God, I thought. So it is true. If a friend says it, it must be true.

Still, I said, "Who is dead?" One always hopes, even when there is little reason to hope. After all, I had heard the news in rather oblique fashion, from Patient Information and from the super in Jiri's apartment.

"You mean you convey regards and don't know the fate of the man?"

I let his prickly remark brush by me.

"Here's the story. We met in shul in New York two Sabbaths in a row. Then I saw him one day at the hospital. Then the hospital refused to give me any information, citing the new privacy laws. It's so frustrating. Oh, my God! Poor Jiri. I'm so sorry to hear this. I liked him so much. I can't tell you how sad I am to hear that he died. What a *mentch.* I only knew him a short while but we established a kinship. He even called me *bruderl,* little brother."

"I know what *bruderl* means."

His third sarcastic remark. Well, at least he wasn't a moron.

"Sorry, I just wanted to make myself clear. I felt I had found a long-lost relative in Jiri. All this in three meetings."

"So you liked him."

If I were combative, I would have said, Isn't it obvious? I just told you I liked him. But I toned it down to:

"As you can see."

I sat down next to the golem.

Wait a minute. What happened to my scenario? He still hadn't told me his name.

"You see," I said, "when they stonewalled me at the..."

"Excuse me, what is this stonewalled?"

"At the hospital, no matter how hard I tried, they refused to give me any information. They wouldn't tell me if he was a patient, if he was well, if he was discharged, if he died. Like a stone wall was put up in front of me."

"Stonewalled," he said, closing his good eye and staring at me, golem-like, with his glass.

"Stonewalled. Good word. Excellent word. I like that word, 'stonewalled.'"

"Exactly. I even went to his apartment afterward to see his wife."

"Wife?"

"Well, it looked like a wife. It sure talked like a wife."

"Jiri was not married. His wife and son were killed by the Germans. He never remarried."

"All right, then. A housekeeper."

"Ah, yes. Keeper of the house. Keeper of the keys."

Then he winked, not with the good eye but with the bad. An eerie, empty wink. But perhaps it was just the lid moving, a mechanical flaw.

"But when I arrived at his apartment the next day," I continued, "the house manager told me the apartment was empty. His housekeeper had moved out."

"And his books, his signed copy of *Meditation*?"

"I know nothing about that." I wanted to tell him about Jiri's and Betty's secret language but I held back.

"And… and…" The golem wanted me to continue. He dangled a word magnet right in front of me and waited. His face conveyed two messages, both contradictory. Puppet stiffness and animation. But on one thing both sides of his face agreed: talk some more. Reveal.

Broke then my resistance, especially when he said:

"Did he tell you any special word?"

"You mean like a password, or, like in banking, a personal identification number?"

The golem didn't answer.

What special word did Jiri give me? None that I could recall. Or should I tell the golem about "nepa tara glos"?

But he had inserted the magic key, turned it, and now the words tumbled, bubbled, out of me, oozing the pleasure of juicy gossip.

"All right, I might as well tell you. Sometimes, in my presence, especially at the hospital at our last meeting, they spoke a secret language I could not penetrate. Well, maybe I did get a word or two."

The golem laughed. "That means they liked you."

What kind of nonsense is that? I thought. If they liked me they would have spoken a language I could understand. Then I considered my relationship with Jiri. There was a difference between he liking me and they liking me. On his own, it was love. Conjoined with Betty, the affection underwent a chemical change.

"I never thought discourtesy was synonymous with affection."

"You are very philosophical. But wrong. I said they liked you. I didn't say they trusted you."

"Another misalliance. Another *moyshe-kapoyr*—yes, I know you know it means upside down—another strange coupling… About what didn't they trust me? Inheritance? Bank accounts? I hardly knew them, for goodness' sake."

"I don't know either. But when people use a secret language…" But he didn't finish his thought.

"And how does a woman who isn't a wife get to know such an arcane language?"

The golem shrugged. "Yes," he said.

"It must have been a made-up language, because it had no affinity to any language grouping I know."

"You'll have to ask him that."

"I'm in no rush to meet him again. But Jiri did say you could be helpful to me, to introduce me to some people."

Should I tell him about the magic pen? No, I thought. Why give him another excuse for sarcastic laughter?

Thud. Thud. Thud. The sudden banging in the synagogue startled us. Someone pounded with a leather paddle on a leather-covered board for silence.

"I'll talk to you after davenning," said the golem softly without moving his lips.

"I still haven't fully expressed how I feel about Jiri," I told the golem later. "Sometimes you know people for years and don't know them and yet sometimes you meet someone and in an instant you feel you've known and loved them a lifetime. I can't tell you what a loss I feel."

The golem must have been touched by my words for both sides of his face softened.

"Let me tell you something about Jiri he never would tell you himself. He was head of archives for the Jewish Museum here just before the Germans came. Since he had a PhD the Germans chose him to head the Jewish Museum they had in mind. The Germans respected titles and even called him Herr Doktor. He was going to be the director of what the Germans would call the Museum of an Extinct Race. Of course, they never told Jiri or any other Jew that name. Every day they brought truckloads of items stolen from the Jews they were killing, and they wanted Jiri and his staff to catalog them. And for cataloging the thousands of items the Germans were pillaging all over Czechoslovakia and surrounding regions, Jiri told them he needed lots of help. This way he was able to save many Jews in Prague. He stayed up nights teaching the Jews what to do so they could prove they were useful. When the Germans complained how many people he hired, he told them, If you want to have an accurate and precise cataloging we need every man and woman here. And the children are especially useful for handling the small items. 'Precise' and 'accurate' were totemic words for the Germans and they relented."

"Jiri never told me that."

"And he never would. I told you that. That's the sort of man he is, was. An unsung hero of the Holocaust, whom we call the Schindler of Prague. But, near the end, they still sent him to Terezin. But thank God the staff he created survived."

I shook my head in wonder.

The golem clapped his hands once. "So! What brought you to Prague, tovarish?"

"A direct flight from JFK in New York."

He laughed a crooked smile, one side of his face happier than the other.

"Rather, I meant to say, what brings you to Prague?"

"My camera. I'm a maker of documentary films. Here I'm hoping to make a film about the Jewish uniqueness of Prague, with an accent on K."

"Uh-huh," said the golem. He licked his lips. "And no doubt you want to begin with this old shul."

"Yes. Starting with the attic." Seeing who stood before me I refrained from saying golem.

"The what?" said the golem.

"The attic."

The golem leaned against the wall and burst out laughing. But not laughing laughing. I mean *laughing* laughing. He laughed out of the two sides of his mouth, a sad twitching laugh on the glass eye side, and a raucous double-barreled laugh on the left side, as if making up for the lack on the right with an extra dose on the left. He held his sides. His belly shook. He was a cartoon stereotype of a laughing man.

"The attic," he gasped. "The golem."

"I said nothing about the golem."

This golem showed all his teeth.

"You don't have to say. You don't have to say. But you said it. You said it without saying it. When you say attic you say golem. And when you say golem you mean attic."

Maybe I'll nickname you Attic, I didn't say.

Then the golem called, "Shamesh! *Kum aher!*"

I never expected the golem to speak Yiddish, although the original golem, the Maharal's sixteenth-century creation, did understand Yiddish; the same golem whose remains presumably lie, untouched, in the dusty attic where no human being has ascended since the Rabbi of Prague, the Maharal, put an end to the golem by plucking the *shem*—the little parchment with God's holy name on it—from the golem's mouth. And yet this tall man with the big head and glass eye and ruddy face of an Irishman, this golem surprised me by using Yiddish.

Approached now the shamesh, a small thin old man with wispy white hair straggling over and around his black yarmulke, a sad old man, a survivor, I saw. I hadn't noticed him before. He must have been standing directly in front of the bimah, out of view when I came in. And because the wooden poles on the bimah blocked my view of him, I hadn't seen him—it was very likely he; who else besides a shamesh bangs for silence?—when he pounded on the table before. The shamesh had survived one them during World War II, only to fall after the war into the hands of another them. But the second them were gone now too, gone three years ago, and Prague breathed freely.

"*Vos iz*, Yossi?" the shamesh asked. What is it?

Aha. Finally. His name. Yossi. Of course. A diminutive of Joseph. I was right. It was a Biblical name. Yossi. Yosef. Joseph. Now I won't forget it. Yossi.

"Shamesh…he wants…" and the golem, laughing, pointed, actually jabbed his index finger toward me, "…to see the attic. The golem."

"I said nothing about the golem," I repeated.

The shamesh too began laughing. Now both of them laughed together. They shook with laughter, these two, moving forward and back, the golem a bit jerkily, like an automaton, the shamesh more smoothly. They held their sides, their stomachs (each his own), tending to a quaking, laugh-shooken belly, adding titters to cackles, giggles to hysterics, until tears ran from their eyes, even the golem's glass eye trickled a tear, and they gasped for breath.

A few of the other worshippers drew near, tentatively. For them the golem and the shamesh repeated my request. Then they too, without even looking at me, subjected me to a cacophony of laughter. They sounded like a synagogue choir for the High Holidays, a bass laugh, then a falsetto, then the entire chorus, then solo voices laughing in alternation until they all chanted their laughter together. They bent forward and leaned back in orchestrated laughter, dipping and rising in a laughter ballet.

I stood there dumbfounded, mingling feelings of anger, shame, and helplessness. I wanted to rush up to the bimah and shout for silence. But I was too old to cry, and too polite to berate them.

"*Yoysher!*" the shamesh suddenly cried out. He leaped up—what agility and speed for a man his age, up to the bimah, doing for me what I only dreamt of doing—grabbed the leather-coated wooden paddle and slammed it down hard on the thick red leather pad on the reading table. "Decency! Justice! What are you, citizens of Sodom? Not nice to laugh at the visitor. He just came. From thousands and thousands of miles. Not nice." And he slammed the paddle again and again. "Shame on you. Foo! Feh! Not nice to humiliate a guest. A young man we see for the first time comes to shul and you laugh at him?"

The laughter suddenly ceased, a radio snapped off.

The shamesh called me out to the anteroom. We stood by the big arched wooden door. I regarded the ancient stone walls. This anteroom, as indeed the rest of this magnificent synagogue, was carefully built by hand, stone by stone, many hundreds of years ago and had withstood invasions, uprisings, wars, the Germans in the 1940s. We stepped outside into the little alley.

"Please accept my apologies for these boors. Bunch of fools. Congregation of idiots. Like King David says in the Psalms, 'They have eyes but see not, ears but hear not.' But, alas, they have big mouths. They are the real goylems, the nitwits, the numbskulls, the fools. The Psalms also says that God protects the fools—but He missed with them." The shamesh dropped his voice, looked around. "This shul is a magnet for the mentally debilitated." Now he brightened. "You know, don't you, that goylem in Yiddish, just like in Hebrew, also means fool?"

I nodded.

"Do you want to see the goylem?" he asked softly, almost seductively.

I didn't know what to say. Perhaps the shamesh had taken a liking to me and, seeing the disgraceful reception I had just gotten, pitied me. In compensation, he would show me the legendary attic that no one in modern times had seen. And then I could bring my camera and photograph the place where the golem had lain. Wonderful! My Prague film was taking shape nicely. K's son; the little museum; the golem; the attic.

"Well?" the shamesh said.

I didn't want to answer too quickly. I pretended I was thinking it over. Even faked a thinking pose by holding my chin with thumb and forefinger.

"All right," I said languidly, desultorily, as if bored, as if it were, if not the last thing I wanted to do, then at least next to last.

"You don't sound very entuziastish," the shamesh mingled English and Yiddish.

"How can one be enthusiastic about a legend? If, for instance, I asked you, Do you want to see Moses...?"

"Him I see all the time. Every time I read the Torah I see him..."

"All right, let me rephrase the question. If I asked you, do you want to see Sholom Aleichem, or, closer to home, K, would you jump up and down for joy?"

The shamesh—I wondered how old he was. Eighty? Ninety?—put his hands on his hips and regarded me. A clever look sparked in his rheumy eyes. He had to be clever, serving as a shamesh here for probably decades, under the communists who, besides their anti-Semitism and anti-Israel Soviet party-line stance, were also anti-religious.

"I see you're a smart yungerman... But tourists always come up to me and ask me, privately, quietly..." Here he put his hand over his lips and said softly, "and they look this way and that way as if on the lookout for spies. Some even slip a folded five-dollar bill or ten-dollar bill into my hand or my pocket and say, 'Take me to the attic. Please. It's my life's wish. My dream, ever since I read about the Maharal and the goylem he made. So, please, please, take me, I'll pay anything.' I look at the ten-dollar bill and say, 'This is anything? Beh! This is nothing. Less than nothing.' Embarrassed, they say: 'I'll add to it. Here.' And they give me a twenty-dollar bill, which I give back. Because I don't take bribes. 'All right,' I say. 'I'll show you the goylem.' And they, their faces are in rapture, as if they've seen the Divine Presence at Sinai. And they don't know the surprise that's coming."

"You actually show them the golem?" I say, astonished.

"I actually do. I tell them I show the golem and I show the golem. I promise and I keep my promise. I am the shamesh."

He stopped. Took a breath.

"You want to know how? Sure you want to know how. Here is how."

The little wizened shamesh put his hand into his jacket pocket and withdrew a little mirror, the sort women carry in their purses. He held it in front of my face.

"Na! Here! Look! I tell them. Here, in front you, is the goylem. *Der emesser goylem.* The true, the real, the authentic goylem. Now you've seen him, is what I tell them. You wanted to see the goylem and now you've seen the goylem." And the shamesh laughed merrily.

Was he reprising for me what he had done for countless others, or was it at me he was now aiming his jibe? He laughed with such joy it seemed he was laughing at me as he was laughing at the foolishness of people who finally got to see the goylem they sought. Still, his little act was so subtle, full of subterfuge, I couldn't figure him out.

But I laughed too, and saw myself laughing at the golem in the little glass. The shamesh, pleased with himself, now put the mirror back into his jacket pocket.

"A marvelous ploy. Terrific. Original. Clever. Unusual. It has the making of legend. It deserves to be filmed...I'll film you. I'll make a movie—I'm a producer of documentary films—a movie of this shul and I'll film you doing just this."

Another great scene for my film, I thought. The scenes were just piling up, one after another. Falling into my lap. And I hadn't even taken out my camera.

The shamesh took a comb out of another pocket, looked at the little mirror again, combed his hair and patted it down.

"I suppose you want to know where the attic is," he said, addressing the mirror. Then he looked down at his shoes. Careful, I said. But I didn't heed my own warning and didn't hear the ambiguity in his voice.

So this time I didn't play coy or hard to get. At once I said:

"Yes."

"And you also want to see the goylem."

"Not a second time," I said with a smile. "Once is enough."

The shamesh too smiled.

"Ah! Now you sound enthuziastish."

"Yes."

"Follow me, yungerman."

We entered the shul again through the anteroom. I saw the other men holding their tallis bags standing in clusters chatting. The man who had let me in nodded to me. The morning service was over but the after-sound of prayers still hovered in the air.

"Look up," the shamesh said. "Do you see the vaulted arches?"

"Yes."

"Do you know how high up it is?"

I looked up, saw the huge, five-part vaulted pillars, purposely architected so that it would not look like a cross. I saw the banner that King Charles V had presented to the congregation in 1357 as a symbol of their independence. No conquerer of Prague had ever removed the flag.

"Um, I'd say seventy feet."

"Not bad…ninety-two feet. Now follow me once more." Again we went out into the anteroom and made a semicircular right turn. Now we were in the tiny women's section, which had only a few chairs and no visibility except for some window-like openings chiseled into the deep stones, maybe fourteen inches high and seven inches wide. The openings were cut into the three-foot-thick stone walls and looked into the men's section. How uncomfortable it must be, I thought, for women to pray here.

"Look up. Up up up. Do you see doors? A staircase? Steps?... Look…look…do you see anything?"

"No."

"You want to look in the mirror again?"

"No."

"Now you understand?"

"Yes."

"Good. Is there an attic up there?"

I felt like Schweik. I was itching to say, Yes.

"Do I get a prize if I answer correctly?"

"Yes."

"What?"

"A trip to the attic.... So what's the correct answer? Is there an attic up there?"

"No."

"Right. You get a prize. I'm apprising you there is no attic. There was no attic. There is no attic. There will be no attic. The Al-tnigh-shul never had an attic. It's a *bobbe-mayse*, a legend, like the goylem... Now, when will you film me? I want to look good, to get a haircut...when?"

Again the shamesh took out his little mirror, looked at himself, fussed a bit with some wispy tufts of white hair.

"I haven't set up my schedule yet. As you know, I just got here. But I'll be in touch with you."

"Wait a minute, yungerman."

I stopped.

"What's your Hebrew name? Next time you come I'll give you an aliya."

"Amschl ben Moshe."

The shamesh gave a start. His head and torso were thrust back. "I haven't heard that name for a long time. But do not worry, I'll remember it. Amschl ben Moshe."

As soon as the shamesh left, Yossi golem came up to me, shaking his head, his lips compressed, a look of disdain on the left side of his face.

"Disgraceful. Those asses. No consideration. And they call themselves God-fearing, observant Jews. Did you see the way they laughed at you, derided you, made a mockery of you? Rocking back and forth in laughter like metronomes. Please accept my apologies on their behalf. But let's forget them. Back to business. I'll try to help you, for you were sent to me by my dear friend, almost a kinsman, Jiri of blessed memory. Now I'm going to send you to another family friend, her name is Eva, and she'll be helpful too. She has lived here all her life and knows people. No doubt that's the person Jiri wanted you to meet."

I wondered why Jiri didn't send me to her directly. Perhaps that was the cause of Jiri and Betty's argument, Jiri stressing one point, Betty another. Perhaps they wanted the golem to check me out. Still, I thought, why did I need a middleman?

"Because," the golem answered, "Jiri wanted me to meet you. He wanted my opinion. He values my opinion."

Opinion for what? I didn't say. I didn't even think it lest the golem read my thoughts again.

"I think you'll like Eva. She's a very interesting woman, a heroine of the Resistance, a pianist, she studied with Dvořák's son-in-law, Josef Suk—"

"I just saw some youngsters carrying a placard for a concert with the violinist Josef Suk. Is he still alive?"

Yossi golem laughed. "No. That Josef Suk died in 1935. You're seeing the name of his grandson, who has the same name, and he's no youngster either… But people do live to ripe old ages, you know. Like entertainers in the US who have gone beyond one hundred. Irving Berlin, for instance?"

"Yes, I know. Chagall at 98. George Burns, 101. Moses at 120."

"Very nice," Yossi said quickly. "But no more obituaries today, please. So. To continue. Eva has plenty of stories about the old Jewish community and sites of Jewish interest here that few people know about. And if she likes you, she will introduce you to other interesting people."

I did some calculating. "Wait a minute. If Eva studied with the first Joseph Suk so many decades ago, she must be up there in years. How old is she?"

"I don't know. She's older than me and I'm sixty-eight."

"No. I don't believe it. You're sixty-eight? Impossible. You don't look a day over fifty-four. Okay, maybe fifty-five."

The golem laughed.

"Well, I'm in good shape, even without my right eye. I'm made of good elements… And when you see Eva, send her my best regards."

Yossi wrote Eva's full name—Eva Langbrot—her address and phone number on a slip of paper, even suggested the Metro line and station closest to her house. Then he said:

"It's all very nice. We have had a lovely conversation, a good time together, but one thing is missing."

"What?"

"Your Hebrew name, tovarish." Yossi golem smiled. "I still don't know your Hebrew name. Suppose one day we want to give you an aliya here."

"It's Amschl. The shamesh just asked me too. Amschl ben Moshe is how I'm called to the Torah."

"Ah," he said. "Aha… A…" and he lifted both his palms up and lowered them several times as if carrying an invisible weight. "A significant name in Prague. A worthy, a serious, memorable name. Amschl… Did Jiri know your Hebrew name?"

"No, but just before I concluded my visit in the hospital he said, right out of the blue, 'Amschl.'"

"That may have been the special word. Sometimes we hear a special word but we don't know it."

"I didn't know it was a special word."

"See? That's exactly what I mean. A name as a special word. And, speaking of names, my name is Yossi, Yosef, Josef Lemberg."

I didn't want to tell Yossi—of course, he probably knew it: how could a citizen of Prague not know?—that the name traditionally given to the golem was Josef. Was it just coincidence that Yossi, who looked like a golem, had the golem's name? Or can we say, like Kant and Kierkegaard, that there is no such thing as coincidence: everything is planned, preordained, destined. How does Spinoza put it? A domino fell, eons ago, and pushed other dominoes, which are still falling.

"Now go to Eva. She'll introduce you to the old man who will sh—"

But he didn't finish the word, for just then another man came up and started a rapid-fire round of Czech, which Yossi matched energetically. I watched Yossi's face. He gave no sign that he was arguing with the man, but there was a give-and-take between them. When they stopped, the other man bowed to me, acknowledging he had interrupted me, and departed. But he did not apologize for intruding into our conversation.

"What were you saying a moment ago? The old man who will—will what? You started a word with 'sh' and then that man burst in."

Yossi looked up, tilted his head, thinking. "I forgot…that chap knocked the thought right out of my head."

Yossi looked away from me. I saw his face in golem profile, the dead side of his face.

"'The old man who will…' Those are the exact same words Jiri used. 'Go see Yossi. He will introduce you to some interesting people, an old man who will…'"

"Will what?" Yossi asked.

"How should I know? That's what I'm asking you," I said with increasing frustration. "Jiri said this at the hospital when he wasn't well. He would say something, drift off, and fall asleep, and not finish what he was saying. After I left him at the hospital that day I never saw him again. But how strange it is that you used the very same phrase he did."

Yossi turned away from me and again I saw only the frozen side of his face.

"Sometimes the dead speak through me," he said with a hollow voice.

"And like him, you didn't finish your thought."

Yossi golem shrugged. The incomplete thought, which annoyed and intrigued me, didn't bother him at all. But I pressed on.

"Try to recall what you wanted to tell me about the old man. 'He will sh—' Will surely? Will show? Will share?"

He shook his head. "I'm sorry. I don't know. But good luck with your visit to Eva and come back to see me again."

As I shook hands with him, I wondered what kind of aborted message both Jiri and Yossi were trying to send me. I turned to go. But I had hardly taken three steps when the golem added another conundrum. I didn't see him as he spoke. The words were aimed at my back, then split and flew by each of my ears.

"By the way, you probably don't know this, but Jiri's middle name was Amschl too."

5

Looking for Karoly Graf

As soon as I said goodbye to Yossi golem at the Altneushul—and disregarding Dr. Hruska's advice not to waste my time—I went to look for the man who claimed to be K's son.

What better way to put a star into my Prague film than to video Karoly Graf? Even if false, his story would still make for fascinating cinema. Let the viewer judge the accuracy of his claim. I even toyed with the catchy title, *K's Son*.

In the taxi to his house, I was already filming. That's where films begin, in the mind's eye, which is both camera and screen. The rest is easy. It's like writing. Not on paper is it done, nor with pen, but on the mind's slate. Only then, a few seconds later, do the fingers guide pen over paper, and often the pen can't keep up with the torrent of messages the mind is sending the fingers. Same with films, or a Mozart composition. It's already fully formed in the head.

I would begin with an overview of Prague, its silhouette, much like the opening of the silent film *The Golem*. Then, after a brief interlude in the K Museum, I'd feature my first star, K's son. I would be careful to note that this is Graf's assertion. But I would also state that to my knowledge no one else has come forward with a like claim. In my segment on the golem, its place in the film not yet determined, the shamesh would be featured. And as a way of getting to know her, I also wanted to include the girl in the blue beret. I could promise to film her but with no guarantee that her scene would be in the final version. If I wanted to blend documentary with fiction, as some filmmakers do, I could pass her off as a grand-niece of K's and coach her with a few lines. It is no secret in the newpaper world that photos, especially remote war scenes, are occasionally staged, like that famous World War II photo of the Soviet flag flying from a building when the Germans were defeated. But I wouldn't, couldn't, do that. My reputation was based on total honesty. Not only has my integrity never been questioned, it's been singled out for praise.

The taxi dropped me off on the quiet side street away from center city Prague. I approached the apartment entrance. No Graf was on the list of names. Déjà vu? Looking for Krupka-Weisz in Jiri's apartment? Are the same events fated to happen again and again to a protagonist, like in an avant-garde Danish film I had seen some years ago? Is there a super here too with minimal English, with whom I (c)(w)ould conduct an absurd conversation?

I stood before the locked, thick glass door covered with wrought iron, waiting for someone to come in or leave. I didn't know the Czech word for superintendent and didn't want to aimlessly ring a bell, for how could I possibly explain to someone who didn't speak English who I was and whom I was looking for? Just then a pretty woman came to the door. Seeing me standing there, looking confused, she smiled and spoke to me in Czech, probably saying, Can I help you? When I asked if she spoke English, she said, "Yes." And what if she had said No? How long would I be standing there? But her answer too was fated, just like my meeting with Jiri. There could be no other scenario.

I showed the woman Graf's card.

"There is no one here by that name, and I am here for twelve months."

"Is there a super here?"

"Super? I do not have reference to such word."

"I mean a house manager. Like a concierge in French apartment houses."

"Ah yes, oh yes. I'll ring him."

She pressed a buzzer and said a few words in Czech.

"He'll be right out."

"Will you interpret for me?"

"Yes, of course."

An old bald man with bristling white eyebrows came out. My helper showed him Graf's card. He said a few words and shrugged.

"He says Mr. Graf, a strange man, moved out more than year ago. He had little possessions but several boxes books."

"Please ask him if he knows where he moved to."

"He says he doesn't know."

"Does anyone in the building know him? Did he befriend anyone?"

I watched both as they spoke.

"The super—" the woman said, and she looked at me with a flirtatious twinkle, as if to say: I got the word right, didn't I?—"the super says he was quiet, shy, polite man but not to share confidences or making friends."

"Is there a central registry of Prague citizens?"

"I don't know...if you will pardon me, I may make observation. If the man wanted really you to visit he could gaven you veezeet kart with good address."

"True," I said, "but he just pulled card out of his pocket in fit of enthusiasm, seeing how much I liked author we were discussing. You see, we just met at museum, so perhaps by mistake he gave"—I almost said gaven—"me an old card."

I was about to reveal what Graf had told me, but I held back, afraid of making a laughingstock of the old man. If the super had known, he surely would have revealed it by now, with words like: Ah, yes, the man who always says he's K's son. Yes, that one, he moved out more than a year ago.

But the woman's observation, despite my attempt at defending him, was absolutely right. Why did Graf mislead me? Or was the museum director's international sign language correct?

Another thing bothered me: I should have asked Graf if he had any brothers or sisters.

I thanked the woman, bowed slightly to the super, and walked away. Then it hit me, l'esprit d'escalier, why didn't I invite her, as an act of gratitude, invite her to the concert?

So Karoly Graf, K's putative son, had moved. Why indeed hadn't he given me his correct address? Or was it really an oversight, a mistake? If he did this intentionally, maliciously, he was truly an oddball. He had proudly shared this astonishing bit of information, without prodding or coercion, knowing full well the effect it would have on a lover of K's works. With one hand he had given me important information and raised my spirits, and with the other—literally stretching out his right hand and giving me his false card—he had crushed me. And without realizing it, he had ruined his chances for a bit of fame.

Did he consider my incredulity an insult? I wondered. But that's impossible, since he had given me the card before I expressed my doubts. But then again, in mystic, golem-filled, K-inspired Prague, time and cause and effect followed no natural laws but an ineluctable order of their own, more determined by string theory's ten dimensions and time-devouring black holes than by age-old laws of predictable nature.

What was I to make of Karoly Graf? Knowing that my next move was futile, but pursuing it nevertheless, I looked him up in the telephone directory; I went to the Bureau of Internal Affairs, Citizens Registry Department, in Prague; I returned to the K Museum and spoke to Dr. Hruska—all in vain.

Confession: I had to revise my "officiousness" depiction of Dr. Hruska, for he welcomed me warmly. Too bad we sometimes form opinions and make judgments of people too quickly.

"Has Graf come back since I last saw you?"

"No."

"Would you kindly call me at my apartment hotel," and I gave him the number, "if he should come by, and get from him his current address and phone number?"

"With pleasure." Then the director repeated his admonition: "Don't waste your time."

"Dr. Hruska, I know I am wasting my time. You are absolutely right. Still, if there is the slightest chance of finding him, I'd like to take advantage of it, for I want to interview him for my film."

"Film? You're making a film?" He brightened. His eyes sparkled.

"Yes."

"Would you consider, I mean, wouldn't you like to include our little museum?"

"Of course. What a question! I had planned to."

Dr. Hruska brushed the side of his hair and temples as if I was about to film him. I wondered if, like the shamesh, he too would pull out a little mirror from his jacket pocket and primp.

I thanked the director and left. A magnet drew me back to the faux address on Graf's card. Perhaps the hope of seeing that pretty woman again. I met a few of the residents, older working-class folk who had probably never heard of K. In halting English—one helped the other, sharing the sixty-six English words they knew—they recalled Graf as an amiable man. But they knew nothing about him. Or had American hospital privacy laws affected them too?

Twice more during the next week I returned to the museum. Each time Dr. Hruska smiled, perked up, thinking he would be filmed that day. No, he hadn't seen Karoly Graf.

"In fact, I myself am now wondering why he suddenly stopped coming. I hope he is well." Then, with a sly smile he added, "I even begin to miss him, for he was a very nice chap, no trouble at all, almost like a mild thorn, well, not quite like a thorn, more like a mild itch on the leg or a tiny canker sore inside your mouth that you get used to, your tongue is always probing there, and that you miss when it goes away."

I had so many things to think of. I thought of the film that was still only in my head. I thought of the girl in the blue beret. Would she show up at tonight's concert? I thought of the golem's acquaintance,

Eva Langbrot, whom I still hadn't gone to see. And if thinking isn't too mild a verb, my head was flooded by thoughts of Karoly Graf, K's missing son.

The whole thing didn't make any sense. Perhaps Graf had indeed inadvertently given me an older card that somehow had remained in his pocket instead of the newer card that had his right address. But then, why had he stopped coming to the museum? Unless, of course, he had fallen ill.

And more, what person, even if his assertion were absolutely true, would immediately share such a confidence with a stranger, even if that stranger loved K's work as much as I did? One would think that such a person would be cautious, first invite his new friend to a café, sit and talk, and then tell him he had something fabulous to share with him about K. And if he were a poor man or in modest circumstances, as Karoly Graf no doubt was, if I were he, I would suggest some kind of quid pro quo, for like time, information or astonishing revelation is also one's stock in trade.

That's what I would have done if I were K's son and wanted to share this bombshell with a man I'd just met at the K museum who was crazy about K. But first I would test that someone, determine if he really understood and appreciated K's writings and if he deserved to be privy to such amazing information. I wouldn't play with him or tease him or draw the revelation out inordinately, as heroes of folk tales sometimes do, or as an older woman does in initiating a young lover into the joys of lovemaking. But if I were K's son, I would not rush. I would bide my time, balancing deliberation and speed.

I must say it felt rather good—for a few moments it made me feel very special—nurturing this fantasy in my mind, turning the tables on Karoly Graf, I becoming K's son and he becoming the layman, the doc filmmaker who loved K and who wandered into the K Museum in Prague and was soon to become the possessor of a stunning secret. A secret that Karoly Graf had revealed how many times to how many people? I reveled in the delights of my fantasy, the secret that I possessed and was so willing to share with a select few—hopefully not like Karoly Graf, who no doubt shared it with the unselect many.

Too bad I couldn't film the delights of my fantasy. Oh, how if the situation were reversed, what a time I would have had in concocting a delicious scenario. Not only would I be K's son, I would create several other children, some living in Prague, others elsewhere. And, why not?, yes, an entire family. And my revelation would not be a simple declarative sentence: I am K's son. My revelation, offered slowly, gradually, would be the equivalent of a complex sentence, with inner and outer clauses, not necessarily balanced, but as nuanced and ambiguous and multilayered as K's prose. And then that astonishing many-phrased revelation could be reduced like a rich broth into the mouth-watering gravy of a crisp, declarative sentence with only subject, verb, and possessive:

I am K's son.

But I'm confident that some day via magnetic resonance, pulse echoes, neurotechnology, or other nano innovations, it will be possible to record thoughts, mental images, scenes running across the screen of one's imagination and preserve them on film.

Maybe even video dreams.

Terrific. I dreamt impossible dreams but hadn't yet pressed a button on my camera.

And while I was thinking of making my own film, I felt that someone else was filming me.

6

Going to the Concert

Instead of a taxi from Karoly Graf's faux apartment house back to my hotel I took the modern, comfortable Metro. It was there I changed my mind. About what? Tell you in a minute. But it was inspired by what I saw in the subway car. There, everyone, men and women, seemed to be a golem. It was as if I had landed on the stage of a theater company and everyone was practising how to mime a golem. In the New York City subway system, aside from the nerve-wracking noise of the cars, passengers spoke in dozens of languages. Some to each other, some to themselves. Some sang out, as if performing, as if waiting to be paid. Others mumbled to themselves as though praying by rote. No one kept still. Even those that kept still, kept still noisily, in harmony with the racket of the rails. The cacophony was so thick you could package it.

But here in Prague, silence. The cars rode on rubber wheels; no one spoke. Nevertheless, in the silence I heard words I couldn't understand. The passengers had stiff, immobile faces that reminded me of the right side of Yossi golem's face. And then, just then, at that moment, I thought of the mobile, expressive face of the girl in the blue beret. And that's when I changed my mind. At the last minute. About tonight's concert.

Why should I sit at home and mope over my lack of assertiveness? When she asked me to buy a ticket, I should have said, I'll buy a ticket, even two, if you'll come with me. A left-handed way to ask a girl out, ass backwards, if you will, but it could have worked. Now she was going—with my ticket—and I was staying home. What a date! I had, without even thinking or planning it, invented an entirely new, heretofore unknown, social engagement: the half date.

Would you like to go to tonight's concert? asks the hero. Why, sure, replies the heroine, cheeks flushed, all—as they say—agog.* Okay, then, is the hero's retort, Here, buy yourself a ticket. A scene out of an absurdist comedy, no? Or the Masochist's Handbook.

Seeing those silent golemic faces, and contrasting them with the lively, animated face of the girl in the blue beret, jolted me. That's when I made up my mind. I was the golem. I was like those people in the car. And I resolved I would no longer be a golem.

I'll go look for her. I'll tell her I cancelled my appointment and want to invite her to—wait a minute! I already invited her. How can I invite her again? Well, then—in this topsy-turvy half-date script—I would tell her I'm inviting myself to join her at the concert I already invited her to, that is, gave her a ticket to. That is, if tickets were still available. And suppose only balcony seats were left? She'd sit with my ticket in the orchestra (it was orchestra, I saw, but I didn't note where) and I'd sit upstairs. Hey, credit me with yet another brand-new social engagement. That's two in two days. The split date. Still, I was curious to see if she'd agree. Split, or half, if she said, Yes, I'd be delighted. Delighted! The understatement of the decade.

So I went out to the huge square to look for the girl in the blue beret, postponing my visit to Yossi's friend, Eva, for another day. I inspected every one of the two dozen placard-holders as I went from one end of the square to the other. Like a pawn on my imaginary chessboard I went up one line, down the next like a castle. I criss-crossed the board like a bishop; moved up, down, and across like

* A word always modified by "all." You never see "partially agog" or "agog" unadorned, unmodified, all alone. "Alone" can be "alone" or "all alone." Not agog.

a queen. No check, no mate, no luck. If I was black there was no white. If white, no black. I couldn't find the girl in the blue beret.

Perhaps some of the placard-holders would know. I approached a tall blonde and asked her if she spoke English.

"A small."

"I'm looking," I said slowly, "for one of your colleagues. A girl from Georgia."

She shook her head. "Not knowing."

"A blue beret," I said, "is what she wore."

Again she shook her head.

"There is so multitude of we here, we who carry plakat for concert. The turnunder of workers is grand. What name is she called by?"

"I do not know," I said, "how she is called by name."

"I am regretful."

Was the blonde sorry that I never got to know the girl's name, or that she didn't know her and can't help me?

"How can someone disappear from this square just like that?"

I thought of snapping my fingers but feared she might misinterpret the gesture.

"Also I regretful not knowing this." Then she said softly through almost tight lips, "Make large favor me. Speedily, please, for my overling draws near, so please farewell a concert ticket now from me."

"I should farewell a ticket?"

"Yes. Please. If you farewell a ticket and give money, I present you ticket. Othersmart, my overling he flames me."

At first, I thought I was hearing a variation of Jiri's and Betty's language in a dialect I thought I knew. Its basics sounded familiar enough, but there was a mystery around its edges. If only I had a converter or a special gearbox. And then, shifting gears to halfway between first and reverse, I got it.

"Why? Why your boss flames you?"

"Yes. Because my overling has big eyes. He grabs me conversationing too muchly with no one farewelling ticket he flames me. Me no wish lose job."

She spoke slowly, the tall blonde. She was about thirty, with an angular face and two long, curved lines in her cheeks from her nostrils to her lips. Not the sort of woman that made heads swivel as men passed her on the square. What exigency had made her, a grown woman, do this sort of coolie work? Then I saw a dictionary sticking out of her bag. The words traveled from the pages, filtered through leather, cloth, and skin and infiltrated her synapses, where an odd short-circuiting took place.

"Your boss grabs?"

"Overling grabs me. He grabs overthing and underwhere. Big eyes. Underling like me caput. I am flamed."

"Aha. Now I overstand. Your overling oceans everything, all the underlings, grabs underthings, overwear?"

"Yes. With big eyes. Grabs me everywhere."

"The swine."

"Eyes all over. He oceans all the plakat-holders. Grabs me conversationing with you, he flames me. I need job. Please. I have no desire..." She stopped. "To be flamed."

I studied the program on her chest and said:

"On the one arm, I don't want you to be fired either. But on the other arm, I have no desire to hear music by Benda, Koželuch, Zelenka, and Reicha..."

She smiled. Looked at me for a moment with her sad eyes. Maybe she didn't understand I had refused her. Was she waiting for a message from, as the Yiddish had it, her words-book?

"You possess top of stepladder Czech compositor pronouncification," she said flirtatiously.

Now she pulled out her dictionary and consulted.

"You double-Czech word?" I asked.

"No. Verb. To look for cinnamon for 'farewell.' One moment." She licked her forefinger in the European manner as she moved from page to page. "Oho. Okay. Please. If you no overstand verb 'farewell' I prostitute other verb: 'So long.' Please, so long a ticket for concert for me, othersmart I be burned."

I bowed my head. "With extreme mournfulness and grand regretification, I no farewell ticket. I no want to so long ticket. I am leaving now. Good-purchase!"

At once the little gleam exited the blonde's eyes. She turned abruptly and walked into the crowd. I too turned to see if I could find her boss. Maybe he would know where the girl in the blue beret had gone. But in the crush of people I couldn't tell overling from tourist. Then it dawned on me: there was no boss. It was just a standard tactic used by the ticket sellers to make a sale.

I stood before another placard-holder, a bearded fellow with long hair. Maybe he would remember a pretty coworker. But he didn't know her either.

"Don't you all work for the same company?"

"Are you kidding?" He laughed. "We are all competitors. Sellers of tickets to the great Mozart Hall, the Dvořák Hall, the Rudolfinium, the small churches."

"But she's been here, in this part of the square. I've seen her a few times."

"People come and go often in this job. The pay isn't so good, you know. A salesgirl might even quit in the middle of a conversation with you. Like this."

And he walked away.

What kind of absurd joke was this? I wondered. Had he somehow rehearsed this scenario and waited, God knows how long, for it to be realized? I watched him move to another spot. I shook my head, still incredulous.

Not far from the K Museum stood a young man just where the girl in the blue beret had been days before. I wanted to imagine it was she but I couldn't bend reality. I didn't have the magic to turn a balding twenty-five-year-old into the lovely girl in the blue beret.

"Excuse me, but do you know a girl who used to work here carrying a placard? A girl from Georgia who wore a blue beret?"

"Georgia? No. But there did used to be a girl here.... You know her name?"

"No. Was she pretty?"

"Yes. Very." And he smiled as if remembering the girl in the blue beret. "Blue beret, you say? Well, maybe she did."

"Ah, good. Finally getting somewhere. Do you know how I can reach her?"

"No. She left."

"Left?"

"Yes. Left."

"You mean she's gone?"

"Gone. Left. Same meaning. Is English your native tongue?"

I disregarded his question, which may have had sarcastic undertones.

"Gone? Like altogether gone?"

"Yes," he said testily. "Like they say in America, gone gone."

"Gone gone where?"

"How should I know? Maybe back home. Lots of students work here from different countries, then they get homesick and go home for a while."

"Did she say where she was going?"

"No. And I didn't know her that well. And who says that—without a name—that we talk about the same person."

"Is she coming back?"

"If the she is the same she in your half of the conversation as is the she in mine, I don't know. She just said she was leaving. Maybe she didn't even say she was leaving and just left."

"She worked for your company, right?"

"Right, and why are you so interested in her?"

"Will your boss tell me?"

"Why should my boss tell you more than me? Why should he give you personal information about employees? We have new privacy laws. You want ticket to tonight's concert?"

"Why? Is your overling coming toward you and you will be flamed for chatting too muchly with me?"

The chap looked at me as if I were loco. Maybe that line I had twice heard before wasn't a ploy after all. Just a coincidence I was misreading.

Frustration needled me. I felt I had walked into a bramble bush. Why didn't I ask her name, the girl in the blue beret? What an idiot! A golem! I had a half date with a girl whose name I didn't know. I wanted to ask her but thought it would be intrusive. If she felt I was becoming too personal, she might turn and walk away, just like that golem I had addressed a few minutes ago. I should have gotten her name and phone number like a normal person and made a date. Well, I did have sort of a half-baked date, didn't I? I wondered if prizes are given by social science foundations for creating new social forms.

Why did I dilly-dally, knowing in the depths of my skin that precisely this would happen—that she would slip away from me, that my lethargy—just call me Oblomov—would do me in? When it came to making my films, I was pretty forthright, even aggressive. Why not with girls? Could it be that the interest she had shown in chatting with me, in saying I looked like Danny K, was just politesse? That she wasn't interested in me at all? I got so used to looking like thirty, I forgot that someone might see me as a man of forty, and what would a twenty-year-old girl want with a much older guy? On the other hand, the few conversations I had with her seemed to be personal, not routine, salesgirl's talk. But who can enter another human being's heart? We try and try but never succeed. I wished I could pull a magical dictionary out of my pocket and with several key words enter another's heart.

Plan A didn't work. Since I couldn't find her on the square, I couldn't buy another ticket from her for the concert. But that didn't mean I couldn't go. And so, that night, at the Dvořák Hall, although I had told her I couldn't attend, I bought a first-row balcony seat. I didn't consider what to say if I met her in the lobby while buying a ticket. No doubt I'd see her during intermission and make up some story about my canceled appointment. But, besides seeing her, there was another, subliminal, reason for my going. I wanted to see if she really would attend and had not sold the ticket again (as I probably would have done) and pocketed the profit.

The hall—where Mozart had premiered his "Prague" symphony, the 38th—was stunning: red-velvet paneling and gold lamé on the walls. From my perch I looked down into the orchestra where the girl in the blue beret should be sitting. But I couldn't find her. I looked left and right. So she did take the money and run. Good for her. Maybe she needed it. Then a wave of applause. Soon the music would begin—Bach's *Brandenburg No. 1* and then Dvořák's Piano Quintet—and I still am scanning the seats row by row. I still hadn't found her. And no wonder. I kept looking for a blue beret. But why should she wear her hat indoors? Then I looked once more, and there, there, there she was, in the left front of the orchestra.

From my balcony seat, I saw her almost in profile. She had short, cropped hair and she moved her head to the rhythm of the music. After the first figure she just stared ahead, mesmerized by Bach, a lovely smile on her face. She was absorbing the music like a sunbather sunlight and it made her happy. How could one not be happy in Bach's Garden of Eden?

Up in the balcony, I deluded myself, amused myself, that I had a date with her. After all, I had asked if she wanted to go to the concert and she said Yes, and I treated her to a ticket and here we were—both of us—in the hall. It was a bona fide half date. Of course, I slyly edit out that first she told me sotto voce to quickly buy a ticket, which I offered her, creating that looney half date—credit me for that invention—to the enrichment of society (a boon to shy or other socially maladept people) and to the detriment of me.

The only trouble was that even though we were both here, I wouldn't talk to her. I decided not to seek her out during intermission, for I didn't want her to assume I was a liar. Telling her my appointment was canceled and that I decided to come at the last minute would look strange. That would look like a ploy, an attempt to upgrade a half date by fifty percent (to seventy-five percent, for those of you weak in math, who think upgrading a half date by fifty percent makes it equal one full date).

But I did look to see if the girl in the blue beret was interacting with anyone, a man to her right, a man to her left. But no, she didn't smile or turn to anyone or acknowledge a shared enjoyment. She was off in a world of her own. But once in a while, I saw her turn a couple of times, as if looking for someone.

Now that I was far from her, the video camera in my head replayed for me what my eyes had seen but not noticed while standing close to her. It was like enjoying the forest without noticing the ballet of individual trees, the colors of the leaves. With the vision of memory, isolating the frames of the video, I saw for the first time those unique sea-green, those long green eyes, eyes made all the more green by the black lashes that framed them and the clear white around them, a leaf green with glamour, in the pristine, shamanistic meaning of the word. I wouldn't say they were witch's eyes, but they were bewitching, or at least so they seemed to me, as if some enchanter chanting cantabile incantations had made me see an underwater sun drenched green in her eyes, eyes that cast a spell in the eyes of any beholder who looked into those long green eyes of hers, the color of water you see when you swim underwater in the Mediterranean when the sun is shining, eyes that I was noticing now only in videographic memory, eyes I hadn't noticed before because I was too busy looking at the whole of the girl in the blue beret.

Another thing I didn't mention: that dimple in her right cheek, and right cheek only, when she smiled.

As the applause began, signaling the intermission, I saw the girl in the blue beret stand. At once I acted. Again I changed my mind. I ran downstairs, saw the first people coming through the doors to the lobby. Sharp-eyed, I inspected every person who came through the doors. Thump-a-thump beat my heart, excited that I would soon see her, finally learn her name, listen to her thank-you while I smiled modestly. I'd speak to her for the first time without her placard.

But although I looked and looked, I couldn't find her. I moved laterally in the lobby, not taking my eyes off the doors. The fifteen minutes passed. Now people were returning. A man walked around the lobby playing a little tinkling melody on a small triangle, signaling that soon the concert would resume.

Upstairs, I leaned on the railing of the balcony. Saw her in her seat. Perhaps she had remained there throughout the intermission. Once more she stood, looked back and waved to someone, then sat down. Who could she be waving to? Perhaps a coworker on the square.

Then I saw the old man with a Van Dyke beard again. Again? Yes, again. It wasn't the first time I'd seen him. I had noticed him the other day on the square, strolling slowly, cane in hand, a dreamy look on his face. He used the mode of strolling with a walking stick that was fashionable at the beginning of the century, a manner I had seen in silent films and musical comedies set in fin-de-siècle Europe: a forward motion with the cane, then a rightward semicircle back to the first position, a way of promenading that bespoke elegance, style, class. Now he walked slowly down the right center aisle of the orchestra, dressed in the same blue serge suit I had seen on him the other day. This genteel elegance, aristocratic stance, made me think of Jiri and his distinguished mien, old men with a history, old men with a past. Here is another old man I'd like to speak to. If not for my desire to look for the girl in the blue beret at the end of the concert, I surely would have sought him out.

Outside, I waited and waited but could not find her. I dreamt of a miracle where she would surprise me, tap me on the shoulder, and I would turn. She smiles flirtatiously. Why didn't you tell me you'd be here? she asks, as members of the orchestra reprise a movement of the Brandenburg, with its dancy rock-and-roll rhythms, and we break into a spontaneous dance.

How could she not have come out the front doors? I wondered, then I answered my own question. Because at the front of the orchestra, on both sides, hung an exit sign. But in my rush to be the first outside, I had not imagined she might leave from the door closest to her.

7

Everyone Disappears

The following morning I looked for her again on the square, but I was just going through the motions, like someone who has lost a ring on the street looks but knows there's not a chance it will be found.

I saw the three ticket peddlers I had spoken to the other day: the tall blonde who spoke an invented English, the bearded guy who demonstrated how a placard-holder can walk off in mid-sentence, and the young bald chap who specialized in privacy laws. We looked at and through each other. Either they didn't remember me, or chose not to—just as I purposely said nothing to them, not even a nod. The girl in the blue beret had disappeared.

What's happening here? First Jiri Krupka-Weisz disappears. Then Karoly Graf vanishes. And now, number three, the girl in the blue beret. A cluster of three, potentially ominous, if one were superstitious, as I am not. Especially if you're puzzled how to number them. Should Jiri and Betty, who also disappeared, be counted as one or two? If two, then Graf is three, and the girl is four. But let's take Jiri and Betty as one. But the girl in the blue beret still cannot be number three for I forgot Danny K. So with him it's either four or five. No longer an ominous three. Still, a lot of disappearances.

When one such incident occurs, you don't think about it. You're puzzled, but you forget it. When two, you begin to be suspicious, which rhymes with superstitious but otherwise has no links. Maybe you're nervous. Could these disappearances be directed at you? Some private message?

But when it happens a third time, you feel edgy. You ask, Why am I being singled out for this? Am I jinxed? Or paranoid? Or is it just a series of strange coincidences scattered over two continents? A haphazard concatenation of events I happened to witness. But, let's face it, if this were happening in a film—of which, let's say, I was the auteur—wouldn't one (you, that is, I) conclude that this was somehow artistically planned, organized, directed? But if it happens in real life, isn't it normal to ask questions? Like, Why is this happening to me? How many people do you know who experienced the disappearance of three, four, five people they knew within a month?

Two of the three who vanished I liked. Jiri I liked as if he were family. Karoly Graf I liked too, more perhaps for professional reasons. Danny K I adored for years. And the girl in the blue beret was simply attractive. Her gentleness and allure caught me. Now all three or four were gone. What was worse, no one could tell me where to find them. Across that wide brook were no stepping stones; no third or fourth parties to suggest a former employer or distant kin. These disappearances reminded me of an Ingmar Bergman film I'd once seen where actors vanish in a split second before your eyes: phhtt, wwwhish—gone.

Gone?

Gone.

How gone?

Gone gone.

All right. In mysteries people vanish. In surrealistic stories characters disappear. In films, a minor figure is never seen again. But in real life? Maybe once in a while. Like Judge Crater, or is it Carter, who disappeared in about 1930? Or, seven years later, the aviatrix Amelia Earhart. But five people in the space of a month or so? Could it indeed be that someone was trying to send you, that is, me, a message? And if message it was, what kind of message? And in what language? Gibberish? Tutu? Half-baked, Double Dutch Ural Altaic?

No impact on me that message, if message it was. The warning meant nothing, if warning. And why should these four or five good people disappear to create some kind of stupid, inchoate message or warning? It was totally absurd. And having concluded that, I realized it was totally meaningless as an interpretative act. All this was absolutely coincidental. And I would continue to do whatever I was doing—look for a vibrant opening, memorable, dramatic, unforgettable, A Major Discovery, for my film on Prague—without inner trembling or change of plan.

8

To Eva Langbrot

During the fifteen-minute underground ride to Eva Langbrot, Yossi golem's friend, the train stopped at five or six brightly lit stations. The walls were sparkling azure tiles, decorated with large, framed reproductions of works by Van Gogh, Matisse, Picasso, Mondrian, and Klimt. But, oddly, no one entered or left my car. No one budged from his seat. Perhaps the lifelike creatures in the car were dolls, installed by the Prague Metro Authority to give new riders like me a sense of security. But it did just the opposite. Why were these mannikins entombed here with me? I thought of asking one of the passengers the time but feared a silent rebuff would unnerve me.

Again I saw golems everywhere, golems with stiff, expressionless faces. Any minute the roof of the subway car would crumple along with the steel and concrete vault of the tunnel, and all the people in the car, now vivified, would simply raise their hands and support the collapse like the golem did in the silent film.

I couldn't wait to leave the Metro. The library silence in the car had become oppressive. Emerging from the subway into the singing sunlight was a pleasant surprise. I was now in the suburbs, even though Yossi golem had told me that Eva lived in Prague.

Up a rather steep cobblestoned street of private villas bounded by flower-filled gardens I made my way. Many houses had wrought-iron fences painted white, blue, or black, with flower-edged lawns in front and gardens in back. At the top of the street I saw a grove of tall pines, no doubt the beginning of a park—a bit of countryside on the outskirts of the city.

Up I walked, up up a slightly curving street. I imagined I was floating through a late-nineteenth-century movie set. Because of the hill, the houses looked atilt. Of course they were not. The houses stood straight. The ground was slanted and the foundations were higher on the downslope. Between the houses I saw hills—and at one point, the Charles River below.

Ahead of me walked someone with a blue beret. Oh my God, was that a placard on her back? What a miracle! Wait, I shouted. Wait, girl in blue beret! I sprinted up the hill, getting closer. But the girl turned out to be an old man; the placard, a grey overcoat. The disappointment slowed me down but my heart still raced. At times we don't see with our eyes. We see what our hearts want us to see. The only thing I saw correctly was the blue beret. And even that wasn't the usual beret, at least not the one the girl wore. Hers fitted tightly. Made of soft cloth, it hugged the shape of her head. The one the old man wore had a stiff leather rim that made the beret sit on his head.

He was rather tall, the old man. One usually thinks of the phrase "little old man" due to the shrinking effect of osteoporosis or degenerative disc disease. But this man was tall and lanky. His walk was neither spry nor slow, but he seemed to be making his way up the street without difficulty, not hesitating but maintaining a steady, even pace that gave the impression of speed.

As I passed him, I turned and nodded. He had a white Van Dyke beard, I saw, a smooth, unwrinkled face, and wise eyes. He was even taller than me. He bowed his head slowly for a moment as if to say, Yes, I acknowledge your greeting, which I now reciprocate. That's a lot of words and imputed thoughts for a slow, slight incline of the head, but the gracious, musical, even dance-like andante nod bespoke Old World cortesia.

Could he be, I wondered, the same old man with a cane I'd seen at the concert the other night, and on the square with his walking-stick pirouette a day or two earlier? But maybe all old men look alike. The old man on the square—with the crush of people of varying sizes, I hadn't noticed his height—had ambled along slowly with a cane, using that unique, almost affected mode of promenading. However, the man I had just passed moved forthrightly. I turned once to look at him but he didn't notice me.

A few minutes later I found Eva's house, entered the hallway. What looked like a private three-story villa was actually subdivided into apartments. I walked up one flight and stood before a nameplate on a door that read: E. Langbrot/Ph. Klein.

I rang. A woman with white hair tied in a bun opened the door. At once her warm, motherly smile filled the space of the doorway.

I introduced myself.

"Ah, yes, hello. Come, come right in, my boy. I have been expecting you."

Clasping both of my hands, she drew me in. I regretted I hadn't thought of bringing her flowers.

I looked at her; she radiated kinship. What is it with people? I wondered. Some you can know for ages and they don't penetrate your heart. And for others my late, beloved father had a three-word Yiddish phrase: "*a liblicher mentch*," lovable person; better, a person you instantly fall in love with. Like Jiri. With a few words and genuineness of spirit, they make you feel you've discovered long-lost kin.

That's what I felt with Eva Langbrot as soon as I saw her round, open face, her light blue eyes, the color of the bright sky I had just seen, a patch of rose on each cheek.

"Yossi told me you'd be coming...I've been waiting for you. Why didn't you come sooner?" Her English, I now noticed, had the same accent as Jiri's.

"I—"

Then she clapped her hand over her mouth. "God gave ten measures of speech to mankind and nine of them to women... Who am I to be asking you why you didn't come sooner?... Come in, sit down. I just put up some tea—and you'll also taste my cookies."

She served me and placed some bright red paper napkins on the kitchen table.

I thanked her and told her about my first days here and my brief friendship with Jiri.

"We all loved Jiri," Eva said. I saw tears welling in her eyes. "Did my friend Yossi tell you what Jiri did during the war?"

"Yes. He also told me you too fought with the underground against the Germans."

Eva made a disparaging gesture.

"It can't compare to Jiri's heroism and daring. Or to Yossi's."

"He too?"

"Yes yes. You saw his right eye? The right side of his face?"

"I did…"

"Yossi was in the Israeli army during the 1973 Yom Kippur War. A tank commander in Sinai. He was wounded when his tank was hit near the Suez Canal but still, in pain, blinded in one eye, he saved all his men from the burning tank."

"And he left Israel to come back to communist Czechoslovakia?"

"It's a long story. It wasn't easy. Another silent heroism of his. But, you see…"

A door slammed. Then another door opened and closed.

Eva lowered her voice. She bent close to me.

"Mr. Klein, the man who lives here, has just come back from his walk.… You'll meet him after he rests a bit. But, shh, please, don't say a word to him."

"About what?"

Eva shook her head as though getting rid of cobwebs.

"Excuse. Don't say a word to him about Jiri. Please. Jiri visited here about two, three years ago and saw Mr. Klein. He liked Jiri very much. I don't want to sadden him, to upset him."

"Of course. I understand. But can I say I met him? After all, it's because of Jiri that I'm here."

"Yes yes. Say as much as you like, but not…" She dropped her voice even more. "But not that." A tear glistened in each eye. "He was such a unique man. There are not many people like him... Well, maybe Mr. Klein."

"He was unique," I said. "I can't believe the bond we formed in just three meetings." And at once I saw Jiri before me, which prompted the thought: What did he want to tell me in the hospital? And via his pen?

"If Jiri sent you to Yossi and me," I heard Eva saying over my momentary reverie, "he had a special affection for you."

Just then the phone rang. Eva answered and had a short conversation in Czech.

"That was my singer," she said when she cradled the phone. "She sings and I play piano for the old people at the Jewish Home. She's coming over tomorrow so we can start rehearsing for our Hanuka program."

"But isn't Hanuka...?"

"Yes, I know it's weeks away, but we want to prepare carefully these old Jewish folk songs."

"I love old Jewish folk songs. Would you mind playing some for me?"

Eva brightened. "Why, happily. Come into the living room..." Then she stopped and turned to me. "But please know I am not professional pianist. I'm just a volunteer in the Jewish Home who plays for the old folks twice a week."

Old folks, I said to myself. She's no youngster either and calls the residents of the Jewish old-age home "old folks." How old could she be? Her hair was absolutely white, but there wasn't a wrinkle on her round, ruddy cheeks. Yet Yossi said Eva was older than he. Was she in her mid-seventies? If she had been in the Resistance in 1943, let's say at twenty-four, now fifty years later she would be seventy-four or seventy-five.

As Eva played these traditional songs I thought: What can one expect from an old lady who probably took lessons sixty or sixty-five years ago. It was commendable—a perfect word: commendable—that she played these homey tunes at her age and made the men and women at the Jewish Home happy. I felt that my effusive praise,

"How nice, Eva, how beautiful!" was patronizing, but I couldn't help it. That's how we were raised, to be polite, to make people feel good, especially the old and the young.

I knew all the songs but one.

"That last song, Eva, it's new for me. Quite enchanting."

"I learned it from some Jewish villagers during the war. It's been sung in the countryside for generations during Hanuka."

"Can you play it again?"

She sang along as she played. The song, Eva explained, celebrated the power of light over darkness, faith over evil. I heard the rhymes but of course couldn't understand the words. In its folk simplicity and captivating rhythms, it might have been a melody Dvořák could have used in one of his Slavonic Dances.

I looked at Eva as she played. She wore a fine, white, long-sleeved sweater over a nicely cut flowered blue dress. I closed my eyes, took in in memory her round, affecting, grandmotherly appearance and imagined she was the grandmother I never knew.

This too has to be filmed, I decided. A previously unknown and traditional Czech Jewish countryside Hanuka song.

Besides the old Bösendorfer upright piano, the living room contained several four-foot-high bookcases. Atop their shelves were little vases, a pair of glass elephants, the caboose of an electric train, a half-dozen typical wine-colored Bohemian glasses and bowls, and a brass Hanuka menorah. Two thick Sarouk carpets lay on the floor. The old leather sofa was cracked like an old woman's wrinkled cheeks. Two plush easy chairs with crocheted ivory-colored armrest covers that Eva or her mother had crocheted years ago stood on either side of the sofa.

The sunshine from the window cheered the room, covered the dusky old furniture with light. I looked out the window into the big backyard with its flowerbeds along the rear fence. The Charles River sparkled and the grey-green hills danced in the distance.

In a moment of silence, when time was suspended and I felt myself motionless, like the golems in my Metro car, I thought again of Jiri. I should have filmed him too, it dawned on me. But now, now, alas, it was too late.

Then, a Bach melody on the piano, the opening notes to his *English Suite No. 2*, overtook my reverie. Who could be playing? At first I thought it might be Eva. But she was standing next to me. So how could she be playing the piano if she wasn't at the piano?

"What's that?" I asked.

"Bach."

"I know it's Bach. *The English Suite*. But who's playing? I know it isn't me and I'm sure it isn't you."

"Don't be so sure." And she made some fingering motions in the air on a make-believe keyboard. Smiling, she said, "It's Mr. Klein."

"He also plays?"

"Yes." And that naughty look in her eyes, the color rising on her cheeks.

"He too has a piano in his room?"

"No." She laughed. "A gramophone."

I marveled at the use of that old word.

"And I do mean gramophone, not phonograph."

Eva walked back to the piano and sat on the bench. *The English Suite* continued. Eva held her hands over the keyboard like a concert pianist about to begin. Her fingers hovered inches away from the keys. Her head ticked to Bach's melody. She closed her eyes. From Klein's room, again silence. The end of a dance. Eva looked at me with a smile that grazed the borders of shrewd and sly. In a minute, I'm going to surprise you, her smile said. Eva's expression seemed so wise and all-knowing I felt like blurting: If you know everything, where's the girl in the blue beret?

A second later, Eva's hands lunged forward in attack and her fingers began to move, as if miming playing the Bach piece. What's going on? It seemed to me I was hearing the gigue in stereo. Now I saw what I had only imagined before: she was playing along with whoever the pianist was, probably Glenn Gould, note for note, trill for trill, arpeggio for arpeggio. Until she, he, both stopped at the same time at the end of the gigue.

I applauded. "This is incredible.... You rehearsed this."

"No. But we have done this a number of times."

Showing off for visitors, I kept myself from saying.

And this too, somehow, will have to go into my film.

Everything will go into my film, I thought.

9

To Mr. Klein's Room

I looked around Eva's living room. Why did Jiri send me here? Jiri to Yossi, Yossi to Eva. Tara pilus. Was it for her I was too young? Did Jiri or Betty actually presume some kind of match between Eva and me? Impossible. One mismatch—Jiri and Betty—was enough, thank you. They were quirky at times, but not mad. So maybe Mr. Klein was the final stop. I recalled the line both Jiri and Yossi did not complete: The old man will sh—

Then the double notes of that Bach gigue came back to me, that enchanting duet Eva had played along with Mr. Klein's gramophone. And I had judged her playing commendable. It was either a musical tour de force she had perfected, or some kind of acoustical sleight of hand. What kind of magic potion was in effect here that permitted an elderly woman who at first played like a solid amateur to replicate Glenn Gould's *English Suite* as though she were lip-syncing? Did she have another recording in her piano that made me think she was actually playing? Was it a player piano? Or was Arthur Rubinstein in there performing, like he had done many times, years ago, inside Vladimir Horowitz's concert grand, when the ailing Horowitz went on tour—remember, Horowitz always traveled with his own Steinway—Rubinstein playing a smaller piano of his own inside his friend Horowitz's while Horowitz just went through the dramatic hand and finger motions?

"I'd like to meet Mr. Klein," I said.

Eva looked at her watch. "I think it's all right now...I shall go and ask him."

As she left the room I looked at the bookcase. I blinked. Little shivers ran up one arm to my neck and scalp. My hair tingled. The title of the book I saw grew larger and larger as if on a five-story screen. I couldn't believe it. Another copy of K's *Meditation*?

Eva came back nodding.

"I'll bring you in."

I pointed out K's book.

"I see you also have a copy of K's first book. Jiri showed me the one in his library, signed by K. Did he get it here? Or was his copy mailed back to you? Did you have two copies and give him one? Is this one signed?"

"So many questions." Eva's eyes lit up with a smile. "I don't know. These books are my son's, who is now living in Brno. But I would think this book can be found in any antiquariat."

"May I see if it's signed?"

"Please," Eva said.

I pulled out the copy and, heart beating, turned to the title page. No signature.

"No. It's not signed."

"Come," Eva said.

"Does Mr. Klein speak English?"

"Yes. Among many other languages."

Then a strange thing happened. Eva bent forward, brought her face close to mine. I thought she was going to kiss me. *Tara pilus, tara glos* ran like a bolt of lightning through me. And a dozen thoughts, swift as that electric pulse, tumbled in my brain. So indeed that's what Jiri and Betty were arguing about. Too old, said one. No, the other. What exactly did they have in mind? Had I known, I too would have fainted in the hospital room along with Betty when I told her I understood every word she and Jiri had said.

Eva bringing her face closer. The skin of her rosy cheeks smelled like freshly picked apples. Why should she want to kiss me? But out of politeness I did not draw back. Was a magical thought, straight out of fairy tales, riding along those neurons and synapses just brushed by lightning, that if she kissed me her enchantment would be undone? Like the kissed green little frog metamorphosed into a young prince, whssht, Eva would become a lovely princess as soon as her lips touched mine—a princess with an engaging smile, dark eyes, a dimple in one cheek and one cheek only, and a blue beret atop her head, a blue beret worn at a fetching angle.

But then, when her face almost touched mine, she drew three short breaths. She sniffed me. Just as I was about to ask why—my lips parting, a slight popping sound—Eva said:

"Mr. Klein is very sensitive to fragrances. He can't stand perfumes—"

I said indignantly, "I don't wear perfume or cologne," then tried to smile to cloak a possible brusqueness.

"—aftershave lotions and so on, so I'm glad you're not." Her voice trailed off.

Then she gestured, Let's go. She put a finger to her lip and whispered, "Remember. About Jiri." And she waved her forefinger.

I nodded. "I remember. Don't worry."

As we entered Mr. Klein's book-filled room, Eva introduced us. First caught my eye what hung from the ceiling: two beautifully constructed model aeroplanes, double winged, from the pre–World War I era. And there to my left, on a little table, the old gramophone.

"So we meet again," Mr. Klein said with that Czech accent I recognized by now. He stretched his hand out to me and shook it with a firm clasp. It was the man with the white Van Dyke beard I had passed earlier on the hill. Now, sans his blue beret, I saw that except for a fringe of soft, silky white hair he was bald. Standing next to him, I realized for the first time he was more than six feet tall.

Eva brought the palms of her hands together. She looked happy, satisfied. "Well, enjoy each other's company. I'm going out now, Mr. Klein. Do you need anything?"

"No, thank you, Eva."

Like Eva, he too looked me over. His gaze seemed to say, I've seen you before. The sort of look you give people you're seeing again after a long absence.

"Were you at the concert," I asked him, "in the Dvořák Hall the other night?"

"Yes."

"And a day or two earlier, strolling in Old Town Square with your cane?"

Mr. Klein laughed. "I'm not the only man with a cane on the square."

I matched his upbeat tone with one of my own. "But how many wear a blue beret and fashion a unique ballet with their walking stick as they amble along?"

"Not many," he allowed.

"So it must have been you."

He pursed his lips and ticked his head, not really admitting but not saying no.

"Why use a cane for level walking but not uphill?"

"I use it for promenading, not as a third leg."

"On the square you walked dreamily, but briskly up the hill."

"If you daydream on an uphill cobblestoned street it may turn to nightmare—that is, a nasty fall. And I always walk quickly up a hill. It saves time. You see, I collect time," Mr. Klein declared.

"You are quite energetic," for an old man, were the words I censored.

"I am blessed with dark energy," he replied, looking into my eyes and behind my eyes. "And anti-gravity too."

Uh-huh, I said to myself. Why was I pursuing this idiotic line of questioning?

I turned to look at the old-fashioned gramophone on the table. Mr. Klein's room was quite spacious, bright with sunlight streaming in through the window. I saw two other doors, one probably a closet, the other a bathroom. Another wall had floor-to-ceiling books. He had a writing desk and chair by the window, an easy chair, a cot, and some lamps. Maybe one of them was powered by his dark energy.

For a moment we blinked at each other in silence, like two people who have no more to say to each other and strain to fill the space of air with empty words. I looked up at those two marvelous model aeroplanes—had Mr. Klein made them himself?—and wondered if I should fly away on one, just like Danny K had wanted to sail away from that dinner on one of his own napkin ships. Instead of asking about the planes, I said:

"I saw the 'Ph' on the door before your family name. What does that stand for?"

"The 'Ph' is for Phishl…officially—accidental pun—Philippe."

Fishl Klein, I thought. Small fish.

"That's right," he said. "Small fish. That's what I am in this world. A small fish."

I wanted to contradict him, to counteract this self-effacing thought, but I didn't know what to say.

"Why the 'Ph'? Why not 'F'?"

"Yes," he said with a pensive nod. Then he added, eyes sparkling, "I suppose you spell 'philosoph' with two 'f''s too."

It sounded logical; it sounded like a good riposte, but I still couldn't figure it out.

"Why are we standing? Please sit down."

He sat in the easy chair and motioned me to the wooden chair next to his writing table.

"What did you want to say?"

I hadn't wanted to say anything, but hearing his soft question prompted me to remark:

"Up in the balcony of the concert hall the other night, I looked down and spotted you. At once I said to myself, I'd like to speak to that man."

He spread the palms of his hands as if say, And so you are.

"The same thing also happened to me in a New York synagogue a few weeks ago. I saw a man who sat in front of me explaining a Torah verse to his neighbor. And I said to myself, I have to get to know this man."

"And did you?"

"I did, and he turned out to be from Prague, the former director of the Jewish Museum, the man who visited you two or three years ago. And it's because of him that I am here now—Jiri Krupka-Weisz."

"Jiri," said Mr. Klein.

At once I saw his face pale for an instant, followed by a slight flush, a bit of discoloration by the roots of his hair and on his scalp. One nostril flared. What have I done? I reproached myself. Maybe I shouldn't have brought him up?

I told him how I befriended Jiri and about the affection between us.

"How was he feeling when you saw him?" Mr. Klein put his hand on his heart as though expecting sad news. I looked at his face, noticed for the first time his long black, youthful eyelashes.

"Good, last time I saw him." A surge of fright rushed through me. I felt my face reddening. "Then I had to go out of town for a while and then I came here."

I was babbling and I knew it.

Mr. Klein drew closer. Again that high color on his forehead. He looked me in the eye, then up over my head.

"He's dead, isn't he?" he said in a low but firm voice that hinted: do not contradict me.

What should I say now? I had given Eva my word I would not mention Jiri's death. In fact, I myself hadn't been absolutely sure until Yossi golem confirmed it.

"He was all right when I left. Why don't you ask Yossi or Eva? They have some links to him."

"They want to spare me sorrow. But I know."

"How do you know?"

"I look at Eva's face. At yours." Which he did as he spoke, reading me like pristine Greek, from right to left, then left to right. "One knows these things without being told. Faces have music, you know. And I hear that sad music on Eva's face. I can read the notes on little lines vibrating on her face when she talks to me, notes that spell out the Kaddish melody. Now on your face too. Lips lie. Eyes don't."

Mr. Klein's face now clouded with sorrow. I stared down at the edge of the Bokhara carpet on the wooden floor. I wanted to cover the sad music on my face, the Kaddish notes in my eyes, but I could not.

"How can you be so sure?"

He looked through my eyes into the screen of my retina and said slowly:

"A father can tell."

I felt a blow on my head. My brain rattled, my equilibrium atilt. Mr. Klein, Jiri's father? How could that be? First of all, they looked nearly the same age. Secondly, they didn't even have the same family name. The only contiguity between Klein and Krupka-Weisz was the letter K. They didn't even look alike.

"You're Jiri's father?"

"Yes."

He's delusional, I thought. Lots of crazy claims here in Prague. Karoly Graf, K's son; Klein, Jiri's father. What's wrong with these people? I felt I had stepped into a wrong room in a rehearsal studio. I better back into the hallway and enter again. Maybe the play I had chanced into would change and I would be in another story. Or perhaps I should commandeer one of the little napkin boats that Danny K had set sail and head for a less absurdist port? I looked up again at Mr. Klein's model aeroplanes. Don't get any ideas, I imagined him saying.

"Even without reading the music in one's eyes and voice, a father can tell. I felt it in my heart, a twinge, a rush of pain into my head, the moment he died. On—"

And Mr. Klein mentioned the day and date I had spoken to Patient Information at Beth Israel. But it still didn't jibe. How can

Mr. Klein be Jiri's father when Jiri himself told me he was eighty? Could Jiri have made himself older than he really was? Not likely. Especially since he remembered seeing the Czech writer, Arnošt Lustig, as a baby in the late 1920s. If Mr. Klein's assertion is true, he has to be over… No. Impossible.

Then again I spoke without thinking.

"May I ask how old you are?"

"Yes."

So I asked again.

Mr. Klein's response was, "Sixty-nine, almost seventy."

Again I had crossed the boundary. Once more I was in the never-never land of Jiri and Betty's language, in a world where numbers were listed alphabetically and alphabets were circular.

Mr. Klein knew I would ask; I saw his eyes twinkling. I could not resist; I succumbed.

"How is it possible for a father to be younger than his son?"

"Yes."

"Jiri told me he was eighty."

"Yes."

"And you say you're sixty-nine."

"Almost seventy."

"Can you explain?"

"Yes."

I waited.

Mr. Klein didn't explain.

We sat in the room, looking at each other. A few minutes ago it felt as if we didn't have anything to talk about, like strangers meeting. Now we had plenty to talk about. But Mr. Klein would have to do the talking. The silence hummed; not like the anticipatory silence Haydn creates between passages, an arc between one lovely melody and another. Here the silent hum soon became oppressive. It didn't seem to bother Mr. Klein that he was ignoring my question.

Finally, as the silence stretched like a rubber band about to snap, he said:

"Too complicated."

The tone of finality to his remark, like an auctioneer's hammer blow, did not invite further exploration. He put both hands out, all ten fingers outspread. Mr. Klein had a wide vocabulary with very few words. His hands, eyes, tone of voice, were his extended speech. If he wanted to elaborate, fine. If not, I wouldn't ask. That's it. I had asked enough. Maybe he would tell me some other time. I looked at Mr. Klein. Yes, he looked eighty, just about Jiri's age, maybe even younger. But if indeed he was Jiri's father, he—no! Could Mr. Klein really be over one hundred? He had to be, unless he had fathered Jiri at nineteen. And walk up a hill in that consistent faux-speedy fashion? It didn't add up. Something was wrong here.

For the last couple of months I found myself in a world where the edges were fuzzy and boundaries between real and dream fluid. Then the Altneushul shamesh told me the fabled attic did not even exist. And that lovely girl in the blue beret gone into the mist. Then a woman suddenly plays a clone duet of a Bach gigue with a recording. And now a man who claims to be sixty-nine tells me he's the father of my late eighty-year-old friend, Jiri.

I just hope the someone who's videoing me caught my facial expressions when Mr. Klein made that statement.

I leaned forward in my chair.

"When I saw you from the balcony the other night at the concert, I had a hunch you'd be an interesting man. But I didn't know you'd be mesmerizing."

Mr. Klein's response was a glowing smile, like a girl praised for her wit and beauty.

"Yes," he said, stroking his Van Dyke once.

If Mr. Klein's assertion that he was Jiri's father was true—and if true, what a chapter in my film; another surprising twist in the narration ongoing in my head—it explained, perhaps, why Jiri and Betty wove that strange language around me. Maybe Jiri wanted to tell me he was going to send me to his father, and Betty, for some mysterious reason, was attempting to dissuade him from revealing this. Now that I think of it, yes, indeed, it must have been so, for when Betty went to the bathroom in Jiri's hospital room and left me alone with him, he said something about how important it would be for me to meet someone in Prague. I distinctly remember Jiri saying the word "my" and then he closed his eyes. Did he want to say "my father" just as a spell of weakness came over him?

Also, could tara pilus and tara glos—too young and too old—have some relevance here? Was Mr. Klein the one who was too old? And too old for what? Too old to reveal his age to me?

What else did Jiri and Mr. Klein share beside the first letter of their last name? Love of literature and—?

Wait. How about head gear? Jiri, like his putative dad, also wore a beret.

I know I'm groping. But even if you're up against a smooth wall you still grope. And pray outlandish prayers, like wishing the tips of your fingers were suction cups. If I had a father who was, or even claimed to be, over one hundred, I would stand on a truck with a bullhorn and drive slowly around town blathering the news at the top of my lungs. If Mr. Klein were my father, at one hundred plus, I'd let everyone know. I'd be proud, not secretive, of my healthy old papa.

And could this old man with the brisk walk indeed be over one hundred and defy most laws of nature? Maybe, like Karoly Graf, he was tugging my foot, as the Russians say. If indeed he was one hundred, then his mode of parading with his cane was not copied from films. He was an eyewitness to that fin-de-siècle style of fancy strolling with a walking stick.

Again a wave of surprise surrounded me, palpable as a blast of wind on your face on a freezing day. Another in the series of surprises that began when I entered the Eldridge Street Shul in lower Manhattan. Surprises that have yet to stop. I now had two parts of the puzzle, the words and their meaning and possibly the person involved—but still the pieces didn't mesh. It just didn't make sense.

So far my stay here was a deck of cards. Every few days, sometimes every few hours, another card was turned over. It was never a deuce, king, or ace. Never a jack or a ten. It was always a special card, one that didn't belong, an interloper from an unknown game, a surprise, like words you don't understand spoken by two people you'd expect to converse in a normal tongue. Each turn of a card from the deck brought odd designs, numbers in an as-yet-uninvented mathematical system, faces that were refugees from a new world of playing cards that had infiltrated a traditional deck.

Still, I felt relaxed, in a mood to get to know Mr. Klein better.

"What did you do all these years, Mr. Klein? Were you a teacher?"

"I was a failed wunderkind." He laughed.

So did I. It was a marvelous formulation, an elegant turn of self-deprecation.

"But let's leave it at that." Then he looked at me with that mild but penetrating glance. "What brings you to Prague?"

"A long story."

"I have time. You see, the time I saved walking briskly up the hill I can now put to good use."

"A mystery. I was drawn here."

"I like mysteries. We are all mysteries, you and I. Enigmas, we."

I nodded. Maybe you more than me.

"So what indeed"—he gazed into my eyes—"brings you here?"

"Basically, my wish to make a film. But underlying that is something I can't put my finger on. Something is driving me. Pushing me. To Prague. A huge magnet pulling me. To complete a circle I myself began."

"How so? Why Prague?"

"I..." I stopped, I stopped, waited to increase suspense. "I...I was born here."

Mr. Klein's eyes widened. His lips formed an O. "How fascinating! Now you surprise me. This you must tell me about."

"My parents were young Holocaust survivors. They met in Italy, then got a job here after the war with a Jewish relief agency. A few years later I was born and soon thereafter they took me to New York. So coming back here for my first visit was like completing a rondo, coming to solve a mystery that like a bubble seems to get bigger every time I look.... And you, are you a native of Prague?"

"That's not what you wanted to ask."

"How do you know?"

"I know. I know lots of things. I have total recall of conversations that never took place and I never forget anything I want to remember."

"Still, are you a native of Prague?"

"Yes."

"And where were you during the war?"

"Here. In Prague."

How did he do it? I wondered. In hiding? Hidden by a friendly gentile? But I didn't want to distract him now.

"Then you must know the K legends, the stories about him."

"What literate person in Prague doesn't?" He waved a hand toward his book collection. "I have all the Czech writers."

I told him about Karoly Graf, his claim that he was K's son.

The old man shook his head, gave a soft, deep-throated chuckle that could have passed as a groan.

"You know," Mr. Klein said, "even if true, children of K would keep it to themselves, guarding the secret like a precious stone. It's not a banner to be waved in the public square, rather a very private matter."

"Really?" I broke in. "If it were me I'd proudly shout it in the village square: 'I am K's son!'"

I looked at Mr. Klein. He didn't react. Then I caught the echo of a word I had missed at first hearing.

"Children? Did you say 'children'? Plural, you say?"

I felt I had stumbled upon a great secret, as if I were suddenly unraveling the mystery of Jiri and Betty's language, which I had actually done for a brief, time-compressed three seconds.

But the old man didn't reply. He didn't say No. He didn't utter his ambiguous, slippery Yes. How much did he know, Phishl Klein? Did he, a lifelong resident of Prague, and surely a graduate of the university, know the juicy legends of Prague that circulated privately among its citizens but which outsiders could never be privy to, facts he wasn't willing to share with a newcomer? Perhaps he had even met, or known, K himself.

"Mr. Klein, do you by any chance know where Graf lives? I haven't been able to find him."

"No. I don't know him. Why do you want him?"

"Well, he's an interesting character. Who wouldn't be who is or claims to be the son of K?"

Mr. Klein looked at me. I was afraid he might say something that would upset me. He could have told me to mind my own business. To stop prying. But that wasn't his nature. His glance was neither stern nor penetrating. It didn't make my heart flutter. He looked at me mildly. I sought a trace of a smile on his unlined cheeks. I found that smile. Not on his lips but in his eyes.

"Who doesn't claim to be K's son? Go to a K convention. Have you gone to any?"

"To one. But only one. I stopped going. All the lecturers seemed to me to be egotistical prigs."

Mr. Klein nodded. "If the chairman of the event would call out, 'If anyone here is K's son, please raise your right hand'—at first people would look around, left and right, regard each other, and then slowly some hands would go up, then other hands would go up, men's and women's hands, until everyone in the audience had their hands up."

And then Mr. Klein burst out laughing. First his lips twitched as if he were holding back a laugh and then he let it go and shook with laughter. He was pleased with his scenario.

"They're all my children," he continued. "Even you, who doesn't go to K conventions."

"Your children?"

Mr. Klein laughed again. "I was thinking as if I were K. I put myself in his shoes."

I waited to hear more, but Mr. Klein was silent. As expostulative as was Karoly Graf, so reticent was Philippe Klein. If he wanted me to catch an ever so slight twinkle in his eye, I did.

"Now you will tell me what you wanted to say before."

I sighed. I couldn't resist. "All right. It's about Jiri. He told me lots of things, but one thing he wanted to tell me he didn't tell me."

"What is that?"

"What is that?" I don't know why I said that. Something made me repeat what Mr. Klein had said.

"What did he want to tell you?"

"I don't know. He didn't tell me."

Mr. Klein laughed. "Now this is either very comic or very funny. Are you sure he wanted to tell you something?"

"Yes. Absolutely. I'm absolutely sure. When I visited him and he began to speak, his housekeeper interrupted him. They spoke a language I couldn't piece together. For a while I felt it was impertinent, but gradually their secretive language enthralled me. Maybe because Jiri was speaking. You notice, I keep wanting to talk about Jiri, but I can't find words to express that special bond created between us during the two or three times we saw each other." Why I said "two or three" I don't know. Of course I knew I saw him three times. But the drive to be secretive after Eva's initial warning persisted.

"I also told Jiri how much I loved the golem legends of Prague and the legendary writer of Prague, K."

"Ah, golem. Ah, K, the man who published too much."

"Too much?" I raised my voice in protest. "Not enough. If only there were more."

Mr. Klein pressed his lips and made a little rocking motion with his head, as if to say, Well, that's the way it is. For a moment he looked sad. Maybe he was thinking of Jiri; maybe my disbelief that he was Jiri's father hurt him. But then he brightened.

"I heard you mention K's *Meditation* before."

"You can hear through the wall while playing Bach?"

"Yes."

Perhaps it wasn't polite to disbelieve him again but I couldn't help it. But maybe Eva had quickly mentioned the book to him in Czech as she was introducing me.

"Why were you so excited to see a copy of K's first book?"

"Because it was his first book. Because so few people know it. Because I saw it at Jiri's house. And with K's signature. My God! K's autograph! I held the book in my hand and literally trembled with excitement."

"I know."

There he goes again.

"You know? How do you know?"

But he merely said, "Yes, I too would have trembled with excitement."

I looked at my watch. It was late. I said it was time to go. I thanked him and bade him goodbye.

"Just a moment." Mr. Klein went to his desk. "I want to show you something."

In his hand he held a thin, light blue airmail envelope addressed to Ph. Klein, sent by Jiri Krupka-Weisz. The handwriting was European, elegant, angular, neat. It was the first time I had seen Jiri's script.

"You don't read Czech."

"That's right."

"But international words you understand."

He took out the letter, pointed out the word "Papa" on the first line and Jiri's name at the bottom.

"It's his last letter, I'll translate some of the lines. 'I am sending you a fine young man I met in shul recently, a man of intellect, a filmmaker. He loves good literature, especially K's works. When I showed him a signed copy of *Meditation*—by the way, he knew the book, even the year of its publication—he literally trembled with excitement. He will come to you via Yossi and Eva. I think you will like him.' That's what my son wrote to me."

How could I argue with that—never mind the age conundrum—except to say, "Very interesting, even convincing. But you have two different names."

"Aha!"

I smiled at him. "You usually say, Yes."

"Aha is Yes to a higher power."

"So that's how you knew my reaction to holding K's book."

Mr. Klein smiled. He looked proud, as if he'd won a difficult chess match with me.

"Now tell me whom else you have met in Prague. What other interesting people you have spoken to?"

"Well, besides Eva's friend, Yossi, I also met the old shamesh of the Altneushul."

Mr. Klein laughed. "Did he do his mirror routine for you?"

I laughed. "His trick is quite amusing."

"And he said something about the attic?" Klein asked in a teasing, mocking tone, just waiting to react to my answer.

"He told me everyone wants to see the golem. Show me the golem, bring me to the attic…but there is no attic, the shamesh said."

Mr. Klein gazed at me for a moment, skeptical. The air hummed. And hummed some more. Like current through high power lines. Then he said, almost in a whisper:

"There is an attic."

"There is?"

"Yes. There was an attic. There is an attic. There will be an attic."

"But he took me inside the shul, pointed to the ceiling, showed me there is no attic. There can't be an attic."

"There is an attic," Mr. Klein repeated.

"How do you know?"

"I know," he said crisply. His stubbornness was stone.

But I, wanting to know, pressed on.

"How?"

He sighed, as though about to reveal long-suppressed information.

"I was there."

A bell rang. A wordless thought moved like a circular staircase through my head.

"When?"

But Mr. Klein merely nodded.

"How did you get there? Tell me. Tell."

"I'll tell you."

"When?"

"Yes," he said.

10

The Dream

That night I couldn't fall asleep. Time was askew, its rhythms off. The little clock next to my bed didn't go tick-tock, like normal clocks. It went tickety-tock, tickety-tock, keeping the rhythm of the opening four-note phrase of Beethoven's Fifth Symphony. The destiny motif. Destiny knocking. Tickety-tock.

Then I slept. I slept and had a dream. I dreamt I was back in Mr. Klein's room. The room was different, Mr. Klein the same.

In the dream he told me again he was Jiri's father, age sixty-nine. The illogic was no more acceptable in a dream than during waking. I was still incredulous. But Mr. Klein wasn't offended by my disbelief.

Since one can be bold in dreams, I said, "I just don't believe it. Sixty-nine minus eighty is a problem in a world of math not yet discovered. People make all kinds of claims here in Prague."

"You mean like Karoly Graf, who claims to be my son?"

The old man was slipping. True, it was a dream, my dream, but still it was the second time Mr. Klein had mixed himself up with K.

"Not your son," I said. "K's son."

"Yes." Mr. Klein laughed. "That's what I meant. That man who claims to be K's son."

"Who disappeared."

"Never mind him. I want you to know the truth about Jiri and me. Watch."

Mr. Klein went to a corner of his room. Only now did I notice that the walls of Mr. Klein's room were not straight but angled out like a rhomboid. I felt we were leaning either forward or backward as we spoke. From the corner he fetched his cane and flung it to the ground. At once it became a serpent. At first it didn't move, but after lying still for a while, its beady, unpleasant little eyes locked with mine, the snake slithered on the floor, creating "esses" that disappeared and reappeared as it slid forward. But since I come from the Show Me State, I don't believe what I see. Even in my dream.

I backed into a chair, trying hard not to fall off because of the angles of the walls. I tucked my legs under me.

The serpent headed for the door.

"Now do you believe me?"

I didn't answer. Just because Mr. Klein could turn a walking stick into a serpent didn't mean that sixty-nine minus eighty wasn't a negative integer. Stick plus snake didn't add up to Jiri plus Klein. Even in a dream.

"Go. Pick it up. By the tail."

Fat chance, I thought.

"No."

"Don't be afraid."

"I am afraid." Even though I didn't believe what I was seeing, I was still afraid.

"It won't hurt you." Mr. Klein seemed to glide on the floor toward me. "Pick it up and give it to me."

I moved toward it slowly. The snake lay stiff, still as a stick. I bent down, approached it gingerly. With my right hand stretched out, I touched the serpent's tail, ready to spring back at its slightest move. But it did not budge. It did not hiss. It did not strike. I picked it up. It hung limp. I gave it back to Mr. Klein. One shake and it turned back to wood.

"Are you a magician?" I asked Mr. Klein.

He tilted up his chin, raised his eyebrows, closed his eyes for a moment. Jiri had a similar gesture when I had asked him how he got his signed copy of K's *Meditation*. A Middle Eastern gesture. Only Allah knows.

"Now do you believe me?"

I still couldn't see the connection between this magic trick and the mathematical impossibility.

"All right, then here's a second sign."

Mr. Klein put his hand into his pocket and withdrew it. The skin was a dead, leprous white.

"Enough?"

"Enough," I said. But I still didn't believe it. He could have had talc in his pocket. There are many magic tricks in this world and many practitioners. Pharaoh's magicians also turned staves to snakes and snakes to staves. Although these two signs defied rational explanation, Mr. Klein's claim that he was Jiri's father was even more irrational. Houdini's feats—being locked into a box which was then thrown into the sea from which Houdini, Jewish trickster extraordinaire, emerged within minutes—were also seemingly irrational. They defied all credulity.

Until it was revealed—and not too long ago—that prior to each of his death-defying adventures, Houdini's wife would always kiss her husband. What was in that kiss? A magic potion? Not at all. Nothing more and nothing less than the key to the lock that could also be opened from the inside of the box, the key that Houdini's wife had in her mouth, which she slipped into his with that loving goodbye kiss.

Here too was something that could be explained. What, I didn't know.

"I have a third sign," Mr. Klein said.

"What are you going to do next?" I said, looking at the water pitcher standing atilt on a little table. "Turn that water into blood?"

"No," he replied rather testily. "You're not Moses and I'm not God." Then he added, "And since Pharaoh's time Jews don't deal with blood, even for magical purposes. From the Middle Ages on, if you know history, blood, the blood libel, has been very disastrous for Jews. Actually, my third sign is the most incontrovertible of all. I'll show you some other time. Meanwhile, I'll let you think of these two. But now it's time to wake up, my boy."

NOTE: For those anxious to learn what happened with the girl in the blue beret, skip to Chapter 12.

But be sure to come back to Chapter 11. If you don't, you'll miss a stunning surprise.

11

Graf. Filming Hruska. Miss Malaprop on Old Town Square.

And Karoly Graf? Was he gone gone too? Listen. One day I boarded a Metro. As I stood by the door facing the tracks, I looked to my left. There he was, Karoly Graf, on a Metro going the opposite way. He too stood by the door. Two pieces of glass separated us. Had the cars stood still, had the doors opened (on the wrong side), had had had, I would have been standing face to face with him. Had had, would have, could have, I could have spoken to him, could have asked him all the questions I was asking myself as if I were addressing him. Why did you give me an old card with the wrong address? Did you purposely do this or was it a mistake? And how come you didn't tell anyone where you were moving? And why did you stop coming to the K Museum? What's wrong with you, Karoly Graf? But all these questions were in vain, for now we were moving slowly, he one way, I the other. Gone gone again, Karoly Graf.

A classic scene from films. Two people who have met, yet lost contact, see each other precisely in this frustrating way. It reminded me of a scene in a novel I'd once read, *Partita in Venice*, where the hero locks eyes with a lovely blonde in a gondola going one way in a narrow canal while he's going the other way. They are about to signal each other when one gondola goes round the corner of a palazzo and the romance is lost forever.

A glimmer, I think, of recognition passed between Karoly Graf and me, he with a slightly startled, even guilty look, and I with a puzzled expression: Why did you do this to me, giving me a card with an old address?

As we were parting, Karoly raised an index finger. Wait, was that a finger Karoly Graf held up as both our trains began to move, his one way, mine another? Or was it a pen top* and not an index finger he flashed at me? To tease me, to intentionally vex and hex me, just as he had teased me, hexed and vexed me with that phony visit card. Or was my desire to see a pen prompting my eye to deceive me into seeing a pen when there was only an upraised finger? And if it was an index finger, what was he pointing to? What kind of message was Graf sending me? Was he trying to tell me something? Perhaps to meet him at the top floor of the K Museum tomorrow? Soon as I saw his raised index finger I quickly put my left fist to my left eye and made circular motions with my right fist—the international sign for filming. Hinting that I wanted to film him. Where, I couldn't tell him. I had no sign for that. His upraised finger could also stand for the number one—to be at the location where we had first met: the first floor of the K Museum. Both signals were one—they pointed the same direction.

Because the whole scene flashed by in an instant, it's one that is imprinted on my mind and seems much longer than it actually lasted. I guess Karoly Graf made an impression on me, after all. Although I didn't believe him, I still felt an affection for him and wanted to see him again. And now I had. And now he had disappeared on me once more.

All the way home I had his image in my mind. Standing in the other subway car so close, yet out of reach. Then it struck me. The real hint. The real hint was the reel hint. That I get to doing what I had come here for in the first place.

---

* But with my pen silent and the top missing I gradually forgot about the pen, using it only on occasion in my apartment (having fashioned a temporary top for it from an old ballpoint pen). Not until much later, during a seminal moment, was I reminded of it once more.

Begin.

Start filming.

For if I delayed any longer I would never begin.

I began by videoing the statue of the Maharal in the city Town Hall, a statue that neither the Germans during World War II nor the Russians during their decades of post-war occupation had removed. They didn't even touch it. I zoomed closer and closer to the Maharal's face, focusing on him from various angles, with a voiceover (added later) of his words, a fine old cinematic trick that gives the impression he's actually speaking.

As I began filming, I rubbed for good luck the little gold ring studded with two tiny diamonds and two tiny pearls my mother had given me. I had attached it years ago to my camera strap and have never removed it. And it has always brought me the good luck I sought.

Now that I had begun I felt a certain ease and confidence, as if a breath of air from a garden full of flowers had flowed into me. A table of contents appeared: Danny K's remarks about his idea of filming "Metamorphosis," Dr. Hruska at the museum, Yossi golem and the shamesh. Then Eva, and perhaps Mr. Klein.

The next day—I knew, I predicted it at once, even in the subway—of course Karoly Graf wasn't at the museum. But at least he was well, alive, and I was glad of that.

At the little K Museum, Dr. Hruska greeted me like an old friend and beamed with happiness as I stood behind the camera and heard him tell me the story of the Museum. He even insisted I talk to his assistant, the receptionist. I thought that was very considerate of him. Originally, I had him pegged as an officious martinet. But my first impressions were dead wrong.

I wanted to talk to Dr. Hruska about Karoly Graf. Something in me was itching to talk about him. What a great addition he would have made to the film. What a missed opportunity. Did he reveal his relationship to K to everyone? I was about to ask. Or did he single me out? But something held me back. I didn't want Dr. Hruska to think I had come here just because of Graf. Next time, I promised myself. Dr. Hruska thanked me several times for coming and filming. He kept bowing and clasping his hands in gratitude. Had he possessed a duplicate of a precious K artifact, I'm sure he would have given it to me.

Outside, I made a sentimental tour of the Old Town Square, seeking you know who. But that wasn't a total waste, for I spotted the placard-holder who spoke an English only Danny K could have concocted. I approached her to say hello.

"Aha," she said. "Here are you."

"Fine," I said, glad she remembered me.

"I was waitressing for you to up show."

"Waitressing? Why not waitering?"

"For in correctly English, 'waitering' is for sex male and 'waitressing' for sex female."

"You are the da Vinci, nay, the Einstein, of Queen's English."

Then she pulled a card out of her pocket and read:

"If you think by conversationing with me you will small by small sail into a intimical relationboat with me, you—"

"I have no intent—"

"—you mistertaken."

"No, you miss-taken." I also pulled out a card from my wallet—Graf's old veezeet kart—and pretended to read from it. "Because me get violentish ocean-ill, I have no intention of boarding a relationboat with you, even for a short, one-day scruise. Are you kidding? You and me? Me and you?" And I gestured to drive the point home. And even added an operatic, villainous, "Ha!"

At once tears sprang from her eyes. Instantly, I felt sorry for her. Sorry I had made fun of her, sorry I had pulled her foot, using her unique take, rather mis-take, on the English language. I put the card away, looked at her again. Why do we hurt people when they are down? I had nothing against her. It wasn't her fault she wasn't attractive. She wasn't a bad sort, just rather pathetic, maybe even down on her luck. Linguistically, an original. But I could not embark. Still, I couldn't help saying it, even though once I said it, I would gladly have withdrawn the words. But the steamroller was on a downhill roll and the brakes were off. It was too late to unsay, having already said:

"Believe me. Not the next–to-last thing in the world, but the very last thing in the world, even more than that, if that is mathematically possible, is for me to embark—"

And I stopped for a moment, took cognizance of the square with the masses of people buzzing in it. People swirling all around, paying no attention to the man and the woman with the placard talking, throwing soft darts at each other—"for me to embark on a relationboat with you. For such a voyeurage I have no tackets, no teckets, no tickets, tockets, or tuckets."

Now the tears rolled from her eyes. She pressed her lips. Tried to stop crying. She even tried to smile. Through her tears. Through her tears she tried to smile and I saw those tears and those tears affected me. I gazed at her eyes, her cheekbones, her lips. Actually, with tears rolling down her cheeks, misting in her eyes, she looked rather appealing. Sadness made her plainness sail away. And then a voice I heard as my own added in perfectly good, non-screwy English, "Would you like to join me for a drink, your choice of beverage, after you finish work?"

"Yes," she said quickly through her tears. "Yes. Off course," she said, drying her tears. "I now, right now, am finish work. No longer in labor." She removed her placard. Now I saw her body for the first time, quite nicely, in fact, very nicely shaped. She walked to the base of the clock tower and rested the placard against the wall. Then, turning to me, she said, "I would affectionate to conjoin with you. Terribly. You seemingly actually very nicely."

I looked at her enticing figure and a wave of heat rose from my hips to the top of the placard, had I been wearing a placard.

"After beverage of your choice," I took her hand and shook it and told her my name and she said hers was Katerina Maria, "we can later maybe conjugalate some sex male and sex female verbs together in my apartment."

"Indeedly, yes. To improvingment my minimalish English I have such large desire."

"And your body English is largely desirable too."

"I am thanking you. I very muchly desire to taking off the heavy cloak of my bad English."

"I will help you take off that heavy cloak, Katerina Maria. And I would love to clock you remove, layer by layer, other unwanted ungrammatical undergarments, understand?"

"We shall ocean if you will layer."

"We shall indeed."

"Goodly."

"As you can ocean, I have similar muchly desire too. Even three," I said.

"Tell, is English you nativity tongue?"

"Why?"

"Because is comedianly."

"My native tongue is Albanian but since I, alas, am in exile now, my English comes out right to left syntactically Albanish."

"Can you to me speak something in Albanish?"

What nonsense syllables should I come up with? I wondered. Then it hit me. Why not use the words I know from Jiri and Betty's language?

"Tara pilus, tara glos."

"What does it meaning?"

I thought of saying, I love you, but then changed it to: "Too young, too old."

"Nepa tara glos," she said, smiling like Mona Lisa only with her eyes.

My head swiveled, then stopped. "How do you know that?"

"On one side, perhaps my front, perhaps my back, I am partial Albanish."

"Do you speak Albanish?"

"No, but the mother of the mother of mine, this proverbialism was in her folk speech."

"I am happified if not horrified to hearing this," I said.

She took my hand and shook it, then said (ex)pertly with tilt of her head: "It is nice to knowing that in both of us Albanish blood runs betwixt us."

"Goodly."

"Come," she said. "Let us to café." And she touched my forearm, held her hand there a moment, then glided it down to my wrist. I love it when a woman touches just like that, on her own. And the desire rose from my placard to the back of my throat.

"Goodly. And I will leg the bill," I said.

"No, I will not allow. We shall cleave it."

Over black coffee (hers) and cocoa-mocha (mine), Katerina Maria told me she had studified drama but could not find labor—hence the placard to support herself. I saw no ring on her finger. She noticed.

"I am not husbanded," she said. Then, looking at me closely, she added: "You look familial."

I was used to that, so I didn't elaborate. "Danny or K?"

"Like Czech author is you resemblement," Katerina Maria said.

"So it is K after all. Plenty people tell me that."

"Not K. Hasek. Writer of *Nice Soldier Schweik*."

"But but," I exploded, frightening her somewhat. "Hasek was short, fat, and not too good-looking."

Katerina Maria shrugged. She smiled into her cup. Maybe she was joking. Maybe she was getting even with me.

I wanted to linger at the café, if only out of politeness, but I could tell she was anxious to pound verbs and stretch nouns.

In my apartment, after a swift English lesson, we reclined on a bed of roses and, with beaps and lounds, boarded the relationboat. Katerina Maria took out her little card and, with a laugh, tore it in two, once, twice, three times. She flung the pieces in the air merrily and watched them float down slowly on us. They fell languidly like thick snowflakes. She tried to catch them with her bare toes.

"Why they fall slow soly?" Katerina Maria asked.

"Because of poor gravity in room. I lowered gravity, increased levity."

Katerina Maria laughed but didn't understand a word I said.

"Do you know differdance between gravitate and levitate?" I asked.

"Differdance?"

"Like what's the reffidance between good and bad?"

"You mean ferdidance," she said.

"Yes."

"No," said Katerina Maria.

"Heavy, light," I explained. "Sink and float. Serious and funny."

"Too fiddicult for I."

By now, I think she was pulling my tibia.

We stopped talking. Her body was even nicer once she unhooked the heavy cloak of her bad English. On her back, silent, her cheeks flushed, she looked good. Her breasts were full and luscious, but one nipple pointed up, the other down. If there was a message there—about English or anything else—I didn't get it. Soon her tender touch made my sin skingle. The walls bent, shook in place, the ceiling rippled like northern lights in the sky. A long loud shriek tore out of one of us, which one I don't know, for our eyes were closed, maybe out of both of us.

I began whispering an endearment into her ear.

"Not presently," she said. "I am still arriving. Did you arrive?"

"Yes."

"I too. I have arrived six multiples and am still arriving."

But sadness was built into her, poor Katerina Maria, for afterward she immediately burst into tears.

"You are not going to ocean me anymore," she declared.

"We'll ocean," I said.

She stopped crying. She looked at me and smiled.

"Know you. I affectionate the way you kiss my kitten."

"Any clock," I said.

"You make goodly use of your language that has gaven me best arrival I ever have."

"Because I speak in tongues, many of them forked.... And I affectionate being naked with you, Katerina Maria."

"And I very muchly affectionate my naked being with you."

Suddenly, she jumped up and rummaged in her pocketbook.

"What's the matter?"

"I possess something interesting in writing. Let me theater you."

She showed me a little handwritten three-by-five-inch card.

"Ocean this," said Katerina Maria.

I looked at the six-word sentence. The words reminded me of a title of one of Borges' stories, "Tlön, Uqbar..."

"Where you achieve this?" I asked her. "And may I copy it?"

"Indeedly." From her bag she took a pen and a piece of paper. "From goodly friendly I achieve this."

"Know you what this means?"

She shrugged. "Is mystery. I possess not the passing-outest idea. Know you?"

"Easily," I said. I read the words aloud slowly, with dramatic sonority. "Oth oiksis alanti ojeca postra aspo."

"Ahh. Your baritonal declamification make me feel eroticlish."

"I am muchly gratitudinous." I pointed out the first word to her. "'Oth' is one of the iconic words in the pan-Gothic linguistic family. Know you what Goth is?"

"Indeedly. I believe in Goth. You do?"

"No no no. That's God, not Goth. Goth is like Gothic cathedral in Old Town Square around which you carry plakat."

"Ahh, goodly. I overstand."

"'Oth' in Gothic, Ostrogothic and Visigothic means I, being, existence, everything."

"Know you Ostrogothic too?" Katerina Maria marveled.

"Muchly. I told you I have many tongues. Ostrogothic is my second tongue after English and Albanish. And Visigothic and Gothic too. There is cunning linguistic relationboat between Ostrogothic, just plain Gothic, and Visigothic. Thusly, every goddam Goth knows 'oth.' Even every Ostrogoth and Visigoth, those brutes."

"Yet you have not eclaired the meaning. Is hardly?"

"No. Is simply. It is the Goths' demand of surrender from the Visigoths who, in turn, sent it to the Ostrogoths in their epic three-sided struggle for the domination of northern Manygerm. You see, the Goths and the Ostrogoths kept switching loyalties so often that after thirty-three years of war no one knew who was on whose side. So, at a peace conference, where they sat around a triangular table, they decided to slaughter one another. Still, there is a problem, linguistically."

"Tell."

"Easily. Although Gothic and Ostrogothic have same vocabulary, many words have different meanings. The note you theatered me can be read as both demand for surrender or a rejection of surrender, depending if you read it in Gothic or Ostrogothic. In Gothic, the line reads, 'oiksis alanti ojeca,' which means: 'I demand you surrender or Goth death doth cometh.' But in Ostrogoth, the same phrase, rather than demanding surrender, is Ostrogothically rendered, 'I do not surrender for I will be all-knowing after death.'"

"You make large impressing on me with your know-shelf of many tongues," Katerina Maria gushed. "You are indeedly very nicely. You possess affiction for books. You are very tome-ish. I affectionate to hangman around with smart, light ineffectuals as you."

"I am honorific to repay compliment. And you, Katerina Maria, are quite lovely. Especially once you are undressed from your plakat. Your eyes are lovely, your cheeks are pinkishly lovely, your red lips, once they are silenced of that angled Manglish, are lovely. And going south on the adorable appurtenances inventory, your neck is lovely kissably, your breasts are nibblingly delicate essen, even if they point in two different directions. And like Demetrius said to his daughter, Ifeelya, 'etcetera, etcetera, etcetera,' down to the celestial Southern Hemisphere. And, oh my goodness, I almost forgotly: you have a massageable, menagable, garagable donkey. I would rather ride on your donkey than in any late-model-year autocar."

Hearing such praise made Katerina Maria blush; the old girl, I couldn't believe it, actually reddened with pleasure.

"I am so gladful my auto body is pleasant to your taste."

"Now I must take my leave of you. Parting is such sugared sadness."

She kissed me on the mouth before she left. "I hope to ocean you again."

What thoughts ran through my mind during the hour or so we spent together? Although she was fun, I saw no place for Katerina Maria in my film. At least not yet. But I must admit that at the height of her ecstasy I was thinking of a placard. Not hers. The one behind which stood the girl in the blue beret.

My missing rainbow.

12

With Marionettes

One day I found the rainbow again.

Walking up a tiny side lane from the great square, a lane I had never explored before, I saw her displaying marionettes in front of a puppet store. She held the handles in two hands and manipulated the dolls so skillfully they seemed to dance on the pavement of their own accord. My heart took a little leap.

"Aha. I found you."

"Hello." It played nicely, that hello. Its music friendly, that hello. A little klieg-like smile, bright and full of wattage, that lit up in me, crinkled in her eyes.

"I thought you went back to Georgia."

"No. Just up the street."

"Why? What happened? Were you flamed?"

"Flamed? What is 'flamed'?"

"Flamed is Georgian slang for 'fired.'"

"No no. I didn't want to carry those heavy signs anymore. They hurt my shoulders. Boring work."

"But meeting such interesting people."

"True."

"I thought you left to avoid me."

If she were pert, fresh, European, she could easily have said: Don't flatter yourself. But the girl in the blue beret said:

"To change jobs just to avoid you? That would be a pretty"—she thought a moment, recalling the word—"drastic thing to do, wouldn't it, just not to see a man? To give up a job? It so happens this jobs pays better and suits my hours. No no, it wasn't personal."

"I've looked for you all over the square," I told the girl in the blue beret.

"Why?"

Now she had me. Now I would have to declare my interest in her. The subtle, mimed, boy-girl ballet could be wordless no longer.

So I came up with, "Because I had nothing else to do."

I looked at her. She burst into a laugh, an understanding smile.

A vague feeling of discontent hovered in me. I was annoyed that she had said nothing about the concert. I waited for her to say just a word of thanks. Or at least mention the event.

I looked at her. I even put my hands on my hips and assumed an "I'm waiting" stance and look, like a father about to scold his naughty little girl.

"What?" she said, knowing she had to do, say, something.

"Did you like the concert?"

"Oh, I'm so sorry for not mentioning it soon as I saw you. Please forgive me. It was wonderful."

Could it be, I wondered, that she was so excited seeing me it just flew out of her head?

"Turns out I was able to make it after all," I said. "I looked in vain for you on the square to buy another ticket…to invite myself."

I thought she would laugh but she looked pensive.

"Where did you sit?"

"Up in the balcony," I said. "And I saw you down in front, in the orchestra."

"So you were up in the balcony. Can you imagine, I sensed it. I felt in the back of my neck someone staring at me. I felt a tingling in the roots of my hair. Did that ever happen to you, sensing that someone is looking at you?"

"Was it a good tingle?" I asked the girl in the blue beret.

But she only smiled in reply, a demure smile, a Cheshire Cat smile, a smile that substituted for words.

"How about you and I actually going somewhere together instead of separately?" Finally, I said what I'd been wanting to say for what seemed like years. Having said it, I couldn't believe I said it.

"Would you mind if I think about it? I made it a principle never to socialize with tourists, for one can get hurt that way. But in this case I want to think it over."

I'm honored, I didn't say.

"How much time do you need? Five minutes? I'll take a walk and come back."

She shook her head.

"An hour or two. A day? Thirty days?"

"Come back in a few days. Let's say four."

A minute later I returned.

"Like in the famous fox fable, I blinked a few times, counted each blink as a new day. And so four days have passed and here I am."

She laughed.

"Actually, I wanted to buy a little hand puppet. Does your shop sell them?"

"Of course. I'll show you one."

She brought out one of Papageno. Perfect, I thought. He'll love that one.

"Is it a gift?" she asked.

"Uh-huh."

"For a man or a woman?"

I could swear I heard a little tinge of jealousy in her voice, a little quaver as she said "woman." Her voice lost its center of gravity when she said that word. I thought of teasing her but decided not to.

"It's for a man." I saw that this pleased her too.

"I ask," she said, "because if it's for a woman, we have a Papagena doll too."

"Look. I want to show you something." I gave the girl in the blue beret a little folded note containing the six words that Katerina Maria had shown me.

"For me?" she said, seemingly delighted. She held her fingers together close to her chest and opened the piece of paper slowly as though she were knitting with miniature needles and read the note as if it were a secret she was keeping to herself.

"How nice! That's so sweet of you."

"You understand it?" I asked

"Of course."

I peered over, wanting to see what she was seeing, but—teasing me—she pressed the note even closer to her chest.

"Why are you doing that?" I burst out. How could she not let me see my own note? "It was I who gave it to you."

"Exactly. So you should know what's in it. So why are you so anxious to see it?"

"Because it's mine. And by hiding it you arouse my curiosity."

"But, but you wrote it," she insisted.

"Then why hide it as if it's a secret note from my rival?"

"Because now that you gave it to me," came the reply of the girl in the blue beret, "it's mine."

"But I may have written something I don't know and I want to find out what it is."

She considered the (il)logic of the request, thought a while, then said:

"All right," and, in one continuous, unbroken gesture, almost musical and balletic in nature, she slid the note across her blouse as she stretched out her hand and gave me the little piece of paper. "I like what you wrote to me."

I opened the note to reread the faux-Gothic words. I turned the paper this way and that. But the paper was as clear of script, as clean of message, erased and white and empty, as blank as it was before I wrote the words Katerina Maria had given me.

13

Calling Mr. Klein

I waited till noon to be sure that Mr. Klein was at home and rested after his morning walk, then I called Eva.

"Hi, Eva."

"Hello, hello, how are you?"

"You recognized my voice?"

"Of course. And also, not too many Americans call me. So how are you doing?"

"Just fine. And you and Mr. Klein?"

"All is well."

"May I say hello to him?"

"Just a moment."

I couldn't hear the words or understand the Czech, but I'm sure she was telling Mr. Klein who was calling.

I was tempted to tell him about my dream, about the staff that became a snake.

"Ah, my young friend, good to hear from you. When are you coming again?"

"Very soon. You know, I had a dream"—there went my resolve—"and you were in it."

"A good dream, I hope."

"Fascinating. Like out of a modernist short story."

"When you come I will show you the third sign.... So, until then, au revoir."

"Thank you," I said without even thinking what I was responding to. When I put down the receiver, only then did shivers spurt over me. Did he say "third sign"? What's going on here? I ran to the bathroom mirror to make sure I was me. I saw my own reflection, slightly pale, staring back. Had Mr. Klein bridged the gap between dream and real, or had I, despite my promise not to tell him about my dream, blurted out all the details in a kind of mind-relaxing stupor, like the one-second, exhaustion-induced dream I had once described?

But reality has to take hold, even if it is Prague. I'm sure I did not tell him details of my dream. And if so, then how in heaven's name did he know of the two signs—signs that really didn't persuade me he was almost seventy with an eighty-year-old son, even though the room was an atilt rhomboid and he was able to turn a walking stick into a snake and withdraw a leprous hand from his pocket? Such magical signs, although they defy reality, still cannot upset mathematics. Applies even in dreams the majestic, inexorable rule of numbers. Even if the world turned upside down and inside out, it couldn't possibly prove the logicality of a sixty-nine-year-old man with an eighty-year-old son.

14

Hero to the Rescue

Early the next morning out of my apartment hotel went I. To take a walk and think about my film. But what happened next was really out of a film.

I step out into the normally quiet, cobblestoned street. Commotion at its edge makes me turn right. A crowd of people watching a struggle. A man fighting with a young woman. He held her by the shoulders, his back to me, blocking her face, and was attempting to force her down. Why are these golems standing unmoved like the wicked men of Sodom and not doing anything to help her?

As I ran toward her, a shout from a rooftop opposite my hotel made me stop. I look up. A man is pointing a rifle toward the crowd. I didn't know whether to run into the hotel and shout to the clerk to call the police or run to the girl. Now she screamed. I looked again. Now I saw her face. My God, it was her, she. But without the blue beret. And no one doing anything. Just standing there. Why?

At that moment all the feelings, inchoate as the wind, impalpable as emotions, all the attraction I felt for her, her pretty face, the dimple in her left cheek, and left cheek only, as she smiled, her fetching blue beret, her dark green eyes, described previously at length and in lovingly precise if not poetic detail, all my feelings for her coalesced like disparate numbers adding up to a preordained sum—as the cute little tyke with the angelic countenance usually seen hovering in the air in the upper left of a Renaissance painting with a soft white leather quiver on his back appeared, unwilling to let slip the opportunity of triumphing over me and my heart, and wished to add that heart of mine to his list of trophies.

And so, the angelic little creature, with the slightly pudgy apple cheeks, baby blue eyes, blond curly locks, and eternally innocent doll-like face, stole up softly and without anyone, including me, seeing him, discharged an arrow from his golden bow that pierced my heart through and through.

Cupid, they say, for I think that is his name, is a blind little boy, but boy how good his aim. Right on the mark. Arrow to the heart omni temporis. Not lung, not liver, not legs, but arrow from quiver to bow, from bow snap straight to the heart. And then the sly, sightless little rascal with the innocent *who me?* face vanished, for he always accomplishes what he sets out to do without being held accountable, since he has been, is, and will always be invisible, his arrows swift and painless—and always, pphht, on target.

And I flew, as if a bow had released me, as if I were the arrow, and not the one arrowed, and shot toward her without thinking and hearing other shouts that I muted out, I at once grabbed the man overpowering the girl in the blue beret and threw him to the ground. He was easy prey, no resistance, and shouts grew in intensity, hurrahs and applause, and I turned to the crowd:

"Why are you standing there like golems when someone is attacked? What's the matter with you?"

Then I turned to the girl and asked:

"Are you all right?"

"You!" she said. "What's the matter with *you*?…I don't know whether to laugh or to cry."

"Cut. Cut. Cut!" someone shouted.

"You just killed my scene," she said sadly.

"Oh, my God!" I looked around, saw the camera, added lamely, "Is this a film?"

"Yes," she hissed.

"Then that sniper on top of the other building, he…"

"Yes. Yes. Yes."

"I'm so sorry. I thought you were being attacked. And no one coming to help you."

I turned to apologize to the man I had thrown down. I helped him up. The guy muttered and walked away. I kept saying "I'm so sorry" to his back.

"Can't you tell when a film is being shot? Don't you know anything about films?"

"I should. I'm a…"

Just then the man who looked like the director was heading our way.

Soon as I saw him, I grew jealous. It's not for nothing that the marvelous English language, so subtle, direct, on the ball, uses the word "grew" with "jealous." Because it's like a wild plant that grows, increases vastly, like bamboo, no stopping it. He's her boyfriend, I thought. A good-looking guy in his late thirties with long black hair combed straight back and a slightly scruffy beard. A movie-star look.

And when I saw her looking at him the jealousy intensified. Now jealousy is usually a bedfellow, and the compound components of that word are apropos here, a bedfellow of possession. I didn't possess her. I didn't even know her name, for goodness' sake. Still, a liquid spurt of jealousy rose to the back of my mouth, bitter as gall, sour as bile, awful-tasting on my tongue, and turned my stomach to knots.

I called her aside, apologized again.

"I have to run now. Quick, tell me. Are my four days up? What's your answer?"

"I'll talk to you tomorrow by the marionette shop."

"Really? And you'll be there?"

"Of course."

"And we'll make arrangements to get together."

She was about to say yes, but she took a breath and swallowed. But I sensed that yes. Oh, how the knots in my stomach dissolved. Oh, how the embarrassment of making a fool of myself vanished.

Oh, how I floated up and looked down at the sniper on the rooftop. He winked at me and I, happy, winked back.

I stood there and looked at her, wondering if I would disappear from her consciousness as soon as I left her.

I wanted to hex her to not forget me. I wanted to imprint an image of myself into her mind; impress myself into her eyelids so that every time she blinked she'd see a little photo of me, but so subtly, so imperceptibly, so below her level of awareness it would be like those quick cinematic ads clever admen created where a frame of a product would flash for a fragment of a second, unseen on the screen, but nevertheless slyly embedding its message.

Thus my wish for her. So she wouldn't, couldn't, forget me.

But what spell or kabbalistic formula to use to realize my wish? Mutter phrases? Pray? Recite incantations? A certain patter of words in an unknown or concocted tongue with my eyes shut, my lips pressed tight, fists clenched too, and my brow furrowed?

I did what I did, thought what I thought, wished what I wished.

No one can fault me for lack of concentration or for not bidding Godspeed to my wishes.

And I ducked quickly into the crowd before the director could castigate me.

Then I remembered. What a dummy I am! Why didn't I give her my phone number or tell her in which hotel I was staying?

14a

Second Version

Or maybe it happened this way, for nothing is made up here. I am recording the story exactly as it happened. As I said at the beginning:

A true story.

Perhaps in a world where there are multiple universes and parallel cosmos, and where one atom can be in two places at the same time, can one event take place in two different versions. Perhaps because of its importance it looms so large and variegated in my memory.

Oddly, I remember it in two ways. In the course of the confusion, I can swear that both took place. But even if one of the two happened, does this mean the other did not?

No.

For both happened, one in real life as I saw it, and the other in memory. But which is which is hard to confirm.

If you read two versions of a story in two different newspapers one of them surely is, if not purposely untrue, then inadvertently false. But this isn't a newspaper, so you can be certain that what I say really happened.

Who says the same event can't happen twice?*

---

* Another approach. One was a dream, the other happened—or vice versa. Or could it be both were dreams, or, even more like a dream, that both happened.

It can.

Here is part two:

I came out of my apartment hotel and walked into a side street fenced off by the police. A crowd is watching a trial. A judge sat on a slightly raised wooden platform. He wore no hat or wig but a black judicial robe. Behind him, stretching far to the right, was a fake wall with a courthouse scene. A man and a woman whose backs were to me—I watch from the far edge of the crowd—stood before the judge. The woman, with a large red kerchief around her head, complained that the man had taken liberties with her in the field just outside Prague.

"He took from me," she whined, "what I have been guarding zealously for more than twenty-five years."

The judge turned to the man and ordered him to reply to the complaint.

"I crossed the field outside of town. All of a sudden this woman came out of nowhere and seduced me. I gave her money but now she wants more and has dragged me to this court, sir. She claims that I forced her, but that is a lie."

"Do you have twenty silver crowns?" asked the judge.

"I do."

"Give it to her."

The woman thanked the court profusely, bound the kerchief tightly under her chin, bowed several times, and departed—but not before she had counted the silver crowns carefully.

Now the judge turned to the man again.

"Go after her. Get your twenty silver crowns back and bring them to me."

I saw the man running after the young woman. He caught up to her and began to struggle with her. She seemed stronger than he. But, locked into each other, both managed to return to the judge.

"This ruffian," the woman cried, "is trying to take from me the coins Your Honor just ordered him to give to me."

"Did he succeed?" asked the judge.

"No! I'd sooner give up my life than my silver crowns. Hammers and chisels won't succeed to get them out of my clutches."

"She's right, Your Honor. I don't have the strength to get them from her."

"Let me see those silver crowns," said the judge.

The woman gave him the coins and the judge handed them back to the man. The judge turned to the woman.

"If you had defended your body as you defend your crowns, not even Samson himself could have overcome you.... Off with you—and don't show your face in Prague anymore."

As the young woman walked off, she removed her kerchief. It was only then that I recognized her.

The girl in the blue beret! Why was she being expelled from Prague? And how could a sweet girl like that be accused of being a tart?

I leaped over the wooden horse and ran through the crowd.

Behind me, I heard the crowd susurrating antiphonally. Some said this and some said that. Was it "tara pilus" and "tara glos" that they were chanting? I couldn't tell because the rush of blood in my head confused my hearing. But I caught up to her—she had turned—and shouted:

"Why did you let them do this to you?" I took her hand. "Why?"

She wheeled. "You! You just ruined my scene. My first chance in films and you ruin it. I was supposed to go back to the judge and weep for mercy."

"Is this a film?" I looked around.

"Yes," she hissed and burst into tears.

I couldn't tell if they were genuine or part of her act. Still, I tried to console her. I reached for her hand. "Don't," she said, "stop," I wishing she would continue to say quickly, "Don't stop. Don't stop."

But just then another man came to her too, and in my haste to get to the girl I tripped over him, pulling him down also. I tried to break my fall by seizing a klieg light I hadn't noticed before—for had I noticed it I would have known what was happening—and toppled that too. It fell through the papier-mâché courthouse wall the scenic designer had no doubt constructed. That plopped back also with a ripping sound, three segments of carton falling in three waves.

Not only were the sounds proliferating, but I could see my bills growing and my budget for my own film shrinking. Still, I couldn't help laughing at this silent film comedy I was scripting without a script. I wondered if others were laughing as I tried to pick myself up. I could swear I heard laughter all around me.

The segment I had seen seemed familiar. Then it clicked. It was the famous scene in *Don Quixote* when Sancho Panza is governor of an "island" and administers justice in a Solomonic way.

Another man ran toward me.

"What's wrong with you, signore? Where you get the nerve to crash a film?...Bruno, Scarpio, escort this man out of here.... Don't cry, Katya."

Two men stood next to me. I looked at the girl without the blue beret—so Katya is her name—admiring her long green eyes. She stood sullen with hands on her hips.

"Why did you jump into my role?" she complained.

"I'm so sorry. I was just passing by and thought you were in trouble. I didn't realize this was a film shoot. Look, I want to see you. Finally. Will you go out with me?"

The two men began marching alongside me.

I turned, heard sounds in a foreign language. Maybe Georgian. Maybe Gibberish. But one word came through clearly.

"Nevah!" she said, although it could have been, "Nepa!"

15

Looking for Katya. Filming the Shamesh. Actor Returns.

The next morning, I crossed the square into that side lane full of stores and stood in front of the little marionette shop, expecting to see Katya outside demonstrating those cute dolls. But she wasn't there. A new girl stood there playing with the marionettes, showing off before a group of six or seven people. She didn't know where Katya was. She didn't know her, had never met her, was just summoned to work late last night.

Back to the square. But she was not there, nor in any of the side streets that shot off Old Town Square. The placard-holders—Katerina Maria, whom I would have avoided, must have been off today—surely thought me an oddball fixture here, a character out of classic myths, the guy who is doomed to keep on looking for a girl in a blue beret. Every town has its loons. Now I was an added screwball landmark on the great plaza.

I returned to my apartment hotel and asked the manager if he knew what production company had been filming here the day before. He didn't know. They were here one day, he said, gone the next. Adults don't cry. But I felt like bawling. Where would I find another girl like that, with a dimple in one cheek, and one cheek only, when she smiled? I don't like to play with destiny, use fancy romantic terms, but I felt she was—all right, I'll confess—I felt there was something between that sweet girl and me. Otherwise, why would I have bumped into her so many times, why was she friendly with me, flirtatious even? Katya, the girl in the blue beret. Katya, now I know her name. Just like I knew I'd get to know Jiri and felt I'd get to know the old man with the cane. I had the same feeling about her.

Did I think she was Jewish? My heart—my prophetic heart—told me she was family. For was I going to give my heart, my life, to a gentile girl, or as the Americans so colloquially phrase it, to a shikse? I, whose entire life and professional career was shaped, molded, stamped, by Yiddishkeyt?

Absolutely not.

She didn't look like the other young people on the square who had flat cheeks, snub noses, and Tartar eyes, the solidly Slav facial bone structure. There was an otherness, as K says in one of his stories, to her features, those long green eyes, the black hair, the kissable lips, and the arrow she had engaged that sightless little boy to shoot into my heart.

Thinking of Katya brought to mind poor Dora Diamant, K's love that could not be. I didn't want Katya to be my Dora. If we weep at films that move us, shed tears while reading, how many more tears should we shed at real life's dolour? No story moved me more deeply than K and Dora's romance. She was his true love; with her he would have found fulfillment. The others were false loves, forced loves. The same arrow the blind little boy sent to my heart he had also sent through the hearts of Dora and K. But other powers, some human, some divine, intervened.

I didn't want my affection for Katya to end up the same way. I didn't want someone, perhaps years later, to pity us, the way I'm now pitying K and Dora, mourning a lost love. But at least Dora survived. Unlike K's three younger sisters, Ottla and Valli and Elli, whom the Germans took and had killed in 1942, young Dora Diamant made it to England in time.

I was glad for K when he fell in love, and I rooted for him and Dora. And I cursed her father's intervention, and even more, her father's Hasidic rebbe, who forbade the match because K was non-observant, even though Dora herself was removed from that world of piety. And I felt sorry for poor K when they parted.

Did Katya intentionally say she was going to be at the marionette shop knowing she wouldn't be there? Or had she been taking lessons from Karoly Graf? Or had something happened beyond her control—in all fairness, we have to take that into consideration—that prevented her from keeping her promise? I don't usually let defeat or disappointment stop me. But if she had indeed disappeared, there was nothing I could do.

She wasn't here; she wasn't there. And there was nowhere I could look for her. So I had to conclude it was not meant to be, she and me, which rhymes, and sounds better than she and I. Because if it was meant to be, it would already have been. So many missed signals, so many missed opportunities. If it was meant to be, she wouldn't have vanished so many times. If it was meant to be, *someone* would have known where to reach her. So many misses hinted that this miss was not for me.

One night I dreamed of Katya. Dreams are like films, with storyline, dialogue, characters, even colors. Except there's no replay or editing. I dreamt I met her. We'd gone for a walk in a park. Suddenly, she broke away from me and, with a teasing laugh, said, "Try to catch me." I ran after her. Then she stopped, changed direction with that provocative laugh, and ran away again. I couldn't catch her. Then a fog, a thick mist, rolled in. She went into it. I followed. The sun burst through. The mist vanished. I looked. She was gone. Gone? Yes. Gone. How gone? Gone gone. Terrified, I woke.

My mother always said a bad dream is just that: a bad dream. Of no significance. What's bad is spit out in dreams. In real life good remains. Which meant that the opposite would be true. I would catch her. No fog. No mist.

Just sunshine.

Early another morning, I returned to the Altneushul.

The cop greeted me, looked at my camera bag.

"What? In? Sack?"

"Big tefillin."

"Ah," he grunted.

I found Yossi golem. He gave me an enthusiastic hello.

"Shalom. So, how are things?"

"Fine. Thanks for the great introduction to Eva and Mr. Klein."

He smiled, pleased. He looked at my bag.

"Big tefillin, huh?"

I laughed. "Camera."

The shamesh came over, also looked at my bag.

"Good. I see you brought your camera." He patted his hair. "We'll start right after davenning, is that all right?"

"That's exactly why I came," I said. "But first I have to interview the first man I met in Prague—Yossi. I'll be with you in a moment, shamesh."

Yossi agreed. I was going to tell him I had learned that Mr. Klein was Jiri's father, but recalling his and the shamesh's derisive laughter, I kept silent. You poor deluded soul, he would say. You believe that? They're almost the same age! Shamesh, *kum aher*! Come here and listen to this! Mr. Klein is Jiri's father, he says!

Yossi examined the strap of my camera, saw the ring.

"Beautiful ring. Why not on your finger?"

"Because it's for good luck, not adornment. It's been there for years."

"Well, may it bring you much mazel."

I asked Yossi why he liked this shul, how often he came, his feelings about the place, its mystery, its history. I asked him to bring me an old Siddur from the bookcase and open to the title page. I also asked about his service in the Israel army.

"Who told you?"

"Eva. Just like you told me about her wartime heroism, she told me about yours. None of you speak of yourselves; you only have nice things to say of others."

"The way it should be."

I listened to him as he talked. But in truth, I wasn't so much interested in his answers as his face, his movements. Maybe it wasn't fair, but art is never fair. It's selective, egotistical. Later, in the editing process, I would make my commentary on his features, accenting the stiff left side of his face, the golemic part, showing the viewer what a golem must have looked like, with similar lumbering movements and a frozen face. My commentary would override, subdue, maybe even silence, many of Yossi golem's words. He would be a fitting prelude to the shamesh's story about the golem and the attic.

At the end of the morning service the shamesh and I sat alone in the synagogue on the bimah. An eerie stillness pervaded. It echoed through the enormous space of the Altneu. I heard the walls stir, the curtain of the Holy Ark rustle, the centuries-old banner up above wave. I told the shamesh I would ask him about his reaction to people requesting to see the golem. He nodded; he understood.

But while the camera was rolling, the old shamesh with the rheumy eyes and red lids, as if he'd had an excess of weeping, this old shamesh fooled me. He didn't speak about what I wanted him to speak about. Instead, he answered a question I hadn't asked—but not before he asked me a question I couldn't answer.

"Do you know how the golem is made to come to life?" the shamesh said, fixing his twinkling, pink-red lidded eyes on me.

I wanted to get to the two points I thought would be most interesting, so I said, "Yes."

"Good. I'll review it for you, in case you forgot."

And as if reading from an invisible manual before him, the shamesh stared straight ahead at the metal music stand that wasn't there with the unseen notes on how to chant the instructions to vivify the golem.

"And you take the golem you fashioned from the clay and loam on the banks of the river Moldau," the shamesh chanted from the unwritten staves, "and you open his mouth…"

Here the shamesh closed his eyes like a violin soloist who knows the score by heart and has no need of notes, and he stood and held on to the old shiny wood of the railing of the bimah as if he were addressing a crowd of worshippers or a class of golem makers.

"...and you take the *shem* written on a tiny piece of kosher parchment," he continued softly, his eyes pressed shut, "the sort on which the *Sh'ma Yisroel* is written for a mezuza, the same sort of parchment which if it was bigger you could write a Sefer Torah on it, and you write on this little piece of parchment no bigger than a thumbnail the holy *shem*, the four letters of the holy name of God, first a *yud* and then a *hey* and then a *vov* and last a *hey*, and you take this tiny parchment"—the shamesh drew a breath, in and out like a sigh—"now called a *shem* because it has the *shem*, or name of God, on it, and you place it under the tongue of the clay and loam golem, and then the clay and loam golem, a shudder runs through him as though he is vibrating, for a special kind of current, the electricity of life, is running through his veins, and then the golem opens his eyes because life has come into him, in other words he lives, with God's name part of him, now he is alive..."

And I'm filming this extraordinary presentation.

Now the shamesh slowly lay down on the wooden floor of the bimah, much like Leah did in the film *The Dybbuk* as she died. At first I thought he had collapsed from the spiritual exertion of his narration. But I was mistaken. He was merely demonstrating for me how it would look if he were a vivified golem. Then the shamesh opened his eyes, blinked a few times, looking confused, his milky watery eyes staring straight ahead, and I have this magnificent scene I hadn't expected to film, in fact, wanted to avoid, because I thought it was extraneous but now realize is central, I have it all on film, including how the shamesh rose, a bit dazed, stretched out his hands before him and walked down the steps of the bimah as if he were a vivified golem taking his first steps in his newfound life. Then the shamesh stopped and turned to me. A shudder went through him and he was himself again and he said:

"...and then the golem takes one breath and then another breath into his lungs and life is in him because the *shem* with God's Ineffable Name, the name that the *Kohen Gadol*, the High Priest, says once and only once in one and only one place, in the Holy of Holies, in the Holy Temple in Jerusalem, the Holy City, on one and only one day, the holy day of Yom Kippur, pronouncing the now lost pronunciation of the letters that make up the Tetragrammaton, the *Shem Havaya*, the *Shem ha-Meforash*, the Ineffable Name, the holy four-lettered name of God, first the *yud* and then the *hey* and then the *vov* and last the *hey*, and life is in him because the *shem*, the *shem* is under his tongue and now he can live and walk and hear and obey. But talk he cannot, no, he cannot talk because he is not a full human being, for he is created not by God but by man. And since he is created by man and not by God he does not have the God-given gift of speech. And that is how the golem is made alive." The shamesh inclined his head and torso forward. "I am finished with my presentation."

He opened his eyes, took a deep breath, and sighed again. From somewhere he uncovered a glass of water and drank.

"Thank you," I said. "That was very beautifully done. You told the story like an actor with great dramatic flair."

"You filmed me?"

"Yes. Didn't you know that?"

"I wasn't aware. For a while I was in the sixteenth century. And anyway, I thought you were going to only film me talking about people asking me about the golem." And he mimed showing me the mirror, as if it were a secret between him and me and he didn't want to share it yet with the microphone that wasn't on.

"That's next. But let's go outside, like last time. Start by telling me about your reaction when people beg you to show them the golem."

Outside, he said, "You filming me?"

"Yes, soon as you begin."

He put his hand into his jacket pocket—

I stopped him.

"No, no. Don't take out the mirror yet."

"Not the mirror," said the shamesh. "This." He took out his comb and combed the little hair he had. "Now I will begin."

"Fine."

"Ready?"

"I am," I said.

"I begin." The shamesh cleared his throat. "Everyone wants to see the famous goylem of Prague. The famous goylem of the Altneushul. They come up to me, for I am the shamesh, you know, and they look this way and that, as if spies were watching."

The shamesh's broad hand gestures and facial miens made him look odd. He was hamming and I told him so, of course not using that word. I suggested he look natural. "Speak like you did last time."

He took a deep breath.

"Everyone wants to see the famous goylem of Prague. The goylem of the Altneushul. They come up to me and secretly say to me, 'Please take me to the attic. All my life I'm dreaming of seeing the goylem. It is my life's wish. Please. I beg you.' They offer me money but I refuse. I don't take a penny. Bribe? Me taking bribes? Of course I refuse."

I stopped the camera again.

"That's not what you said last time."

"What I said last time?"

"Last time you said you do take a five- or ten-dollar bill but the twenties you give back."

"Last time I wasn't being filmed."

"You say one thing to me and another to the camera?"

"I don't know. I never been in a movie before. Can I see it before it goes to Hollywood?"

"So which is the truth? What you said last time or now?"

"Both."

"How can both be the truth?"

"We're in Prague, my boy."

I sighed. I couldn't argue. He had already given me precious, unexpected footage.

"Please continue. What do you do when they insist that you show them the goylem?"

Hearing the word pronounced the way he said it, the shamesh brightened.

"They say to me, they insist, 'Show me the goylem, show me the goylem. Please! I beg you! I have been waiting for this special moment all my life.' Finally, I say, 'All right. I'll show you the goylem.' Their faces are in rapture, as if they're seeing God's holy presence, the Divine Shekhinah at Mount Sinai. And they don't know the surprise that's coming."

"You actually show them the goylem?"

"You know I don't..."

I stopped filming.

"...I told you already the last time what I do," the shamesh said.

"Of course I know. But for the film I'm pretending that it's the first time I'm hearing the story."

"Aha! You mean the film is pretend. Not real."

"Both," I said. "We're in Prague."

He raised a finger, shook it once, as if conceding a point.

"You right."

"So we'll start again, from the moment I say, 'You actually show them the goylem?'"

"I actually do. I promise and I keep my promise...'I promised to show you the goylem and you will soon see the goylem,' I tell them. 'In a moment.'"

Here the old shamesh put his hand inside his jacket once more and withdrew the little pocket mirror. He held it not in front of my face but in front of the camera lens.

"'Nah! Here! Look!' is what I tell them. Here in front of you, in front of all of you who are meshugge to see the goylem. Here, now you see *der emesser goylem*, the true, the real, the authentic goylem... You. All of you. Every single one of you has now seen him. Look in the mirror. Know. Realize. *See*! The goylem. See the goylem. Nah! You've seen him. The goylem!" and like a pro he hesitated a moment, "Is you!"

And the shamesh, laughing delightedly, put the mirror back in his pocket.

I stopped filming.

"How did I do?"

"Marvelous."

"You caught me saying what I was supposed to?"

"Yes."

"Now we continue?" the shamesh said.

"Yes. Now I want to ask you a question. And film your answer. You told me how the golem is vivified. But I know that according to the golem myth he also died. How?"

The shamesh seemed pleased with my question. He rested one lip on the other. He looked satisfied. Gone the sadness. Did he have a wife? Children? He never spoke of them. I didn't ask. Maybe, like other survivors, the Germans had killed his entire family and he went through life alone. Alone, yes. But not defeated. Like other Jews, he climbed back to life.

"The golem didn't die," was his answer. "He was made unalive. You understand the difference? I'll tell you how they did it. I quote from the memoir of the holy Rabbi Yitzchok HaCohen Katz, son-in-law of the Maharal, the Chief Rabbi of Prague, the rabbi of this very shul: 'And the Maharal took all three of us who had been present when the golem was formed, when life was breathed into that creature of dust and loam and clay, and he took us to the place where the golem lay sleeping in the attic of the great synagogue…' In other words, right here in the Al-tnigh."

"But you just said there is no attic."

"Wait. I'm still quoting from Rabbi Katz's book. 'And just as we had stood at the golem's feet and faced his head when he was created and we walked around him seven times from right to left, as the holy Hebrew tongue is written from right to left, and just before the seventh circuit, the most potent circuit of them all, we placed under his tongue the *shem*, God's holy name on a tiny piece of parchment, and then completed the seventh circuit and he began to breathe and stir—so now, to undo the creation, to bring him back to clay and loam and dust, we stood at his head and faced his feet and walked around him six times from left to right, as though the holy Hebrew alphabet were written backward, and just before the seventh circuit, the most potent circuit of them all, the Maharal bent down and removed the *shem* from under the sleeping golem's tongue, and we finished the seventh circuit and the life spirit of the golem was gone. He breathed no more.'"

"Shamesh! Sir! Please wait! You describe a scene from the memoir of the Maharal's son-in-law and yet tell me there is no attic in the Al-tnigh. Explain. Please."

The shamesh scratched his cheek. "Maybe in his day it was a phenomenon created just for that purpose. For that one time. Like the Torah says about the earthquake when the earth opened up its mouth that one time and swallowed up Korah and his band of rebels. Remember what Moses said? 'And if God now creates something entirely new, a new phenomenon, you will know that it is the deed of God.' So that is what it probably was. A phenomenon. Created tem-po-ra-ri-ly."

"Then it went away."

"Maybe. Could be. Perhaps." The shamesh thought a moment. "Absolutely. For sure and for certain. Because for sure that attic isn't here now.... Now you want me to tell Hollywood how there is no attic?"

"Yes. Please."

"And..." The shamesh hesitated. He bit his lip, looked at me shyly, questioningly. "How to say it, is there any payment for an actor in a film?"

"Not for a documentary. I'm not a big Hollywood producer."

"You not?"

"No. I'm a one-man operation."

"You also a doctor, chirurg, surgeon too?"

I laughed. "Operation is another word for business. I'm a very very small businessman. I do everything myself."

"So it's not Hollywood."

"You disappointed?"

"Is all right."

"How much money did you expect? Want?"

He looked over my shoulder, gazed out into the distance. He blinked his red-lidded eyes.

"Twelve dollars."

"Why twelve?"

"I figured two times the five dollars people offer me and a twenty percent bonus."

"You know what? I'll make it eighteen."

"Okay. But why eighteen?"

"I figured twenty dollars for the twenty you refuse as a bribe, less ten percent discount. And, anyway, eighteen dollars is *chai* for life."

"Very nice of you.… Plus a copy of the film."

"Fine. You have a VCR?"

"What's that?"

"A machine you put the video in."

"No."

"You have a television set?"

"I don't watch television."

"But you need both to see the film."

"So you need two machines? A VRC and a television?"

"Yes."

The shamesh looked disappointed.

"Show me the attic," I said.

"I told you last time. No attic."

"I know." And I laughed again. "I meant, let's go inside and you'll tell me again all about it."

I began filming.

Inside, he showed me the banner King Charles V had given the Jewish community, the arched vaults, and the women's section, pointing to the ceiling each time, saying:

"Look. Up there. Do you see a ladder? A trap door? No, right? Nothing. It's a *bobbe-mayse*. Fantasy. Legend. There is no attic. There was no attic. There will be no attic. Everyone thinks the goylem is in the attic. Maybe if there was a attic there would be goylem. But there's no attic, so obviously there is no goylem. Except the one in the mirror. So even if I wanted to take you to the attic to see the goylem, I couldn't. There is no attic. Hence, no goylem. The only goylem—"

Here he went into his pocket and took out his mirror again.

"—the only goylem is you, dear viewer. The one in the mirror. You. You. You."

Here the shamesh surprised me. By pulling out his mirror, he did something a good director would have done, tying together theme A and theme B, making them one in essence.

"Thank you. Thank you very much. That was wonderful, shamesh. Superb. Thank you."

Just as soon as we walked outside a man wearing sunglasses rushed towards me.

"You," he said.

"I," I replied.

"It's you."

"True. I'm the only you here except for you."

"And you're a cameraman and don't know when a film is being made."

"Do I know you?" I asked him.

"You should know me. You knocked me over the other day and I don't like it."

He took off his sunglasses and handed them to the shamesh.

"Here, hold them for me."

I had no intention of getting into a fight. I hadn't even fought when I was a child. I couldn't stand the idea of one person hitting, hurting, another. Fighting is for beasts and human lowlifes.

"Why didn't you react," I asked him, "when I tripped over you?"

"I don't fight when I'm working."

"Well, I'm working now," I said.

"But I'm not," he said and began pushing me, once, twice, three times.

"You can push all you want," I said, brushing his hands off my chest. "I don't fight. I'm not going to fight you. I don't fight, neither when I'm working nor when I'm not."

"Watch out!" the shamesh cried in a voice tinged with fear. "Here comes the goylem." He took the mirror out of his pocket and flashed it.

The actor stopped, as if frozen.

"You were scared to start up with me," I told him, "when everyone was looking the other day. You didn't want to make a bad impression. You didn't want to risk being fired."

"You fell over me, knocked me down, and didn't even apologize."

"I certainly did. That's the very first thing I did. I begged your pardon and said it was an accident. But you walked away and didn't even turn around."

"Mmm," he said, apparently mollified. Maybe he was considering what to do next.

"Aha! Ahem!" the shamesh shouted.

My antagonist turned. The shamesh flashed his little mirror again. I don't know if it was the reflected sunlight that stopped him or if indeed the shamesh had a magic mirror. In any case, the fellow's attitude completely changed. He became a lamb, like the wild beasts in Mozart's opera when the beautiful melody is sounded by the magic flute.

I shook him.

"Where is Katya?"

"I don't know."

"What do you mean you don't know? You make a film with her and don't know where she is?"

"She was hired at the last minute. She's not part of our crew."

I shook him again. He didn't resist.

"Tell me where she is. No one in the entire city of Prague knows where she is. How can a girl disappear like that?"

"If she liked you so much, she would look for you, just like I looked and found you.... Is Prague, mister. City of mystery. Things disappear. I don't know where she is. And even if I knew, I wouldn't tell you."

I let him go. "Go," I said.

The shamesh put his mirror away.

"I wish you to disappear," the actor grunted. He turned to the shamesh. "May I have my sunglasses?"

"What sunglasses?"

"The glasses I gave you a few minutes ago. To hold."

"These?" The shamesh pulled his old horn-rimmed specs from his jacket pocket.

"No. Those are your glasses."

"I know they are my glasses. That's why I didn't give them to you."

"I meant my sunglasses."

The shamesh tapped his pocket. "I don't have your sunglasses, mister."

"But I gave them you. Come on, those are designer glasses."

"Oh! Designer glasses. That's a different story." The shamesh turned to me. "Did you see him give me designer sunglasses?"

"No," I said. "The sun was in my eyes before. I couldn't see."

"What's wrong with you?" the actor shouted at the shamesh. "I just asked you to hold my glasses." Then he turned to me. "And you heard it too."

I didn't say a word.

"Maybe," the shamesh said, "you asked me, but you never gave them to me. Why don't you look carefully in your pants pocket?"

The actor automatically tapped his trousers pockets and pulled out the sunglasses.

"How in heaven's name…?"

The shamesh said a few words to the actor in Czech and then translated them for my benefit.

"Next time, don't accuse an innocent man. Now go."

"Go," I echoed.

The shamesh put his mirror away, an enigmatic smile on his face.

The actor went.

The shamesh assumed I'd ask about the sunglasses, but I knew what the answer would be.

Is Prague.

16

Dream, Again

I woke up in the middle of the night. For a moment I was so disoriented I didn't know where I was. I thought I was back home in New York. But it was too quiet. A moment later I was fully awake, the question, in two parts no less, perfectly formulated, the question dancing on the English supertitles in my mind. You might even say the question woke before me. Maybe I dreamt the question. Or maybe it bridged the sleeping and waking states, starting in one, leapfrogging into the other.

Why did I meet Danny K so late in life? And why did fate tease me with Karoly Graf, K's putative son? Danny K I met; my other hero, the other K, I was born too late for. Sometimes we belong to one era but are born in another. One of my professors once hurled an insult at one of his colleagues (behind his back of course) by saying, "He should have been born in 1250; he has a perfect medieval mind." For a person like me, who knew Maimonides and Chaucer, that put-down wouldn't have fazed me at all. But that question quickly led to others I'd asked before. Why did Jiri disappear? And Danny too? And Karoly Graf? And, most frustrating of all, the girl in the blue beret? I just hoped, as I closed my eyes and tried to sleep again, I hoped that one day I wouldn't wake up and not find myself in bed.

Then I slept and dreamt again. And again. And again. Three times I had the same dream. Three separate dreams, in chapters. They echoed the A Major Major Discovery message the two placards had sent me on the great square, one of them held by Katya. I hadn't had a continued dream since I was ten. And I had never met anyone else who dreamt this way. You dream, wake up, fall asleep again and the dream continues, like a bookmark placed in a novel. You go away, return later to the book, and the story continues. But this was basically the same dream. At least the same message in each chapter. Three times. You will find a treasure in Prague.

A dream dreamt once you maybe remember, maybe forget. Twice, it takes you by the shoulders. Three times, shivers run down your back. You start believing in dreams.

So I pondered:

Graf? Was he the treasure? Now out of reach, perhaps irretrievably lost.

The girl in the blue beret? Was it she?

Klein?

Maybe all three. One for each dream.

Or maybe it was the shamesh. Or Yossi. Or Jiri, also gone. Or Eva Langbrot.

Maybe all of them. After all, if you believe in dreams, you give up logic.

A time will come when you can order dreams. They won't be as haphazard and chancy as today's dreams. When you order dreams you'll savor those who are gone and undo errors. I'll dream of my parents. Talk more to Jiri. Explain to the girl in the blue beret. Find Karoly Graf, the man who claimed to be K's son.

Oh, there are dozens and dozens of dreams I would dream.

17

Visit to Mr. Klein

My next visit to Eva's house, as you will soon see, was crucial. It revealed to me why I had come to Prague, why I was drawn to Prague, what possible treasure I could find in Prague.

Usually, Eva Langbrot opened the door. This time is was Mr. Klein himself. Eva was traveling, the old man said, visiting relatives.

"Anyway, welcome, welcome, how nice to see you," he echoed Eva's affability. "Would you like something to drink? No? Then come right into my room. What's this? A Papageno puppet? Why, thank you. How kind of you. *The Magic Flute* is my favorite opera."

"Mine too."

"I'm putting it right on my writing table and that's where it's going to be. And now…"

I started talking about the weather—but I sensed Mr. Klein's impatience.

"I want to tell you something," he interrupted me. "Sit down."

I sat at the edge of the chair and looked up at the tall, slim, white-bearded man.

"I think the time has come," Mr. Klein said without any drama in his voice.

Were this a suspense film, the camera would focus on his face, and by the light of his eyes, a lift of eyebrow, flare of nostril, crease of lip, we could gauge if the words were ominous or ironical, neutral or enigmatic. But this wasn't a film and from a glance at his face I could not predict what would follow.

"Yes. The time has come."

For what? I wondered. Would he show me a magic trick? Open a door, either one of the two in his room, or perhaps the hallway door, behind which—surprise!—like in the old-fashioned early TV shows, *This Is Your Life*, a long-forgotten beloved friend or relative would appear, and behind this door, yes, indeed, the time has come, he would show me a smiling, shy, eager, waiting-for-me Katya, and we would fall into each other's arms, and she would never disappear from me again?

"Jiri and Eva and our friend Yossi all like you. And I too. So I won't delay any longer."

Mr. Klein went to his desk, opened a drawer, and pulled out a letter.

"My late, beloved son Jiri also wrote that you have an instinctive affection, a simpatico, as you put it, for our family. He liked that. I like that too.... That's why I'm going to share a secret with you, a secret that few people know."

He put up his hand as if to stop any questions.

"Jiri was touched"—he looked at the letter—"touched by how sad you were that K never had any children, never married, never had the good fortune of living out his life with his beloved Dora Diamant. Jiri was moved by this sensitivity for another human being so removed from you in time..."

"I was just thinking of Dora Diamant the other day," I cut in. "It still affects me, that failed, that tragic romance. Every time I think about it I shake my head in sympathy and pain."

"But I have some good news for you," said Mr. Klein.

"You do?"

What could he tell me? But then I weighed the words "good news" and "share a secret" and decided that perhaps Mr. Klein would reveal that K indeed had a son and that that son was Karoly Graf and now he could share the secret, the good news, with me and tell me where to find him.

Wait! Maybe Klein would tell me where the golem was. That he had seen him during his stay in the Altneushul attic. That he would short-circuit the shamesh, do an end run around him and, lo, bring me to the golem in the attic. What a coup for my film! Unless, of course, all of this was just an old man's delusions.

But Mr. Klein surprised me. What he brought me was indeed good news—good but problematic—but it wasn't about Graf, it wasn't about the golem.

"I want to tell you who I am," is what Mr. Klein said.

"But I know who you are."

"Who am I?"

What an easy quiz! Would I get a prize, and what prize would I get for the right answer?

"You're Philippe Klein, also known as Phishl, ex-proofreader who corrected so many other writers' books—Eva told me this—he began to think he wrote them."

Mr. Klein gave me a genial smile. He closed his eyes slowly, as if savoring his proofreading past, then reopened them. The smile was still on his lips.

"Wrong! I'm not Phishl Klein."

"Then who are you? Are you going to tell me you're Phishl Krupka-Weisz, who for some good reason changed his name. Maybe politics, maybe safety, I don't know."

"That's right. You don't know…I'm not Krupka-Weisz."

"Then who are you?"

"I'm—"

And he told me.

I couldn't help it. I knew it wasn't polite, and even as I was doing it I knew how wrong it was, how it violated all I'd been taught by my parents about elemental decency, courtesy, respect, especially for elders. But now I couldn't restrain myself. I burst out laughing at the absurdity. Right, I thought when he told me, and I'm Danny K's son.

And then I apologized.

Mr. Klein took it well. "It's all right. I understand. I expected it. You're not a believer. You come, as Yossi tells me, from the Shawmee State."

"I didn't say that to Yossi. I said that to Karoly Graf when he told me he was K's son."

"Then how come I heard it from Yossi?" Mr. Klein asked.

I spread my hands in confusion. Perhaps Graf had contact with Yossi or with Mr. Klein, which the old man hadn't told me about or simply didn't want to. On the other hand, if both Karoly Graf's and Mr. Klein's absurd claims were true, then contact between them wouldn't be that absurd. It reminded me of what I'd learned in geometry, maybe algebra: multiply two negative numbers and you get a positive. Here too. You add up two absurds and get one truth.

Wait! We're getting sidetracked. We've just—maybe—discovered the Rosetta Stone, and like idiots we're quarreling about a broken chisel.

"You also didn't believe I was Jiri's father."

I couldn't argue with that.

"Well, now I suppose I believe it.... But how can I possibly believe you're K? True, you may be a K. K was a common name in Prague. I once even met a Jew in New York with that name."

"But I am he. The one," he insisted.

Hearing this, I blurted out: "But you died."

"But I didn't," he said, his voice low and unhurried. Still, in his polite reply I sensed a sharpness. "And if you notice, my dear boy, you said 'you,' not 'K.'"

What can one say in the face of such an absurd (pronounce it "ab-soord")? And I meant it as a noun, not an adjective. In the face of such an outlandish, irrational assertion? Should I play along with him? Humor him? Condescend? Should I make believe I didn't hear what he said, or should I use a rational response like: But it flies in the face of historical truth?

"Flies in the face of historical truth should be brushed away," he said. "Facts on the ground sometimes contradict historical truth."

My breath was captive. I felt dizzy. My tongue cleaved to the roof of my mouth.

"So you're K," I whispered.

"Yes."

I resisted the temptation, oh that awful pleasure of sarcastic laughter again, to tilt that seesaw we always ride, to stand up and loom over him, lord it over this poor old simp with derision and whatever other superior airs we can pull from our nasty sleeves.

"The writer."

"Yes."

"'The Metamorphosis.'"

"Yes."

"What else did you write?"

"Yes."

Now what in heaven's name was that supposed to mean? Was he some kind of robot or automaton programmed to say only one word?

"What else?" I repeated.

The old man looked at me, trying to assess if I was testing him. Of course, any literate person could rattle off K's novels and stories. I, for instance, could do just that, having read every word he wrote. Does that make me K? Or K's kin?

"America," he said. Yes, that was one of his books, published by Max Brod after K's death, and spelled with a "k." But then he continued and said, "That's where you come from. The Shawmee State."

I shook my head. But this time I did not laugh.

"I don't blame you for not believing. If, for instance, K tried to reveal himself to me I wouldn't believe it either."

That was loopy, dead-end reasoning, for if Mr. Klein were really K, how could another person "reveal" himself to K as K? Of course he wouldn't believe it. It would be like someone approaching me on the Metro to tell me he was me. Would I believe it? Of course not.

"And besides, K died in 1924."

Mr. Klein smiled. He played with the hairs of his Van Dyke.

"And if he had lived, the Germans would have taken him like they took his sisters," I said.

"You know about my poor Ottla and Valli and Elli?"

"Yes."

"Few people know that."

"Those who love K and know the Holocaust also mourn K's sisters."

"It is for this love that I just told you what I told you."

I looked at Mr. Klein, puzzled, astounded. I wished I had a thesaurus, a dictionary to look up words to express my astonishment, incredulity, disbelief, a fountain of shifting emotions, as if fragments of mirrors were passing before me, I racing past them with barely a glance.

"K's death in 1924 is a rather big hurdle to overcome for a man who claims to be K. It's much easier to claim one is K's son, like Karoly Graf."

"Didn't I tell you I didn't die?"

Still, even assuming the surreal, the absurd, the impossible, the nature-defying—let's assume K didn't die—today, in 1993, he would be exactly 110 years old.

I don't know, but I might have muttered his age aloud, for Mr. Klein exclaimed, "Bravo! How did you guess my exact age?"

"Then why keep this a secret? Why not also share it with the world?"

"You remember I wanted Max Brod, that traitor, my beloved friend, to burn my manuscripts?"

"Yes. Everyone knows that."

"I wanted to burn everything. Bridges. My budding fame. I wanted to live quietly. In peace."

"How could you have lived in peace during the war? You hinted last time that you survived in the attic. But even if there is an attic, how could you escape the Germans? They were everywhere, spreading like a cancer."

"They heard the shamesh's story. 'There was no attic. There is no attic. There will be no attic.' And they believed him," was Klein's laughing reply.

I walked around the room, glanced up at the two model aeroplanes that stirred slightly, as if they had just exhaled, leaned my two hands on his desk as though it were my own, and looked out the window.

I stood before Mr. Klein and gazed up into his clear blue eyes.

"All right, presuming all this is so, how can I resolve for myself the question of your age? Last time you told me you're 69 going on 70 and have—"

"…had."

"…had an 80-year-old son. Now you tell me you're 110."

"Going on 111. Three straight vertical lines. Isn't that a remarkable number? A magical cipher. An unforgettable integer. Three in a row. One one one. Three magnificent beginnings. One, the perfect number; the one-ness of God. *Sh'ma Yisroel*, the Lord our God, is one. No more, no less."

That's all very nice and mystical, I thought, but:

"You still haven't explained how you can be both 69 and 110."

He could have said: I really don't have to explain anything.

"Yes."

"So which is it? 69 or 110?"

"Yes."

I wanted to stamp my foot in frustration but was afraid one or both of those gorgeous two-winged model aeroplanes would fall. I might also damage the arm of his gramophone. Or, worse, it might start to play Bach on its own. That's all I needed now, music to accompany my frustration.

"I mean, isn't it *either or*, even though the *either* is absurd…and come to think of it, so is the *or*."

"Both are true, and you'll soon see why."

I stood. I faced the door. Then I wheeled quickly and asked my question in a booming voice, dramatically, like I had seen prosecutors do on TV shows.

"Can you prove you are who you say you are?"

"Can anyone? Can you?" Asked like Karoly Graf. Like father, like son.

"But I'm not making an incredible claim."

"Are you, my boy, who you think you are? Maybe not."

I showed him my business card.

"Anyone can print a veezeet kart," he said. "If I showed you my veezeet kart, would you believe me?"

Klein understood my silence.

"Please, Mr. K—" But I couldn't finish his name. The "lein" got stuck in my throat. "Your claim is—who will believe it?"

"Yes," he said.

Again that laconic, irritating, sandpaper-on-skin yes.

"*You* will believe it," he said. "I don't care about anyone else."

I looked at him. For a moment I thought he would make his skin dark brown and his back chitinous; he would elongate himself, lie on the floor or cling to the ceiling with hundreds of tiny suction-padded hair follicles. But if he did that, who knows if he would be able to reverse course and become himself again? What a piece of theatrics to prove a point, to persuade a skeptic about the truth of his words, the veracity of his very existence.

"These books." He pointed to his packed bookcases. "All of K's works in the original and in many translations are not enough for you. No. Of course not. Any serious collector, you will respond, any fine library would have them. Even a madman who thinks he's K. I can understand it stretches reality to assume that a man who died is alive and, what's more, has lived so long. But imagine how frustrating it is for me to share this news with you, which perhaps only a handful of people close to me know, and for you not to believe me."

"I'm honored that you're sharing this with me." Then I looked at my watch. I stood up to go. "I have an appointment."

"Tomorrow you will believe what you haven't believed today."

"I'll be here in the morning," I said. So as not to offend him I didn't call him Mr. Klein.

He inclined his head. "Thank you again for Papageno."

But as I crossed the room he ran after me. I was astonished at his nimble stride. He's going to confess, I thought. I was just teasing you, he'd say.

"What if I were to pull off my plastic face mask and reveal myself, show you my true face?"

I tried to gauge the timbre of his tone; serious or mocking? So I said:

"And what if I were to show you *my* true face, make my voice an octave higher, like this, remove the onstage mask I'm now wearing, and reveal myself to you as your long-lost daughter?"

"If you pull off your mask I'll pull off mine," Klein said.

"Fine," I said in falsetto. I put my hand under my chin. Then a wave of fear chilled through me. My God, what if when I start tugging a mask really comes off? "I'm ready."

Mr. Klein did the same. He moved both hands to his throat. He curled his fingers, about to pull—then stopped. With a warm, self-deprecating little glint in his eye, he said, somewhat sadly, "I don't have a mask."

"Neither do I."

We both laughed. He clapped me on the shoulder as I opened the door.

But my head was a carousel. Leaving his room, I bumped into the doorpost of the outer door, so dizzy was I. Had Mr. Klein said something I didn't hear? The hallway was spinning. Not only spinning, but the walls, like in my dream of a few days ago, the walls were angled up and out, like in an amusement park's hall of mirrors, hall of fun, where distorted reality throws you off balance, makes you bang into walls.

The fresh air outside did not mitigate my agitation. If anything, it sharpened the conundrum. First he's Jiri's father; now he's K. First one man tells me he has the honor of informing me he's K's son. And now another tells me he's K. In other words, if both are to be believed, Mr. Klein is Karoly Graf's papa. Maybe I should bring these two fakers together for a faux father-son reunion.

As these thoughts buzzed, my mind's-eye camera was rolling. Even if this is not true, it would still be fascinating. An old man claiming to be K's son, followed by a supposedly very old man claiming to be K. It fit right into Prague, golem, illusory logic. Right into my film.

It was only when I boarded the Metro that I realized Mr. Klein hadn't shown me the promised third sign.

18

In a Dream State

I departed in a dream state. I felt I'd been sedated, anesthetized, was walking about half asleep. Klein's claim had put me into a different world.

Once out of the Metro, I headed for the great Old Town Square and walked around, trying to calm down. I tried to take in slowly the crowds, the tall clock tower, the people streaming in and out of the little lanes. I blended memory of the square—Katya in the blue beret wearing her placard, Katerina Maria and her fractured English—with what I was witnessing. I imagined I'd bump into Katya again, but deep down knew she would not be there.

As much as I wanted to think about Katya, I was overwhelmed by Mr. Klein's secret. Klein K? The twentieth century compressed? I couldn't absorb it. History was an express train running past me. What would, what could, Klein do tomorrow to persuade me? Don K's clothing in the style of his photos from the late teens or early 1920s? Show me a family photo album? Display his handwriting and compare it to K's memorable slanty calligraphy? Or maybe summon Max Brod back from an ethereal abode? What could he do? What would I do if I claimed to be K and had to convince a recalcitrant visitor? Or what proof could I provide if I claimed to be K's son? I'd turn to pages of mystical texts and invoke some potent magical formulae.

Klein had shown me a letter from Jiri with the word "Papa" on it, ostensibly proving Jiri was his son and he Jiri's father. Would he show me a letter tomorrow from *his* father, or one from him to his father with his signature? But that still didn't prove anything. Rare book dealers did a thriving business selling letters from famous people. And even signatures could be forged.

That day I spent several hours in the Czech National Library looking for proofs. I inspected old photos of K and various memoirs to see if I could find something personal. Did he limp? But that's easy to imitate. Was he cross-eyed? Did he have a birthmark on his face or hands? Did he stammer? Also easy to mimic. Were his earlobes large or attached? Alas, there were no surviving family members. The Germans had taken and murdered K's sisters and their families. I could find nothing. I even asked Dr. Hruska of the K Museum if he had anything in his archives or in storage. I could see my question hurt him. His eyes dimmed, as if not the museum but he himself had been insulted.

"We have no back rooms, no storage, no archives, no space, no revolving exhibits. What we have on view is what we have."

If I could convince myself that Mr. Klein was K, I would run out to the streets and cry: K lives. K's here. K's back. People of the street, good citizens of Prague, do you know who is living among you? But I know I would be taken as a madman, in the same league with those who shout Jesus lives, or the Messiah has come, or those who claim, I am K's son. People would stare at me, smile indulgently, and move away.

And what if he wasn't K? What if he had taken someone else's identity? There were plenty of stories of people assuming another's identity after the war. Folktales had plenty such stories. Shakespeare is full of switched identities. The great Italian storyteller, Franco Sacchetti, has an amusing tale where an abbot who can't answer questions put to him by the local lord asks a smart miller to don his hat and cloak and switch identities. And there's a famous story about the Baal Shem Tov and his coachman switching places, just for a lark. When they come to a village and a local asks the faux

Besht a hard question, the clever coachman just laughs and says, "That's so easy even my coachman can answer it."

One mitigating factor in favor of Mr. Klein's story was his fingers. He had long elegant fingers, a fact noted in biographies. A voice one can imitate; stance, walk, even personalities can be copied. A writer's works can be memorized; lists of the imitatee's friends, names, places, bios, can be learned. But the length of a person's fingers, like the classic birthmark that identifies a child of royal birth in the folk stories, *that* cannot be replicated. Those ten digits were a kind of birthmark: singular, unique, inimitable. Like fingerprints or DNA.

Of course I would return the next day. But Mr. Klein had a mountain to climb to convince me.

19

Back to Altneu

The next morning I went back to the Altneushul for a morning minyan, but I felt trepidatious. After what Mr. Klein had told me, I now saw Yossi in a different light. Yossi knew Mr. Klein; after all, he had sent me to his friend, Eva. Still, Klein puzzled me, saying he heard my remark about the Shawmee State from Yossi, when actually I had told it to Karoly Graf. It showed some contact between Graf, Klein, and Yossi. But now I knew something that perhaps Yossi didn't know, and I certainly wasn't going to share it—especially since I was still skeptical myself.

It wasn't Yossi I wanted to see but the shamesh. However, since I sat in the back with Yossi after the service, I asked him:

"Did you ever hear of, or meet, a man named Karoly Graf?"

Yossi thought for a moment. The good side of his face lit up; the damaged side stayed flat, unmoved.

"I can't say I have.... Why do you ask?"

"I met him at the K Museum and, seeing how enthusiastic I am about K's works—"

"You like K's works?"

"Of course. That's one of the reasons I'm in Prague. Didn't Jiri tell you that?"

Yossi shook his head.

"Anyway, when Graf saw how much I love K, he told me—as we stood outside the museum—he told me he has the honor of informing me that he is K's son."

As soon as Yossi heard this he let out a roar of laughter. The same raucous cackle as the first time we met, when I said I wanted to see the attic. This time both sides of his face flushed. Even the glass eye gleamed.

"K's son!" He tried to stifle his laughter with his hand. "That's hilarious. Ab-so-lute-ly hi-la-ri-ous!"

"So you never heard of him?"

"Who?"

"We're talking about Karoly Graf, who said he was K's son."

"Oh, him. I'm so busy laughing at the wild idea of it that I forgot there was a man behind it."

"Mr. Klein told me that you told him that I come from the Shawmee State."

"What state is that?"

"It's Missouri, but never mind that. I told that to Karoly Graf when he told me he was K's son."

"He told me that you told us that we told him. My head is spinning. You have to be a genius to follow all these tolds. I never said that. I never even heard of the Shawmee State. The old man must be mistaken."

"Then how do you know he's old?"

"Only an old man could be so demented."

"So you never heard of Graf?"

"By name, no. But now that I think of it, I may have heard of a man who claimed that. I mean, there aren't too many people around who have the honor of saying that. How old a man is this Graf? Fifty?" And he slapped his knee and burst out laughing again at his own joke.

I too had to smile.

"Or perhaps he's ninety," and again Yossi laughed. "Yes, ninety. Old and demented."

I waited, annoyed. Yossi saw this and calmed down.

"Do you really want to know how old I think he is, or will this be another occasion for more derisive laughter?"

Yossi's face fell. He had never seen me angry and he apologized.

"I would say in his mid-seventies," I said.

Yossi looked thoughtful.

"But you'll admit," he said, "that there is something funny about this." And he began laughing again, this time more subdued.

Now the shamesh approached.

"I heard laughter, Yossi. When I hear laughter, especially yours, I have to know what's funny."

"He asks me if I heard of a man named Karoly Graf."

The shamesh pouted, shook his head. "And that's funny? That's not funny to me. Usually, when you laugh, it's something funny. So why are you laughing?"

"He says he met Graf in the K Museum," Yossi explained, "and Graf told him he has the honor of informing him he's K's son."

"K's son? Now that's funny." And the shamesh began laughing and Yossi joined him and the laughter invaded both sides of his face. His cheeks shook and both the good eye and glass eye shot sparks of laughter and delight. I thought back to my first visit, when they both began cracking up at my desire to see the attic, the very reason I was here now, to discuss the matter with the shamesh. One man's mirth bounced off the other's; each enhanced the other. Two merry men were they.

Soon, from somewhere, although I hadn't seen any of them, the chorus of fellow cacklers would appear and approach and join in, and the shamesh, after all of them had laughed themselves out, would quiet them and scold them for humiliating and making fun of a guest. I realized how wise it was that I hadn't told Yossi that Mr. Klein claimed to be Jiri's father. I didn't need another bundle of sarcastic laughter. And only a certified masochist would have shared the news with Yossi about Klein insisting he was K!

"As if we didn't have enough to laugh at in Prague," the shamesh said, out of breath, red in the face from the exertion of endless laughter. "Now we have K's son."

Which prompted both men to initiate another round of laughter.

"I was trying to find out where he lived because I wanted to see him," I blurted out against my will, unable to subdue the fool within me pushing me to reveal everything. "You see, he gave me his veezeet kart, but when I went to the address on the card—" I should have stopped but didn't.

"—he wasn't there!"

But it wasn't me who said that; it was Yossi, gleefully, bursting out again, joined by the shamesh who, with tears rolling down his cheeks, cried out, "I knew it. I knew it. Of course he wasn't there."

"And why not there?" Yossi asked. They both quieted down now, but I could see they were keeping in another salvo of laughter, doing their best to restrain themselves.

I imagined myself spinning around, turning my back to them, and walking out, insulted, waiting for their apologetic cries: We're sorry. Come back!

"I don't know," I said. "The house porter told me Graf had moved out a year ago.… Perhaps he mistakenly gave me an old card."

"And you don't know where he is?" the shamesh asked.

"I saw him for a few seconds again on a Metro the other day that was going the other way."

"Which means," the shamesh said with a professional detective mien on his face, "that he's still in Prague."

"I thought that perhaps you know him or of him, or if he's registered with the Jewish community."

"I don't. He's not. And who says he's Jewish?" the shamesh said. From his pocket he took out a tiny notebook. "Give me his name again. If I hear anything, I'll let you know."

"Karoly Graf."

The shamesh wrote his name. "Could be a Jewish name.… And why do you want to see him so badly?"

"For my film."

The shamesh drew back, hurt no doubt by another competitor for attention in the film.

"But he's a faker," Yossi said.

"Still, he'll be an interesting character for my documentary. And how do you know he's a faker?"

But Yossi just laughed again and the shamesh joined in. No chorus echoed their laughter—still, it rang in the benches, the walls; even the old banner fluttered near the vaulted ceiling.

When Yossi left, the shamesh and I gazed at each other. Sooner or later, he would ask me about the film, his role in it, to see what he looked like.

"The film, shamesh, is in its very early stages, so I have nothing to show you. It will take a while. But I guarantee you, I won't forget you. You will get a copy of the film."

I was still musing whether I should tell him what Mr. Klein had said about the attic. But that is the very reason I had come to the shul this morning.

"Shamesh," I began. "I spoke to an old man the other day and he also said there was an attic here."

"Yeh? Who is this man what spoke to you?"

"A Mr. Klein. He said he knew there's an attic." I didn't want to tell him Mr. Klein was there lest I get inundated with another barrage of hilarity.

"And maybe that man, maybe he also seen the goylem?" the shamesh said, ticking his head like a fishwife arguing with a petulant customer.

"That he didn't say."

"I don't know a Mr. Klein." And he clapped his hands twice to signal: end of story.

"But he knows you," I persisted.

"More people know me than I know them. I am the shamesh."

"So we have a contradiction, don't we? You say no attic, but last time we spoke you recited from the memoir of Rabbi Katz, who described the Maharal undoing the golem in the attic of the Altnigh.... Was he lying?"

"What? Who? The holy Rabbi Yitzchok Katz, son-in-law of the saintly Maharal, a liar? God forbid!"

"But you also showed me there can be no attic here. You said, and I quote you, I quote you like you quote the holy Rabbi Katz, 'There was no attic, there is no attic, there will be no attic.' So how can it be and not be? It can't be true and not true at the same time. It's not logical. So we have a contradiction, don't we?"

"You know physica, yungerman?"

"Physics? Yes, a bit."

"Did you know that scientists discovered that one of Newton's basic laws has been ab-ro-ga-ted? The law what says one thing cannot be at two places at the same time?"

"Yes."

"But they discovered recently that one atom *can* be in two places at the same time. Quantum physica."

"So?"

"So you just answered the question. Solved the riddle. So!" he concluded, imitating me.

I don't buy it, I thought. I don't accept it. Something is fishy here. Then it dawned on me: perhaps the shamesh had created a myth of his own in telling people there is no attic. He was old, tired. Didn't want to be pestered anymore. Golem, attic. Attic, golem. Enough. There is no attic. And you're the golem. Period.

"But Mr. Klein told me he heard of someone who was up there. During the war."

"Okay. So God made a miracle for him," the shamesh said with a sarcastic singsong. He either didn't believe me or he didn't believe Klein. "And He created the alleged attic, which as any in-tell-i-gent person can plainly see, and as I've shown you, does not exist. And, moreover, the Maharal, who created the goylem, gave an order that has the force of a Torah law and has been strictly obeyed for more than four hundred years that no man ever dare set foot in the attic, the which we all know does not exist." Then the shamesh added, "You will send me film when done, yes?"

"Of course. I told you I would."

"I know." He smiled. "I just wanted to hear it again."

Then he hugged me goodbye and kissed me on both cheeks.

His parting words were, "If God wants to create an attic for his purposes, who am I, a simple shamesh, to say no?"

20

The Chase

As I was coming out of a little vegetarian restaurant—rustic wooden tables, cozy atmosphere, no smoking, imaginatively prepared food—and made my way along a little lane that led to the great square, I heard a cry "American!" I turned and saw someone running toward me from the top of the lane. That cry spurred me to run first and think later. It had to be someone local, for an American would have called me by name. Who could be running after me? I thought, as I sprinted ahead.

Sensing someone loping among them, people made way for me. For those who didn't, I nimbly stepped left and right, hopped, pivoted on one foot, and pressed ahead.

Who could be calling me "American"? As storefronts moved by and behind me, I felt I was a camera dollying forward in the middle of the street. Now the shops whizzed and blurred by until I was in the crowded open square, where it was easier to elude a pursuer.

It could be the director, after me for damages I had caused his set; it could be that huffy actor. He had said he would meet up with me and he was right. I turned. My pursuer, whose face I couldn't see, was running too. I didn't want to meet him again. I owed him nothing. I had apologized. And the shamesh wasn't here to help with some kind of magical powers to give me an edge in a confrontation, which I didn't want in the first place.

Or maybe it was someone Katerina Maria has sent—Katerina Maria, angry that I hadn't made contact with her again and had abandoned the relationboat we had launched together. Or maybe it was her papa after me for other, more complicated, reasons: leaving his daughter, making false promises, placing his thirty-seven-year-old virgin in harm's way, embarrassing the entire extended family now that she, unattached, unspoken for, unmarried, was in the family way.

All these thoughts—again came the urgent call, "American!"—flitted in my head as I danced, leaped, jigged, and ran. Hadn't I done this before, when I was in pursuit some time ago after the girl in the blue beret?

It was good the crowds were thick and I was able to blend into the crush of people, moving quickly, unobtrusively, now at the edge. On I ran. Ran on and on. I ran and ran. It seemed I was running all over, through, and around Prague, crossing bridges, streets, up the hill and down the hill, passing the Altneu on Parizska Street, running along the Moldau, traversing the great plaza again, dodging crowds, my adamant, unknown pursuer well behind me, always letting me know that he was still near, with his recurrent shout, "American!" showing that he had not given up, was relentless in his chase, but was well enough behind me to keep out of sight and shroud his identity.

Could that actor in Katya's little film still remember that alleged slight so well that, despite my apology, which he refused to acknowledge outside the Altneu, he still harbored such a fierce determination to strike back at me? Or was I dead wrong? Could it be someone else who wanted to harm me? But if he had so much energy to run so far, why had he not caught up to me? Or was he doing it on purpose to keep me off balance? To frighten me? Weaken me so that his confederate, lurking nearby, could surprise me from the side?

Now I was running on the square again. The K Museum was coming up, and I hunched and moved to the side, like 007 in a

James Bond movie, crumpled myself into a ball, and rolled into the museum doorway, pushed the door open with my feet, turned and crawled in.

The surprised receptionist saw me. It was not the one I had filmed. Her I had never seen before.

"What's the matter?" she said in Czech.

"Do you speak English? Someone is after me. Don't be afraid. I know Dr. Hruska. Is he here?"

"In vacation. Business trip. To Brussels and Amsterdam. Come quick. Behind desk. Go in door. Closet."

In the door, heart pumping. I touched the wall for a light switch. None. Swooshed my hand in a circle in the air for a pull string. Found one and pulled. The light went on.

I tried to calm down. I looked around. It was a little utility room. Brooms, deep sink. Another door within—the toilet. I washed my sweaty face and neck, still heard my heart pounding.

Ten or fifteen minutes later the girl opened the door.

"Are you feeling well?"

"I'm all right."

"You want to still stay?"

"Well, it's hard to look at a mop and sink for long."

"I think you can come out. You know Dr. Hruska?"

"Yes. But I haven't been here in a while. Are you new here?"

"Yes. Started two weeks ago. Why you scared?"

"Man chasing me."

"Man he is gone."

"What man?"

"Same man chasing you. He came. He said, 'Is American here?' I said, making believe, 'What American?' He said, 'Man, running. No come here?' I said, 'No man coming here.' Is what I said to protecting you."

I was so overcome at this sweet girl's spontaneous and creative help that I embraced her and said, "Thank you. Thank you very much."

"To protecting you, I said, 'No one comes in here.'" She smiled at me, happy at the collusion.

"What kind of man was it?"

"Czech man. Spoke Czech."

"Young? Old?"

"You know, he crashed in here, 'Is American here?' so fierce, anxious, and I afraid and astonished, and I, not telling him truth, first time such thing happen to me."

"Lying."

"Yes, lying, but also standing up, confused by sudden ask for help, big excitement in this boring job, so I no pay much attention to looks of man, but he has strong voice."

"Did he leave right away?"

"He looked once to left, look once to right, here, right here by desk, and left."

I looked around. No one was in the K Museum.

"Did he want to go upstairs?"

"Yes, but I tell him, 'Upstairs close. No guards there today.'"

"Is there a back door or a back entrance? A side door? I would rather not go out the same door. Maybe he's waiting for me."

"Is good idea. Use back entrance. I show."

I looked at her. A bland Czech girl with typically Bohemian features. Probably in her late twenties. Sort of pretty, blue eyes, upswept blond hair, pert nose.

"You from Prague?"

"No." She smiled sadly, as if ashamed she wasn't from the big city.

"Been here long?"

"Only few months. Need to make money. To help my mama and papa. Improve my English."

"When do you finish work?"

"Six p.m. in evening."

"Are you free?"

"No, I am not free. Me you must to pay."

I didn't show it, but I smiled inwardly at her misunderstanding the American idiom.

And then she broke into a laugh.

"Yes, I free. You want to take me someplace?"

"No. I just wanted to know if you are free or if you cost many kroner."

Now it was her turn to be astonished. I saw a little downturn on her face. And then I burst out laughing.

"You protect me. I want to reward you. You go, come, with me to concert tonight."

"Yes. I go, come, with you to concert."

"Show me back entrance. I return and meet you there at 6:01 p.m. in the evening."

21

The Transformation

"All right," Mr. Klein said without preliminaries as I came in. His face glowed. He had just bathed, trimmed his Van Dyke. He wore a suit and a tie I hadn't seen before, as though dressed for a special occasion. Later, I understood why.

"Two signs you saw already: the serpent and the leprous hand. Now for the third. Since you don't believe me, I'm going to reveal myself to you."

Was he some kind of angel or Elijah, I thought, to resort to revelation?

"I believe you, but—" Then I realized: he had just mentioned the two signs in my dream!

"Ah, there's that 'but' that sticks in the throat," he said with a cadence. "But you still want proof. Now watch."

He took my hands. A warmth flowed through me. As if by clasping my hands he sent a wave of fatherly love into me. As if by that touch of hands he turned from a charming, friendly stranger into welcoming kin. Then he went to his high chest of drawers. He stood with his back to me, bent down, opened the bottom drawer. He quickly took something out of a little brown leather box.

What next? Would he metamorph himself? Surprise me again by changing his mask? What would I see now? He would point his old wooden cane up to the ceiling and I would see an enormous bug, five feet long and a few inches wide, with sticky, suction-cup legs, crawling on the ceiling—a creature similar to the chitinous one I had imagined last time I was here. That would prove his contention.

But would he be able to undo that metamorphosis and change himself back again? I was worried about this before and I was still anxious now. Changing back was always a problem. A double maneuver. One change was miraculous enough. But who said the return trip would be successful? Who knows how many animals now walk the earth that used to be human beings with a failed round-trip ticket?

Or would he show me more letters? He made a motion near his face. Did he look into a pocket mirror? Take a pill? But he didn't drink. Even with the swift movement of his hand I noticed he held something tiny, perhaps the size of a nickel. I looked intently and saw a piece of parchment. His jaw muscles moved once or twice. Although he put that parchment in his mouth, it was I who was affected. I felt an electric jolt. When I was in high school I had a portable radio that gave me shocks each time I flipped open the cover. But this shock was stronger, an infusion of volts. Mr. Klein straightened up, turned and faced me.

He wasn't showing me letters.

No.

Something else was happening.

I looked.

I stared.

I saw.

My hands fell to my side. A frisson ran up and down my back.

So quick was the event I couldn't react. His face was changing. When I saw what was taking place, I closed my eyes for a minute or two like a Jew does when the *kohanim* bless the congregation.

Klein became younger, as if shedding skins, born anew. As he reached my age, it seemed as if I were looking into a mirror. Had we switched identities?

Skeptics will say that I turned away from Mr. Klein for a moment and looked in the mirror and saw myself. But to skeptics I say: There was no mirror in the room.

Had he put on a mask, similar to the almost realistic faces one sees in a wax museum?

He gazed at me.

I tried to speak. No sounds came from my mouth.

"A mask, huh?" he said.

It was only then he showed me the transformation. What I had seen was just the quick preview. A coming attraction. First, back to Mr. Klein. He did this in an instant, so quickly as if I'd been drugged for a minute. Then the years just dropped off him. So stunned was I by what I was witnessing, I couldn't see, focus, on anything else. Not his collar, not his neck, not his sweater. I didn't even know what he was doing with his hands, moving them to enhance the hocus pocus, or add/detract from abracadabra. It was the reverse of that famous scene in the classic Frank Capra film, *Lost Horizon*, where as soon as the people leave the magical kingdom, Shangri-La, and step out of the enchanted Tibetan paradise, they suddenly age. Years leaped on to their faces. Wrinkles etched in skin. But here, now, with Mr. Klein, the years fled.

It began with his white Van Dyke beard. When photos are developed, the image slowly materializes. Here it was just the reverse. His beard began fading. Soon nothing was left. His hair darkened as though an invisible black rinse were washing through it. Black hair covered his head. He became a man of fifty or fifty-five.

Then, for a few magical moments, I saw the young K—yes, now I called him K—before me. The dense black hair parted in the middle. The angular face. The slightly protruding, pointy ears. The straight thick black brows. The high cheekbones giving his big sad eyes, luminous and piercing, an almost Oriental cast. The cheeks fuller. The long, compressed lips. Gone the almost feminine softness of the old man's lips.

Had a spell come over me? Had he cast stardust into my face, a sprinkling so subtle I hadn't even seen it? Did the Sandman put me into a sleep trance that made me believe what I thought I saw?

But while K's face was transforming, something was also happening to me. As I looked at him I sensed something shift in my head, a wall appearing, and a movement, maybe me, sailing to the other side, then realizing I too was someone else, somewhere else.

I heard music, music on a different plane. Music thick and compressed, like the music I had heard in Jiri's hospital room, a forty-minute symphony, the spaces between the notes gone, condensed to four seconds. Music so dense I floated on it, as if on thick water. Then I sank. But it was not like drowning—descending is the better word. It was like descending into Champagne-like bubbles, between which one can breathe, then rise. Between the bubbles, I was Josephine the mouse; a carapaced insect on the ceiling looking down at my sister, my parents; in the courtyard of the castle, standing before the bar protesting my innocence; I floated to the Great Wall and walked along it; fasted in the cage for forty days and forty nights; then found myself in the synagogue, watching the furry little brown animal crawling in the woman's gallery.

Then K began to speak. I had heard recordings of people who had lived in the late nineteenth, early twentieth centuries: Sholom Aleichem, Edison, Mark Twain, people who were older than K. But I had never heard a recording of his voice. They either didn't have machines like that in Prague—or, if they did, K never made use of them.

He stood straight, looked even taller than before. His eyes sharpened, danced brightly. A wise look glowed in his blue eyes. He took a deep breath. He put his hand to his mouth, a gesture people use when they try to remember something, four long, elegant fingers over lips, or index finger upright, pressing against the cheek, bent middle finger near the lower lip. However, it seemed to me that K put his index finger and thumb between his lips for a moment, a quick movement whose significance I would understand only much later.

"I would have you understand, ladies and gentlemen, that you know more Yiddish than you think you do. So many of you are so frightened of Yiddish one can almost see it in your faces. But there are powers in you that make you understand Yiddish intuitively and, if you bear that in mind, you begin to come quite close to Yiddish. Relax—and you will suddenly find yourselves immersed in it. For Yiddish is everything: the words, the Hasidic melody, the theater and songs. And once the language has taken hold of you, you will forget your former reserve. Then you will understand the true unity of Yiddish."

"Your famous speech in the Prague Jewish Town Hall. When you arranged an evening for a poor Yiddish actor and his troupe."

"The only speech I ever gave.... Now you know who I am?"

I couldn't say anything but "Yes."

So this, then, was the A Major Major Discovery that awaited me in Prague. The treasure my dreams told me I would find. Jiri's and Yossi's unfinished remark.

And just then, at that "Yes," something lit up in my head. Flashed a cynical thought, calculating, exploitative: in my mind's eye I saw a leer on my face I wasn't accustomed to. One really strange to me. Still, it was there, side by side with that light still glowing in my head.

I had to video this man. I must. Nothing should, will, stand in my way. What an event a video of him would be! Of course, no one would believe it. Why should they? Just because I and my subject claimed that he was K? But with proof, the same proof he had just shown me, the news of this astonishing discovery, this miraculous revelation would become known all over. The Rosetta Stone with a human touch. What a video! My God, what a documentary! Earth-shaking. Worldwide news headlines. Features. Intergalactic publicity. The find of the millennium. If the three-inch, one-time headline of the *New York Times* in 1969, MEN WALK ON MOON, was astounding, wait till people see K FOUND ALIVE IN PRAGUE. And it wouldn't be a *National Enquirer* scandal sheet fake story either.

But would K repeat that proof for me with the camera on?

I hope my relationship with him won't change, I thought. That I won't look at him only in one way. As a subject. To be exploited. It had to go one way or the other. I couldn't have it both ways. Was this why I was sent here? Yes, sent. And if so—I had no choice.

Then into my reverie came his voice.

"Now you believe me?"

"Yes."

"That I was telling the truth?"

"Yes."

"That I'm not delusionary?"

"Yes."

"Like Karoly Graf?"

That I wasn't sure of. But since I had established a rhythm, I said, "Yes."

"Now you sound like me," K said.

"Yes."

We looked at each other. We should have smiled at this in joke, at this little affinity in our personality, but we didn't. But maybe there was a hint of smile in our four eyes.

Now it was my turn to lead, to take the steering wheel.

"You kept the 'K' in Klein."

"Yes."

"Even the 'f' sound in Phishl."

"Yes."

"But you disguised it a bit so others wouldn't suspect."

"Yes."

"Who would have suspected anyway? Unless they knew your story."

"Yes."

As I looked at him, I sensed again I was staring into a mirror. It was not the first time such a phenomenon had swept over me in Prague. It had happened before and I paid scant attention to it, ascribing it to the excitement of being in Prague and listening to gorgeous music in one of Prague's revered halls. It was a Brahms string quartet, where the first violinist was the legendary Josef Suk, great-grandson of Dvořák. I started looking at the faces of musicians. Odd, a certain face seemed to float from one player to the next, not changing it but superimposed, as though a semi-transparent mask. That face? K's young face. And yet my own. The face of K. His/my visage. First on Suk's face, K's pointy nose, high cheekbones, and slightly protruding ears. Then it moved to the cellist who played with a serious, high-voltage gaze. The musicians took short, insucked, passionate breaths. Then came a magic moment when all four faces were mine. I don't know if they noticed three clones of the same face. Perhaps, if they did notice, each thought it was a passing mirage, passing strange.

Then K took the parchment out of his mouth and replaced it in the box. The black hair slowly whitened, hair by hair. Some vanished. The bald spot returned. The Van Dyke beard grew back. He became the old man he had been. I don't know how long this transformation took. It seemed like two or three minutes; perhaps it was a quick dream later. Oh, if only I had had a camera in my eyes to record this scene.

Still stood time.

I had lived through this before, intensely, swiftly. I felt again what I had felt in Jiri's hospital room, when I hissed to Betty that I understood every word she said. Soon as I said that I broke the code. Felt a surge. A flow. A current. Everything they said in that strange language made sense. I had understood then, for fifteen intense, lifetime-long seconds, what I had witnessed now. And then the dense secret vanished.

K didn't say a word. He didn't say, See? He didn't gloat. I took a deep breath. I had my identity back. A few stray palpitations quieted down. I wanted to sit but realized I was already sitting. Like I had wanted to stand in Jiri's hospital room but then realized I was already standing.

I waited for K to speak. But he was looking out pensively into the middle distance. Perhaps this sudden change affected him too. What do I mean, perhaps? Of course it had. It had taken his breath away, as it had taken mine. Didn't he need a glass of water?

"Shall I bring you something to drink?"

K shook his head.

What odd thoughts, images, ran through my head. I thought of the International K Society, the *K Quarterly*. Even your image is ubiquitous, I thought. Almost as widely disseminated as Einstein's. And the adjective your name has shaped: K-esque.

"Well?" he said, a proud little gleam in his eyes.

"Yes," I said.

"Yes yes?"

I nodded.

"Then I am satisfied," he said.

And then, as I realized that one of the greatest writers of the twentieth century stood before me, a warmth—not a bodily heat, but the excitation, heat, of intellectual energy—rose in me.

"And you've written over the years." Not a question. A declaration. Affirmation.

He looked at me.

"You have, haven't you? I hope you have. Will you show me?"

He still looked at me. He stared into my eyes. The intensity of his gaze increased, sharp, penetrating, ray-like. As if he were warning me to desist. I turned away—and stopped asking.

Then something, a rustle, a swoosh, a presence outside, in the hall, attracted my attention.

I looked to the door.

K's door was slightly open, perhaps two or three inches. A quick, thin slice of a back of a head I'd seen a number of times in town flashed by. A waitress in a restaurant, receptionist in a museum? Strange, but when a face or the shape of a familiar head is seen away from its usual setting, we have difficulty placing it. Where do I know you from? is the question we usually ask. It's amazing, even miraculous, to meet someone for a second time in a city where miracles have occurred, just like the miracles in K's recent past, surviving his illness, surviving the war. It's like seeing a train running backward or a scene in a film run in reverse. Time recaptured.

I jumped out of my seat, as if ejected from a fighter jet, and while talking with K, I ran to the door and opened it.

In mid-stride, away from the door that was now open, in mid-stride in the hallway, on her way to another room, the door just shut behind her. I hadn't even caught a glimpse of her. But I was certain it was a girl.

I returned to K's room, apologized.

"Somehow she looked familiar. Do you know who she is?"

"I think you better ask Eva. That's her department."

I could see he didn't want to tell me any more.

Then, to distract him (and me), I said:

"I once attended a K conference in Montreal some years ago sponsored by the International K Society, which I heard about while doing a film there. A strange thing happened in the auditorium. Actually two. During the first session, in the middle of a lecture on 'The Metamorphosis' entitled 'Angst and Anxiety: Psychological Ramifications of Change,' an old man in a beret just like yours, holding a walking stick, ambled down the aisle of the lecture hall, stared at the speaker, even raised his cane and called out, 'Nonsense. It's a comedy, you fool.' Then he turned abruptly and walked out of the hall. Was that you, by any chance?"

"What year was it?" K asked.

"I was just out of college then. Probably 1971 or 1972."

"No, it wasn't me."

"Why, what year were you in Montreal?"

"I was never in Montreal."

"Then what difference does it make what year it was?"

"I just wanted to know what year I wasn't there." And K leaned back and laughed. "But I must say, the old chap imitated me quite well.... And he was quite right."

"Okay. But later, during the afternoon session, something even stranger took place. It was during a break. I was in the hallway. An older woman approached, sort of tentatively, and looked at me. Then she drew closer, almost up to me. She blinked, moved her lips, and uttered a curt, 'K!' and slowly buckled. She fell to the floor in a faint. An attendant from the hotel came by and helped revive her. Luckily, a crowd had gathered and I was not the center of unwanted attention. I never attended another K conference again. I didn't want to be gawked at, nor did I want to be distracted."

"Did you ever find out who that woman was?" K asked.

"No."

K looked over my head, nodded slowly, an enigmatic, dreamy smile on his face.

My God! I thought. If he is K, then K had a son. My dream wish for him was fulfilled.

"Wait a minute," I burst out. "If you're Jiri's father, then Jiri is your son. Which makes me very happy that K had a son."

K nodded. His eyes sparkled as if ironically praising my sentience.

"No wonder he had a signed copy of *Meditation* in his house."

"I gave it to him years ago."

"But the one in the other room is not signed."

"I don't autograph every book."

"Does Eva know?"

"Know what?"

He knew very well what I meant.

"You know what I mean. This."

But he did not reply. In my mind I heard his spokesman saying, K neither confirms nor denies this.

Now I understood why all the whispering, why Jiri and Betty spoke that strange language. Tara pilus. Tara glos. But I still didn't understand who I was too old or too young for. Maybe K would know why Jiri and Betty spoke that language. Did Betty also know that Mr. Klein was K? That he was Jiri's father? She must have known something; otherwise, why the secret tongue? But perhaps K knew nothing about Betty, so it was better not to ask.

"Now you understand why I said I have good news for you."

"Can you imagine? About a week ago I dreamt that you told me."

"I did?" He sounded like a surprised little boy. "What did I say?"

"I dreamt I was rebutting you about being Jiri's father. I said people make all kinds of crazy claims here in Prague. And you said, 'You mean like Karoly Graf who claims to be my son?' Then I corrected you, saying: 'Not your son, K's son.'"

"I'm more careless in dreams," K said with a laugh.

"In my dream I didn't pay too much attention to your slip of the tongue. But had it happened in the real world, I would have caught it."

"There is no such thing as the real world," he said. "It's all a dream."

"But you just said you're more careless in dreams."

"Yes," K said.

Was what I had just witnessed also a dream, a phantasmagoria prompted by extreme exhaustion, like those exhaustion-induced quick visions I wrote about before? If I could have looked at myself I would not have seen a man with a straight back. I would have seen a man shaped like a huge question mark. My lips, my tongue, my eyes, my brain were all question marks. Supple, bent, ready to spring. Ready to ask. But I held back. I didn't want to intrude.

I was confident that Klein/K would tell me his story. Why was I so sure? It was the classic *a fortiori* reasoning. Which meant: how much the more so. The *kal va-chomer* of Talmudic disputation. If a man can lift fifty pounds, *a fortiori, kal va-chomer*, how much the more so, he can lift five pounds. If Klein had chosen to share his amazing secret with me, it stands to reason he would tell me how all this happened to him. Did he die and come back to life? No, impossible. We haven't yet reached Messianic times and resurrection of the dead. Or did K not die at all? Was his illness a sham? And how is it that he had lived this long? And in total silence?

I looked up into K's eyes. Yes, up. Those who know K only from his photographs have no indication of his height. In fact, no full-length photos exist of him standing next to someone else. I too had imagined him to be of middling height. Jews in Europe are not known for being tall. In Poland they tend to be on the short side. With his well-known slenderness I had imagined K to be about five-seven or eight, but six feet tall! K a six-footer? Star of his high school basketball team?

Ask any K expert, How tall was K? A glazed look will come over his eyes. He will shrug, with perhaps a supercilious smile on his lips, indicating an irrelevant, even idiotic, question, and say: How should

I know? It's his works that are important, not he. And I, who stand five-ten, had to look up into his eyes. Age had not diminished his height; age had not shrunk his frame; age had not bent his back. And old age, advanced old age, had not compromised his skeletal structure. He still held himself erect and was the full six feet plus he was reported to be. No little-old-lady shrinkage, no osteoporotic diminution of spine, neckbone, femurs. He was as straight and thin as ever. And those blue eyes still radiated a special light. One can fake identity cards, accent, vocabulary, even language. But height, like long fingers, is unique and inimitable. So K was either real or a superb sorcerer.

The last thing I saw as I bade him goodbye were the two models of the early double-winged aeroplanes that moved slightly with the invisible breeze in the room. Then I remembered K loved planes. He had gone to visit early demonstrations of flight and even wrote a little essay about planes in Brescia.

K didn't have to tell me to come back. We both knew I'd come back. Can paper clips resist a magnet? But with all the excitement in his room, I had forgotten to ask him to reconcile his two ages.

22

The Extra Kroner

The next time I came K was already holding his walking stick.

"Come, let's go for a walk."

Now he's going to tell me his story, I thought. We'll walk in the park near his house and he'll tell me what I was waiting to hear.

"It's so beautiful here. This entire city is just stunning."

"You really like Prague, don't you?"

"I love it."

But what I loved about it couldn't be put into words. How can I describe that floaty, delicious feeling, that air of possessiveness, that pride I felt when I was in K's room. When I was with him, I glowed with the thought that it was I, me, who was spending time with the greatest writer of the twentieth century, and only I knew it was he. And I could not shout it out from the rooftops either. I myself couldn't believe I had the privilege of seeing him almost every day. And during my visits I sometimes felt myself levitating from the high of being with him. And at night, when I wrote about my hours with K, a special thrill of joy came over me, a feeling no doubt that drunkards or drug abusers feel, they're sitting on top of the world, everything going their way, that touchdown with thirty seconds to go, that bases loaded, game-winning home run at the bottom of the ninth. Or, best of all, a Golden Globe Award or a Cannes Prize for a documentary film you've made.

I was spending time with K. Who would believe me? And soon, when—if (again that magical, slippery IF)—I put him into my film, everyone will believe it and envy me for having known him, brought him to the attention of the world.

No wonder I loved Prague.

"I love it. If I had arms big enough I would embrace it. But tell me, where is the mystical Prague? Where is the ethereal, golemic, middle-ages magic of the city? Tell me, is it travel-brochure talk or is it real?"

"So you want to see something mystical, something at the cusp of the real and the unreal."

I marveled at K's use of the word "cusp." But if I were to marvel at everything he said, I would be marveling all day long. Wasn't everything about him, his very presence before me, a marvel?

But I didn't want to sound overly enthusiastic. For I knew quite well what was considered mystical in Prague. The touristy mystical. Which had as much connection to the truly mystical as the popular version of fast-food, I-want-it-now kabbala in America had to the true study of the onerously difficult authentic Aramaic kabbala. You know what the touristy mystical was? A walk around the Altneushul with a sprinkling of legends about the golem. The clock on the Jewish Town Hall with its Hebrew letters, which run backwards. The grave of the Maharal.

That's why I said,

"Yes, I would,"

slowly, with absolute self-control, no tremor in my voice. But as I was to learn later, I had unfairly denigrated K's offer. It wasn't a tourist site at all. In fact, "cusp" was an exaggeration. What he showed me was squarely, firmly, in the lap of the unreal.

"There's an unusual synagogue I want to show you, which no tourists know about."

"Too bad you didn't tell me before. I would have brought my camera."

"Impossible. Good you didn't. Photography is not permitted."

We walked along residential streets I hadn't seen before, then turned into a small, busy shopping street.

"Here's the post office. Wait. I'll be right out. I need some stamps."

Meanwhile, I watched the parade of people passing by. Now, with freedom (my finger slips and I type "g" instead of "f," a good word "greedom," showing the Czechs' pent-up fascination with wealth and goods), the sunshine suppressed under the Soviets burst through the grey fog. People moved with a buzz of energy, heads up. Not quite like actors in a Hollywood musical, a smile on every face, a song on every lip. Still, the sun shone in their eyes. Gone the grey.

Here came K.

"Just a minute," he said, standing next to me. He looked into a little leather change purse. "I must check something."

Maybe in old European black and-white films or early twentieth-century novels do you see a man putting coins into a small leather purse, with no metal clasp, closed by a little leather tongue that slips under a strap. It must have been a hundred years old, K's purse. He took the coins out and counted them.

"Oh my, she gave me an extra kroner…well, I have to go back."

K stood in the line again—this time I joined him—and returned the coin to the surprised girl.

Outside, K pressed his lips and shook his head. He took out the purse and counted the coins again.

"Turns out she gave me the correct change in the first place. Sorry." He licked his lips, wondering what to do. Return to the window again? But by now the line was longer. Ten people stood waiting.

"Forget it," I suggested.

"But it's wrong," K replied. "It's not the kroner, Max, it's the integrity. Just as it was wrong for me to take an extra kroner that didn't belong to me, so is it wrong for her to take an extra kroner that does not belong to her. And, anyway, who knows what problems this could cause her at the end of the day, when they discover extra money in her till?"

I countered with: "But if in your heart you declare it now belongs to her, a gift you've given her, then it's no longer a fault. She didn't take the kroner. You gave it to her."

"But don't you see it's a matter of honesty? Like a coin, honesty too has two sides."

I liked the ring of the metaphor, even though I didn't grasp its meaning at once.

Suddenly I was overwhelmed by a sense of déjà vu. The scene was familiar. Was I reliving something? Waiting at a post office. The mistake with a returned coin. Had I experienced this before myself or with someone? Or had I read about it as an illustration of K's absolute sense of honesty?

Wait. Something had passed me by. I had heard it only with an outer ear, like a remark absorbed absently that surfaces only later, delayed like a bright light on the retina seen when the light is gone. K had called me Max. So I was right. He had done something like this decades ago, more than seventy or seventy-five years ago, with Max Brod present, and I must have read about it in my unrelenting, omnivorous passion to read every word K wrote and every word written about him, in order to recreate him in my mind. Could I have known that I would invade a special time zone, bridge the impossible gap, the years between the death of my hero and my own birth and, miraculously, magically, meet the man I had always wanted to meet?

And so K stood in line for a third time to get his kroner back, while I waited outside again and observed the citizens of Prague. The merry sound of children with their mothers added music to the scene. Then a sudden tweak in my heart. I watched a tall young mother in a blue beret pushing a double baby carriage. Of course it wasn't Katya, but fantasies are sweet.

A couple of shops down from the post office I noticed a video store. I ran up to K.

"I'm going to buy some batteries. See that video shop two doors down? I'll meet you either here or in there."

I entered the small shop. An attendant addressed me in Czech.

"English?"

"Little."

"I need some batteries for a video camera."

"Good. Moment."

I felt a tap on my shoulder. I turned. Froze as I saw who I saw. Oh, my God, another fight, like the one with the actor I had knocked over by mistake. I wished I could have run away again from the director like I did last time. But now, here, trapped in the little shop, nowhere to flee.

"I'm Michele Luongo." He smiled as he stretched his hand out to me.

I shook his hand.

"How fortunate," he said with his Italian-accented English. "This coincidence is out of a Russian novel. I was just thinking of you but of course had no way of contacting you, and here you are.… Why did you run away that day?"

"Embarrassed."

"Oh, come on."

"The trouble I caused your film."

"A Cannes Prize winner, embarrassed?"

"You know me?"

"Of course. I recognized you right away. I saw you at the Cannes Festival two years ago, but you don't remember me."

"I'm sorry about the trouble I caused you. And I'm prepared to reimburse you for damages." I felt my face flushing. The heat rose in my neck. "In fact, I asked at my hotel how to reach your film company but they knew nothing. They said these film crews appear one day and disappear the next."

"Forget it. We left that scene in. It's hilarious. It gave our film a slapstick turn we never even thought of."

"I'm so glad." I took a deep breath. "By the way," I said with as much innocence as I could muster, "do you know where the girl is?"

"Katya? No. We engaged her for that one shoot but then she disappeared."

"She keeps disappearing. That's the third place she disappeared from. And some other people I know have disappeared too."

"Maybe it's you." And Michele Luongo laughed.

"You know, I actually thought of that."

Luongo lowered his head and looked over glasses that weren't there. "So you have a thing for her. I don't blame you. She's quite an unusually pretty girl."

"Well… Did she ever mention the place she was headed for?"

"No. I told you…she just left. But when I interviewed her before the film, she said she had studied in Brno. Who knows, maybe that's her hometown. Look, why chat here? Let's get together and continue the conversation."

"Wonderful. How much longer you going to be here?"

"About three weeks. And you?"

"Probably another month."

"Here's my card," Luongo said. "You can always reach me on my cell phone."

"Terrific. I'll call you." And I wrote my address and phone number for him. "By the way," I added. "Is that actor still around? The one I accidentally knocked down?"

"Stacek?"

"I never got his name. That good-looking, aggressive fellow who played alongside Katya."

"I suppose so. He doesn't work with me anymore. Why do you ask?"

"I think he was stalking me a few days ago. Yelled 'American!' at me and chased me through the little lanes and across the square and then I eluded him."

"What's wrong with him?"

"I don't know. He's probably still mad. Did you know he sought me out at the Old New Synagogue about a week ago and wanted to pick a fight with me?"

"No! I didn't think he was that touchy."

"I apologized to him right away. He seemed to accept it, grudgingly. But he's still harboring an enmity. Now I keep having to look over my shoulders to see if he's following me."

I looked toward the shop doorway. Suddenly, K materialized on the threshold.

"There's an old gentleman looking at you. You know him?"

I did what Schweik would do. Pop a lie gratuitously. On the spot. "He's my grandfather."

"Don't give me that salami. He doesn't look old enough to be your grandfather. Dad, maybe." Luongo looked at his watch. "Oof! Late. Got to run. See you soon, eh?"

We shook hands.

"Let me introduce you quickly on your way out.... Mr. Klein, look who I met here? My friend, Michele Luongo, a film director. Meet Mr. Klein."

"Please to meet you, signore. You have a very talented grandson. Sorry, but I have to rush off to an appointment. Ciao!"

K nodded to him, then looked at me quizzically. I watched Luongo run off, weaving in and around people on the sidewalk as if heading for a train he had to catch.

I shrugged. "Italiano. Loco, but with great imagination.... Done?" I asked K.

"Done," he said, triumphant, and held up the kroner like a trophy. "Circle closed. Now we can move on." He slipped his arm into mine as we walked. Do you folks know who is moving among you? I sang to the people passing by. If you knew you'd fall to your knees in obeisance. I smiled but they didn't know why I was smiling.

K pointed to a bearded man sitting on the sidewalk, leaning against a lamppost.

"You see that beggar sitting there. He tugs at me, for my sympathies are with the poor. But at the same time I wonder why an apparently healthy man has to sit there without doing an honest day's work. Look how many coins he already has in his hat."

K stopped and observed the beggar.

"Soon he'll take them and hide them, for it isn't good policy to show the public how good is a beggar's treasure. See? He's putting most of the coins in his pocket, the rascal."

But as we passed him, K gave him the kroner he had retrieved.

"Why did you do that?" I asked. "Your entire line of reasoning showed you weren't inclined to give him a penny."

"Man's rational thinking and his emotions often run on parallel tracks. And anyway, my mother always said, better to give to a beggar who you think doesn't need it than not to give to one who might need it. That's the Jewish way."

K still hadn't said a word to me about his past. Was he deliberately doing this to keep me in suspense, or didn't he think his story was important enough to share with me? I decided to wait a bit more and then ask him to solve for me the riddle of his life.

We turned into a side street and passed a classical three-story building set back on a spacious lawn adorned with flowers and attractive shrubs. On the iron fence I saw a plaque with a Star of David and words in Czech I could not make out.

"I see it's a Jewish institution. This isn't the synagogue you had in mind, is it? It doesn't look like a synagogue."

"No. It's the Jewish Children's Home, the famous old orphanage."

My heart stopped. I held my hand to my throat.

K fixed his gaze on my face. "What's the matter with you? You're white. Are you all right?" He clasped my shoulders. "Come, let's sit down here on the bench."

What made him bring me here? I wondered.

"I'm all right." I sighed, looked at the building. "But now it's time for *me* to say to *you*: It's time. I have a secret to share with you."

He looked into my eyes, waiting.

"Remember I told you I was born here?"

"Yes."

"And that my parents, both young Holocaust survivors, met and married after the war in Italy and then were assigned to work for the Joint Distribution Committee here for several years?"

"Yes, I remember. And then, after a few years, you were born and then all three of you emigrated to America."

"True. But what I didn't tell you, and what I wanted to tell Jiri but never did, is this: I was adopted. My parents couldn't have children and so they adopted a Jewish baby."

"How fortuitous, then, that we passed here. It is very likely they found you here. Didn't you ever want to know who your real parents were?"

"Not really. As far as I was concerned, my parents were my real parents. I wasn't part of that generation that moved heaven and earth and spent years trying to find out who their birth parents were."

"I can understand that. And perhaps it's no coincidence that you revealed your secret here. Still, maybe now is an opportune time to go in and make inquiries."

"Absolutely not. Come, let's turn away. My usual equilibrium regarding my birth is being tested. Is being upset. Come, please."

K took my arm—for a moment I felt as if I were the old man and he the younger—and we walked back to the shopping street. Was it here that I was adopted? But no feeling of sentimentality overtook me. The place didn't tug at my heart. On the contrary, it made me nervous. I didn't sense that something was pulling me there. Prague pulled me, yes, but not the Jewish Children's Home. And even if I went in I would likely face martinet bureaucrats who specialize in procrastination and probably in the new privacy laws: I'm sorry, we cannot give you any information without the express permission of the adoptee. But that's me, I say. That may very well be, but how do we know that? You know you're you. I know you're you. But do the authorities know you're you?

Back on the shopping street I felt better again. I took a deep breath. K, that dear man, noticed and gave my arm an affectionate, sympathetic squeeze.

But when we reached his house, K withdrew the offer to see the synagogue.

"Not now," he said, taking a deep, slow breath. "I think we have had enough excitement for one day, and I have walked enough. We will visit it another time."

23

A Message from the Shamesh

When I got back to my hotel a voicemail message waited for me.

"Hello. Hello? Okay, you not there. So I will leave message. This is the shamesh. It is funny speaking one way into the air and nobody answers me. Me talking to a machine and the machine tells you what I said. Nu, we will see if it tells you exactly, word for word, what I said, or just gives you summary. Come to the shul in the morning. I have something for you."

Typical Prague fashion; no details. What could he have for me? An admission that there was an attic? Special permission to see the golem? Or was it something else to enhance my film? Wait! Don't tell me he found Katya. But how could the shamesh have found Katya if I didn't tell him I lost her?

In the morning, I greeted Yossi golem, who said laconically, as though that dry, cheerless tone were studied, well-rehearsed, "I hear you're really becoming pal of the old man and Eva." But in his voice I think I heard a trace of plaint, a hint of sarcasm, as though somehow I was taking up too much of their time.

But instead of justifying myself or arguing with him, I reversed the table on him and said:

"I can't thank you enough for introducing me to Eva and Mr. Klein. It's been one of the most fortunate encounters I've had in Prague, along with meeting you and the shamesh."

Yossi, the big man with the ruddy cheeks, smiled with both sides of his face. Then the shamesh approached. I wondered what they would have to laugh about now. If I were impudent or bold enough I would have articulated my thought.

"Ah, there you are. So you got my message. It is strange, no?" and he looked down at a note in his hands, maybe a jotting of what he had told me, "talking and no one talking back. It's like talking to the wall. And someone else hears it later than when you actually said it. Amazing. Come…guess what I have for you."

He gestured to the Holy Ark. I excused myself from Yossi and followed the shamesh.

"Um…" I said, resisting the temptation to say: a passage to the attic that you finally found. "I can't guess."

"What did you want? Remember?"

"What did I want?" I said aloud, starting to reckon my wants. "I wanted to film you and I did. No, the film isn't ready, not finished yet. I wanted the attic, but that is laughably unavailable, along with the golem." I wanted Katya but I wasn't going to share that with him. "So what else did I want? I don't know. Please remind me."

"To find someone you asked me. You forgot already? So important that someone is to you? You asked me to find him, even if I didn't know he was a Jew."

"Graf!" I exclaimed. "Karoly Graf! You found him?"

"What you think?"

I made believe I was thinking. Like Rodin's *The Thinker*, I put my hand to my face and thought.

"Yes, I think you did find him."

"You asked. I looked. I f…"

"So you found him. Bravo!"

"Well, no," the shamesh backtracked. "I didn't found him."

Then why was he teasing me?

"Then who did? You just gave me the impression you found him."

"I didn't found him." The shamesh paused. For drama. For effect. "Actually, he found me."

"How? Where?"

"I am the shamesh," he asserted slowly. "Here." He gave me a slip of paper with Graf's name and address. "Go. He waits for you. Tomorrow. Two p.m." And the shamesh told me precisely which Metro and which connecting bus to take for the twenty, twenty-five-minute ride.

"You're a miracle man. A modern Maharal. How did you do it, shamesh?"

But he just smiled.

"Thank you, shamesh. Thank you so much. You don't know how much this means to me."

I looked down at the name and address.

"Did he give you a phone number?"

"No. No phone. Just address."

I hoped it wouldn't be another wild goose chase.

24

How He Got Better

K sensed me at the other side of the door. I didn't even get a chance to knock. He began to speak as—even before—he/I opened the door.

"Two crucial events occurred within days of each other. In the year I died of tuberculosis, Dora Diamant and I wanted to get married. She wrote to her father for permission but her Hasidic papa didn't want his daughter to marry a Jew who wasn't Orthodox, even though Dora herself had long ago moved away from that tradition. And never mind I was much older; I could have been her father. She was only eighteen or so at the time. But the papa didn't want to say no without consulting his rebbe, for Hasidic Jews like him don't make a move within any arena of consequence—family, marriage, business, job, education—without consulting their rebbe, their spiritual leader, their all-around guide. So Dora's papa went to the Gerer Rebbe, who said one word, No! With rebbes there is no arguing, no negotiating, no compromise. No maybe. No let's see. With them it's either Yes or No. So No it was. Which meant I couldn't marry, couldn't have a family within the framework of a traditional Jewish family structure.

"Even though I had found happiness with Dora—why are you standing? Please sit down—that I had never had before, the rebbe's No smothered my happiness, robbed me of my future, exacerbated my illness. Yes, his decision made me sick. And not metaphysically.

Actually sick. Doctors now agree that a psychological blow has its physiological consequences. Further examination seemed to show the tuberculosis spreading to my larynx. But Doctor Klopstock said he would await final word from the laboratory report that would come back in a week. Perhaps, he said, his observation with the naked eye was wrong.

"At this time Dora decided to make one last personal appeal and see her father. And I told Doctor Klopstock that I'm going back home to Prague for about ten days. I needed to get away from the sanatorium. I needed the pretense of normality. Medically, there was nothing I could do. I needed home. Space. The ambience of family. I hadn't seen my parents and sisters in months, for I had discouraged them from coming to the sanatorium in the outskirts of Vienna until I felt better." K stopped, looked out the window as if seeing Prague, 1924, in black and white. "It was good to be home. I tried to expunge from my mind the suspense about the laboratory report. Meanwhile, at home, everyone said how much better I looked; how the fresh air of the Vienna woods agreed with me, helped me. Whether it was true or wishful thinking or conventional lying I could not tell. I didn't even get to see Brod. He hadn't known I was coming and went hiking in Slovakia. At the end of my stay I kissed my parents and my three sisters goodbye. I did not tell them the extent of my illness. Would I ever see them again? I asked them not to accompany me to the train. Train station departures are too emotionally wrenching. And banal too, straining out the window, waving a silly handkerchief.

"On my way to the train station I asked the taxi driver to stop for a few minutes at the Altneushul. At that time it was always open. I hadn't been there in years, since my bar mitzvah, and I wanted to bid goodbye to it. I sensed that this would be the last time I would be in Prague. Little did I know the synagogue would be my place of refuge less than twenty years later. I had always been impressed by its antiquity, its grandeur, its odd architecture, the magic it exuded, the legends infused in it."

"The golem," I said.

"Yes."

"And the Maharal."

"Of course. The legendary Rabbi Loew, Chief Rabbi of Prague, creator of the famous golem who, so the legend goes, lies undisturbed under a mountain of torn pages from holy books. Until he is needed. In this shul Jews had prayed more than eight hundred years ago. I walked up the three steps to the Aron Kodesh, approached the curtain that covered the Holy Ark. I saw the Ten Commandments embroidered on part of the curtain. I bent forward and brushed my lips on the First Commandment, 'I am the Lord your God.' Then I turned and walked down the three steps and made my way past the bimah to the door. I thought: I am not an observant Jew, but my faith in God, the Creator of the Universe, is unshakable.

"At first nothing untoward happened. I felt the same. But as I approached the door, ready to return to my waiting taxi, a line of electric energy ran through me, as if a new vein or artery had been placed in me. I felt a jolt, as if a bolt of lightning had entered one part of me and exited from another. But it was not the pain one expects from an electric shock; it was its mirror image. Joy. A thrill. An uplift. An infusion of light, of happiness, a giddy feeling of wine in me, as if suddenly I could walk on air. I was filled with new oxygen.

"As I took a deep, deep breath, I could feel clean mountain air filling my lungs. Oh, that uplift, that surge. I felt it like sweet laughter. I felt energized. Not a dark energy but a bright energy, as though I had been touched, blessed, with a beneficent light, a benison. I was vibrating. Not shaking, vibrating. Vibrating with the light within me."

K paused, bent his head, looked down at the floor, then raised his eyes and looked at, through, me. Tears stood in his eyes. His eyes were moist with happiness.

"I felt elevated. I felt I was up there on the slanted old ceiling looking down at myself. I felt I was floating. I felt myself rising even higher to the attic that was or wasn't there. I felt I was a miniature man walking between the lines of the Torah, sailing horizontally near the slightly raised letters written with gall nut ink. I felt I was the eyes of the lions that guard the top of the Holy Ark in the small shuls in

Prague. New sensations ran through me. Sensations I had never felt before. Or since. I was melody. I was a cluster of notes, triplets, trills. I, who cannot carry a tune. I, of whom Max Brod, who was also a famous composer, said, 'He can't tell the difference between Bach and Offenbach,' I suddenly was able to lift my voice and sing—and my throat did not hurt as it did an hour ago. Nor did any coughs rattle my chest and take my breath away. And I sang the verse from the Psalms, 'God has tormented me but did not give me over to death.' Days earlier, as I died slowly, a different verse from the Psalms flashed before me, 'The bonds of death surround me. I have only trouble and grief.' Every day I watched myself die. But now that the thrum of electricity was like a flood of lifeblood in me, other verses from the Psalms rose before my eyes: 'I shall not die but live,' and 'You rescued my soul from death…I shall go before the Lord in the Land of the Living.'

"Now I felt a sense of well-being, yes, health I had never felt before. At first I thought I was dreaming. How could it be? So used to malaise was I, I closed and opened my eyes, assuming the dream would go away. But it was no dream. I felt well. That was the first magical moment in my lonely and blessed life. I returned for a moment to the Holy Ark. And I sang out, facing the Aron Kodesh, I sang into the ancient and holy space of the Altneushul, '*Sh'ma Yisroel*' and 'Blessed are you, O Lord, who cures the sick.'"

K stopped, took a deep breath. His face shone as he relived those nonpareil moments. I thought he would continue the rhythm of his remarks, but he surprised me with:

"You know there is such a thing as unreal numbers."

Yes, I thought. For instance, sixty-nine minus eighty.

"In higher mathmatics, mathematicians use math to calculate the inconceivable, the undetectable, the nonexistent, the impossible. There even exist equations that represent things that not only can we not visualize, we can't even imagine being able to visualize them. They are beyond visualization. Beyond imagining.

"When that jolt of beneficent energy went through my body, killing at once, like a powerful antibiotic, all bacteria in me and restoring me to health, I was in a special time zone that physicists today call flowing time and textured space, but I didn't know it then. I was in a realm of unreal numbers. And in that special moment, all I knew was that for the first time in my adult life I had a sense of well-being.

"On the train back to Vienna and to the sanatorium I couldn't wait to share my good news with Dora, who said she would be back before me. I rehearsed my words several times. Like in a modernist drama I froze time and said the same thing in several different ways. I also hoped she would have good news for me: her father had relented; the rebbe had changed his mind and was giving her permission to marry me. One miracle would join another. We would both surprise each other with good news and I would marry her, not in illness but in health.

"When I returned, Doctor Klopstock met me at the entrance, a concerned look on his face. I didn't see Dora and assumed since she didn't know when exactly I was returning, she had gone to spend some time in Vienna. Doctor Klopstock did not comment on how I looked, which—I admit—annoyed me, for I thought that the change that had come over me was visible on my face. I thought it shouted wordlessly right out of me. So I concluded that my feeling of good health was illusory, that it was just an anaesthetic my body was producing to cloak the approaching end. It often happens in severe illness that there is a momentary surge of feeling well just before one dies. I didn't tell Dr. Klopstock I felt fine, for when he heard a remark like that he would comment drily, 'That's what they all say.' What he said next explained why he had made no comment about the way I looked.

"The doctor said, 'I had hoped the laboratory report would be different, but sadly it shows that your larynx and epiglottis have been infected. I am sorry, but there is no hope for further medical solutions, except painkillers, morphine, or pantopen.'

"I was silent. This was not the time to tell Klopstock how good I felt. Instead, I asked about another patient, a man without a family who also had an advanced case of tuberculosis. 'Johann? Not well,' said Doctor Klopstock. 'Johann Eck probably has no more than three or four weeks left to live.' And I? I asked the doctor silently. But maybe he read my mind. He raised his eyebrows and looked up, as if to say, Only God knows.

"I looked out the window into the garden of the sanatorium. The owl I had previously seen in a tree was no longer there."

K stopped. But I knew this was not, could not possibly be, the end of the drama. There was another player to account for.

"And Dora?" I asked.

"Yes, Dora," K said. "When I asked Klopstock where she was, he said: 'I thought you knew. Didn't you get her letter?'

"'What letter?'

"'She said she wrote to you.'

"'I got nothing. So she didn't return?'

"'She did come back,' Klopstock told me, 'but spent only a day or so here and then announced she's going back to Poland and would write to you.'

"'I didn't get a letter.'

"Again Klopstock said, 'Dora said she would write to you.'

"Well, we could go on repeating those two lines forever. That's it, I realized. She abandoned me. Her father's wishes have prevailed. She succumbed to her father's demand to return home and leave me. Dora was brave, rebellious—but as far as I was concerned, not brave and rebellious enough. She abandoned me; my heart abandoned her. Alas, I learned much later the real reason for her leaving, written in a letter that was much delayed in the post. Had I had that letter when I returned to Vienna, my history, perhaps hers, would have been different. I was waiting to surprise her with my return to health but she had another surprise waiting for me. And that's when I decided to die," K said sadly.

"What do you mean?" I interjected.

"I told the doctor, 'I'm as good as dead.'"

"But you said you didn't die."

"Didn't die in one sense. Did—in another. It was at that moment, learning that Dora had gone, at that very moment the idea that fixed my destiny came to me. I knew I would die. She knew it. Her father knew. His rebbe knew—maybe he even wished it. I have no doubt he wished it. Then the idea spun quickly in me. All the details. Let them all assume I was dead. The wish that people in rage always have: I'll die and then they'll be sorry. I was cured but heartsick. Dead inside. With Dora leaving me, the lifestuff in me was sucked away. I had no desire to live. To write. To go over my manuscripts. I was finished."

For a moment K looked up at the two model double-winged aeroplanes as though he wished to fly away with them.

"I loved Dora but I was furious with her. True, she was young, but she always seemed mature for her age. But why didn't she have the courage to stay? The father summons her home, forbidding the marriage to a non-observant sinner, a secular Jew like me, and she obeys like a little pussycat. Why couldn't she free herself, is what I thought at the time, from the shackles of her father, who himself was chained to his Hasidic rebbe? Although my attitude softened over the years, especially in the thirties and forties, when I mourned for her, thinking she was one of the six million, but at that time she was dead for me and I would be dead for her. Let her think I was dead and the separation would be complete, on my side and hers.

"I didn't receive her letter until much later, but by then it was too late. Doctor Klopstock had assumed she had written to Prague. But she didn't. She wrote to me at the sanatorium and, in one of those mix-ups that occur in cheap romantic novels, the letter got lost and surfaced many weeks later. I didn't read that letter until I went to visit Klopstock much later—he met me in Vienna, of course, not at the sanatorium. The letter had just come, but he didn't want to take a chance forwarding it to Prague lest it get lost again. Had I had that letter earlier I would have lived out my life as the real K."

"You still are the real K," I said.

He took a deep breath, responded obliquely: "In any case, it was there, at the sanatorium, when I returned from my ten-day visit to my family that the thought, the idea, came to me. You recall I asked Klopstock right away about the man without family who was nearing death. He was a slightly retarded man who had been cared for by an elderly housekeeper in Vienna before she died. I stayed at the sanatorium three days and asked Klopstock to examine me. He couldn't believe it. 'What miracle happened to you?' he asked me. I told him what I knew. He shook his head. 'I've never seen anything like this.'

"'Still,' I told him, 'I want to die. Officially.'

"Fortunately, Klopstock was a *mentch*, a friend. He had nursed me, helped me, nurtured me, even babied me. Klopstock and I looked at each other. It was as if the same thought came to both of us at the same time.

"'I have a life-and-death favor to ask you,' I told the doctor."

25

A Thirty-Minute Trip

It took me thirty minutes to get to Graf's house. Of course, I took my camera. Now the problem was—would he be there? This was certainly a marvelous turn of events, I mused. If one of the two people who disappeared in Prague was found, could the second be far behind? It was a good omen, a fine omen, an excellent omen. Provided of course I actually laid eyes on Karoly Graf, K's putative son.

Yes, in the foreroom of the apartment house Graf was on the list of tenants. So the address was correct. I wondered if he had a family, for the concierge of Graf's old apartment building had referred only to Graf alone.

I rang the bell. A man's voice spoke in Czech. I told him in English who I was, "sent by the shamesh."

"Wonderful. You're here. Happy, happy, happy am I. Come up. Fourth floor. Sorry, no elevator."

A smiling Graf waited for me by the open door. He was clean-shaven, had lost that haggard, grizzly look he had had when I first met him outside the K Museum and mistook him for a beggar. He was tall and thin as ever, with a prominent Adam's apple. But his cheeks were no longer hollow and he didn't give me the edgy feeling I was speaking to one of life's unfortunate creatures.

Graf greeted me affably and invited me into his small, light-filled apartment. Books everywhere. In bookcases, on wooden shelves propped by bricks, on the floor. An entire section, I saw at once, devoted to K.

"Come in, come in, man from the Shawmee State, who pays homage to K. So happy to see you."

"I too. But I must ask you—"

But he interrupted me with, "Why did you not come to see me?"

So he beat me to it. I was just waiting to express my righteous indignation, but Graf got to me first.

I could have—I wanted to—explode with: What's the matter with you? Why did you give me a card with the wrong address? Why did you do that to me after you so excitedly and passionately told me you're K's son? I took my camera with me and was prepared to video you, to make you a leading figure in my film. I can't understand why you invited me and then gave me a wrong address.

But I said nothing. Like Joseph before his brothers, dying to speak, I controlled myself. I merely—and with marvelously understated dramatic flair—pulled his card out of my wallet and showed it to him.

"I tried," I said softly.

He gazed at the card and gave me a puzzled look. "But this is my old veezeet kart. No wonder you couldn't find my house."

What is one supposed to do with this Alice in Wonderland topsy-turvy behavior?

"So how could I possibly find you if I don't have your current address? This is the address you gave me."

Suddenly, he slapped his head. He looked at me with contrite eyes. "Oh my God! Please, please forgive me." He sounded like he would soon fall down on his knees and plead for pardon. "Forgive me. I gave you an old veezeet kart. I am so apologetic to you I am nearing to cry. I was wondering why you didn't come next day to visit me."

"I went to your old address and the house manager said you moved out more than a year ago and he didn't know where you'd moved to."

"That is true. I did not give my new residence and since I didn't hear from you, I thought maybe you went back to America. Until—"

"Until you saw me in the Metro. You did see me, right?"

Karoly Graf clapped both my shoulders.

"I did see you. And what a pleasant coincidence. Something that happens only in cinema. But now, at this moment in time, I must state I have a cartilege to pick with you."

"Why?"

"Why? I tell you why. And you tell me why you ran away?"

"What?"

"I said, why you ran away?"

"When? Where?"

"That day I tried to catch up to you. Near the Old Town Square. But you flew like a wind."

"Was that you?"

"I think it was me, yes."

"Shouting 'American'?"

"Yes. Why you ran away?"

"I thought it was someone else who is after me, chasing me."

"I finally see you close by and not in Metro going in opposite direction and you run away from me. I thought you ran into the K Museum but receptionist said you're not there."

"Never mind," I said. "Main thing is you found me and I found you. Now the question is—how did you do it? I looked and looked for you, tried all kinds of municipal registries, but you were not listed anywhere."

"And to myself I thought, how do I find a visitor? Then I remembered I met you at the K Museum. So I went to see Dr. Hruska if he saw you. He said he has not seen you in a long time and, misfortunately, has misplaced phone number you gave him."

"And then?"

"And then I thought of going to synagogue because you said you were interested in Prague, in golem, in K."

"How smart! How clever! How right!"

Graf smiled. "You see, I very much wanted to see you."

"Wonderful. Brilliant. Now tell me what you tried to signal me during those few seconds we saw each other on the Metro."

"I lifted up one finger," said Graf.

"Yes, I remember that." Should I tell him I first thought it was a pen top? No, that would only confuse him. "But a raised forefinger can have so many interpretations. I thought it meant we should meet on the first floor of the K Museum. I went the next day but you weren't there."

"And Dr. Hruska didn't tell you I was looking for you."

"He was away on a trip to Holland, I was told."

Graf nodded. "I know a gesture can have many interpretations. But how could I invent speed language that would tell you what I wanted to say? With lifting one finger I wanted to tell you: one station. I'll go one station and wait for you. Did you see me making a gesture with my thumb, indicating out, that I would get out first station?"

"That I didn't see."

"I got out at next station and waited. It was a small chance, I know, but I did it."

"Why didn't you leave your address with Dr. Hruska and ask him to give it to me when I come?"

"I don't think he likes me. So it's very hard for me to bother him."

"May I video you while you talk?"

"Yes. Of course. Please."

As I took the camera out of my bag and set up the tripod I asked him:

"Did you see my gestures to you?"

"Yes. You put fist to one eye and made little circles with your hand."

"Right. How did you interpret that?"

"By covering your eye, you say you didn't want to see me. And circles around your ear, why everyone knows that—it's the sign I am crazy."

I burst out laughing. "Oh no. No no no. My fist to my eye plus the right fist circling around my ear meant I wanted to make a movie of you. One hand was the lens, the other the old-fashioned reel camera. It's a common sign for moviemaking."

Graf laughed too. "What a mix-up!" He looked closely at my camera. "Very nice.... What's that?"

"A ring."

"And you keep such a nice ring hanging from your camera strap?"

"Always. For good luck. My mother gave it to me years ago."

Graf shook his head. "I saw rings on fingers, rings on noses, but never rings on camera straps."

"It helps me film better, which I'd like to begin with you now. Ready?"

"I am ready."

"Okay, let's begin. I'll ask you to tell me what you said when we first met. We will have a normal conversation.... Try to forget the camera. Just look at me. Okay, I'm pressing the start button. Go!"

Without hesitation, Graf said, "I have the honor of informing you that I am the son of K."

"This is Karoly Graf," I said, "citizen of Prague, who has a fascinating story to tell. Please repeat what you just said."

"I have the honor of informing you that I am the son of K."

"How do you know that?"

Graf looked at me. "Am I supposed to prove to you? Last time you also didn't believe me."

Should I shut down the video, I quickly thought, and explain to him, like I had explained to the shamesh? No. I'll record the natural flow of his remarks; I'll let him speak unimpeded. Then I wondered if his giving me the wrong address card was a direct result of me not believing him. No, I went through this already. He gave me his card first and then, later, I asked for proof.

"Well, as I told you, I'm from the Show Me State."

"And where is exact location of this Shawmee State?"

Perfect, I thought. He's recreating our first conversation, which I would have loved to film but of course could not.

"It's just an American expression. It means: I'd like to have proof. Show me. In other words, show me something to prove your claim to the world."

"Do you have to prove to others you are your father's son?" Graf's voice trembled as it did last time.

That's an interesting question he's throwing at me. Fact is, when you get down to it, I am *not* my father's son, at least not the son of the man who is generally acknowledged to be my father. But I gave Karoly Graf the same answer I had some time ago.

"No, I do not. But then again, I don't go around saying I'm K's son. Or Danny K's son, even though people have told me I look like him."

"You also look like the young K."

"I've heard that too, but not from the same people who tell me I look like Danny K. But we're getting sidetracked.... You see, if you make a radical claim you have to prove it."

"Prove it! Prove it!" Graf exploded. Good, I thought. We need a little drama, lots of excitement. He began pacing back and forth. I stood back, filming him.

"By the way," I said, "do you know a Yossi?"

He wheeled. Faced me.

"Yossi? Which Yossi?"

"The Yossi in the Altneushul. A friend of the shamesh."

"No. Why do you ask?"

"Because a friend of his quoted Yossi saying, 'Where is exact location of Shawmee State?'"

"So?"

"So, what do you mean, so?" I told Graf.

"So what it has to do with me?"

"Because I used that expression only with you. So it was weird hearing someone say that Yossi said it. That's why I thought maybe you told it to Yossi."

Graf shook his head. "Some mistake is happening here. Something, as you say, weird."

Then he went to his bookcase and took out a folder.

"Here. See. Look. It will make all residents of Shawmee State happy as they see the proof."

He held a beige envelope, thin at the edges from too much handling. He took out a sheet of paper and showed it to me.

26

The Life-and-Death Favor

"So I told Dr. Klopstock," K continued his narration, "'I have a life-and-death favor to ask you.'"

"'Anything,' he said.

"'You said that Johann Eck, that slightly retarded man, will die soon. He has no family. He's all alone in the world.'

"'He's dying alone and will be buried alone,' said Dr. Klopstock.

"'We can arrange a good funeral for him. This is my request. We shall switch identities. When he dies, arrange to have the coffin sent to our family plot in Prague. And we will give the word out that K has passed away.'

"Klopstock seemed stunned. I told him, 'The life I wanted with Dora can never be. Not in sickness nor in health. All my life I longed for a stable, traditional family life, wife and children. It won't happen with her. And if it won't happen with her, it won't happen with anyone. I am incapable of living with any woman but her. Will you do it, Klopstock?'

"Doctor Klopstock pressed his eyes shut. 'This is to be expected from a man with a fantastic imagination like yours…but the fact is I agreed before I even heard your request. But you must first return to inform your parents and sisters. I cannot consent to this extraordinary arrangement if you don't do that.'

"At once I cried out, 'Willingly! I wouldn't have done it any other way.'

"'And what about your appearance?' Klopstock said. 'Won't people recognize you?'

"'Don't worry. I thought about that too. I won't look like this. I will grow a Van Dyke beard. I will crop my hair short in the German style and will wear a blue beret. I will become my own distant kinsman,' is what I told Klopstock.

"You see, my young American friend, I grew a beard not only to disguise myself from others but also to hide from the Angel of Death. True, I was feeling fine—but maybe he hadn't been informed yet. If he came after me again, he wouldn't recognize me with a beard. It was something the religious Jews do when they are deathly ill. They change or add to a Hebrew name in order to fool that angel, who is never fooled. When he seeks someone by a certain name and presumably can't find him because that certain someone has changed his name, he finds him anyway. For that angel's arrows, like Cupid's, always find their mark."

"But you were called Mr. Klein," I interrupted, seeing before me his Ph. Klein name plate.

"But my Hebrew name," K continued, "I didn't change. Just my face." K smiled, chuckled softly and whispered, "It seems to have worked," and he broke into a laugh. And I laughed with him.

"When poor Johann Eck died they prepared the coffin. Meanwhile I returned to my family. They almost didn't recognize me, but they were delirious about my recovery. But their mood changed when I told them about the staged death and the funeral that would follow. I had a row with my father. I told him to appreciate my return to health rather than criticize me for my drama. 'Mad writer,' he called me. 'Looney Bohemian.' I told him I could have pretended to have died and then at the funeral of the lonely man revealed myself. But that probably would have killed him. To make a long story short, they buried the poor fellow in a grave whose tombstone read K, 1883–1924, and my parents and sisters went through the shiva while I took a room somewhere."

"And you didn't share this with your beloved Max?" I said and felt myself sailing through the decades in the space of K's sunny, book-filled room.

"No, I'm sorry to say. For then I would have had to include several others in our group and then secrecy would have been impossible. It was a hard decision, but I kept to it."

"And how did your parents explain your presence at home later?"

"Aha. Good question. I was passed off as a distant cousin from Hamburg who had come to help out at the business. If people marked that I looked a little bit like poor, beloved K, my sisters would say that Philippe Klein had always been known as a K lookalike."

"Is it possible you did what you did to get back at your father?"

The old man's face turned white, as if in a backstage dressing room talc had been smeared over his face for some special actorly effect. I thought he would die now. So I hit the nail. It was all done for his father.

K stared at me, anguish in his eyes. The color returned slowly to his face. Behind the retina I detected a faint look of disdain. He said nothing. Not a word. Just gazed at me. After a long period of silence—how discomfiting that angry silence—he declared:

"I loved my father and my mother. And they reluctantly, and not without arguments, complied with my wishes. For me, to go along with my madness, they had to undergo the torments of a sham mourning, my father and mother and sisters, sitting shiva for a ghost. So make no mistake. Don't be a literary pseudo-psycholog. I loved them. You of all people, you're a creative artist, you say you make films, so you should know that you can't read fiction as biography or autobiography."

I licked my lips, took the rebuke, then said softly:

"And what about the funeral? Tell me. Was Brod there? Did he speak? Were *you* there?"

"I'll tell you about the funeral."

27

An Old Document

As I videoed Graf, and before he gave me the document, he asked:

"How old do you think I am?"

With his cheeks fuller and shaven, he looked younger than last time, perhaps sixty-five.

"Fifty-five," I said.

"Very kind of you. But I am sixty-eight years old. I was born at the end of December, 1924, several months after K died. Dora Diamant's departure created a vacuum and so K befriended Miriam, one of the devoted nurses, a very beautiful, tender woman, and when it was time to have the baby, that is, me, she had it in the Jewish Children's Home. For reasons of privacy she didn't have the baby in Vienna. And for reasons of sentiment she had the baby in Prague. You see, as a single woman, working full time, she was unable to care for the infant. And the document I'm holding testifies to this point."

I looked at the paper, filmed it. It stated that the baby boy named Karoly was born to the nurse, Miriam Graf, religion Jewish, of the Vienna Woods Sanatorium, in the Jewish Children's Home Adoption Center, and placed there for one year, then reclaimed by nurse Graf.

"This is fascinating," I said.

"See? See? I told you you would be impressed."

"But nowhere in this document does it state that K is the father."

Karoly Graf looked at me as if I were a moron.

"But that is obvious! As obvious as you looking into a mirror and seeing yourself."

"Sometimes I look into a mirror and don't see myself."

"I'm talking about normal people. It *is* obvious because K stayed on at the sanatorium for about a month after Dora Diamant left for Poland. He was ill, lonely, depressed. Within a month he would die. The staff was very kind to him. Everybody loved him, including my mother, with whom K had a special bond. They formed, how shall we say, a union, and nine months later, by this time K was already dead, Karoly came into the world. Think of it. How many people beside K stayed at the sanatorium and lived in Prague?"

"Probably not many."

"No, not many. No one but K."

"Interesting," I said. But I wasn't convinced. Klopstock could have been his father, or another patient. Or someone else entirely. And the fact that nurse Miriam Graf sought out the Jewish orphan home in Prague proved nothing either.

True, Graf was tall. But he didn't look like K, or Jiri. And why was he the only one to announce his special relationship to K, whereas Jiri kept silent? Or could it be that Jiri had wanted to tell me but Betty stood in his way? Obviously, Jiri and Karoly Graf were different personalities. And then I recalled that I had once said, and to Mr. Klein no less, that had I discovered I was a son of K, I would have hired an open truck with an amplification system and shouted, "Listen, folks, I'm K's son." I wouldn't keep it still. So if I would have done such a thing, why shouldn't Karoly Graf? So, why should I criticize Graf for doing something that I would gladly, proudly, have done myself? Never mind the penchant we have for criticizing in others the very fault we ourselves possess.

Of course, criticism aside, the only problem here is veracity. Is Graf telling the truth? Or, if not wittingly lying, then taking facts and extending them like strudel dough to come up with his (now not so fantastic) claim.

"Tell me, Mr. Graf, do you go around telling everyone that you're K's son?"

"No. Not everyone. But if I find a K lover, like you, I certainly do not hold back from sharing the news."

"I mean, are you known in Prague as the man who goes around saying he's K's son?"

"I don't know what reputation I have in this city. I do not have, how do you call it, a relations public consultant. As for the phrase 'goes around saying,' I would heartily disagree with it.... Here, let me show you something."

Graf rolled up the left sleeve of his sweater and then the sleeve of his shirt.

"See? Near where the arm bends, this dark brown birthmark. That's another sign. And another one just to the left of the navel."

But I laughed. I couldn't help laughing. I felt like Yossi golem and the shamesh who laughed at me. But now I was doing the laughing.

"So what does that prove?"

"You know in fairy tales and folk stories, the birthmark proves a baby is prince or princess."

"I still don't understand. In the stories the baby has the same birthmark as the king or queen. How is your birthmark connected?"

"K had same birthmark."

"How do you know?"

"I know."

This conversation, although absurd, was being filmed, recorded. What a delicious bonus for my documentary!

"Do you have a photo of K bare-armed? I've never seen a photo of K without a suit jacket on."

"So I was told."

"Is it documented anywhere?"

"Yes."

"Okay. Where?"

"In oral tradition."

I shut the camera. I thanked Graf heartily for letting me talk to him. And then I remembered his mother, the nurse Miriam. And I started filming again.

"Did K ever see your mother again? Acknowledge the baby? Take responsibility?"

Graf looked at me, astounded.

"But he died! What are you talking about? Your question would be valid for a man who lived on and did not acknowledge his paternity."

I shook my head. "Of course, you're right. I was so engrossed with your fascinating tale that I forgot the facts."

"When can I see the film?"

"Actually, I've just begun. It will take a while, but when it is finished you will surely get a copy."

28

The Eulogy

"The funeral, you say? Yes, the funeral. At my own funeral, I maintained my stoop. My Van Dyke beard and mustache, of course, were fully grown. I made sure to show my bared, closely cropped head of hair that I covered with a dark blue beret, the one I've been wearing for decades, for almost seventy years."

"The only man I know of," I said, "who attended his own funeral."

"Well, it also happened in Mark Twain," K reminded me, "either in *Tom Sawyer* or *Huckleberry Finn*."

"Wait a minute! Did you say you're wearing that beret for almost seventy years?"

"Yes."

"Sixty-nine, almost seventy, right?"

"Yes."

"Then I think I've solved the mystery of sixty-nine minus eighty."

"Congratulations," K said drily.

"Now I get it. The year of your death is also the year of your rebirth, so you also mark your birth year from 1924. Which means that you are now sixty-nine, almost seventy."

K smiled.

"But I interrupted you. The funeral, you were saying. Was Max Brod there?"

"My parents called upon Max to deliver the eulogy. It was Max who began. He looked down at the open grave and said:

"'My dear beloved friend…you…'

"And I felt a tweak at my heart. So guilty to that childhood friend who was so close to me I felt he was another me…I almost felt like rushing forward and saying, 'Max, dear Max, it's all a horrible mistake. I'm not dead. It's me, here I am…' But I bit my lip hard and waited to hear more.

"Once more Brod said, 'You…'

"And then—silence. One moment. Another. A chill wind blew through the cemetery that early June day. Everyone sensed the silence. Heard only the mournful wind. Brod swallowed. The sound of that loud, difficult cluck hung in the air. We waited. The stillness of empty space became heavier, as though a cloud had come over us, growing darker and darker and bringing gloom as it descended, until the silence became unbearable. Then Max broke down and began sobbing. From the back of the circle of mourners I saw the tears running down his cheeks and, feeling so sorry for his grief, I felt sorry for myself and my lonely life, and I too began to weep…

"Brod broke down, he broke down, my beloved Maxie. He had hardly said a word and everyone was already sobbing. At first he wept openly and then he covered his eyes. His shoulders shook. Two men approached and held him. Max wiped his eyes. He tried. He bent forward, opened his mouth, but he could not continue.

"I looked at my parents, my sisters, my relatives. All were dabbing their eyes.

"'Forgive me, Franzl,' Max Brod whispered in a choked voice. 'Please forg…'

"And with that word stuck in his throat, he backed away from the grave.

"It was at that moment that I stood on the precipice. As in a dream I tottered at the edge. I could go this way or that. The slightest wind. There, then, my resolve was tested. If I did not reveal myself then, I could maintain my charade forever. But what would happen if I revealed myself? How many heart attacks and traumas would I cause by my dramatic, egoistic gesture? For a moment I imagined that I'd rip off my false paste beard and mustache, which really were not false, take off my beret, and say theatrically, 'No, I am not dead. I still live.' My father, my iron father, who had the strength of *his* father, an innkeeper who once picked up two gentile attackers, one with his left hand, the other with his right, and cracked their skulls together, my iron father—who knew what might happen to him seeing his son's second wild gesture? Again changing his mind. No, I could not do it. There was no backpedaling anymore.

"I kept silent. Perhaps at some later time I would contact Brod. Just then, beyond the edge of the mourners, I saw a little bonfire and, in an excited, overstimulated frame of mind, I thought of it as a memorial candle for me. In all likelihood it was the cemetery caretaker burning refuse.

"As I was thinking this, someone came up to me and asked me, as a relative, to say a few words. To my counter-suggestion to ask the father or a sister, he replied that it might be too much of a strain. If Brod broke down, how much the more a close relative. So he begged me, saying since I lived in another city and wasn't that close to K, I could maintain my equilibrium and say the few words that K deserved to have said about him and that must be said on such an occasion.

"I agreed.

"If anyone noticed how much the distant cousin, Philippe Klein, looked like K, he said nothing. But of course who would believe, who could possibly believe that the real K now stood at the gravesite of his own funeral? And, in any case, I had a dark black Van Dyke and mustache and wore a navy blue beret that K had never worn. I had on glasses and affected a slight stoop to make myself somewhat shorter.

"I stood where Max had stood. I looked at him. He wasn't standing now where he had stood before. I nodded, bowed slightly in the Mitteleuropa manner, but saw no recognition in his moist eyes. And I reviled myself for betraying my brother and for being such a reprobate.

"Then I gazed down at the open grave and thought of the miracle that had been granted me: life. For normal human beings it is either life or death—but for me, uniquely, now it was both, and at the same time."

K looked pensively at his bookshelves and, for a moment, up at his two model aeroplanes; he held his chin, remembering.

"I really didn't think of what to say. The words tumbled out spontaneously. Before I began to speak I made an effort to change my voice. I lowered it. Under the circumstances, no one would have noticed, but it would have been too eerie for people to hear K's second cousin delivering a eulogy about K in K's voice. Also, K spoke rather quickly because he thought quickly. He, I, hardly formulated one thought, one phrase, when another came leaping along like a cheetah. So I deliberately spoke…slowly…in…my…newly…deeper…voice,…as if…carefully…gathering my thoughts.

"'How awesome is this day for us. The book of life is closed and yet, strangely, open. In the last days of his life K no doubt thought of the words Jews recite on Yom Kippur, Who shall live and who shall die; who shall come to a timely end and who to an untimely end; who shall be at peace and who shall be tormented? Dear K, you passed through this world and beyond. You wanted justice in this world. You wanted happiness. He was a quiet man, was K.' I looked over the heads of the mourners as I continued speaking slowly. 'A good man, a lonely man who had wonderful friends. He loved his family, adored his friends.' Thinking of my friends, I was overcome for a moment and I stopped. '"It was worth coming into this senseless world," K told me, "for the precious friends I have. Blessed with friends am I," he said.' And I looked at Max as I said this, and tears spurted from his eyes once more. 'K loved books and writing. You loved Judaism and began to study Hebrew and Yiddish to strengthen your bond with your people. You loved laughter and elicited laughter even in your most absurd stories. In your work you fulfilled the prophet Joel's prophecy that old men will prophesy and young men will see visions. And you, a young man, had visions of a world where people are oppressed and where the individual is lost.'

"I looked down at the grave. I found myself in a puzzling, enigmatic situation. I was delivering a eulogy for myself but also had to pay my respects to the poor, lonely, abandoned Johann Eck who actually had died in the sanatorium and was now being buried.

"Jews believe in the continuity of life. So do I. K's life will continue. Now let us weep for this unheralded man so few knew; let us weep for this unknown man.... May the soul of the man who rests here be bound up forever in the bond of life.'

"But Brod interrupted.

"'K will be heralded. K will be known.'

"And then, before the rabbi had a chance to say it, I began the Kaddish for the poor man who was taking my place in the earth where I should have lain but for the miracle:

"'*Yisgadal ve-yiskadash sh'mey rabbo...*'

"When I finished, I looked up. People were weeping again. At the end of the service people I did not know, that is, Philippe Klein did not know, came up to me and took my hand in theirs, pressed it warmly, lovingly, put their arms on my shoulders and said, 'You captured his spirit.' But how could I capture his spirit if it was of myself that I was speaking? Can a man capture his own spirit? And in any case, in retrospect, it was an uninspiring bundle of banal sentences I put together. Not moving. Not touching. Not spellbinding. Not extraordinary. I hope to do better next time I am called upon to deliver a eulogy for myself. But because it was a funeral, people were moved. The emotion of the moment cloaked rational thinking. Even Maxie shook my hand and thanked me. At that moment I felt again I had betrayed my best friend and I looked down at the ground. People thought it was in sorrow—but it was actually in shame."

Then K brightened. He looked around his warm, comfortable room as if searching for something. He turned to me and said, "And Franz was there too."

Was he mixing himself up with himself? Having divested himself of one life and assumed—maybe even arrogated, but that might be too strong a word—another, was he now referring to his former self? Or was he referring to himself now—as a new person—in the third voice?

"Franz?" I said. "But you're Franz."

I saw no flicker of anything on his smooth face. An absolutely neutral reaction to my challenge. My God, I thought, and an epiphanous feeling swept over me, a sad spirit, a sad breeze. Maybe he *was* Phillipe Klein and all his long life he had lived a charade, a pretense, something akin to Karoly Graf pretending to be K's son, conning his family and few friends that he was K. Klein, having delivered a eulogy in 1924 and convincing himself then that he was K, Klein just kept on with the lifelong pretense.

K waited. He waited until I had puzzled out my suspicion. Then he smiled.

"But there's another Franz. My good friend, Franz Werfel." Now he laughed. "Of course, he didn't recognize me. If Max Brod, whom I would see twice daily, didn't recognize me, how could Werfel? And anyway, if you're going to the funeral of K, even if a newcomer from a distant town, some kind of second cousin, somewhat resembles the deceased, what can one say? You look like the lately departed?" Again K rolled a full phrase of laughs. "No one in his right mind would say anything like that. One's human nature acts as a mask of self-deception. I was, my dear boy, absolutely in the clear.

"One more thing I should tell you. I go to my gravesite every year on my yorzeit. I light a yorzeit candle on the anniversary of my, that is, his, Johann Eck's, burial, and I say Kaddish for the poor man. He was not a Jew, but I still say Kaddish for him anyway, for the man who was buried instead of me and who has no grave marker of his own. And because of that the light of my own life was temporarily relit for me.... Do you want to see the letter?" K said with almost no pause.

"What letter?"

"*The* letter. The one that came too late. The letter Dora wrote to me."

"You have it?"

"Yes."

"Where? Here?"

"No. It's in a safe place. Would you like to see it?"

"Oh yes. Absolutely."

K rose. He got his coat. "Then come. Come with me."

"Wait," I said. "Sit down for a minute."

K laughed again. "Are you like the peasants in a Chekhov story who before they set out on a journey sit down for a moment to avert the evil eye, lest a demon who spoils trips goes into action?"

I laughed too. K seemed in a good mood. He had told me much, in splendidly K-esque precision—not all, but much, of his story.

I was sure he would share many other details with me. Now, when he was so upbeat, was the time for me to ask him a question.

"You know my profession, right? You know what I came to do here. So I want to ask you a favor."

K's normally relaxed face tightened. He could feel what was coming. "Yes?"

"Please. I would like to film you. It would be such an important, riveting, even earth-shaking film."

K started shaking his head as soon as I began. "No, my dear boy. I can't do it. I must say no."

"Like the Gerer rebbe said no to Dora's father."

That hurt, that comparison. But K didn't flinch.

"You want the world to know I exist." He gave me a sad smile of understanding.

"Yes, very muchly, to quote a Prague friend of mine. You would make such a great subject."

"I'm sorry. I can't. I won't."

"But why?"

"There are too many X's and Z's that surround that why. I would have to give you one hundred ten years of history."

"I'm willing to listen."

"I have protected my identity for decades. Please don't spoil it for me. I trust you."

"I would like to see you get the Nobel Prize."

K gave a start. As if moving forward to me. A shift in his psyche. Had I hit a sympathetic chord?

"No doubt about it," I pursued my lead. "You'd get the Nobel Prize."

"The Nobel Prize is given to living writers."

"So?"

"But I am considered dead."

"That's where my documentary will play a role. K lives."

"They won't believe it."

Was I winning? Was he relenting?

"You can show them what you showed me."

"They'll think it's trick photography. You'll lose your reputation as a maker of true documentary films."

"But let's give it—"

Sharply, he said, "The answer is no." Then in a more moderate tone: "It would go against the grain of everything I've lived and believed in. I am very sorry."

K went to the hallway, picked up the phone and dialed. He spoke in Czech for a minute or so.

"Come. It's all set. I'll show you Dora's letter."

29

In the Altneu Again

Once we emerged from the Metro, K took me up Parizska Street, past the Schweik sculpture, to the Altneu. The main door was open.

"Sit down here," K said.

He walked up the three steps to the bimah, bent down, opened the two doors below the wooden reading table, reached in and moved his hand in the cabinet. He held up an envelope.

Then he approached me, opened the envelope and pulled out a single sheet of paper. He stood before me like a lecturer reading his notes to his class.

"I will translate Dora's German." He smiled. "Her German was never excellent. She grew up with Yiddish and got some education in Polish. Here is what she says:

"'I'm sorry I have to say goodbye to you this way. But our relationship is doubly doomed. My family, as you know, is against us. And now that you are away, one of the nurses…'"

At that last word—"nurses"—there was an infinitesimal hesitation. Its duration was no longer than the hesitation a ball makes when it's thrown up in the air and stops for a fraction of a second before acknowledging gravity. But I caught that hesitation. I caught that fractional stop and it intrigued me. Why did K hesitate? Why did he stop? Was it the memory of one of the nurses that made him pause?

"'...secretly told me that the laboratory confirms Doctor Klopstock's diagnosis. I should be with you at this time but I cannot witness the ebbing of your life. I just cannot. The days I spent with you were, are, the happiest in my life. I want to remember the joy, the life, not the departure of life. I do not have the courage to be with you. Forgive me. Please forgive me. All my love. Your Dora.'"

I absorbed the words but still couldn't fathom what difference it made if she left him because of her father's intransigence or her own lack of courage in being with him when he died. But for K it was apparently crucial. He felt Dora had abandoned him. Many years had passed; he had made his decision. I couldn't question him on this now.

"Thank you for sharing this with me. She writes so touchingly, so lovingly." Then I asked him:

"Why do you keep that letter here and not at home?"

"As I told you. Because here it is safe. Despite evil regimes, nothing has ever happened to this synagogue in all the years of its existence. And nothing ever will. It is safer here than at home."

K walked up to the Holy Ark, kissed the curtain, and returned.

"The last time I did that was sixty-nine, almost seventy, years ago." He looked up at the soaring space of the synagogue, admiring the source of his salvation, as if beholding it for the first time.

"If not for the Maharal, where would I be?" he said suddenly into the silence. "Sometimes I think he breathed his spirit into me."

Did K mean this or was it just a metaphor? Maybe wishful thinking.

"Especially during the war years," he added.

I looked at him as if to say: Come on now, really! He caught the skepticism in my look. Suddenly he raised his hands. He stood taller than ever. In the synagogue's chiarascuro light it seemed as if gauze were appearing between his outspread hands and his hips. K spread his wings.

"I am the Maharal," he boomed slowly. His voice frightened me. I felt chills running down my spine.

I stepped back, saw the word *emet*, truth, glowing white on his forehead. Three Hebrew letters, *aleph, mem, tov*—the first letter, the middle letter, the final letter of the Hebrew alphabet.

I blinked, rubbed my eyes.

K dropped his hands, laughed again. "Sorry, I was just joking. How can anyone but the Maharal be the Maharal? But, still, I felt that something of him had rubbed off on me in the attic, protecting me."

"What attic?"

"I told you. The attic of the Al-tnigh-shul. Here. Upstairs." And he rolled his eyes up to the ceiling.

"But there is no attic," I chittered. My voice laughed of its own accord, rolling the laughter around each word.

K laughed too, but I couldn't gauge the timbre, the import of that laugh.

"So God made a miracle for you."

The words that came out of my mouth had a familiar ring. But these words were someone else's. Not mine. I heard sarcasm in those words, a sarcasm that belonged to someone else. Who had told me those words?

"The shamesh told you," K said. "And where is he?" K looked at his pocket watch, one he may have had from before World War I, and then to the door. "That's the shamesh's position: 'There is no attic.' But there was an attic when I was there. Either that or I was living on thin air."

"A miracle," I repeated. I said it gently, bemusedly, admiringly. "How did you get up there?"

"A ladder."

"Whose?"

"Jacob's."

I wanted to ask him if he met any angels descending as he climbed up.

"You ask how I got up into the attic. It's not so simple. It's like asking how one gets to the fifth floor of a three-story building.... Do you know *The Guide of the Perplexed*?"

"Not well."

"In it, Maimonides writes that only a small, serpentine letter marks the difference between 'comic' and 'cosmic.' If you look at my story from a cosmic point of view, it's not too strange at all. The light we see from the moon is one and a half seconds old. But the light we see from some stars is already millions of years old. In some cases, the light we see is shining from a star long dead. When we look up at the sky we look back in time. If you are aware, you see how the parameters we normally deal with are mixed up. Do you see?"

I said yes, but I didn't see.

"And more, there is a force in the world called 'dark energy,' which accelerates the expansion of the universe."

"I remember you once told me that you are blessed with dark energy. So what's the connection?"

"It's this dark energy that helped me get into the attic."

"But you said the Germans came looking for you."

"Yes."

"How did they get there?"

K leaned forward. He brought his face close to mine. His lips became thin. Anger suffused every pore of his face.

"How did they get everywhere? How did they spread like a cancer to every village, every town, every city, street, alley, and lane in Europe? How did they get to every house, cellar, attic? Who taught them such organizational skills? Does water have to be taught to run downhill? Do cows have to be taught to come home from the meadow? In a village in Bohemia, on a trip with Brod, I once saw a cowherd bringing the cows back from a day in the fields. Once he was in the main street, it was like a magic show—each cow, on its own, branched off into a side street, into its own yard, like a worker returning home. If you like, you can call the Germans' power of searching, sniffing out, finding, instinct. Their penchant for evil. How else did they get to every house, cellar, attic?"

"Not by Jacob's ladder."

K moved his head a bit to the left, a bit to the right, hard to say if agreeing or not. Perhaps his gesture said: I do not know.

He took a breath and said, "If you noticed, I spoke Czech to Eva, not German, the language we were all educated in. Since the war I do not let those execrable sounds cross my lips." He stopped for a moment, then continued: "When they talk of miracles, survivors always say, It was a miracle I came through alive. But you also have to consider anti-miracles, the negative side, events and incidents powered by an infernal machine. Theirs. The anti-miracle. Like death and murder, which for them was ordinary. Usual. While for us, life, survival, was extraordinary." He nodded and said, "Yes."

"Then what did you do to avoid them?"

"To repel them I cast at them a spark of impenetrable darkness. In that spark there was enough light energy to drive out those dark, evil forces."

"And you were able to survive there in the dark? With no windows, no natural light?"

"Yes. No natural light. Do you know the verse in the first chapter of Genesis, where God says: *Ye-hee or!* Let there be light?"

"I do."

"It wasn't the light of the sun, remember. The sun wasn't created yet. It is a special light, a divine light. A light that was no light. The sort of day that wasn't day and wasn't night."

"Then what made the light?"

"The *sheymes*. The loose torn pages from prayer books and other holy texts that contain God's name. Because of their sanctity they cannot be thrown out, so they are either buried or stored. There were hundreds of them up there in the attic. They prompt a strange kind of bioluminescence, like the dying elephants of Africa whose tusks glow in the dark as they go instinctively to their secret burial grounds. The light doesn't necessarily come directly from the *sheymes* because they don't like to reveal themselves, but their light glows elsewhere, in different spots, like a referred pain, which does not come from the place of the hurt but from somewhere else. Do you follow?"

"No."

"Yes," said K and nodded, as if saying: I'm glad you're getting it.

"Okay," I said. "That's the cosmic point of view. What about the comic?"

K smiled. "Read my 'Metamorphosis.'"

Just then the shamesh came in.

"Yes, I'm late. I know. But I told you I would be late, so it's not too bad, right? Mr. Klein, I'm so glad to see you again."

"So you do know him?" I said.

"Of course I know him."

"But when a few days ago I asked you, Do you know Mr. Klein, you said no."

I wondered if he would again say, Is Prague.

"Why didn't you say Phishl Klein? You know how many Kleins are in Prague? Some Jews, some not. There are more Kleins in Prague than frogs." And he laughed. "Phishl Klein of course I know." The shamesh said a few words in Czech to K, then turned to me and said, "Mr. Klein has been very generous to the shul over the years, and I thank him again for that."

K bowed his head in appreciation. "Shamesh, do me a favor."

The shamesh looked quizzically at him, as if about to scold him for something. "So you want to show him the attic, is that it? But I already told the yungerman there is no attic here."

"But I already told you I was up there. I spent the war years there. There I was saved."

"I know you told me that. Maybe you were. But now there is no attic there."

"And it is up there, in your nonexistent attic, that I studied English." K turned to me. "As you can see, we have had this argument before."

The shamesh was silent.

"May I go up?"

Who said that? Me or K?

"Of course," the shamesh said. "Just by yourself." He shook his head, exasperated. "I don't understand you. It's all a myth." He turned to me. "I showed you there is no attic there first time I met you, right?"

"We live and die for myths," I said.

"And, anyway," the shamesh continued, "the holy Maharal forbade anyone from going up there, a prohibition in effect for more than four hundred years." He stopped for a moment, then added, "Look, I don't deny myths. I don't deny the power of words, but they cannot create a ladder to nowhere."

"Do you have a ladder here?" I asked.

"No."

"With or without rungs?"

The shamesh said, "Without."

The vast space of the Al-tnigh hummed as we looked at each other in silence. What would happen next?

K spoke.

"Would you like to hear about miracles? About incredible, unbelievable events?"

"I collect miracles," the shamesh said. From his jacket he pulled out a little hand-painted wooden box. He lifted the lid. "Speak and I'll store it here."

"Only in quantum physics can you encounter something that spins while standing still," K declared. "Or an object that is both solid and fluid at the same time. Or an atom that can be in two places at the same time."

At this the shamesh gave me a quick look of complicity—his eyebrows wagged up and down for a moment—as if to say: Remember what I told you about the atoms and quantum physics?

"Seems to contradict laws of nature, right?" K continued. "Miraculous? And only on one planet in a universe composed of 220 billion stars was life formed, and only here is it sustained. Now if these incredible, impossible things are true, why can't an unnatural event such as occurred with me take place, in an attic that is and isn't there?"

The shamesh looked down at the floor. He put the lid back on his miracle box and returned it to his pocket. His eyes were moist. Was it his normal weepy look, or had K's words touched him?

"Do you want to see it?" the shamesh asked laconically.

"Not anymore," said K.

"Did you see the golem?" the shamesh asked him.

I thought K would pull out a little pocket mirror and hold it before the shamesh's face.

"Who do you think fed me?" K replied.

Was that a joke? Or was that also true? For I remember K telling me that Elijah's raven had brought him food.

K stretched out his hand and bade the shamesh goodbye. "Thank you, shamesh. Stay well. Continue your good work for many years to come.... Now come, my boy, I want to show you something you've never seen before."

"That synagogue?"

"No. Not yet."

From the little alley on the side of the Altneu we turned right into Prague's Madison Avenue, Parizska Street. A few minutes' walk away was a statue I had seen before of a seated Good Soldier Schweik, sitting in amiable fellowship at a round metal table with two friends. He had obviously had a mug or two of beer. K stopped in front of Schweik and began softly to speak to him. All I needed now was for Schweik to answer and it would have sealed my membership in Prague's Theater of the Absurd.

Did I see Schweik wink, or was it my overheated imagination, seeing things that couldn't be seen? The language K spoke wasn't Czech or any other language I didn't understand; it was more like the language Jiri and Betty had used to confuse my thoughts.

"Is that Czech?"

"A version Schweik understands. The working-class dialect."

"I see. And who are the two chaps with him?"

"I know only one. The chubby fellow next to him is the author, Hasek."

"Do I look anything like him?"

K's glance said: Why in the world are you asking that? But he looked at my face and at Hasek's.

"No. Not at all. Why?"

"A girl here told me I looked like him. I didn't like being compared to that fat guy."

"She meant it as a compliment. In Prague slang, a good-looking man is always compared to Hasek."

I don't know if I bought it. I looked at K. At that moment he had the innocence of Schweik. How could I not believe him?

"By the way," he said, "did you know that Hasek owes his worldwide fame for *The Good Soldier Schweik* to Max Brod? With his typical generosity of spirit, he worked enthusiastically on Hasek's behalf to get the book published."

I nodded, listened with half an ear, but I was interested in something else.

"May I ask you a question?"

He must have sensed what I was about to say, for he gave me a warning look.

"Not about that. That is a closed issue."

"It's not about that. It's about what you did. It's still hard to believe," I said, "hard to understand why you cut yourself off."

"I didn't want to be K anymore."

I shook my head. "Please forgive me for pursuing this. But your friendship with Brod. You loved him. You appreciated his generosity of spirit. He was like a brother; more than a brother. I read his book. You were like Jonathan and David. Inseparable."

"Yes. That was the most difficult. I regret it to this day."

"So please, please explain it."

"I can't. I cannot. I try to come up with reasons. I think about it. I can't stop thinking about it. It's a regret that spins like a never-ending top in my mind. It haunts me. I can't explain it."

"Maybe it was ego."

"Maybe," K said.

"Or desire for drama."

"Could be. But I still can't explain it."

"Not only the false death that Doctor Klopstock agreed to. But to continue the sham for decades."

"Then I had a reason. Dora. But in retrospect I can't explain it. It has run its course and now it's too late to change. I don't know. I admit it. I just don't know."

Tears sprang into his eyes. No wonder the word "sprang" is used with tears. They did not well up slowly, reflecting the slow buildup of feelings, the eyes moisten, then the tears coming. But here "sprang" is correct. Like a sudden hemorrhage they came, the tears.

"There are lots of things I know," K continued, "but this I truly don't know. Celine writes about the gratuitous act. This may be one. It's like a runaway train on a downhill run. Once started, no turning back. Don't you think I've asked myself countless times, Why did you do it? Why did you fake your death? I have no answer. Or, rather, different answers at different times, which is the same answer as no answer. Sometimes in the middle of the night it becomes absolutely clear to me. In a dream. But in waking, when I want to grasp it, to recreate the thoughts, the words, they elude me."

"Maybe a moment of madness, which even Klopstock, loving you as a friend, admiring you, overwhelmed by your miraculous cure, acquiesced to."

"That's what it was. Undoubtedly. Maybe a moment of madness. But I hurt many people with that moment of madness, most of all my beloved friend Max..." K stopped, gazed at me, somewhat shyly, it seemed to me, and added, "When I met Brod I apologized to him."

"You saw Brod again?"

"Maybe I'll tell you some other time."

And he smiled, in a good mood again.

Like a desire, that good mood of his sent a warm feeling through me. Perhaps I could ask him again. My argument would be: Filming you would be like undoing your mistake. It would help explain to yourself why you did what you did. It would undo your regrets. But K sensed what was going through me and I saw the subtle transformation on his face. It became stiff, suspicious.

K had me. I kept silent.

But other plans, inchoate still, but schemes nevertheless, were whirring through my brain like wild winds.

30

Quandary

I was seeing K practically every day and he still eluded me.

I was torn between ambition and politesse; goals and *mentchlikh-keyt,* simple decency; the drive for a world-resonating scoop and my affection for K and my desire to protect his privacy. What do I do?

Sometimes I felt like a character out of a book—torn, not between ambition and politesse, but torn as if torn from pages of a book, torn out of that novella, *Ladies and Gentlemen, the Original Music of the Hebrew Alphabet,* where Isaac Gantz, an instructor of musicology, wants to get the manuscript of the music of the Hebrew alphabet from a poor, lonely, crippled Holocaust survivor, and finally make a name for himself and perhaps get tenure at his two-bit college.

Me, it wasn't tenure I was after or a one-day halo of fame. What I was getting at was the entire rainbow—and then that word, shaped like a rainbow in my mind, brought back the other rainbow, the first rainbow I was hoping for, another person who was eluding me, the lovely Katya—a rainbow spanning east to west, in glorious Technicolor, sunrise and sunset at once, the cosmos spinning on my fingertip.

So what do I do? How do I preserve for posterity this living legend, in all caps or in italics, if not through chicanery? Then it caught me, that word. It caught and shamed me. I stopped, beheld my eyes behind and above me like a searchlight and, blinded by the beam, beheld myself. Is chicanery the only path? What is the correct path for a man to choose? asks the Ethics of the Fathers.

Had I met Rashi in Troyes, Maimonides in Fez, Mozart in Vienna, Mark Twain or Sholom Aleichem in New York long after their recorded death, wouldn't I have raced to my camera and started the film rolling? Shoot first, ask questions later is not only a Special Forces order, it's the photographer's First Commandment.

Do we owe any debt to history—that is, to the future, to the public at large? Or is anything that is considered historically important discovered by a man of flesh and blood tainted with ego, the self-aggrandizement and ambition of the historian, the mediator between historic/legendary figures and the public?

In short, is the correct path ethical consideration or historical truth? And if precedent is our teacher, the guide that holds a single candle to light our way through darkness, we have Max Brod with K's manuscripts willed to flames, but saved. Because Max was true to history, to literature, to K himself.

I should consult someone, I thought. Talk it over. Get the ethical slant from someone slightly removed. But with whom? I wish I had a rebbe to consult like Dora's father. I had no friends here. And anyway, no matter how good, how objective the advice, no stranger, no friend, can make such a crucial and—in my case—life-changing decision for someone else.

And there was yet another quandary, a quandary wrapped in an enigma, to paraphrase (wrongly, you'll say, and right you'll be) Churchill's famous phrase about the Soviet Union: in the very articulation of my ethical quandary, I'd be revealing, perforce I'd have to reveal, the details of my amazing discovery. What a trade-off!

In the attempt to gain peace of conscience, I would compromise my intellectual proprietorship, give up my scoop. Unless, somehow, I could cloak the ethical conundrum in a different garb, disguise the players, use cunning, otherspeaking, wield a magic wand and cast facts into parable, truth into fable.

And maybe, in trying to be as objective as possible, in trying to look at myself at a remove, maybe in seeking advice, I was subconsciously wishing to slough off the responsibility for my plan of action by, if not having an outsider make the decision for me, then at least nudging me this way or that. Another voice is good; always good is another voice. Even kings and presidents have advisors.

But then again, I thought, why consult? Why listen to other voices? I had other voices in plenitude in me. Proven by my quavering wavering from this side to that. In fact, so many were the voices, each with a different opinion and slant, I could have opened my own consultation service. One voice, you know this one, said, Go ahead. Its opposite, this one you know too, said, Don't. Not too exciting these voices, right? Not voices that shatter glass or make you inhale suddenly with astonishment. No subtle variations; neither glorious bel canto nor sultry contralto. No surprising trills or miraculously sustained high notes. Just a monotonous, mundane Yes or No.

And in between—nuanced signals, many of them flying a little breeze-blown banner. But on the other hand… No wonder Harry Truman—sick of economic advisors who said, On the one hand we should do this, but on the other hand—quipped, Will you please find me a one-armed economist?

As my pendulum swung between Yes and No, I decided to postpone a decision for a couple of days. I needed time to think it over (even though one part of me, the larger part to be sure, already knew what the ultimate decision would be—I may be nice and kind and ethical, but I was nobody's fool), for this was a matter that had historic echoes and ramifications. Page-one news: FILMMAKER DISCOVERS K ALIVE. But as I reread the headline in my mind, my stomach sank. It smacked of the *National Enquirer*, not the *New York Times*. Perhaps I would have to get a new headline writer.

But then my decision was put on hold because I was distracted by someone. Not only is the world at large full of surprises; one's little world has them too.

31

The Letter

The next morning I went with my camera bag to the morning service in the Al-tnigh. When everyone was departing, I asked the shamesh:

"May I stay here alone for a while to meditate?"

"Fine with me." Then he laughed. "But don't let me catch you going up to the attic."

I laughed too.

Yossi, standing near me, smiled. "So he wants to meditate," he said.

"Yes, meditate. Alone," the shamesh said. "Maybe the attic will magically appear."

They're starting again, went through my mind. But I'm going to keep my cool.

"Or maybe the golem," said Yossi.

Look who's talking, I thought. You look more like the golem, Yossi golem, than the golem does.

They both began laughing. But it was a weak, an artificial laughter.

"So he can film them, the attic and the golem. For his film," Yossi added, pointing to my camera bag.

"And meditate."

"Maybe he wants to rewrite K's first book, *Meditation*," Yossi said.

"Enough!" I screamed. "Men of Sodom! I've had enough of your nasty sarcasm."

They retreated. They backed up and pressed against the wall. As though a storm wind pinned them there. Mouths open. Pale and frightened. But they didn't say, Sorry! As I turned angrily away from them they slunk out quietly and I was left alone. The silence in the vast space of the shul had its own melody. I don't know how long I sat there in the humming silence, mesmerized by the ambience of the old synagogue. Fifteen minutes? Twenty? Perhaps half an hour.

Then I went up to the bimah. I looked around. Heard, saw, no one. I bent down quickly, opened one wooden door, felt in a crack deep in the cabinet, and took out the envelope with Dora's letter. If I couldn't film K, the letter—which no one knew about—would be a small substitute. I held the sheet of paper. From my knowledge of Yiddish I was able to make out the German. Why had K hesitated after the word "nurses"? That hesitation intrigued me. I looked at the first few lines and found the answer to the mystery. A phrase that K had left out when he translated Dora's letter for me. He had said, "Now that you are away, one of the nurses secretly told me that the lab confirms Dr. Klopstock's diagnosis." But looking at Dora's letter I saw that after the word "nurses," K had skipped a telling phrase: "you know, Miriam, the pretty one." Why had K censored the remark pertaining to Miriam, whom Karoly Graf claimed was his mother? There must be a reason. The full sentence should have read: "But now that you are away, one of the nurses, you know, Miriam, the pretty one, secretly told me that the laboratory confirms Doctor Klopstock's diagnosis." Here we have another fascinating wrinkle in K's story. It is Miriam who breaks the news to Dora about the severity of K's illness. Ulterior motive on Miriam's part? A purposeful elision by K because he remembers his affair with her? His censoring that phrase certainly adds another dynamic to the film. Karoly Graf had indeed said his mother was beautiful and Dora confirmed it; this entire scenario certainly tilts credibility to Graf's claim. But enough speculating, I told myself. I have to get moving.

I spent a while trying to figure out where best to video Dora's letter. Finally, I decided to place it on a slanted wooden Siddur holder and film it first from the back of the bimah, with the Aron Kodesh in the distance, getting in the reading table, the iron grating of the bimah, and in the distance, the great, majestic Holy Ark. And then I would zoom in for a close-up, holding it there until a viewer could read the entire text, which later would be shown in translation.

Just as I was bending down to take the camera out of the bag, I felt a tap on my shoulder. Scared out of my wits—I thought the golem had come down from the attic—I dropped the camera. It gave one bounce and landed on the floor three steps below.

I wheeled. And faced K.

"That wasn't very nice. Never, never, did I expect something like this from you. You astonish me. You disappoint me. You upset me. Why didn't you ask for permission?"

K's face was ashen. His mustache trembled. Anger glistened from every pore of his face. I placed my hand on my heart and, near tears, said I was sorry.

"Why did you do this?" K wasn't crying, but his plaintive tone was as close to tears as words could get.

I swallowed. My reply came out from a distant speaker.

"You said no to my filming you. I wanted this historic document at least."

K gripped the railing of the bimah. His knuckles were white.

"I am very disappointed. I trusted you. I trusted you.... Why that odd look in your eyes?"

"I'm wondering how you found out."

"I have people close to me here. I got two calls this morning."

Who told you? I wanted to ask. But K's voice was weak; now wasn't the time for normal conversation. But K answered me anyway.

"First, my friend the shamesh. Despite our divergent views on the attic, we are very close. And I also heard from another man I'm close to."

Now I didn't hesitate. "Who?"

"My relative."

"You mean the other man? Yossi? How is he related?"

"He's my father."

That's it. This is too much. I've put up with every absurd thing he's told me, including his claim that he's K. But this! This is too much. He's in la-la land. Writing a K-esque novel.

I swallowed. Tried to remain silent. Restrain myself. But I just couldn't let it pass. The words jumped out of me of their own accord.

"Yossi your father, huh? It was hard enough for me to believe Jiri is your son. How do you expect me to believe Yossi is your father?"

K gave a little smile. "I don't expect you to believe anything. Yossi is my father.... All right, my son told me."

It seemed to me I heard "son." Yes, I did hear "son." Once more the word "son" echoed in my ears. "Son?"

K bided his time.

"I thought he was dead," I said.

"My other son."

So Karoly Graf is right. But Graf wasn't here.

"Yossi? Your son?"

"My father because he protected me. My son because he cared for me. A relative, metaphorically speaking. But above all my friend. Guardian. Angel. One who helped me. Saved me."

I thought K would change faces again. Become the golem. Scare me. Hurt me. Punish me. Teach me a lesson. I thought he would spread his wings and become the Maharal.

"Looked out for me in the past as he looks out for me even now. This morning."

The word "How?" came out of me as if I were an automaton.

"By feeding me. In the attic. During the war. When I was in hiding."

I shivered. No. Impossible. But maybe I had sensed it. With his size, his face, his lumbering movements.

"Yossi?"

"Yes. Yossi. Yes. Yes."

"The g..."

"Him."

"But I thought his face. The glass eye. From the 1973 Yom Kippur War."

"He came to help his people. Was wounded, yes. But he returned to be near me."

So I was right. By calling him Yossi golem I had inadvertently hit upon it. But there is no inadvertence. Only intuition. But, then again, maybe K was pulling my leg. Teasing me. Trying to frighten me.

"You have sidetracked me, my boy. Let us shift the conversation back to you and what you have done. They called me and I had to run down here with a taxi to stop you."

"Please forgive me."

K didn't say a word. He didn't look at me. He took Dora's letter and put it back in its place inside the reader's desk. That he did this in my presence made me feel better. He trusted me not to take the letter again.

"No one will touch this letter anymore." Now he turned to me. His blue gaze chilled me. "Except..." and he tapped his chest three times.

I nodded. I closed my eyes in contrition. "Yes."

Then, without bidding me goodbye, K left the Altneushul.

I ran to the door, then stopped. I wanted to ask K if he had ever contacted Dora Diamant again. If I could see him again. Once more that "if" that creates parallel universes in us.

But I was afraid of his answer.

32

The Old Man Is Out. Guess Who's In?

Trepidatious, my heart higher than it's ever been, pumping in back of my throat, I rang the bell.

Eva opened the door. We were so happy to see each other, we embraced spontaneously.

"I missed you," I said. "How was your journey?"

"All right," she said, but not with her usual upbeat tone.

"Is Mr. Klein in?"

"He went out for a walk."

For the first time something predictable, rock solid, immutable, a set order, like the old man always at home, had been broken. Come whenever you want, he had once told me. I'm always at home. So why wasn't he at home now? Or was he at home and didn't want to see me?

As if reading my thoughts, Eva Langbrot opened the door to K's room.

What is it with these people that they can hear unvoiced remarks?

"How long has he been gone?"

She looked up at the kitchen clock. It was 11:30. I usually came about this time and stayed till it was time for his lunch.

"Since 10:30."

"Did he tell you where he was going?"

"No."

"Is he usually gone this long?"

"No."

"And you're not worried?"

"No."

Eva smiled at the mantra of her short answers.

Again I thought: maybe he's not as old as he says he is. Healthy men in their eighties, even nineties, can and do go out on their own. But someone 110?

Eva walked me into his room.

"Make yourself comfortable. He should be back soon."

Eva and I stood facing the open door to the hallway. I glanced at her and bemoaned the wasted time. For me time was like oxygen. If I'm stuck in traffic—the worst waste of time—I feel my oxygen depleted and I choke. Now precious minutes were lost. What should I do now? Wait, or go back to town? I was so much looking forward to seeing K today I had even rehearsed an apology and a speech that would make him change his mind about the film. It included letting K preview the video and cut anything he didn't like.

Eva saw me looking at her. A moue of guilt appeared on her face, as if K's absence was her fault. She shrugged, as though to say, Sorry, but what can I do?

Just then a girl breezed by in the doorway. Just like last time, I caught only a scant glance of her: back of her head and shoulders, swish of dark skirt. But what I caught was with a camera's eye. I captured that fleet move and, with neural gear shifts, converted it into slow motion. It was odd. Even though she moved swiftly, the girl's beauty moved slowly. As if a faint image of her was stripped from her and floated behind her. How shall I describe that sensation that bridged the palpable and the evanescent? Even though she had gone out of view, a transparent replica of herself had settled in my mind. I didn't see her face, but I caught the aura of her presence, and it was enough to tease and allure me, to make me lose my focus on K for a moment. I dashed to the door but there wasn't even a hint of her, not a faint click of a door closing, a trail to follow, a rung to a perhaps nonexistent ladder.

But my focus on K returned soon enough. Through a haze I asked Eva, still seeing that girl lighting up the haze:

"Did Mr. Klein tell you where he was going?" even though I was dying to ask another question: Who is she? Likely she was a boarder, a college girl from a small town renting a room whose location I wasn't yet aware of. But it wasn't nice to be nosey.

"But you already asked me that." Eva smiled.

"I did? Sorry…and what was your answer?"

"He didn't tell me," is what she said.

I moved to the door, about to say goodbye.

"Where are you going?"

"To look for him."

"Where?" A look of alarm crossed her face, as if I were intruding on a private domain.

"I don't know. He's an old man. He may get lost. He might fall."

"You would be amazed at his vitality."

"But that doesn't make him any younger."

"It does," Eva said.

If I hadn't known Eva was Jewish, I'd have assumed she was a Czech farmer woman, round-faced, well-fed, and genial. She invariably beamed. Even her hair smiled. But as she stood before me now, resolute, her arms folded on her chest, her softness vanished. Despite her affability, I now saw an elemental force in her. It probably served her well in the Resistance during the war.

Then she took my hand and guided me back into the room.

"Sit and wait as long as you wish," she said. "He will be, he is, fine. Just don't move anything. He can't stand if things are moved. It's as though he has a photographic memory. His toothbrush has to be on the right side of the sink, not the left. And he won't eat without a tablecloth. If the tablecloth doesn't cover the entire table, if a part of the table is bare, he won't eat. And once he couldn't find his shabbes glasses."

"What's that?"

"Glasses he uses only for the Sabbath. A fine pair of glasses with a thin, elegant gold frame. Otherwise, he won't read. And once I moved his wastepaper basket from here," she demonstrated, "to here. Just a foot away and he got upset.... Just wait a while longer. He'll be back soon."

"I understand. I don't like my toothbrush moved either. And open windows have to be perfectly aligned."

"Just like him." Eva gave a broad smile. "You're not related, are you?"

I sat down, not in K's easy chair but on the wooden one next to his writing table where I usually sat. It moved back an inch as I sat down. I moved it forward.

"That's right," said Eva. "Mr. Klein is very, how you say, metic—?"

"Meticulous?"

"Yes. Meticulous. He likes everything in order, like I told you. He even combs his hair before he goes to sleep."

"In case he meets a pretty woman in his dreams."

"Not any pretty woman, but—"

Eva was about to say, I could swear a name was at the tip of her tongue. But she held back.

"Maybe someone he loved in the past," I helped her.

"Could be," Eva said.

Later, I thought about it and concluded that she wanted to say Dora—but for some reason kept still.

I didn't think I would wait as long as I did. Every fifteen or twenty minutes I told myself, I'll wait just ten minutes more. And every time I rose to leave, I would think, Suppose he comes back during the next few minutes and I miss him. I was dying to apologize about the Dora letter incident and then give my little speech. Then I decided: Since I waited so long, I might as well wait a bit longer.

At one point I heard a Mozart piano sonata. Probably Eva practicing.

While sitting, I was torn between curiosity, noting everything in the room—no radio I could see (perhaps he had a transistor under his pillow) and no television—and etiquette, hesitant to intrude on his privacy. Restraining myself from looking about too much, I actually felt my neck stiffen, the muscles of my hands and feet charley-horsed. How I wanted to open drawers, doors, to see how much farther I could penetrate the quiddity of K.

Then I looked at my watch. My God, it's already twelve thirty. I stood. If I stayed longer, Eva would offer me lunch, and I didn't want to impose. I stretched. Relaxed my tense limbs. Swiveled my neck left and right a few times. Enough. Time to go. I'll go out and see if I can find him. Maybe he's sitting in the park up the hill.

At the door, the recurring doubts about K's story assailed me again. They actually crept on the skin of my hands, tiny prickles, moving goosebumps, that spread upward to my face. Could Mr. Klein be taking all the information about K, his entire gestalt, his persona, from perhaps a little-known Czech or German or Slovakian novel about K, a book perhaps entitled *K's Son* or *The Children of K*, and it was this that fed his appetite for the grand drama, the luscious theater of his life? Could he indeed be a fraud like Karoly Graf, with his pathetic proof that he was K's son? Too bad K couldn't show me a birthmark on his abdomen or forearm that everyone would recognize from a well-documented source that would reveal him to be the lost princess of the classic fairy tales. Then that phrase that K had censored surfaced—about the pretty nurse, Miriam—and made me rethink Graf's claim.

K really had me. I couldn't even discuss my doubts, never mind the ethics of secretly videoing him, with anyone lest, if his story was true, I would betray his secret.

Then it dawned on me that one crucial question could be answered by Eva, who had probably known him for years.

The piano sounds had stopped. I went out to the kitchen, where she now was sitting reading a newspaper. I thanked her for her friendly welcome and, without even giving myself a chance to catch my breath, asked:

"Do you by any chance happen to know how old the gentleman is?"

"No. I don't. But he's certainly older than me," and she laughed. She knew I wasn't going to ask her age.

"But, in any case, I make it a practice to protect the privacy of people who live here. You should really ask him yourself."

"It isn't polite."

She smiled at me an admonishing smile, scolding me pleasantly.

"Neither is it polite to ask behind someone's back."

I had to admit she was right. But her attitude closed the door to any further personal questions.

Then she was back to her smiling, grandmotherly mode. "Look, since you waited so long, why don't you wait another fifteen minutes? Why take a chance on missing him? And meanwhile I'll make you some lunch."

"That's what I've been telling myself the past two hours. And no lunch, thanks."

"You know what? Try just another fifteen, twenty minutes. Maybe they will be beneficial."

"Okay." I sat in K's room, my mind a blank, staring at K's old framed print of a wheat field, fearful that my staring might shift the angle of the frame and cause K discomfort. I ran out of fingers and toes counting the fifteen-minute chunks of time I'd lost.

Suddenly an idea popped into my head. Inspect K's *shem*. Bottom drawer. Perhaps this is why Jiri sent me here. To get the *shem*. Jiri liked me and wanted to reward me. I imagined K standing in front of his chest of drawers, his back pressed against it, as if to say: Nothing doing—guarding his treasure like the fiery angel with the revolving sword who guarded the Garden of Eden to prevent the exiled Adam from returning.

But now I was drawn to that chest of drawers like a nail to a magnet. A wave of enchanted desire swept over me. Pulled me forward a force greater than my power of resistance. I wanted to, I had to see that piece of parchment. I wanted to hold it, inspect it, gaze at it, get my fill of it. But a strange thing happened. Not that I ever watch horror movies or suspense shows on TV, but sometimes as you switch channels you catch a moment of suspense or horror and an odd feeling begins on the nape of your neck and rills down your spine and a fright as though you're in mortal danger overwhelms you. That's what happened to me.

As I drew closer to the drawer I heard a hum: something vibrating. A combination of sound and touch. An electric thrum. The sound you hear on electric wires or telegraph lines in the countryside with total silence all around. First I heard it, then I felt it in my body, as if a tuning fork had been pressed against me and I caught its vibrations and moved in sympathy with it. And then the tinge of vibrating pain, first mild, uncomfortable, a subliminal pain, then stronger, as if I were holding on to a live wire or my finger were pressed into a bulb socket. A painful electric shock, a burn that made me step back quickly.

I looked to the door. No one. In one swift movement, as I imagine taking the *shem*, K enters and says calmly:

"But it is inefficacious."

"What is?"

"Please don't pretend."

"I don't understand."

"Yes," he says. That frustrating Yes of his.

"What are you talking about?"

"The *shem* in your pocket. In your hand. It is only a blank parchment."

"But I didn't take it."

"Yes."

I looked at him.

"But you thought of taking it."

I was tempted to say that Yes of his.

"Take it out. You will see that it is blank."

From out of my pocket I took the parchment I thought of taking but didn't take.

"See?" he said.

It was blank.

K said, "It only works for me."

Thinking of the *shem*, I recalled telling K once:

"You were so lucky to have that *shem* to sustain you."

He said he was fortunate, doubly blessed. "You see, I have two of them," he said with a soft shyness that was not characteristic of him.

And then he said something that made him sound like a faith healer, a spiritual guide. But it wasn't facile, gimme-a-donation TV spirituality. He spoke out of experience. He meant what he said.

"You know what I learned over the years. Everyone has a *shem* in him. You just have to know where it's hidden, where to find it."

At once I moved my tongue in my mouth, exploring, like someone searching for a canker sore. I touched my upper lip, the upper palate. I went above my front teeth to the gum line, below my lower teeth, to the inside of my cheeks. I stretched the limits of the tip of my tongue, curled it, again searched the roof of my mouth, probed all around as far back as it could go. But I found nothing. Where could it be? I wondered. Maybe it wasn't in my mouth at all. Who said the *shem* had to be in one's mouth? But where else could it be? It wasn't on my forehead. For if it were it would have been obvious to outsiders and plucked off long ago. If I had a *shem*, perhaps it was somewhere else. Maybe it couldn't be found that easily. Maybe, like a magic elixir, one had to search hard and long before one discovered it. And maybe, like the fountain of youth, you had to search all your life only to discover, finally, when you looked in the mirror and were shocked, that it didn't exist, but that, nevertheless, the search for it and the confidence that one had a *shem* was the blessing.

I turned to follow the singing sunshine in the room. Saw K's writing table. Its one drawer was slightly open, like a woman's parted lips, signaling, hinting at invitation. I stood; the chair moved behind me. Remembering K's penchant for neatness and order, I brought the chair back carefully to its original position. I drew near the table, then backed away, pretending I was thinking about my next move but knowing that I would open the drawer. Without even turning, confident that K was nowhere near, I opened the drawer some more.

Jiri's letter lay there, part of a packet of his letters held together by a rubber band. I recognized Jiri's handwriting. Did K leave the drawer open on purpose? To tempt me? Test me? To see if I had learned my lesson or if I was an incorrigible recidivist?

At once—and you can't imagine how quickly: as quick as movie frames, each of which is a still photo, running through a projector—at once the scenario for my film changed. Soon as I saw Jiri's letter it changed. My film would not open with the statue of the Maharal in Prague's Town Hall. The film would reflect my beginnings with Prague in New York. It would open with the building where my first encounter took place, the Eldridge Street shul. The image, in black and white, would linger, silently, like a long sustained note. I would video the synagogue from a roof across the street and capture its elegant Moorish, Romanesque, and Gothic façade. The audience would see the synagogue longer than they would normally have patience for, and with no commentary. Next I'd talk about Jiri and tell his story.

As I looked down at the drawer I wondered if K had left it open in compensation for not letting me have Dora's letter. So there were two ways of looking at this: as test and as gift. If I passed the test and touched nothing, my reward would be a photocopy of Dora's letter. I wanted…

I wanted, oh how badly I wanted to resist.

I wanted, oh how badly I wanted Jiri's letter to his father.

I compromised. I didn't take the top letter. I carefully removed one letter from the middle of the stack. I left the drawer open precisely as K had left it.

I was calm. My heart did not burst with fear as I took the letter, folded it once, and placed it in the inside pocket of my jacket.

The twenty minutes were up. K still had not returned. I rose and left his room.

At the front door of the apartment I said loudly:

"I'm leaving now, Eva. Goodbye."

By the sound of my voice bouncing off nothing except walls, I could tell no one was at home. The stillness in an empty house is different from the absence of sounds when people are present.

I went down the stairs to the front of the house. As I stepped outside a girl emerged from another door at ground level at the corner of the house.

I don't know if I said No! aloud or to myself. It cannot be. I must be dreaming. Are prayers really answered in this world? Just as I was lamenting the wasted hours, the useless trip, in one instant my lost time, my irretrievable hours, turned to gold—but it was not the gold of the earth; it was the gold of heaven. So the old lady was right again. The extra minutes I had spent staring at K's print in his room were not only beneficial; they were as golden as the wheat on the framed picture.

For before me, immobile now, not gliding, stood the girl who had swooshed by me before, seen only from the back, like the vision presented to Moses as God's glory passed before him. The girl with the oval face, alluring smile, and one dimple, and one dimple only, when she smiled. The girl whose long green eyes were sunshine. She had changed into slacks, the way she usually dressed when on the square, the girl from faux Georgia, the girl in the blue beret.

"What?" she and I cried out.

"You?" I and she exclaimed.

"Is it?" said either she or I.

Then we both said, "What are you doing here?"

"This is incredible," I probably said, because it's one of my favorite words.

Her mouth was open.

"Let me see," and I took out a make-believe book from my pocket, licked my forefinger in the European manner as I turned nonexistent pages. "Let's see on which page of the novel this astonishing, surprising, incredible meeting takes place, for it can happen only in a novel where a guy looks all over town for a girl and finds her in the house he's been visiting for quite a while."

I looked at Katya.

We both stood still.

So many questions burbled in my mind, I didn't know where to begin. I put the book back into my pocket.

We faced each other. Now, for the first time, she wasn't wearing a placard, demonstrating a marionette, or acting. Now we weren't on the square but in the flowering little garden in front of the house, far from the tumult of town. Who had ordained that here, in K's house, I would meet my lost rainbow, the girl in the blue beret?

Then, like out of a teenagers' handbook, came simple, tentative, halting questions.

"Do you live here?"

"I have a little room on the ground floor."

"But I saw you passing by upstairs. At least the back of you."

"I was getting some milk from the refrigerator."

We both started saying something at the same time, then fell silent for a long moment.

Then Katya asked:

"And you? Do you live here?"

"Well, I spend enough time to qualify as a resident."

"I don't mean in this house. I mean in Prague."

"I'm renting a studio in an apartment hotel for a couple of months while I'm working on my film."

"But where do you really live?"

"In New York."

"Oh," she said.

I looked straight into her eyes long enough for her to lower her eyes.

"You're not from Georgia, are you?"

Said, still with her eyes down, "No…but you already guessed that."

"Then why did you say that?"

"Do you know how many dozens of men, young and old, stop to chat with me? Everyone wants to take me out. Few are interested in concerts."

"That's what they get when they hire a beautiful girl."

"I have neither the interest nor the time to meet and befriend strangers. So that's why I said Georgia. When they ask to meet me after work, I say I'm going back to Georgia in a couple of days."

"No wonder you weren't impressed by my Georgian dishes.... Don't people see you a few days later and ask how come you're still here?"

"Do you know what the average stay in Prague is? Two-three days. And if by chance someone does see me again, I make up a wild story."

"Why don't you just say no?"

"I don't want to hurt their feelings. Maybe there's still a chance they'll buy a ticket to a concert."

Maybe she also makes a little commission on sales, I figured.

"I've come here quite a number of times. How come I haven't seen you before?"

"I work during the day."

"Which is now. During the day."

"On Wednesday I have a few hours off. And anyway, I was away for a while. I had to return home."

"Am I interrupting your plans?"

"No. Not really. I was going to the museum. And what are you doing here with the old man?"

I noticed she didn't call him by name.

"I love talking to him."

She said something like, "Uh-huh, mm-hmmm."

Again we were silent for a while. It was a nice crisp fall day. The sun was shining. The sky was blue. I was happy. My rainbow had returned.

"By the way, I bumped into Michele Luongo the other day. I thought he would be furious at me but he wasn't at all. In fact, he wondered why I ran off."

"He told me all about you. Why didn't you tell me you're famous?"

"First of all, I'm not famous. And second, famous people don't go around telling people they're famous. And anyway, you never gave me a chance. You kept disappearing." I stopped for a moment, cleared my throat. "The four days are up."

Katya smiled.

"I had an emergency. I was called back home to Brno."

"That's the capital of Georgia, isn't it?"

"You're funny," she said affectionately.

"Is everything all right at home?"

"Now, yes. My father wasn't well."

Why did Brno sound familiar? Yes, K had told me that's where Eva Langbrot had gone, to visit relatives.

"Curious, that's where the landlady Eva went too."

"Why curious? Why shouldn't she go there?"

"How should I know? It's just curious that both of you went to that same little town."

"But that's where my parents live. That's where I grew up before I moved here to continue my university studies and seek work."

"But what about Eva?"

"Eva also went to Brno to help tend to her son who wasn't well."

Maybe I was thick but I still didn't understand.

"But wouldn't you say it's curious, or coincidental, that two women who live in the same house travel to the same town to help with two sick men, in one case the girl's father, in the other the woman's son?"

Katya leaned back and laughed. She clapped her hands, kept on laughing.

"Logic is not one of your strong points, is it? It's not two men, silly. It's one man. One and the same man."

The little bits of info tumbled like scattered leaves settling in my brain until they sorted out.

Click. Every day I learn of new relationships.

"Oh, my God, am I thick!... Your father, her son. Eva Langbrot your grandmother?" So Katya is Jewish. My prophetic heart. "Lucky you, having such a talented, wonderful woman as your grandma. When I got tired of waiting for the old man, Eva told me to stay another fifteen minutes, and then another fifteen minutes. It will be beneficial, she said. And how right she was. Had I left earlier, I wouldn't have met you."

"Oh yes, you would have. If it is destined that two people meet, neither fire nor flood can stop the meeting. Anyway, you would have seen me on the square or near the square."

"But that's not the same as in the house. In the garden. Here. Now. And on the square, as you yourself say, you wouldn't be so friendly."

"But with you I was friendly, right?"

"You were, and that made me very happy."

"What are you doing now?"

I heard the hint in her question, but I was worried about K.

"Do you know where Mr. Klein might be? I want to go look for him. I'm worried he's been away for so long. Eva doesn't seem to be worried, but I am."

"No need to worry. He'll come back. And where in this huge city will you look for him?"

"Do you know where he went?"

"Do you want me to tell you?"

"Of course."

Katya licked her lips, thinking, deciding. Her tongue wet her lips once, briskly. She didn't move it slowly, provocatively, over her lips.

"When he needs spiritual refreshment, he goes to the synagogue not too far from here, a synagogue that few people know about."

"I thought I knew all the famous synagogues in Prague."

"This one you don't know."

"Maybe that's the one he said he would take me to."

"He did?"

"Where is it? I'd love to see it. One day we almost went there but after our walk he grew tired and said, Another time. Do you know it? Can I ask you to take me there? Do you have the time? I'm not imposing, am I?"

She ticked her head and pursed a smile, the girl in the blue beret. "My my, so many questions." Katya seemed to repeat them in her mind as she lifted her fingers, one, two, three, four, five. "Five quick questions."

"Well, do you?"

"Plus one makes six." She gave out a merry laugh.

So did I.

"So you'll do it? I mean..." and I dropped the question mark. "So you'll do it."

Again Katya laughed. "Seven is a perfect number."

How lucky I was, spending so much time with her. My mirror monologue had materialized. I listened to every word individually and then to the trope of the phrases and the arc of her little speech, its melody, each note vibrating on a plane of its own. My eyes glowed. I looked at her with admiration. How beautiful, without a drop of paint on her pretty lips, no makeup on her face. Even though I paid attention, I didn't pay attention to what she was saying, but her words washed over me like a beneficent wave, a benison, until I only heard fragments of words in a language I didn't understand, a tongue like the strange tongue Jiri and Betty spoke in my presence. Nepa. Tara. Glos.

And I thought, even before I formulated the thought, even before I gave myself permission to fathom the thought, even before I could weigh in my mind's balance scale if I could, if I should, let this thought fly—I thought I heard myself uttering the words in my mind: If you let me, Katya, you won't have to lug those concert signs, a sweet, bright, lovely girl like you, and there still will be a smile on your luminous face.

Did I say what I wanted to say? Or were those words only subtitles in my mind? If I did say those words, she didn't react. And if I did, why should she react? I had overwhelmed her at our first private meeting with an overbearing personal remark. If I did say those words and she heard them, she wisely let them pass and vanish into the air like skywriting smoke.

"So why did you do what you did?" I asked her.

"Do what?"

"Carry those signs?"

"I can't stand sitting in an office."

"Can you sit standing in an office?"

Katya thought a while, translated the words into Czech, reflected on the English and then, understanding, smiled.

"You went to college, I imagine..."

"Yes. And specialized in literature. But you can't make a living from literature."

And from carrying placards you can? I thought.

"Then teach."

"I will go back to it. But on a university level. In middle school the students get stupider from year to year.... And your field is film and that's why you are here."

Katya made a circular motion as if encompassing all of Prague and then pointed emphatically to the ground where she stood. "Here."

"But why are we chatting so much? We wanted to go and find Mr. Klein."

"Then let's go," said Katya. "The synagogue is not far from here. But it will be quicker by tram."

33

In the Mystery Shul

"Come," Katya said, "we have to buy a ticket at the tram booth for the Caspa District. It's only three stops."

I rushed up to the agent so that she wouldn't offer to pay.

"Do you speak English?" I asked the sympathetic-looking man.

"I have studied in school."

"Two tickets to Caspa District."

The man held the tickets but did not give them to me. "Why do you want to visit there?" he said kindly.

"We want to see the synagogue."

He lowered the tickets. "Well, hmm, I don't know..." he muttered, not looking at me. "Are you sure you want to go there?"

"Of course I'm sure.... Why, is it a dangerous place?"

"Oh, nonsense," Katya, now at my side, interjected. "It's perfectly safe."

"Shalom," the man said. "I am Jewish too.... Be careful." He handed us the tickets. As we boarded the tram, Katya made a face as if to say: What's wrong with him?

The synagogue was not a freestanding building but blended into other apartment houses. From the outside one could not discern that it was a shul.

"It's beautiful," I said, once we entered the vestibule. "Why isn't it known?"

"The congregants don't want tourists. They have an agreement not to list it in the tourist brochures or guidebooks. It's the only private synagogue in Prague."

I saw no extra yarmulkes in the stand where they kept the prayer books.

"May I borrow your beret, Katya?"

She took off her beret and placed it on my head, angled it and smoothed it down. I liked those gestures and thanked her.

"I'm going up to the women's gallery," she said.

I had forgotten about Jiri's letter in my pocket. But once inside the shul I became mightily aware of it. On my chest, on my bare skin, I felt its glowing heat, a hot little rectangle burning against my heart. Maybe the letter wasn't even there anymore, and only the oblong form of heat remained, like the shape of an object stays imprinted on the retina almost photographically in bright sunlight and you still see it after your eyes are closed. I patted my chest. The letter was there, but my hand felt warm.

The men's section was long and narrow. No windows on the sides because they abutted the walls of other buildings. But from a window above the Holy Ark and from seven skylights light streamed in.

On the bimah, a little four-year-old boy stood singing Yiddish songs. So why the need to be careful?

He had no audience but still he sang. Then I spotted K sitting in the first row behind the bimah. He too wore his beret instead of a yarmulke.

On top of the Aron Kodesh were the two traditional small lions with tiny red bulbs in their mouths—the Lions of Judah—their paws supporting, protecting, the Ten Commandments.

I looked up and saw Katya gazing down at me. She smiled and waved. I watched K and wondered what to say to him. He sat with his head bent. Was he reading from a Siddur or just meditating? Meanwhile, the little boy had finished singing and ran from the bimah down the aisle to the back of the synagogue, where a man picked him up and kissed him.

A low growling sound made me turn my head, left and right. Where could that sound be coming from? Was it the rumbling of the tram? I looked up to Katya. She pointed to the lions atop the Aron Kodesh. The brown color of the plaster lions was fading. They emerged from their sculpted state. Bigger they became. Their fur bristled. They yawned like the MGM lions and their red bulbs dropped. A chill rippled down my spine. After turning their heads this way and that, the lions let out a mighty roar.

The shamesh rushed toward the door. He stopped to say a quick word to K, then continued running.

I tapped him on the shoulder as he ran. "Excuse me, shamesh, but what's going on up there?"

But he didn't stop. I followed him.

"Shh," he said, hurrying along, "those are the Lions of Judah, who protect the Jewish people."

I realized these lions were the model for K's story "The Animal in the Synagogue."

The shamesh returned from the vestibule with two leashes and ran back to the Holy Ark. The lions sprang down from atop the Aron Kodesh and stood immobile as the shamesh leashed them. They dashed forward, pulling the shamesh with them.

K turned and saw me. Then he looked up and nodded to Katya.

Strained forward the lions; the shamesh tried to hold them back. In an MGM film the lion soon vanishes and the film begins. Here the lions remained. They moved down the aisle closer to me. I ran to the rear row and stood in the corner by the wall. The great green eyes of the lions were mild, their great big mild eyes were green, but when I heard their bestial roars their mild green eyes were no consolation. Wide open were their mouths. I had never seen such huge sharp teeth before. Two pink uvulas vibrated deep in their throats as they growled at me.

I was too frightened to cry out, but every part of me was trembling.

When the lions stood before me, their maws open so wide and deep, I saw a new, visceral world. I thought to appease them with the letter they no doubt were after.

But I resisted. If they wanted it, come and get it. I wasn't going to give it up on my own. Especially with K here. It made me think of the classic line, perhaps the most famous one in radio comedy, when on the *Jack Benny Show* two holdup men accost Benny and say, "Your money or your life." The famously cheap Benny does not answer. That alone prompts a swell of laughter. "Well?" the men finally say to him. And then Jack Benny grouches, "I'm thinking, I'm thinking," getting one of the biggest laughs in radio history.

My sentiments went one step further than the equivocating Jack Benny. I'd rather they gobble me up than give up the letter, even though it still burned a postcard-sized patch of heat into my heart.

Then the shamesh began to speak to the roaring lions. He spoke in a mixture of Czech and Hebrew, while I thought: I'm also a member of the Jewish people. Why aren't you protecting me? At that moment, when I thought I'd disappear down the mouth of one or both of them, I promised I wouldn't bother K anymore with the video. Maybe K had arranged all this to scare me. Otherwise, why did he nod to Katya? Or maybe this was the work of that aggrieved actor, Stacek, who sought to get even with me. I looked up to Katya. She was no longer in the women's gallery. But the letter, oh no, that I wouldn't give up.

I felt myself molded to the corner, my heart thumping, a lemony, acidic taste in my mouth. Nevertheless, at that moment, I still wished I had my camera with me to record this scene. I could have made a great documentary from all the scenes I didn't film, from all the opportunities I had missed. Why is it that at crucial moments I don't have my camera?

Now K stood by my side. But he said nothing. As the lions drew closer, oblivious to the shouts of the shamesh, K took one step toward them.

"Stop!" I cried, holding him back.

But K wriggled out of my grasp and moved toward the lions.

At the doorway, her face contorted, Katya shouted, "Stop, Grandpa! Down Gur, down Aryeh," she called to the lions.

But K moved forward. With his right hand he gestured in front of the lions' faces. I didn't see what he held in his hand—could it have been a *shem*?—for at once the beasts ceased roaring, crouched down, then turned and ambled back slowly to the Holy Ark. The shamesh walked alongside them.

Now that I was safe an even greater wave of fear came over me and my heart raced with a fury I had never known before. I sat down. I couldn't control my palsied legs and shaking hands. I looked at them and willed them still; in vain. The blood pounded in my ears. Although the lions were far away from me, fright and astonishment mingled in my head. I didn't know which emotion to quash first.

To the front of the synagogue walked the shamesh with the lions. After he removed their leashes they leaped up to the top of the Holy Ark. Now smaller and smaller they grew until they shrank to their former size, brown-painted porcelain lions with red bulbs in their mouths.

For the first time K spoke to me. Or maybe it was to the charged air around me.

"They have never threatened anyone before."

"Thank you," I said.

But that was the last thing K said to me. He walked past me and out of the synagogue.

I cried, "Wait!" but he did not turn.

And another Wait! cried out in me. A louder Wait. A Wait that shook the foundations of my being. A word I heard more clearly in echo than in its original sound. "Grandpa." If K is Katya's grandfather, and "Grandpa" wasn't just a term of affection for an older man, much like "Uncle" is for an older family friend, then I was right. Eva was K's wife. But why were they hiding this relationship from me?

Everything is hidden here. Starting with Jiri, yes, my beloved Jiri, who hid from me that he was K's son, to Yossi and Eva, even K himself. Every day a new discovery. Surprises never cease in Prague.

I turned to Katya. “Why did those lions threaten me? I thought I was going to die.”

“This has never happened before.”

Then why did that tram ticket clerk warn me to be careful?

The shamesh approached Katya. He spoke in Czech but kept looking at me.

“He wants to apologize for the lions frightening you,” Katya explained. “It is most unusual, he says. They are usually very good creatures.”

He put out his hand. “Shalom. I am very sorry for incident.”

I answered, “Shalom.” But I did tell Katya, “Remember what the ticket agent said? He must know something.”

Katya was silent. A feeling of unease churned in me. I looked up to the Aron Kodesh, but the lions rested there peacefully, holding the Ten Commandments.

“And the shamesh told me they protect the Jewish people. My stomach is still in knots. And what’s more, Mr. Klein is angry with me.”

“Why?”

What should I say now? How could I answer and still be discreet?

“I wanted to include him, as an older man, with many memories of Prague, in my film on Prague.”

“Don’t worry. He won’t be angry long. Next time you come, bring him a box of dark chocolates. He loves chocolates.”

At the doorway I returned Katya’s beret.

“I heard you calling him Grandpa,” I said, trying to control my tremulous voice, “I didn’t know he’s your grandfather.”

She was still. Maybe it was a family trait to assume a stubborn silence to a question they didn’t want to answer. I felt on edge. A chill in the air.

“So I was right. Eva is related to Mr. Klein. Just as I suspected—she’s his wife.... Why didn’t you say that? Why all the secrecy?”

Katya bit her lips.

“Why don’t you answer me? So he’s your grandfather.”

“No. I just call him that.”

"Why?"

She blew air out of her lips; a kind of sigh. But then she smiled at me. That smile made me feel good. That sudden smile of hers put sunshine into me.

"Out of respect. It's like calling him Uncle. He's been living with my grandmother for so long you expect me to call him Mr. Klein?... And she's not his wife."

I didn't realize we were already on the tram. I had been swept along with the aftereffect of fear and the swirl of astonishment.

"And, anyway," Katya added, "I don't have a grandfather. And I like him. That's another reason I call him Grandpa..." Katya stopped and laughed. "Do you want a fourth reason?" She gave me a happy naughty smile. "If I liked you, I would call you Grandpa too."

34

Resolve and Dissolve

The lions taught me a lesson.

I would leave K alone. Forget about filming him. I had plenty of material for my film about Prague: the Eldridge Street Shul, a bit about Jiri, the statue of the Maharal in Prague, the shamesh, the Altneu Synagogue, the K Museum, Dr. Hruska, Danny K's story about "Metamorphosis," Karoly Graf, Yossi golem, the Schweik statue. I would get Eva to sing that Czech Hanuka song. If I could get her to recreate that Bach gigue with K playing a recording that would be a bonus. Before I filmed Eva singing I would add the house and her living room. Maybe K's room too if he was out. There would be other material, more material. In a supermarket I had discovered a dishwasher liquid called "I Golemu." On the label was a Czech Mr. Clean, the golem himself doing, according to legend, the domestic tasks he had originally been created for in the Maharal's house four hundred years ago. I figured this could be an iconic image, perhaps repeating as a motif between segments.

But that lion lesson was not to last too long. Like an addict, I began yearning quickly. It was a powerful pull, that yearning. As mighty as lust. As strong as love. Stronger than death is love. Stronger than love is ambition. Stronger than ambition is destiny. A few days later, my desire, my ambition to film K returned. Not only did I forget all about the old man's plea to leave him alone, not only did I forget my terror at the open-mouthed lions and my earlier resolve to drop the matter, I redoubled my efforts to capture K on film. He was just too tempting a subject; if I didn't pursue it now, I would regret it forever.

But then a tweak in my heart and I stepped back. I saw the lions again. I stood in the middle of the seesaw. Now I will have to decide. I can't say it came down to either me or him. I don't want to reduce this emotional, ideational turmoil in me to a cops-and-robbers motif. But the truth is it was something like that. I reminded myself of what K said and did regarding giving charity to the beggar near the post office. He argued against it. Why give money to an apparently healthy man who can go out and work? Yet he dropped a coin into his hat anyway. So we are torn. Which way to go? I found myself in a like situation.

If I chose the ethical path, I would let the prize of the millennium slip through my fingers, never to be had again. I wanted to be fair to K, to be considerate, not to make him run away again, to be true to his wishes. After all, it's his life, his secret. What he possessed, right or wrong, was his alone. One man—me!—did not have the right to deprive another human being of his essence, which for K was his privacy. For if I videoed him that's what I would be doing. It would be a kind of theft. No, not a kind of. Outright, downright, inright, not right, plain and simple theft. A thievery of mind.* A deception. I would rob him of something precious he'd been guarding for decades. I'm not saying he didn't tease the public, taking obvious delight in making occasional appearances at K symposia. But if I did what I so badly wanted to do, I would be a robber, a thief, a sneak, a pickpocket, a picksoul—picking at his soul.

And for this there can be no restitution. If you stole five dollars from someone, then regretted it, you could return the five dollars. But if you revealed someone's secret, a secret he'd been carefully guarding, like telling someone he had been adopted if the parents

---

* Which is exactly the phrase in Hebrew, in rabbinic literature: genevat ha-da'at.

didn't want it known, why for that there can be no restitution. Nor for humiliating someone in public. And if I filmed K there would be the accusation of self-aggrandizement under the cloak of historical truthfulness. Coattails fame. Oppportunism. Exploitation. For that there was no rebuttal. Except perhaps to say that even the greatest biographers ride on the coattails of their more famous subjects.

What to do?

What should I do?

I decided to think it over, weigh the pros and cons, for a day or so. Stand on the middle of the seesaw and see which way it would bend.

But I knew very well I was fooling myself. I know, you know, we know, what my decision would be.

35

Exchanging the Secret

We stood in front of her house.

I looked at Katya. She looked at me. Neither of us spoke. But—always a good sign—we did not feel ill at ease in this silence. We were getting to be comfortable with each other and silence sans discomfort is one of the markers.

"I was worried before about Mr. Klein, but I see he has the stamina of a young man.... Do you know who he is?" I said quickly, hoping to trigger an answer from her before she had a chance to think.

"If he lives with my grandmother," said the clever girl, "how shouldn't I know who he is?"

"But *who* is he?"

"I'll tell you." She tapped her forefinger playfully on my chest.

I waited. It would be fascinating to have what I knew confirmed. Otherwise, I was living in a dreamworld. On an island. If only one person knows something it's as if no one knows it.

"He's a wonderful old man."

"Very funny. I don't mean that. I mean: Who *is* he? Really. What is the essence of his is-ness? What's his real name?"

Now Katya stopped, mute. Now she understood the import of my question. Now she understood something she hadn't understood before. Now she realized that I must know something that few others, maybe no one else, knew. Now she didn't say a word.

After a pause, Katya asked lamely:

"Do you know his fake name?"

"No. Or rather, yes. Maybe it's Mr. Klein."

"Did he tell you anything about himself?"

I noticed how carefully she worded that question. As if framed by a trained diplomat. Or a clever lawyer. For she could have asked, but didn't: Did he tell you who he was? But a question like that would have tipped her hand, given more answer in question than an answer itself.

My reply too rode on a tightrope, scrupulously balanced.

"Yes. He introduced himself to me."

"How? Why?"

"I was sent to him," was my response, "through two intermediaries. You may know them or have heard of them: Jiri and Yossi. It took a while but Mr. Klein finally introduced himself. Which, by the way, amazingly, I haven't yet done to you. You still don't know my name and you haven't even asked me once. Do you realize we've met so many times and have now spent a couple of hours together," finally, finally, I thought, "and we still haven't introduced ourselves?"

"My name is Katya Langbrot. And I know your name, for Michele Luongo told me." And she gave a proud little smile. So there, it seemed to say.

"Do you know what my name for you was before I knew your name?"

"What?"

"Girl in the blue beret."

We shook hands—hers was a European woman's handshake, firm, hardy, tough even—with exaggerated formality, as if we were spontaneously satirizing one of mankind's oldest conventions. It took a while for me to let go of her hand.

"If you know who the old man is, tell me," Katya said.

"I don't know if I should."

"Aha, so you don't know after all. So why do you keep coming to visit him?"

"Because I like and have always liked old European Jewish men—and young, pretty women."

She smiled a smile that bridged shy and assured.

"Do *you* know who he is?" I asked.

"Yes," Katya said. "Of course."

"Then tell me."

"I'm not at liberty without his express permission."

"I have an idea," I said. "Since we both know but are afraid to say it, suspecting the other doesn't really know, why don't we both write it down on a piece of paper and exchange notes?"

"Fine," she said.

She took a piece of paper from her pocketbook, gave half to me. She turned her back; I did the same. We exchanged, in ceremonious fashion, almost with little bows, the folded notes.

"Let's open them," Katya said.

We did.

Both papers were blank.

We burst out laughing.

"Looks like someone doesn't trust someone else around here."

"Not me," she said, to another round of laughter. Then added: "Yes." K's yes. A familiar yes.

"This is no good," I said.

Katya agreed.

"Why don't we count to three," she suggested, "and then say his name?"

"Okay. But by now it's obvious we both know it and are not revealing any secrets."

"Okay," she said. "One…two…as soon as I say three, we blurt out his name…three!"

We both opened our mouths as if to draw a deep breath and held back, not even exhaling. I watched the blank O of her lips; she regarded mine, a faint, knowing smile in her long, cat-green eyes.

I shook my head. "This is too frustrating. We need a United Nations intermediary. Someone neutral. With big ears. To this third party we will both whisper the old man's name and he'll write it down and show it to us."

"But then we may have to share a confidence with a stranger that must be kept top secret."

"Right," I said without enthusiasm.

I didn't want this to continue. I was beginning to feel that that special aura between us, that bond I wanted to wrap around us, was becoming frayed. I sensed we were contending. A chill was spreading. I felt it on my skin. A chill different from the one I felt when the lions were at me, but nevertheless a chill.

We still hadn't budged. I looked past her up the sloping street where a grove of trees stood, a miniature wood, a little park where cool breezes blew and from which high vantage point one could see the winding Charles River below. And Katya looked past me down the curving street, with its private two- and three-story houses, not far from the Metro stop. In our immobile state, from far away we must have looked like sculptures.

"You're right," I said. "Here's my last offer. How about this? I promise to write the name the old man gave me on a piece of paper. Do you?"

"I do. Do you really really promise?" Katya asked. "I don't want to be disappointed in you."

"I really really do. And do you promise too?"

"I do. I do. I do."

We exchanged vows—and pieces of paper. And, like in the legend of the Septuagint translation of the Bible from Hebrew to Greek where the translations of all seventy translators matched word for word, here too the names on the paper were exactly the same.

Smiling, laughing, celebrating, happy as if we were long-lost relatives finally meeting for the first time, finally trusting each other, we spontaneously embraced, I pressed my face to hers, smelled her skin, her hair, her beret.

"So he confided in you…I'm impressed. He doesn't do that with anyone. And who are you that you are so privileged to know this astounding secret?"

"I'm the son of Danny K, the other K's favorite showman and, if I remember correctly, your favorite too."

"No. You're Danny K's son? You're not. I can't believe it."

"Neither can I." As I laughed I watched Katya's eyes crinkling with laughter too. "I know," I added. "I'm really honored and privileged. Maybe I'm special." Then I smiled to modify the boast.

"I'm sure he thinks that."

"But now he's angry with me."

"Just remember the dark chocolate…do you like dark chocolate?"

"It's my favorite. And you?"

"I love it. I could eat it all day.… So, remember the dark chocolate. And the fact that he confided in you."

I appreciated her attempt to make me feel better. And if you let me, I thought, you won't ever have to carry signs on your back again.

"Isn't it a miracle?" Katya said, looking dreamingly into my eyes. I had never seen that look, almost intimate, before.

"What is?"

"Everything. Him. Us. Especially him. We're all miracles and mysteries. Like how does one cast away a fatal tuberculosis? How does one survive the Germans? How does one live in the attic of the Altneushul when there is no attic? How does one attain a Biblical old age?"

"How," I continued, "does one turn back raging lions with a wave of a hand?"

"How does one survive with only the golem or ravens feeding you? How does a girl like me earn a living by walking around with a heavy sign on my chest and back advertising concerts and still come home with a smile?"

"Because that lovely smile is an expression of your inner spark…"

She gave me her warm smile. Her eyes drew me and I could sense my eyes warming too.

Katya was right. We are miracles and mysteries.

"A gorgeous Georgian smile," I said.

With my own eyes warming I could not see anything around me except Katya's beautiful face and that lovely dimple just out of view.

"Remember that Papageno doll you sold me?"

"Yes. I saw it on Mr. Klein's desk. You gave it to him."

"Uh-huh. Do you have a female version?"

"You mean a Papagena doll?" Katya asked.

"Yes."

"I think they had one. Why?"

I looked at Katya and smiled. I put my heart into my smile. I said nothing. I didn't have to. Katya understood me.

I didn't feel myself moving closer to her, but before I knew it the eighteen inches between us melted away and my arms were around her and I brought my face close to hers and then I held her face and brought her face to mine and I kissed, oh, for the very first time I kissed those beautiful lips, and her long green eyes became my entire horizon and I felt now her arms around me and we pressed to each other, oblivious of the sidewalk and the house in front of us, and the low flame of my love for her that I had kept tamped down within me burst into full blaze, for she kindled it with her kisses and now it was no longer one-sided anymore, and with the flame two-sided it was now mirror reflected in mirror, with light added to light, and she held my face and kissed my lips, my cheeks, she did not stop kissing my face, singing a little song whose melody I did not know but which was composed of little sighs, little moans, happy moans, strung together like a song, the universal song of lovers in a scale that had no earthly notes.

"I dreamt of this," I told her. "Twice I dreamt of kissing you before we kissed."

"When?"

"Oh, a long time ago."

"Really?"

"Even longer than that."

Now I felt a serenity, a joy I had never known before. I tasted the sweetness of the magic persimmon tree in the heart of the Garden. I saw her. I spoke to her. I wanted her. I lost her. I found her. I found my spark. I had her. What more can a lonely man want who passes through this world once, and only once?

I opened my eyes. She opened hers. We opened our eyes and found ourselves in a new country, green and sweet and full of trees. I had thought the treasure I would find in Prague would be a different treasure.

I told her this and added, "But it turns out you're the treasure. Remember, the first day I saw you on the square you carried a sign that said A Major Discovery. Did you know that you were that discovery? That sign sent me a message and that message turned out to be you."

She smiled, was about to say something, but I continued:

"If you let me," I whispered, for my voice—I could not speak with my normal voice—did not respond to my will, "you will never have to carry those signs again."

She rested her head on my chest. I held her close.

"Only marionettes from now on," I said. "I promise."

Katya shook with laughter, making me shake as well. She looked up to me.

"You know," Katya said, "ever since the last time I saw you, I can't get a picture of you out of my mind. It's as if a little photograph of you is imprinted on my eyelids."

There were tears in her eyes. Then, with two of her fingers, she wiped the tears from mine.

36

Why the Old Man Fled

Katya took me by the hand. "Come, let's go to his room."

She knocked; he opened the door, saw both of us. We stood there, holding hands. He looked down at our hands. I saw the scene clearly, cinematically. He zooms down to our clasped hands which fill the entire screen. I wondered what thoughts were running through his mind at that moment. I couldn't read his face. Was he astonished to see me or annoyed?

"First of all, thanks for rescuing me. And why did you run away from me? I came and you weren't here."

"Do you really want to know?"

K looked at me with his clear blue eyes. I licked my lips. A look of understanding passed between us.

"I didn't want, I don't want to be filmed."

I was grateful to him that he didn't humiliate me in Katya's presence. Instead of berating me for attempting to get Dora's letter he brought up something relatively harmless.

"I'm sorry for being the cause of your flight. It makes me feel terrible."

"You were going to make a film of him? As K? Of K?"

"Yes. I wanted to. Still do," I said with the enthusiasm now drained out of me. "I think it will be astounding. A world success. K lives!"

Katya nodded. "I think it's a wonderful idea, Grandpa. He's a famous filmmaker who has won several international prizes. I'm sure he'll make an excellent film. Don't you think it's time?"

I couldn't believe my luck, Katya's sudden support.

"No, Katya. I want to live out my life the way I want—and not be managed by television people, publicity men, directors, historians, and especially professors who think they understand my work. I have lived this long, following my own path, and I want to continue that way. Once it's known that I'm alive—and if it is believed—I will never again have a peaceful day. American television, radio, Israeli television, Russian, Czech, Slovak, France, England. I can go down an alphabetical list of the world atlas. Constant cameras. You will deprive me of tranquility. Who knows what the strain can do to me? It will be the end of me. I know it. Think about that."

"But suppose we won't say where you live?"

"It will never work. People will recognize me. I don't want to be discovered again."

I looked at Katya as I directed my question to K: "Don't you have a sense of history?"—hoping for more support from her. But now she was silent.

"Don't you have a sense of ambition?" K asked me.

"You didn't use a pseudonym."

"Yes."

"Like you," and for the first time I addressed him by his first name, "I too love myths. And I want to share them."

"For personal gain, money, ego, fame."

"Publication is ambition," I reminded him.

He agreed. He nodded. He said, "Yes."

"I would be willing to remove my name from the credits. Like you see in novels sometimes written by Anonymous."

K looked down at the floor. He was saying no with his head.

"Please tell me, what's wrong with letting the world know?"

"You don't understand. I placed limits on my ego. You know that I forbade further publication. I willed that Brod burn my manuscripts."

"You knew, and scholars for the past seventy years have also come to the same conclusion. You knew that Brod would never carry out that wish.... And from decade to decade you watched your fame grow."

I looked at Katya as I said this, noting that I scored a point.

"Yes."

"And even forbidding publication is ego of a different kind."

He didn't say Yes; he didn't say No. Maybe he agreed. Then, looking at me, not with reprimand, but with a kind of neutral tone, he said:

"I see you like to play with words."

"Like father, like son. My father too liked to play with words." I took hold of his hands, noted again the long slim fingers. "It's for you. Don't you understand? Not for me. I want you to get the Nobel Prize. The whole world will give you a standing ovation. What's more, it would help explain to yourself why you did what you did. And if you have regrets it would help undo your regrets."

"No and no. I do not want it."

I looked quickly at Katya. She made a face that said: What can I do?

"I have to run off now." She looked at her watch. "My train leaves in an hour."

"Wait," I cried. "When again?"

"Next Wednesday, at noon, here. I have to go back home to my parents in Brno for a few days."

She kissed K on the cheek. I wondered if she would kiss me too. And at once she did.

I turned to K and said, "Excuse me for a minute," and I walked out with Katya.

In the corridor I held her in my arms, looked into her long green eyes, and said:

"I have to tell you this. Every time I leave you I take a little piece of you with me and I leave a little piece of myself with you."

"That's so sweet," she said.

"You like that, huh?"

"Yes."

Katya stopped and smiled. She was touched by that sort of romantic remark, one that was foreign to my nature but which this lovely girl inspired in me. I, who was so hesitant to articulate feelings, with her the floodgates of words were suddenly thrown open and two unabridged thesauri of sentiments ready to use rode like epaulettes on my shoulders.

Writing this takes longer than the thought, for hardly had I time to gratulate myself on my endearing and perhaps even original formulation than Katya said in a sparkly voice:

"Then pretty soon all of me will be with you, and all of you will be with me, so in order to know who's who we will have to negotiate a prisoner exchange."

Then, reading my expression—I didn't have to say, Don't make fun of my tender feelings, words I indeed held myself back from saying—seeing that her flip remark had taken the wind out of me, Katya said, "I'm just kidding." She hugged me and pressed her face to mine and said, "I'm sorry," so softly I could hardly hear her. "I can't wait for next Wednesday."

She kissed me on the lips, then went, I could have sworn she was sailing, out the door. I returned to K and begged his pardon once more.

Seven days. I'd have to wait seven days to see Katya again. And a sour taste in my mouth spread to my heart. But then at once I berated myself. You fool, thank God you found the girl in the blue beret at your doorstep. Thank God you are one of the few people on Earth who knows this twentieth-century icon is alive.

Bow your head in gratitude, I commanded myself.

And I listened to the voice within me.

"Why are you bowing your head?"

"Because I am thankful I met you, and I'm thankful I met Katya. I'm grateful to have met Jiri and Yossi and Eva. And how lucky I am to discover Katya at your house."

"If you are happy, I am happy too."

Yes, I was happy, but my nervous system was still on edge, as if a vibrato voice were thrumming inside me. The image of the lions with their huge jaws open kept returning like an unwanted ad on the screen of my mind. I wondered if K thought about this too. Why is it that the same picture is larger than life in one man's imagination and soon forgotten in another's?

"Tell me, please. Why did those lions attack me? My insides are still quivering."

"Because."

"Because?"

"Because they felt threatened."

I began laughing, part amused laughter, part sarcastic.

"They? Those huge lions felt threatened? By me? I thought they protect the Jewish people."

"I'm Jewish too," K said. "They felt threatened for me. They also protect me."

"From what?"

"From outside incursion. You see, they sensed you wanted something of mine that I wasn't prepared to give you. But—"

K stopped, as if cut off in mid-word.

He smiled.

"But now I am."

My heart leaped. My prayers answered. Katya *and* the video.

"Where are you running?"

"To get my camera."

"No no no. Not that. It's something else I had in mind. We'll talk about it when Katya comes back."

Maybe, I figured, he's relenting on Dora's letter. My heart surged. The fear running through me like an alternating current abating. Good. Everything will work out.

"Tell me, dear K," I said in a friendly, almost pleading tone, "now that we're alone, tell me why did you really run away? I mean, you could have just refused to see me."

"Uh-huh."

"What do you mean by that?" I said impatiently.

"Other things happened because of that." K brightened suddenly. "You'll admit it was not a wasted day after all.... The synagogue and..." He gestured to the spot where Katya had stood, a sly, conspiratorial smile in his eyes.

"You planned it? Purposely?" I couldn't help blurting out.

"Yes."

"How did you know what I would do?"

"Do I not know you, my dear boy? We have spent quite a bit of time together, don't you think?" There was a warm, almost fatherly, golden glow in his clear blue eyes as he said this. I thought he would put his hands on my shoulders and embrace me. "I knew you would try to find me, and Eva kept you here as long as she could until Katya was ready to leave."

"Thank you. Thank you so much." I stopped, swallowed, then came out with, "But I still—"

"I'm sorry. Please understand. I would like to help you, but as much as I like you I cannot go against my own nature."

"All right," I said half-heartedly.

"Sometimes I see things differently. If you read my work, I'm sure you are aware of that. Like Paul Klee's famous *Window Display for Lingerie*, where a highly stylized woman with a helmet hat is seen from the front from her knees up, yet from the knees down, as one can tell by the seams and the back of her high high heels, she is facing the other way. That is how I sometimes see things."

"In imagination or reality?"

"Yes."

I looked at him.

"It's the same thing, isn't it?" K said.

And then I said something absurd, to match the Klee painting. "And that's how you get out of your trouser leg you've put your wrong foot into, right?"

"Correct."

"You become the Klee model and simultaneously face forward and back, a Janus in half a pair of trousers."

K began chuckling. "You are quite clever, my boy."

I just was hoping, praying that K wouldn't now say to me: Now, promise me, my boy, that you will no longer pursue the idea of a film.

I would not have been able to make, or keep, that promise. But I wanted so badly to keep my other promise. To return Jiri's letter.

If only K would leave the room. And at once he seemed to read my mind, that darling man.

"Please excuse me for a moment."

As soon as the door closed, I replaced Jiri's letter in the drawer. At once departed the halo of heat around my pocket, gone the stone about my neck and the unease pulsing in my heart.

37

Calling Luongo

Things have got to get moving, I thought. I've been here long enough. I felt I was that eponymous Russian character, Oblomov, taking sixty-seven pages to get out of bed. Time was flowing over me, both quickly and slowly, as if I were atoms in some string-theory experiment, where opposite and contradictory physical laws shared the same space. I was in a slow-motion film where everything proceeded lugubriously, and yet my kinship with K was rushing forward like a raft on churning whitewater. To what else can I compare this odd feeling? I'm on a high-speed train, the countryside a blur. Still, I walk slowly, hesitantly, from one end of the lounge car to the other.

I had a plan. At first it was like an invisible seed, a nanoscopic thread. But like undersoil growth, little by little, in the tiniest of increments, it grew. Of course, I had been vaguely aware of the plan all along; it danced somewhere in the behind-the-curtains recesses of my mind. Then leaped out. Video him. Sew a small video camera inside my baseball cap, like something out of a *Future Science* comic strip from years ago, or maybe what CIA operatives use today—but decided against it. Tricking K in his own home wasn't right.

But despite his impassioned plea, I decided to go ahead. To bow to the pressure of history. If I am a burglar, a bandit, a cheat, I thought, I would also be considered burglar, bandit, and cheat if I cheated posterity of this amazing turn in history. And I would be remiss to historical truth—another ethical flaw—if I did not let the world know what I knew.

I loved K. I loved him very much. But I would have to hurt him. And even though Katya had supported me, I would not tell her what I planned to do.

Everyone and everything I needed was out there, waiting for me to film. K and me, Michele Luongo, the vegetarian restaurant, all pieces in a scattered jigsaw puzzle. But the final picture, solid, neat, colorful, was in my head. Needed were a few moves to pick up the pieces and put them in place.

K waited 110, almost 111 years, for me. How much more could he wait? How much more could *I* wait? My time in Prague was not infinite. I knew what I had to do.

First, I visited K. When I entered, Eva thought the box of Godiva chocolates I held was for her and began thanking me, effusively too (had Katya spoken to her, told her all?). I felt my face flushing as I told her it was for Mr. Klein.

"If you like chocolate, I'll bring you a box next time."

"Oh, I love chocolate. Dark. We all do. It's one of the secrets for a long, healthy life."

"I'm sure Mr. Klein will share with you."

Eva laughed. "Oh, I don't know about that." Then, shifting gears, added, "But perhaps he will."

I knocked on K's door. I handed him the chocolates.

"Mmm, Godiva!" he exclaimed.

I marveled that this late-nineteenth-century man knew about Godiva.

"Yes. For you. With my renewed apologies."

"All right, my boy. I don't like anger. I prefer love and affection. But I don't like to be disappointed in someone either."

I looked K in the eye. "Who does?" I said mechanically, but in my mind other words were flashing, repeating: I found her. I found Katya. Right here. Coming out of this house.

I put my hands on K's shoulders. "Let's celebrate our reconciliation. Here's an idea. We have never gone out together. I'd like to take you to a nice vegetarian restaurant."

For some reason K looked at his watch. "Not today."

"Not today," I repeated enthusiastically, glad he had agreed in principle, and gladder he didn't say, Fine, let's go now. "I'll make a reservation to be sure we have a nice private table. I'll call you when I arrange it."

As I left I heard him say something in Czech to Eva. Since I understood the word "chokolat," I assumed he was asking her to come and taste.

I didn't wait until I got back to the hotel. I began dialing as soon as I stood outside. I called Michele Luongo, praying I wouldn't have to leave a message. Luckily, he picked up on the first ring. I told him I wanted his help. He would be paid, of course. At first, he refused to accept money, but I said I won't continue unless he takes a fee. But he would have to get another cameraman as a backup. In case something went wrong. They would do only video, no sound. I would handle the audio.

I thought it was rather clever to separate the two and thereby preserve my secret and K's as well.

Then I went to the restaurant and spoke to the owner, Pavel, a big, fleshy man, not the sort you'd expect to run a vegetarian restaurant. The physical layout there was perfect. The dining area was on the ground floor. Steps led up to a half balcony to accommodate overflow crowds or a private party. I offered Pavel money to erect a wooden partition with a little hole by the overhang side of the balcony, behind which a photographer would stand with a video camera.

The jigsaw puzzle was taking shape. I hadn't been so busy in years. Sailing with energy. My feet touched the ground as I moved, but I felt—like Reb Nachman of Bratslav in the novel *The Man Who Thought He Was Messiah*—I was levitating. So many people to see, so many things to arrange. Soon all the pieces would be locked in place. The cost was high but miniscule compared to the return.

I met Michele and his colleague at the restaurant to show them where they would stand.

"Day after tomorrow, I'm going to interview a friend of mine, a shy, elderly man, about his wartime experiences.... You met him. So don't be surprised when you see him. It's the old man I jokingly said was my grandfather and you said was more likely my father. I'll be here at 1 p.m., when it's less crowded. But you guys should come forty, forty-five minutes earlier to set up. You see that partition on the balcony? Michele, that's where you'll be. There's a little hole in the wood for the camera lens. And you, excuse me, what's your name?"

"Johnny."

"Johnny, see the cashier? There will be a long black curtain hanging there next to him, with a little slit. From behind it you'll also secretly video our table."

"How long will you talk to him?" Michele asked.

"About an hour, maybe more. I won't rush it. And when we finish, we'll both get up and leave—without talking to you. Michele, I will call you later that day."

"Fine. And throughout the meal, you want us to just keep filming."

"Right, I'll have the old man facing you. You can focus on close-ups of the old man, keeping me out of the film. Johnny, you can zoom in on hand movements, facial expressions. You'll have a lateral view of him. Afterwards, I'll edit and mix.... Oh yeah, I almost forgot. There will be an *International Herald Tribune* on the table. I'll fold it to reveal the date. Make sure you zoom in on it, so that the date of the paper is perfectly visible."

Don't think that my heart wasn't palpitating with fear. Don't think that a sour feeling of guilt, gall rising in my throat, didn't wash over me like an unwanted ablution. But, on the other hand, I didn't hesitate for one moment. Understand the conflicting feelings within me. Tricking the old man, betraying him again, luring him, stealing him—yes, to all of these. But overriding all this was truth, responsibility to history, devotion to literature, the journalistic, the artistic, imperative. K's story, his existence, had to be told. Believe me, it wasn't vanity or opportunism, not riches nor overweening ambition that made me want to film him. I merely wanted this miracle to be preserved forever.

Can you imagine meeting the legendary K, long thought dead, and *not* recording this historic moment, not preserving this golden slice of time for posterity? *That* would be a crime. Filming him wasn't a crime. Doing nothing was the crime. Like chucking the only extant photograph of Columbus as he set sail, or the one video of George Washington taking his oath of office. We owe a debt to history, don't we? Each of us is a little thread of history, making up the grand tapestry that is the story of the civilized world. Take out, or omit, a thread, and history begins to unravel.

38

Filming in Restaurant

I called for K in a taxi. The driver, a typical Prague cabbie, sped ahead quickly and furiously. I had to shout, Slow down! At times he seemed to round corners on two wheels. I put my hand out in front of K's chest to protect him from sudden stops. During the twelve-minute odyssey a wild thought came to me. It showed how agitated, hyper, I was. I should have been in heaven, calm in Paradise, after sealing my relationship with Katya. But I wasn't. I didn't consciously put her out of my mind; she just slipped further back while I was planning the K video. A startling inner voice, maybe like the ones madmen hear, was sounding a question akin to the dumb one grownups ask a child: Who do you like better, your father or your mother? But that question was no match to the one that flew into my head: If you had to choose only one, would it be Katya or the film?

Of course it was a foolish question. Dumb and idiotic. Stupid too. Everything was set for the video, and Katya and I had hit it off. My finding her in K's house, and related to Eva, was not only a miracle, it also signaled that K and she were mine. So how could such an absurd, unrealistic question come to me? But my unknown interlocutor insisted: choose.

I hesitated.

The question pressed like a migraine. And you know what? I had to answer.

And the atoms running helter-skelter in place made me say, I have to make a triage, and I shouted silently into the void, scattering the demons:

The film.

Then another thought slid in on the slippery coattails of my reply: Who knows? Perhaps for my hubris I'll get nothing.

Not this, not that. Not her, not him.

The taxi stopped in front of the restaurant.

We entered. Good. The lunch-hour rush was over. Again that sour taste in back of my throat. I couldn't hear but sensed the buzz of the hidden cameras over the soft hum of conversations at a few tables. The black curtain hung next to the cashier. On the balcony, the wooden partition was in place. As K sat down I patted my jacket pocket where the microcassette recorder was hidden. I scratched my chest to hit the start button.

"How nice," I said. "They prepared a paper for us." And I held it to reveal the date. "Do you get the *International Herald Tribune*?"

"Sometimes I read it in the library."

K turned to the menu and I put the paper away.

"So many interesting dishes," he said.

"Have you been here before?"

He shook his head. "I rarely go out to eat."

"But you do go out? I remember seeing you once at the concert at the Dvořák Hall."

"Oh, yes. For concerts and plays, yes."

Then I shifted at once to the topic at hand.

"Didn't you used to go with Brod to little resorts in the countryside when you were younger, or go out with him to restaurants?"

K's face blanched. He turned this way and that, afraid that someone may have overheard the question which would somehow compromise his identity.

"Don't worry," I said softly, "no one hears us and no one here would know who Brod is."

K leaned forward. "Then at least say 'Max,' if you mention him again."

I nodded, delighted with this little unexpected interlude. It was a kind of proof that K was who he said he was, that he was still protecting his identity.

"Yes," K said. "We did go to resorts and, during the years I knew Max, we would go to some vegetarian restaurants."

"What years was that?"

"From 1903, I would say, when we studied at the university."

"Was Max a vegetarian?"

K laughed. "He was when he was with me."

"Do any of those restaurants still exist?"

"I doubt it. But some were around till before World War II."

The waiter brought our dishes. We ate in silence. K had ordered a lentil soup and stir-fry vegetables and I a lima bean soup, spinach quiche, and salad. K ate with appetite and commented how good, how inventive was the fare. Like old friends, we exchanged little portions from each other's plates.

While planning this lunch I have the outré idea of inviting Karoly Graf and introducing him to K. This is the man, Mr. Klein, who claims he is K's son. Tell it to him, Mr. Graf. I imagine this scene so powerfully I convince myself I'm filming it and when Karoly bares his left arm and lifts up his shirt and shows his brown birthmark to the left of his navel, just below the rib cage—I'm watching K's face while Graf is speaking—I notice that K's face pales and his hands involuntarily go from the table to his stomach as if to protect that part of his body from a sudden attack, a surprise lifting of his shirt that would show the very same birthmark on his abdomen. And I wonder if nurse Miriam Graf, Karoly's mother, had intentionally nudged Dora Diamant to leave the sanatorium and return home.

For my film, revealing that Mr. Klein was K wouldn't come at the outset. The discovery—just like my own—would come slowly. Yes, the film was a documentary, but its structure, its aesthetics, would be like fiction, a gradual revelation.

I didn't look up once to Luongo or Johnny. I was confident they were doing their job.

As the videos were rolling I started imagining. Then I held myself back. No, I would not imagine. I would not project. I won't be like that musicology instructor I once read about, who saw himself on page one of the *New York Times* for discovering the original music of the Hebrew alphabet before he even saw one page of the manuscript. I didn't want to raise my hopes beyond the fact that two cameras were working and I had K before me.

Until I had the video in my hands, I wouldn't have the film. And I wouldn't have the video until I viewed it and saw it was done, finished, the task accomplished, K's famous life and story imprinted forever in color. Only then would I feel secure, confident, happy, delirious.

I began to talk to K about Jiri. Later, I would interpolate some remarks of my own about him.

"Do you have an extra photo of Jiri that you can spare?"

"I'll find one for you."

Super. That meant I'd have Jiri in my film too, and not only my remarks about him.

I was about to ask K how many children he had but some self-censor in me aborted the question. I turned to some crucial events in his life, asking him to describe his feelings during these important turning points. I accented feelings, for I didn't want him to say, But I already told you these stories. And so K narrated the stories once more for me.

He told me about the magical encounter with the curtain of the Holy Ark in the Altneushul and that electric jolt that he believed cured him. Then I asked him how he felt about staging his own death and how he told the news to his parents and what thoughts ran through his mind at his funeral.

I couldn't believe this was happening. K's story was being taped and filmed. I was recording every word he said. He spoke of Max Brod, the sanatorium, an occasional K Conference that amused him. He spoke of artistic drive and the lack of it that swept over him during his second life. He spoke of the joy of keeping his identity secret.

K was telling me stories I had heard before but enjoyed hearing a second time for the video. But one was totally new for me. It balanced out the moral quandary. For that story alone I would have sold my conscience.

Here is how it began.

39

About Dora

I was dying to ask K about Dora Diamant. I've already noted how much I regretted, for his sake—I felt as if it had happened in my own family—what he had lost: no wife, no children with her, the things he wanted most in this world, even more than writing and publication. And since he couldn't achieve what he really wanted to achieve, what good was the achievement he had achieved without really wanting it?

How to go about asking K? I wondered. What approach to use? Start subtly? Or proceed circuitously. Then I decided: the direct approach is the best approach. I took a deep breath and said:

"Tell me about Dora Diamant."

"Yes," K said.

If his other Yeses were in C major, this one was in C minor. It didn't have the spectrum of possibilities and infinities of nuance that he usually compressed into that monosyllable.

K did not look surprised. He apparently wanted to talk and was just waiting for the opportunity.

When K began, I felt a shiver rolling over me, a wave of sensation shaped like those crisscrossed long waves we used to draw as kids in penmanship exercises.

"What's the matter? Are you all right?" K leaned forward. "You look startled."

"I'm okay."

"I saw your skin moving. Most extraordinary."

"The skin and body act on their own. For instance, you can't control blushing. The body does what it does in response to outer stimuli."

"But why the fear and trembling as soon as I mentioned Dora? One might almost think you were in love with her yourself."

Again an unusual feeling enveloped me. This time it was a swirl of dizziness, as though I were just coming to after being sedated.

K looked at me as if awaiting a reply. What had he asked? Then the last words of his remark echoed in my mind.

"I was in love with her for you. If you know what I mean."

"Yes."

"Reading the biography I kept rooting for both of you to fulfill your destiny."

"Kabbalists say there are many sparks in the world, as many sparks as stars in the sky, and only one of these sparks, a fragment of the Divine Name, is your spark. But with faith and determination, that spark can be yours."

He stopped for a moment, then continued:

"Do you know she survived the war in England, my darling Dora?"

"Yes. I read that. I read all about you and her. Isn't it amazing how books permit you to climb into a person's head?"

"Yes."

He looked over my shoulder, as if for a cue—perhaps, who knows? someone did signal him to continue. I looked up and back at the wooden partition behind which Michele Luongo was standing, filming everything we were doing.

"All right," K said, as if concluding at that moment to reveal what he hadn't thought of revealing before. "I'll tell you a fascinating story."

I felt the tension in me ebbing, my nervousness about broaching the subject of Dora melting away. An air of calm and satisfaction encompassed me. The sun streamed through the restaurant windows. I was in a different world. Happy, at ease. I was filming this. I looked down upon myself from some empyrean height. This was as incredible as K's life itself. The happiness buzzed in my capillaries. I had not a care in the world.

"I already told you that every year, on my yorzeit, on the day the world assumes I died, I go to my gravesite to visit the poor man, Johann Eck, who died alone, without kin, without even a name on his tombstone. I go early in the morning before others come, because others do come, to place flowers by the tombstone. They come to show that K hasn't been forgotten. And I come to show that Johann hasn't been forgotten. I come early and say Kaddish for poor Eck and I light a yorzeit candle for him at home."

I admired K for his faithfulness, for his devotion to the lonely man who died with another's name. I was about to ask him what connection this had with Dora when he surprised me.

"A few years after the war, I think it was in 1950, early in June, around the time of my yorzeit, I saw a news item in the Prague daily that Dora Diamant, once the fiancée of K, was visiting Prague and staying at the Parizska Hotel. I was astounded. I read the item a dozen times to make sure my eyes were not deceiving me. But it was so. Dora Diamant in Prague. Dora alive! I had not known she survived. I thought she and her entire family were victims of the thorough German killing machine in Poland."

"My God, you hadn't seen her in twenty-six years. What did you do?"

"Believe me, I was torn. I felt myself tearing in two, like a piece of paper, and both pieces of paper were me. The love of my life. Young as she was, the only woman I felt absolutely comfortable with. But she was torn from me and I closed the book on her. Should I tear open an old wound?"

Yes, I almost cried out.

"Notice how often the word 'torn' appears in my thoughts, and in how many variations. I imagined myself going to her hotel room, introducing myself. She doesn't believe me. I tell her what happened, the first person outside my immediate family with whom I share the news. She still doesn't believe me. As you didn't believe me. Which is natural, quite natural. I understand. I mention names of nurses at the sanatorium we both knew. She looks at me bewildered. How can this man remember so many names? she thinks. And how does he know all this? This is where my fantasy ends. I was tempted to go to the hotel and ask for her but I didn't go."

Why? Why? I hold myself back from shouting. I have to grip the edge of the chair with both hands and press hard to keep my lips sealed. Why did you do that? Destiny must play itself out. The huge maw of destiny must be fed, its hunger assuaged, its great thirst slaked. Go for it, K! Please go for it!

"Why are you so agitated? You look uncomfortable, distressed."

"I'm rooting for you. For her. For both of you. Go. Go for it, K. Please!"

"We cannot undo the past."

"We certainly can. Films reshape the past."

"Films preserve. They change nothing."

"Fiction reshapes the past."

"Has it brought back one of the murdered?"

We both were silent.

Then I said, "Your life, rebirth, is a shaping of the past."

"It's all academic. What happened happened. Listen."

"You don't know how badly I want you and Dora to reunite," I interjected. "I feel it in my blood and bones, in my marrow and in my soul."

K gave a little smile. With both palms he brushed down his mustache and Van Dyke.

"You are a good Liebes Direktor, a good manager of love."

"I always thought of your love as the love affair of the twentieth century. K and Dora, the love affair that could have been but never was."

K drank some water. He put the glass down and then drank again.

"Common wisdom has it that, despite Proust, the past cannot be recaptured. Especially in my case, after the great divide of my death.

But you know the expression, '*Der mentch tracht un Gott lacht*'? Literally, man thinks and God laughs. Or to make it rhyme in English: Man proposes, God disposes."

"I remember Jiri also using that phrase in New York."

K laughed. "You see. It shows he's my son."

He closed his eyes for a moment. As old as he was there was not a wrinkle on his smooth face. But I think I've mentioned that before. So what? An important observation can be repeated. Alexander Pope said it better in a rhymed couplet but I can't recall it now. In any case, I wondered what thoughts were going through K's head. Was he reliving his imaginary encounter with Dora? Perhaps after my provocation regretting he didn't make the one move he could have made—to retrieve his spark, take that short ride to destiny on the Metro from his house to the Parizska Hotel, just down the block from the Altneushul, another destiny-laden landmark in his life, and reintroduce himself to Dora? It would have been hard but I was sure the spark of love between them could have been reignited. How many regrets can a man bear without battering his heart?

"For some reason I cannot now recall," K continued, "on the day of my yorzeit I didn't visit the gravesite early. I usually went at eight, or half after eight the latest. But that day I arrived close to ten, fearful I would encounter several people who would intrude upon my private meditation. Remember, I passed myself off as my second cousin, Philippe Klein, who had always resembled me. Isn't it strange, my sisters didn't look at all like me; my first cousins didn't look like me, but my father's first cousin, Flora, who also didn't look like a K, had a son I had never met—he lived in Hamburg, then migrated in 1935 to Sweden—and it was family saga, and pictures proved it, that he resembled me.

"As I approached my tombstone I saw a figure crouching down, holding two roses. I looked closer. It was a woman. And once again I felt that electric shock in me. Could it be? For a moment I thought of fleeing."

"No, no," I shouted. "Stay." I saw heads turning in the restaurant.

"But I felt I had become a tree," K said. "Immobile. Rooted. I took all the air of the cemetery into my lungs. Although I could have backed away I did not. Because I realized now it was fated that we meet. Hearing someone approaching, the woman rose.

"Dora," I said, this time trying not to attract the attention of the few other patrons.

And K repeated:

"'Dora,' I said.

"The woman looked at me. She rose from her kneeling position.

"'Are you not Dora?'"

K closed his eyes, continued his narration, reading his script.

"'Do I know you?' she said.

"'I will answer in Jewish fashion with another question. How can I not know you? How can I forget you, Dora Diamant, daughter of Mendl Diamant, follower of the Gerer rebbe?'

"'Who?' Her voice in tremor; fear quavered in her voice. The woman looked around for other people. But there were no other people. 'Who…are…?' Her voice in trembling was altered, higher pitched; a thin, frightened bird was her voice. 'Who…are…you?' she asked. But she knew. I sensed it. Deep down she knew.

"Was it her words that made me think of a wind blowing through the cemetery, or was there really a wind? There should have been a wind. It would have been fitting had there been a wind.

"'Don't you know me, Dora?' The word 'darling' was bubbling on my lips but I was afraid to say it. How I wanted to say it. How at that moment I was overwhelmed with the miracle of her life and of our meeting and the love I had for her flowing in my veins like another magical elixir. 'Have I changed that much from the days in the sanatorium, Dora Diamant?'

"The woman's eyes fluttered. Her head sank to her chest. Slowly her legs buckled. 'Water, water,' I cried. But no one was about. Neither person nor water. Just the chill wind blowing between the tombstones. But I caught her in time. I caught her before she fell. I caught her and held her in my arms like a baby.

"I said, 'Dora, Dora,' several times. 'Dora, Dora,' I sang to her. She opened her eyes.

"'Is it…? Can it…? No, it cannot. Go away, ghost. Return, dybbuk, to your rest.' And her eyes, I saw the whites of her eyes. I tried to stand her up. She seemed to look right through me.

"'It is me,' I said. 'Don't be afraid. I'm alive.'

"'You died,' she said in a hoarse whisper. 'A ghost. He-elp! I'm seeing a ghost.'

"'No.' What could I do? I pinched my cheek. 'See? Flesh and blood. I'm alive.'

"Now we both sat on the ground, on my grave, near the tombstone.

"'How can it be?' she said. 'It was in the newspapers, Brod sent them to me.'

"'I will explain,' I told her. 'But not here. Let's go back to your hotel.' She was so overcome she didn't even ask me how I knew this. 'I'll tell you everything. When I finish you will know that K is alive.'"

K opened his eyes.

Knowing he was quite adept at this, I said, "And you obviously proved it to her."

"Of course. In her room. She recognized me."

"How did you do it? Same way you did with me?"

"No, no. With Dora it was different. I won't go into details. But you know from fairy tales and folktales that princesses or lost children are recognized by some special sign; for instance, birthmarks."

Again I felt I was trembling. Birthmark. Karoly Graf.

"What kind of birthmark? Where?"

"I would rather not discuss that."

"How clever," I said. "How fascinating. How lovely. A birthmark. A storybook ending with a writer using a storybook motif."

K took a deep breath. "A storybook, yes. An ending, yes."

"So destiny played itself out. The sought-for spark."

"Yes. Dora and I did get together." Now K's eyes lit up. For a moment he looked years younger. Then he said somewhat shyly, "We were married that day."

In my joy, in my naiveté, I exclaimed:

"On such short notice you got a rabbi to come?"

K laughed. "You silly boy. Did Abraham have a rabbi when he took Sarah? Did a Herr Rabbiner officiate when Isaac brought Rebecca into his tent? Jacob waited seven years for his Rachel. I waited nearly sixty-seven for mine..."

In my happiness for him, for them, I jumped up, ran around the table, and hugged K.

"Hooray! And the audience leaps to its feet and cheers the lovers, happy for the happy ending."

"Happy ending? Not quite," K said. "But it was worth dying to spend those five days with her." Now a rueful smile was more in his eyes than on his lips. "But not quite a happy ending. Her Hebrew name was Ra-ch-el."

Saying her name, K's voice caught. A sob slid in between the letters of her name. It was the first time I saw K sad. He looked down at the restaurant's old oaken floor, as if slowly reading letters on a tombstone. Still, I didn't follow.

"And you never saw her again?"

"I didn't say that."

"Did Dora remain with you?"

K's voice was a whisper, as if afraid it would break if he spoke louder. I leaned forward to hear every word.

"Her trip to Prague that year, in June 1950, was only for a few days. She had to return to London, where she was caring for an elderly aunt, repaying her kindness in sending an affidavit in 1938 for residence in England, thereby saving her life.... But the following year she returned. Meanwhile, Dora's aunt had passed away."

K broke off. He shook his head, driving away the thoughts he was reading inside his head. He closed his eyes. "I cannot tell you anymore."

"I'm so glad she came back to Prague." I pressed K's hand. I felt the warmth, the sadness, wafting like a small cloud from him. "Did she ever marry?"

"Never," he said. And then he dropped his voice again and whispered, "Her Hebrew name was Rachel."

I stopped. I cupped my ears. But he told me that already. At first I didn't understand. My happiness for K and for the destined Dora-K (re)union made me too thick to penetrate the hint.

I looked at the old man. He sat in his chair, hunched, his face fallen. His plate, empty of food, looked so pathetic. K resembled a balloon with the air draining slowly out of it. Was I witnessing the ebbing of K? His second death?

He gazed at me, breathing evenly. To my unspoken question, Are you all right? he nodded.

Only when he added an Aramaic phrase, "*Die le-khakima be-remeeza,*" with its inadvertent English pun, and translated it as "A hint to the wise suffices" did I finally understand.

Dora was pregnant.

"And the child?"

"It lived," he said. "A precious child. The child that almost never was. The child who, like Dora and me, defied history."

I stood. "Excuse me," I said. "I have to step outside for a minute." And I said it loudly enough for Michele Luongo to hear me. As I passed the cashier, I said to Johnny behind the black velvet curtain, "I'm coming back in a minute."

I stepped out of the restaurant into the street and breathed out a heavy sigh. A host of opposing emotions gyrated in me: rain and shine, up and down, left and right, glad and sad churned until the edges were fuzzed and they all jumbled together like wash in a dryer. The fresh air cleared the haze in me. I looked at the flower boxes hanging on the windows of the restaurant. The reds and whites and yellows of the blooms cheered me. From the roof swallows flew and darted, chirped their calls, singing their songs. In my sigh I sucked in the breath of life and joy that follows weeping. K and Dora had come together; they had defied destiny. They had outwitted the Germans' decree. There was joy and there was grief and, like in Samson's riddle—out of the strong came forth the sweet—there was life.

I finally understood K's hint.

In dying, Dora had brought life into the world. She lived as Dora, died like the biblical Rachel, giving birth at forty-four.

40

Filming, Continued

I returned to the table, drank some water, and continued as if there had been no interruption.

"Tell me, please, did you ever show anyone who you are like you showed me?"

"Never. To no one.... But you I wanted to show, to prove, who I am."

"Why?"

He didn't answer.

I didn't press. Silence was a magnificent answer too.

But he didn't speak of his children. He never said, "My son," or, "My sons."

While K sat there, occasionally sipping water, images of him, permanent images of K, in color, were being created. And on two cameras too. This is why I had been drawn to Prague, yes, drawn in the mystical, kabbalistic sense of the word, as though some emanation of spirit had sucked me Pragueward. To meet K in person and make this film. To astound the world.

I decided the title would be *K's Son*. A title is a magnet. It attracts attention and intrigues critics and viewers. *K's Son* would be for me what *Lolita* was for Nabokov, *Catch-22* for Joseph Heller. My groundbreaking creation.

But as I spoke to K, it dawned on me that all the pieces did not fit. There was an enigma in his life. Something hidden he was not telling me. What had he done all these years? How did this creative man spend his time? He must have written. I was sure of that. Seventy years without a manuscript? Impossible. There had to be a treasure of his manuscripts waiting to be revealed—in the attic, in the Aron Kodesh, somewhere—with instructions to his family to have them published after his death.

So I asked K bluntly, without preambles or excuses or hesitant politesse, not building up to it slowly like a prosecuting attorney carefully presenting his argument and then, like a serpent, springing the trap question that confounds the accused. No. It was done without subtlety. I didn't say, Have you written? I took it as a given.

"May I see," I asked, "some of the manuscripts you've written over the years?"

He didn't say:

I don't have any.

He didn't say:

There are no manuscripts.

He didn't say:

What are you talking about?

He didn't say:

I told you I stopped writing.

There are lots of things he didn't say. Pages and pages of blank pages he didn't say.

Instead, surprising me, as I had surprised him, K said:

"No."

I had never seen him looking so tough, hard, obdurate, determined. That No chiseled in stone. A cold "No" sculpted in ice. An acid "No" etched on metal. An iron refusal in his eyes. An iron glint that sent out tiny ferrous rays. Rays that hexed me. That paralyzed. Little ferrous rays that wound around my wrists until I heard a metallic click.

I was unable to say, Why?

Unable to utter: I knew it all along.

"And you asked me this once before." Great plains, vast spaces, stretched between each adamantine word.

My heart trembled; no doubt his too. We stared unwavering into each other's eyes until we no longer could stand the intensity of the other's gaze. Then both of us sighed.

I remembered we were filming all this.

It pained me having to fool the old man. Even Michele Luongo and Johnny didn't know the truth; only a faint glimmer of it. The scenario I had concocted was like a perfect spy story. No one knew all the details—some people knew nothing; some, part of the puzzle. Only I knew every detail.

For more than ninety minutes K recounted for me most of the memorable events of his miraculous life. I even got him to explain, he enjoyed that, how he could be both 110 and 69.

One remark he made stands out in my mind. One of his most quotable lines. I asked him how he created his stories, like "Metamorphosis" or "The Penal Colony," and he replied at once:

"I didn't create my stories. Like Mozart's music, they were always there, waiting to be plucked out of the cosmos, waiting to be discovered."

Then K grew tired. He stood.

"Time to go back home. Thank you. This was a treat."

"For me too."

I didn't look back as we left the restaurant, but I felt Johnny's and Michele's eyes on me. I had arranged with Michele to call him after I brought my guest home.

A taxi took us back.

At the door to K's house I thanked him for talking to me. But I added:

"Remember, the other day you said you were prepared to give me something. You suggested that previously you were not willing, but, in your words, 'Now I am.' And yet before, in the restaurant, when I asked you to show me what you've written, you gave me a stony No.... Why?"

"What you think I've written and what I want to show you may be two different things. It's a bit complicated. But in essence I do not like to be asked. To be pressured. I don't like pressure. When you ask, it's No. When I offer of my own accord, it's Yes."

When we parted, K bent forward and—for the first time—kissed me on the cheek.

41

Listening to the Tape

I couldn't wait to get back to my room. I could have heard it walking. I could have heard it on the Metro. But it was like the chocolate icing you save for last. I was itching to play it but I wanted privacy. In my room, alone, I felt a spurt of saliva in my mouth, like a child before the first bite of birthday cake. My hands trembled as I rewound the tape to the beginning. I pressed the play button.

For a moment or two, silence. Oh no, I said in a panic. All lost. I waited. Then the sounds began. Clear were the first few sentences, the banal exchanges about the newspaper and if K goes out to eat. Clear too was his response to my question if he attends events. "Oh, yes. For concerts and plays, yes." But as soon as I asked him about Brod the clarity vanished. Instead of conversation, I got broken phrases, bent at the terminal ends, middles missing. I got garbled words. Sentences in what sounded to me like basic Icelandic with raggle-taggle Tagalog. Still, the rhythm was vaguely familiar. Where had I heard this language before? Where? Where? For indeed I had heard it. I thought I had it. It's...then it slipped away, like a dream remembered in inconclusive jigsaw-puzzle fragments. Oh, the frustration of half-remembered dreams. I replayed the strange sounds. Then it came back to me: the stip-stop, glip-glap lingo Jiri and Betty had spoken in the hospital, with insucked words, backward syllables, fractured syntax, accelerated, syncopated, truncated exchanges. And the scythed words that came from Jiri's pen once the cap was gone.

Hearing the audio I already (fore)saw the video. The two were linked. That too would fail. For the same lifeblood ran through both. Though physically separated, they were still linked like Siamese twins. I had no hope for the videos. Despite two cameramen. The foeboding—then I correct the ominous, message-laden typo and write "foreboding"—tied knots in my stomach. And I would lose Katya too, pumped my darkly prophetic soul.

I dialed Michele's cell phone. Every time I make contact I fear the worst. I was constantly fearing the worst. I feared it even before I put on the audio tape and my fears were right. Michele didn't answer. But knowing I would call, he had prepared a message for me. I had to be grateful for that.

"Sorry, I got called to Vienna. Trouble with a production. I'm leaving the videos with the restaurant owner.... Please say you heard this message so I can erase it. Thanks."

"Michele. I heard. Call when you get back."

I ran to the restaurant. Again the nervousness, again the fears, again the foreboding. The audio and videotapes are related. They're made of the same tainted molecules.

The beefy owner, Pavel, stood inside. Seeing me, he smiled. Ah, that's a good sign. He's expecting me. I breathed out a ton of air, felt better.

"Hello, Pavel. My cameraman said he left the videos here."

Pavel's smile disappeared. He thought I'd come to order a meal. He pulled his lower lip down, grimaced, and shook his head.

"With me?"

"Yes, with you. That's what he told me."

"I did not see that man again after he left."

"Is it possible he left the videos when you were out?"

"Is possible."

"Please. Please look. Those are valuable videos. They can't be made again. And I haven't even seen them yet." I heard my voice.

My pounding heart was raising my pitch. I sounded like a tape speeded up.

Pavel looked near the register; he searched a couple of shelves. He went to check in his little office. He shouted in Czech to a waiter and a cook.

"They say no one came in. I am sorry. There is nothing here."

"Nothing? How can that be? He told me it was here."

"Please, mister. Nobody left nothing here. I look. You see I look. Nothing."

"I can't understand it. Those were his exact words: I'm leaving the videotapes with the restaurant owner."

"Maybe another restaurant. Not me. Look, I don't know you. I don't know him. How I know, how you know he tells the truth? Please leave me alone. I got work."

"But..."

"Mister, I did what you asked. Partition? Put partition. With hole? With hole. Black curtain by register? Black curtain by register. Too much time. Too much work."

"Excuse me, Pavel, but you will recall I offered you a generous sum of money."

"But now time is up. I have no more time. No video here."

"Can I call you in a couple of days in case it turns up?"

"Call."

"I'll also write down my phone number at my hotel. Here. Please."

"If I find it, I will call. But I swear I don't have videos."

I backed out of the front door, crushed.

I held the phone. I took a deep breath. I didn't know if I would be able to talk. I didn't know where my heart was. It wasn't where it was supposed to be, for it was thumping everywhere. Between my ears, a heartache in my head. In my feet. In the pit of my stomach.

"Michele. Listen. I just left the restaurant. The...videos...are not, repeat, *not*...there. Pavel looked, searched, found nothing.

Claims no one came in to give him or anyone on his staff the videos. He was rather testy and impatient. What did you do with them? Who did you give them to? Did you see where he put them? Call me. Urgent."

I wished I had Johnny's number. I didn't even get his last name. Again I screwed up. With all my careful planning, getting Pavel to set up two partitions, getting K to the restaurant and speaking for one and a half hours, even arranging a second video man as a backup in case something went wrong with one camera—but I didn't have enough foresight to get another telephone number as a backup.

One day passed. Two. Three. I kept calling Michele. No answer. I stopped leaving messages. He'll call me when he returns from Vienna, I consoled myself. I don't know how I got through each day. If I ate or not. If I slept. Maybe I wasn't even breathing. I called Pavel a day later. No videos here, he said crisply. Never was. Never will be. I felt removed from the world. Looking at it through the other side of a telescope. I didn't call or visit K. I was so depressed I couldn't even conjure up the image of Katya to cheer me.

Finally, when I thought my soul had drained out of me, the phone rang.

"Hello, it's me. Oh, God! Sorry, just a moment, trouble in Vienna again. Wait."

"Do you—?"

I couldn't even squeeze in my desperate question. Soon as he said, "Hello, it's me," I should have said, "Where are the videos?" But he was already off the line. The phone dead as my heart.

When I dialed back, I only got his answering machine. I felt like throwing my cell phone, smashing it against the wall. But I held back. Why ruin my only chance at connecting with the world? Was this a scam? ran through my head. Was Michele in league with that aggrieved actor, Stacek? Would he tell me he gave the two videos to Stacek and now I would have to deal with that unpredictable, vengeful fool, the rogue of Prague?

Who knows? Prague was still a city of mystery. Who knows what kind of intrigues took place here? True, Michele was an Italian, but still, maybe something of Prague had—under the influence of Stacek—rubbed off on him. Despite his kind words, Michele might still be smarting from me disrupting his film.

When one is pressed against the wall, drained of hope, one thinks desperate, hopeless thoughts.

I looked at my watch; I looked at the calendar. Oh, my God. It's Wednesday. I promised—rather, Katya promised to see me.

The loss of the two videos, my entire hope, my dream, the core of my film on Prague, devastated me. I didn't want to see anyone. But I had to pull myself up. I didn't want to link the loss of the tape, the video, with the loss of Katya. It had been my fear—yes, my gloomy prediction. But it was my choice not to let it come true. The audio and the video were now beyond my control. But it was up to me, my will, to either hold on to or lose Katya.

I boarded the Metro and was in K's house twenty minutes later.

42

With Her

Katya answered the doorbell and welcomed me with an affectionate hug. I bent down to kiss her lips.

"Is anyone home?"

She said Eva had gone out shopping with K.

From the way she looked at me I sensed the good feelings we had last time were holding. I'm always afraid that when I leave a girl I like I'm going to disappear from her heart, and the next time we meet we'll have to begin from square one. But now, here, there was no need for trepidation. Nevertheless, sadness subsumed me. A melancholy, grey as fog, palpable and damp, misted through me. I had to pull my soul up from somewhere near my ankles and suppress my sadness. The videos. Again the videos. The videos I expected and had not yet gotten created a cavernous emptiness in me, a gloom, a grief.

Then the sunshine of Katya's voice broke through the fog.

"Do you want to go somewhere?" she asked.

"Not really. I just want to spend some time with you alone."

She gave me the kind of warm smile, sly and sweet, one lover gives to another. Holding my hand, she took—led—me down to her little room. As soon as she closed the door she pressed up against me and threw her arms around me.

"Look," I said, and took out of my pocket a bag of dark, high–cocoa-mass, chocolate pistules I had bought at Capek Chokolat, Prague's celebrated chocolatier.

Katya gave a little cry. "We must be telep…is that the correct word?"

"Pathic?"

"Yes, telepathic. Look! Look what I have for you." And from under her pillow she took a bar of chocolate she had bought me at the same shop.

But suddenly, a host of negative associations assailed my febrile brain. Chocolate made me think of K, and K led me to the video. Once more, a wave of emptiness overwhelmed me.

How could I rid myself of those blue-tinted low spirits? Could I will them away?

"Bless me," I told her.

"With what?"

"Success. Luck."

"You have success."

"I want more."

"I bless you with success. More and more."

"Unsadden me, Katya. Gladden me."

Her eyes told me: kiss me.

First we sat on her bed and then stretched out side by side.

I kissed her lips. Her eyes. Her cheeks. Her throat.

As I kissed her I felt that same jolt of energy K had felt when he kissed the curtain of the Aron Kodesh in the Altneushul and was restored to health. I felt Katya's soul energy flowing into me, our two sparks locking, and I knew I didn't have to hold her to know I loved her. I always loved her. I loved her before I met her and I loved her even before I knew her. And this love flowed up and overwhelmed the cup of my soul.

"Isn't it strange—actually, beautiful—how the heart opens up and starts blooming like a tree in spring. And you feel as if you're a tree, a flower, a bird that can fly anywhere. And it's always sunny and warm and that flower in you is happiness."

"They call it love, don't they?" Katya said. "And I feel like a flower too," she said and smiled a naughty smile at me.

"Your blessing is working. All my life I have been looking for you without knowing who or where you were. And then, like magic, I found you…under"—I laughed—"a blue beret."

"So how did you find me now that I'm not wearing it?"

I disregarded her rhetorical question.

"Remember that note I gave you at the marionette shop? Remind me what it said."

"Oh, you know what it said. That was so nice, written in the Old South Bohemian dialect. It said: 'Oth,' as everyone knows means 'I'…'I never met anyone I liked as much as you…' Where did you get that phrase from?"

"A native linguist wanted to show me an interesting line in Old Czech."

"Did you really know what it meant?" Katya asked.

"Everyone, even a wild Ostrogoth, knows that 'Oth' means 'I.'"

Katya brought her face even closer to mine. "Once you gave me those sweet words I knew you really liked me."

"So why didn't you want to show them to me?"

"Because they were mine."

"You are mine," I said, and I slid my lips over every atom of her mouth. Our tongues touched, embraced. I took her bottom lip between my lips and slowly ran my tongue over it. "You are so delicious, Katya."

Even with my eyes closed I felt her lips stretching into a happy smile.

"Next to listening to a Bach *Brandenburg Concerto* or a Vivaldi guitar concerto, this, now, here, you, is the best thing."

She gave me a teasing pinch in the waist, then raised her head from the pillow.

"Do you think I'm pretty?"

"Pretty?" I laughed. "You're gorgeous.… No." I stopped. "I take that back."

At once Katya opened her mouth in astonishment. But she must have sensed I was joking, for I saw her sparkling white teeth; let's call it an astonished smile.

"I have a better word," I said. "Lovely."

"I like the sound of that word."

"Yes, lovely, Katya. That's the word for you. It encompasses everything about you—your soul, your personality, your beauty and your wit and your mind.... All of these combine to make you radiate with loveliness."

And she kissed me again. She closed her eyes and bound herself to me.

I couldn't help it. The words just poured out of me. "I've never felt anything like this before, Katya. It's as if you've opened a magic door and I've stepped into a blessed never-never land, a magic garden where cupids play."

"Really?" she said in a low voice that sounded like a song.

"Yes, really," I whispered.

Katya pressed closer to me. She hugged me so tight I was amazed at her strength. She put her hands around my back and pulled me close. I had never felt a hug like that before, a hug that said, Now that I found you, I will never ever let you go.

Later, she got up to go to the bathroom. When she returned I told her I missed her.

"Even these few moments?"

"Yes."

"That's called separation anxiety," said Katya.

"I never heard of that. Where did you get that from?"

"A course in psychology I once studied."

"But I wasn't separated from you. We're both here. If you have to give this new disease of mine a name, rather call it return anxiety. I was worried if you'd return. Or even better—presence anxiety. I was worried that one of us present, me or you, wouldn't be here when you or me returned."

"So you really missed me?"

"Yes. Even for a blink of an eye. Look." I faced the other way for a moment. "See, I miss you again."

Katya thought I was joking, but the truth was I missed her even those two seconds I turned away from her. What's more, when I woke in the morning the first thing that flashed in my mind was Katya's lovely face, in full color no less. I open my eyes and—zhoop!—there you are. What you wear is unclear, because you appear like a passport photo from the neck up. But the blue beret is on your head and your dimple is perfectly in focus, even though it's early in the morning when your visage comes to me. But all this I didn't yet want to tell her.

"Do you ever miss yourself?" she asked.

"Only when I'm away."

Katya gave me a sleepy, contented smile.

"Put your arms around me again," I said. "I can't get enough of your heartfelt kisses."

Where, I wondered, did that adorable ardor, that from-the-depth-of-the-heart loving come from? Was it really me who inspired all this? I felt like a kid. Yes, like a kid. And I, who am usually shy and reticent, I shared my feelings with Katya, saying words to her even before they came into my thoughts.

"Do you know why I keep kissing you so much?"

"Tell me."

"I'm making up for all the years I didn't know you and should have known you."

"That's so sweet," Katya said. But the truth is, I expected her to say more. But as for me, I couldn't stop talking, sharing, confessing:

"I love being with you, Katya. I love holding you. I can't get enough of your lips, your long green cat eyes, your throat, that soft skin by your shoulders. I say things to you I've never said before, and feelings swirl in me I've never felt before. I know it sounds like a song from a musical comedy, but it's true. I can't get enough of you, Katya. I love to kiss you. I love to touch you. The more I kiss you, the more I want to kiss you. The more I see you, the more I want to see you. The more I kiss you, the prettier you become. The prettier you become, the more I want to kiss you."

Again, as she pressed her body against mine and slipped her knee between my legs, again came that softly intoned, "Really?" That "Really?" of hers, a sweet mélange of eros and incredulity.

I moved my hands slowly over her body and said, "You don't say much, sweet Katya, but even in that tender and incredulous, song-like 'Really?' I sense you're agreeing with everything I say. It's as if you can't believe the nice things you're hearing. That you're surprised to hear such words, words you've maybe never heard before. As if you're unsure of yourself and are wondering if these lovely words are really really being directed at you...

"You know, if I could eat one word it would be that sweet and musical and, yes, erotically charged 'Really?' of yours and at once become like Chaucer's Criseyde who, taking one look at the handsome Troilus and feeling she's drunk a love potion, exclaims, 'Who hath given me drinke?'... So open up, Katya, let me hear more. Don't hold back."

Katya cocked her head at me with a humorous glint in her eye, as if preparing me for another "Really?" But she fooled me, did clever Katya.

"You make me feel so weak," she said. "I've never been kissed like this before."

"Exactly what I was thinking. Probably one of the thoughts I wanted to say but missed saying: I've never been kissed like this before.... And you know what?"

"What? Tell me." Again that low, pussycat-fur whisper, in a slightly different key signature than "Really?"

"Your eyes are glowing," I said.

I imagined hearing her tender "Really?" again.

But Katya said softly, "Yes, they're glowing, and—you know what?"

"What?"

She smiled. "We fall into the same rhythm, don't we?"

"Yes. What? Tell me."

"I love the way you touch me," said Katya. "You have such a beautiful, tender touch."

"It's not really me, it's you. You inspire me. After all, you're the touchee."

"Still." And then she laughed. "Touchee. I like that word too."

"Kiss me," I said.

She rolled on top of me and bent her head over mine. Slowly, fervidly, with touching deliberateness, she kissed my lips, going from one edge to another; she kissed every centimeter of my cheeks, she kissed my nose; she brushed her lips over my eyes; she kissed my temples, my forehead, my chin. She moved unhurriedly, brushing her hair back once in a while, and I heard each kiss, rhythmic as a pulse. She kissed and lingered on my earlobes, and then, with a little moan, returned to my lips. And I felt her love overspreading me like a soft blanket of stars.

"Listen, Katya, I want to tell you something…"

"Mmmm," she said, not opening her eyes.

"There is nothing better than this. Forget what I said about Bach and Vivaldi. Nothing in the world. Nothing. Not riches, not fame. Not ambition or success. Not films. Not prizes. Not power or honors. Not the Cannes Festival or Golden Globes or Academy Awards. Not glory, not achievement. Nothing. This. This is the sine qua non. The top of the ladder. To lie next to someone you love who shares your feelings. It's almost too good to be true. When we're like this, we stop time, don't you think? We remove ourselves from space-time and create our own little celestial cocoon universe. Isn't that so, Katya?"

"Yes," she said. It was a still Yes, a nuanced Yes, a Yes, where the "e" went up, then descended, and the "s" was breathed out softly, slowly. "I love it when you say my name."

"Really?" I said, and she—aware that I was teasing—clasped her hand over my mouth.

When she let go I kissed the palms of her hands and the tips of every finger.

"We're on the same wavelength, Katya. Like giving each other dark chocolate at the very same time and buying it in the same shop. It's unbelievable. Incredible. We're one heartbeat."

"Yes," she said.

I gave her a look, waiting. She understood.

"We're one heartbeat," Katya repeated.

"Remember what I said before? The more I kiss you, the more I want to kiss you. The more we kiss, the more I like you. The more I like you, the prettier you become. The prettier you become, the more I want to kiss you. Does that make any sense?"

"Yes. Yes yes yes. Yes, it does. It does."

I hesitated, but then I said it. "This happens to a man only once in his lifetime."

"That sounds like it comes from a book," Katya shot back at once.

"Maybe it's something I wrote. And somebody swiped it. It's probably Leviant. The minute I write something, that word-thief nabs it and puts it into one of his thoroughly unreadable, certifiably meretricious books. Then, when *I* say it—*my very own words*—people, into which category you fall, assume I've arrogated someone else's thoughts. As if I can't come up with—"

"I was just kidding—"

"—let me finish. As if I can't come up with an original phrase of my own once in a while, an original remark like, and then he drops his excitable little voice to a passionate murmur like this: This happens to a man only once in his lifetime."

"You're sneering," Katya said, but a smile danced at the corners of her eyes. "I've never seen you angry before."

"I'm not sneering. I'm hissing. But, regrettably, Leviant doesn't have any sibilants in his name, so I can't even hiss. If he had a normal name like Stanislas Cystos, I could hiss to my heart's content.... The fact that some plagiarist swiped my line doesn't make the remark any less true."

Katya, laughing throughout my mock narration, now gave me one of her delightful smiles.

"Katya. Sweet Katya. My darling Katya. Kick that door shut—that magic door you pulled me through into that magic garden of that enchanted never-never land—and keep me, Katya, and hold me there."

She shut her eyes dreamily. In slow motion she shut her eyes. She shut her eyes to let the wave of my words inundate her.

"Would you like to hear that 'There is nothing better than this' speech again?"

"Yes," she whispered, and hugged me so tight I felt I was part of her.

"There is nothing better than this. Nothing in the world. Nothing. Not riches, not fame. Not ambition or success. Not films. Not prizes. Not glory or honors. Nothing. This is the sine qua non. The top of the ladder." I spoke into her hair, her ear, her cheeks. And I felt her nodding. Yes, yes, yes.

Then, from the floor, she picked up the bag of chocolate I had given her. She took one pistule and held it between her teeth. She lifted her chin and gestured to me. I drew near and bit off a piece.

"Outwardly you're happy," Katya said. "But I still feel a bit of sadness in you. I see it. I feel it." She placed her hands on my cheeks. "Your sadness makes your cheeks cold. Why? Tell, tell me."

"You're right. I've tried to forget it while I'm with you but it keeps surfacing.... You see, and that's why I wanted your blessing, I made an important film and my cameraman didn't deliver the video."

"Did you call him?"

"Yes. He doesn't pick up."

"You'll get the video."

"You think he'll deliver it."

"Yes. He will."

"You sure?"

"Yes...I missed you." She ran her index finger from my temple to my lips. I kissed her finger. "At first, when we met, I didn't think twice about you."

"After we met I thought maybe once about you," I said. "Maybe less than once."

Katya smiled and said: "But then, the more I saw you, the more I understood you were someone special."

"Special or very special?"

She smiled again. "Very special. Someone who makes a very special effort to ruin my only scene in my very special first film."

"So why did you disappear, Katya? I thought I lost you forever."

"But I knew where to find you."

"You did? How?"

"I saw you that day in K's room."

"Oh, my goodness. I sensed something floating by, caught just the shadow of a shadow of you. Thought it was someone familiar. I even asked K who it was, but he said, Ask Eva; that's her department. But I never did ask her. Can you imagine? I thought it was a waitress or a salesgirl I'd seen once."

"It was. The marionette salesgirl."

And she gave me that radiant smile with the dimple in one cheek.

"So why didn't you stick your head in and say hello? It would have relieved me of lots of worry and stress."

She shrugged. "It had to play out differently. The way it did."

"Destined that way?"

"If you wish. Yes."

"Katya, sweetheart, would you like to hear my little speech again?"

Actually, this time my request was a little joke, a kind of self-parody. I really didn't expect her whispered, "Yes, of course."

And I said those words again as she pressed me tight.

"There is nothing better than this. Nothing. Nothing in the world. Not fame, not riches. Not prizes or honors. Not films or festivals. Nothing. This is the sine qua non. The top of the ladder. The best thing in the world."

Where was I now, with that tight, ever-tightening hug of hers? Had I become skin and bone of Katya?

"I love those words," Katya whispered into my ear. "I just love the music of them."

"Have you forgiven me for ruining that film scene of yours?"

"Oh that! Of course. I'm finished with that.... It wasn't for me. I want to teach literature. Now I want to ask you a question. Please tell me. Will you go back to America?"

"Do you want me to stay here?"

"In Jewish fashion, you answer a question with another question."

"Do I really?"

Again she laughed.

I held her close and asked, "Am I too old for you?"

"Nepa nepa nepa. Nepa tara glos," she said, holding my face lovingly as if I were a newborn.

I didn't ask her where she learned that phrase.

"And you are nepa nepa nepa tara pilus for me.... And don't forget, the difference between Dora and K was much greater than the age difference between you and me."

I thought she said, "Aye," assenting in the older English form of Yes. But then I realized she was just attempting to correct my grammar.

43

Finally, Michele

Finally, Michele called. He apologized.

"What happened? Do you have them? Where are they? They're not in the restaurant. I went there. Pavel said he didn't have them, didn't see them. He got very huffy right away."

"Easy! Easy! I know. I didn't bring them there."

"But you said you would. Do you have them?"

"I know, but I changed my mind. I said I'm leaving the videos. I didn't say I left them. I decided not to trust anyone with them. Given what you just told me about Pavel's reaction, it's lucky I changed my mind. I thought the best thing was to hand them to you in person. And then, sorry, I was called away."

"But do you have them?" I said with a hysterical shriek in my voice. "You still didn't answer me. You don't know how depressed I am. Do you have them? Do you?"

My heart stopped—

"I have them. I have them. Don't fear."

—then pumped rapidly.

"How did they come out?"

When I first took Michele and Johnny to the restaurant, I thought of asking them not to look at the video. But I knew it was an unrealistic request. That alone would prompt, tempt them to view it. Now I was glad I hadn't said that. So I said:

"How did it come out? Good?"

"I don't know."

"You didn't review it?"

"No. You didn't ask me to and I didn't think I should. I mean, it's your film."

"When can I get them?"

"I live in the outskirts of town in a friend's house. You want to meet me tomorrow?"

"No," I said rather harshly. "I've waited for days. Make it today."

"Okay, how about later this afternoon, around 4 p.m.? By the Schweik statue on Parizska Street."

"Fine. See you there."

I arrived first, turning this way and that. Minutes dragged on. Then a car door opened and Michele came bounding out, holding a paper bag. He apologized again and again. His words went in one ear, out the other. I looked at the bag. Now I had the videos in my hand. But a suspicion rolled over me. He had taken the originals and substituted others; soon I would hear from Stacek, offering the videos for an exorbitant sum of money. Or maybe Michele would use the videos. He had overheard my exchanges with K, discovered who he was. But I knew I was fantasizing. I knew it.

I thanked Luongo and we parted amicably. I went back to my room, put one video into the VCR. I'm not going to drag it out, make a Job-like excursus into mourning. Again my battered heart. What an organ! Able to take so much stress without complaint.

I run the tape. I see myself sitting at the table absolutely clearly, in full color. But the chair where K sits is empty.

No. Michele would not have done that. Could not have.

And so it went for another hour or so.

Again, there I was, seemingly animated, talking to someone unseen.

Although I had told Michele and Johnny not to focus in on me, it was good they did, for at least it was proof they were filming.

Did K's plate, you ask, have less and less food on it as the film progressed?

Yes.

K's disappearance from the video wasn't Michele's or Johnny's doing. Another force, a hex, was playing here.

I was disappointed, distraught, but not surprised. Once I saw what happened with the audio cassette I had a feeling that the videos would fail. But then I looked, as eventually I always did, on the plus side. I had a few lines uttered by K on the audio, and the unretouched video of K's plate slowly emptying of food was captured on the film. You'll make good use of both, I told myself. This is not the end of the world. Had this happened to me three weeks ago I would have thought it was the end of the world. But not now.

When viewing the videos I had planned to feel happy, secure, confident, delirious.

The rules say three strikes—one audio, two videos—and you're out.

But I also told myself, I won't let it happen.

In my gloom, my pessimism, I had tied my fate with the K video to Katya. If one went wrong, so would the other.

But I vowed, No. I would override the earlier message of my darkly prophetic soul.

For the new ballgame I changed the rules.

No more three strikes and you're out. It could be four, five, six or more.

I will not lose her.

Katya would be mine.

I felt her lips kissing me, felt it so powerfully a shiver of pleasure ran through me. I thought of how success and failure can intertwine in one day. In my dream triage I had given up Katya for the K video. Now I didn't have the video but had her. Would—must—keep her. Real life had blessed me more than I could imagine.

Losing the tapes was not the end of the world.

Knowing lovely Katya was its beginning.

PART THREE

SEVEN ENDINGS

SEVEN ENDINGS

1. At the end of the road 387
2. "Yes." 390
3. "You don't go by Amschl…" 394
4. "What's your favorite piece…?" 398
5. Katya close 400
6. I unpacked 403
7. The pile of pages 407

ENDING 1

I was at the end of the road (not the end of my rope). Any other filmmaker who had had such a golden opportunity for the film of a lifetime and lost it would have jumped off a bridge. Me, I jumped off a curb. Setbacks make me grumble for a while but I always bounce back. The truth is there was no more I could do. Could I appeal to K? Hardly. On this he was adamant. One way or another, he sent his uncompromising message to me via the audio and the film. But he did say he would let me photograph his room. My world-stunning documentary did not happen—but it was not totally dead.

I took my camera and the pages of notes I'd taken since meeting Jiri in New York and came to K.

I rang; he, not Eva, opened the door. In his room he embraced me. I felt like a lover reconciling with his beloved after a quarrel while knowing his other mistress waits for him in her apartment.

First, without saying a word he gave me two photos of Jiri: one as a younger man, in his office as director of the Jewish Museum; another, a more recent picture.

"And here's a letter for you."

The envelope, postmarked Brno, was addressed to Amschl c/o K.

My heart leaped; joy was a tiny boat racing in my bloodstream.

As I tore open Katya's envelope, I glanced at K. He was amused at my excitement.

"I miss you," she wrote. "I can't wait until next Wednesday. But I want to share an idea I had now. You told me that you still didn't get the video you were promised. I hope you did, but if not, how about this? When I was making that little film with Michele Luongo, one of the technicians mentioned seeing a documentary about a documentary. So I thought that maybe your film could be about the film you are making. Maybe at least part of it—with the title: *A Film of a Failed Film*."

I leaped up into the air. I thought I would stay up there. Gravity couldn't bring me down. I almost bounced into the seat of one of K's model aeroplanes and flew off into the vast blue yonder with the joy of Katya's suggestion. What a brilliant idea! She'd just saved my film.

"So she likes you, eh?"

"Yes." I laughed and laughed. "She does. She does. And thanks to you."

Katya, you're amazing, I thought. I would make use of the flawed audio, the failed video, just as I had planned to, but with a different slant. I would include K's room, the house. Of course, now I would include Katya—not knowing, of course, how much she would say for the record—and Eva too. Everything I had videoed so far would be included. Johnny, Luongo's assistant, had focused on the table where K and I sat but, cleverly, he took in an overview of the restaurant, including the balcony and the wooden partition. That too would be in my "failed film." But I would not use Katya's title. Perhaps the film's name would be *Imagining K.*

Then I interrupted my own reverie with: "How did Katya know my Hebrew name?"

"I told her."

"And how did you know?"

"Think about it."

I thought and thought. I shrugged.

"Jiri wrote me."

That was strange. How could he have known? Jiri Weisz-Krupka had stepped out of the synagogue when I was called to the Torah that first Sabbath we met. What kind of secret communications network did these people have?

"Amschl is a rare Hebrew name," K said.

"I know. I've never heard anyone called up to the Torah with that name. And I've never seen it on a shul memorial tablet."

"Come to shul when I get an aliya and you'll hear it. Or visit my tombstone."

"Really? Is Amschl your Hebrew name too?"

"Why so surprised? I thought you read everything I wrote and everything written about me?"

K's clever eyes, the penetrating eyes of the early K photographs, encompassed me.

"It's in Brod's biography," he said. "On the second page, where he quotes my diary, 'My Hebrew name is Amschl.'"

"Imagine! I completely forgot that. But Jiri did say 'Amschl' twice last time I saw him."

ENDING 2

"Yes."

Of course it was K speaking. Again that ambiguous, enigmatic Yes. Oh, that slippery Yes, that monosyllable with as many notes as the musical alphabet. That Yes of shifting tonalities. That continuum Yes. That multihued Yes, green and red and blue. That Yes of snowcaps and verdant valleys, of scald and ice. That Yes of assent, of silence and negation. A Yes that slid and jaggled on a wobbly-legged ladder from Yes to No.

And you know what? I don't even remember the comment that prompted that Yes. Then my frustration, which I thought I had reined in, thought I swept away, suddenly surfaced.

I looked at K, felt so close to him. We had the same Hebrew name. I couldn't help my plea, couldn't restrain it. Maybe he would have pity on me.

"I want to live. To make films." Perhaps the period wasn't there and I said, "I want to live to make films." And then I swallowed and added: "To succeed. To live. Like you. I love books. Your books. Your life is unique. There's only one person who can record your story. Me. May I…?" But I couldn't finish the sentence; rather, to my own surprise I shifted key, changed tonality, elided it to: "May I have…I want…I need…your blessing. Will you give it to me?"

Did I mean, were my words otherspeaking for, Please let me touch the parchment?

K looked at me. Who did I see in his face with the longish, pointy nose and Van Dyke beard—an old man or K? The man who really was K, at one hundred ten or one hundred eleven? Or did I see myself in the mirror of my hopes and dreams?

He looked at me. He looked at me with what I thought was beneficence in his bright blue eyes. He looked at me and said:

"You didn't get the video of me you wanted, you know my view, but I have something else for you. It's in the synagogue. Get it."

"The Altneu?"

"No. The other one."

"With the lions?"

"Yes."

"Uh-uh. No no." Just the thought of that place sent shivers of fear through me.

"It will be all right."

"Where in the synagogue is it?"

"In the Aron Kodesh."

"No. I'm not going there again. They don't like me. I don't know why, but they don't like me."

"They won't come down again. I promise you."

You can promise all you want, I thought. But can I rely on their promise?

"No. I won't do it."

"You'll go. You'll get the folder. Copy it if you like, and then put it back."

"No…what's in it?"

"You'll see."

"Why can't you get it for me? You go there from time to time."

K looked at me. K looked through me. K looked at me pityingly, as if I didn't understand the simplest equation.

"Don't you see?"

"No. I don't see."

"It's a test. Remember Tamino, from our favorite opera?" K went to his desk and picked up the little puppet of Papageno that always stood there. "You too have to pass the test.... If I bring you what I'm sending you to fetch, it won't be much of a test, will it?"

As I turned to go, K added: "And, ah, by the way..."—now I faced him, and a shy, kindly look waved across his face like a patch of sunshine suddenly appearing between moving clouds—"I have one more thing for you. And this you can have without undergoing a *Magic Flute*–like test."

He went to his little writing table, opened the drawer, pulled it out as far as it could go, and from the very rear took out a small item.

Looking closer, I saw it was a pen top. No, not a pen top. *The* pen top. The top of *the* pen.

K raised it and gazed into my eyes.

I understood.

He understood.

We understood.

Although I wanted to, I didn't ask him how he got it—and I smiled inwardly, proud of my restraint. But I imagined. For imagining no restraint needed. Imagining is my middle name. It may have been Betty who brought it to him. But I didn't, wouldn't, ask. Or perhaps there hadn't been a Betty, not in the airport lounge, not on the plane. Perhaps it was a trick of the imagination, with me balancing, as I occasionally do, on the tightrope between the real and the dream.

K brought his hand toward me.

"Here. Take it. It's mine. Yours. Ours.... The top of my, Jiri's, your pen."

I bowed my head in gratitude. I did not even have to say, Thank you.

Betty—the instrument in all this commotion, on the ground and (maybe) in the air—K did not name at all. It dawned on me that Jiri had never mentioned Betty to his father. And if Betty did not exist in K's imagination, who was I to intrude her into K's life?

And, of course, as I discovered later, the pen—complete now, whole—was, as I knew it would be, absolutely silent. Totally inefficacious. Sans Jiri's voice. For I had already gotten to, destiny had brought me to, my destined destination.

And, in giving me the top of the pen, the way K handed it to me, bestowed it to me, presented it to me, transferred it over to me in almost formal fashion—a balletic gesture like a swan bowing her long elegant white neck; a hand gesture that has replayed itself over and over in my mind—in giving me what he gave me, I felt like young Elisha standing before the older prophet Elijah.

Receiving his mantle.

His tallis.

His quill.

His pen.

ENDING 3

"You don't go by Amschl, do you?" K said.

"No, only for aliyas."

"Curt is a nice crisp name."

The first time in all these weeks that he had articulated my name.

"I like the way you pronounce my name the European way… Koort."

K's unsaid Yes looked through me then looped back around my heart.

"Curt," K repeated. He seemed to savor that one-syllable name. Perhaps preferred it to the eighteenth-century flavor of the first Rothschild's name, Amschl.

"And you're not a filmmaker, are you?"

"Yes."

But that Yes wasn't a Yes of assent. It was a Yes that said: I exist.

Then K rattled off a series of words I could not understand. From the inflection I gathered he had asked a question. For a while his words sounded like Jiri and Betty's words, when Jiri was about to reveal something to me, words that ran backwards, had their centers cut out and attached to the beginnings and ends of other words. I waited a moment. The words reassembled.

"And you created all of this, this entire scenario: About being born in Prague and being adopted. You made this whole thing up"—he drew wide circles in the air with his right hand—"from, or out of, how do you say it in your beautiful, evocative, mellifluous English tongue, which given my history, my past, my survival, is a word I prefer to the word 'language.' You concocted all of this out of entire fabric."

"Yes," I said. "Together we wove this magnificent fabric. We made it up out of whole cloth."

K frowned. "Cloth with holes? Moth-eaten?"

"No." I laughed. "With a 'w.' Whole cloth."

"Ah," said K. "Just as I said. Entire fabric."

"Yes."

"Even me," he said.

Did he mean that I had made up even him, or that even he had participated in the weaving?

"Yes. Me and you. You and I. All of us. Both of us. All of this. Together we wove it."

"How did you do it?" K asked.

It was not a question I expected from the master weaver himself. And in any case, I couldn't answer. Shall I tell him the letters hang in the air, in sunlight, and one by one we pluck them, sometimes stretched on tiptoe, sometimes by leaping up to a distant star to seize a shining letter? Or a destined spark? And if we miss, fall back to Earth like Icarus. Or, if we are lucky, the letters fall into our palms like rose petals, perfumed and velvety, ripe and ready to be used.

How did *you* do it? I was about to say. How did *you* weave your magic? With one word spun around another, like stars with satellites and moons. They call it writing, K, but they're wrong. It's not writing. For writing one doesn't need paper. One doesn't need pen. We write when we walk. We write when we talk. We write when we dream. We write when we sleep. We write when we hold, like Goethe, our beloved in our arms; while she is hugging me tight, we write. Sometimes we don't even write when we write, for we are just jotting down what we have thought earlier. For what people call writing is really thinking. Calling us writers is a misnomer. We're thinkers. First we think. Then we weave.

K probably thought I didn't hear him, so he repeated:

"How did you do it?"

I was about to say Yes again, that slippery K Yes I had learned from him, a Yes that was at times life-affirming, at times ironical, at times meant silence, at times meant No. Instead, I decided to tell him the truth. About magic. Divination. Divine assistance. The mystical sparks that float about unseen until with a swift lucky move we snag them.

"How, you ask? Like this," I said.

(to be continued)

[this page left blank intentionally]

ENDING 4

"What's your favorite piece of writing?" I asked K.

He looked at me and nodded. His head moved up and down several times. The loose skin beneath the chin you see on old men wasn't there. I still couldn't get over how young he looked. The shape he was in. The way he rose out of an easy chair into a standing position without grabbing his back or groaning or getting up in three or four installments. He had the movements of a vigorous man forty years his junior. I remembered reading how much K liked swimming and boating and hiking. Even decades later, the salutary aspects of physical exercise showed. Then again, maybe he was lying. Maybe he wasn't 111. But maybe it was in the genes. My beloved uncle Monia, who used to take me to see Danny K in New York and looked more like K than I ever did, when Monia was in his mid-eighties and ill, he also jumped out of his chair into an erect position. And he never exercised a moment in his life. Unlacing his shoes, taking his pants off, and lying down to sleep at night was his most strenuous physical activity. Not too many people knew about K's penchant for sports. Imagine how much time he lost from writing. Had he spent less time on sports and outdoor activities he could have written more, much more. He could have written "The Good Street," "A Day at the

Circus," "The Lottery Agent," and "In the Synagogue Courtyard," the latter a major tale.

K regarded me. He still had not replied to my question. Was he thinking? Would he put me off? Give a definitive answer?

"You, and everyone else, will no doubt expect me to say: 'The Metamorphosis' or *The Trial.* But I won't say that, no." And he nodded again.

But I was insistent. "Then what will you say?"

K put his index finger to his lips.

Then I realized that I had phrased the question ambiguously. "What's your favorite piece of writing?" could refer to his work, my work, or the work of others.

"I'll have to think about it," K said.

(to be continued)

ENDING 5

I held Katya close to me.

"Do you know who the man you respectfully call 'Grandpa' is?" I asked her. She smiled at the private joke between us.

"Yes," she said with that storybook Mona Lisa smile, a smile so wide it encompassed all the Ifs in the world. She thought it was a game I made up and she willingly played along.

"Shall we both say it at the same time?" I said, laughing. "Or write it on a piece of paper?"

Playing along, again she said, "Yes."

And I thought of the magnificence of K's analysis of "If," the magic word that made the world spin on its story axis.

"If," I said, but I didn't know what I meant.

"If," she said, in absolute synchrony with me.

Then together we said it both.

I said to the girl with the blue beret:

"Give me your hand."

I thought I heard her say:

"And not the rest of me?"

Which prompted me to say:

"May I? May I ask for your hand?"

But she didn't understand the idiom, for she said:

"Why ask if you already have it?"

"I may have it," I replied, "but I don't possess it."

From somewhere came piano music. Bach. Upstairs. Eva was playing the gigue again.

I took Katya's hand, her right hand, then took her other hand, her left hand, and brought both of them close. Touched now all four hands. I saw those sparkling long green eyes, those delicious lips, lips that lied early on that she lived in Georgia, the smooth high cheekbones, the soft enigmatic smile, much more sharing, giving, caring than Mona Lisa's, the red lips on a face unsullied by, that needed no, makeup.

My lips approached hers.

They touched. Sparked a charge of voltage through me; surged my blood; rose my soul.

I felt the parchment under her tongue.

At once, we both pressed each other close, tight, in possession.

"Yes?" I said.

"Yes," she said.

And at that moment I knew what K meant when he told me that everyone has a *shem* in him, he just has to know where and how to find it. When she said "Yes," I discovered mine.

"Yes," she said, taking my *shem* with her tongue and giving me hers.

"Yes," we said.

ENDING 4, CONTINUED

"Well," I asked K. "Have you thought about it?"

"About what?"

"What I asked you last time. Your favorite piece of writing."

"Yes. I have now thought about it." And he gazed at his two aeroplanes, his gramophone. He turned his head and regarded his endless shelves of books.

"And it is?"

He pointed.

I spread my hands, questioning.

He pointed to the book he was reading.

I was reading.

You are reading.

ENDING 6

I unpacked my camera bag.

"You said I could film your room."

"Yes. But not me." K stood next to me, ready to move behind me.

"I understand."

I lifted my camera.

"What's that?" K said, holding the strap, looking intently at my ring.

"A ring."

"I know it's a ring. Beautiful. Unusual. Where did you get it?"

"I got it when I graduated college. It's actually my mother's."

"I know it's your mother's ring."

"How do you know?"

"I know everything."

"You sound like the shamesh."

K laughed. "He knows everything too."

"Come on. Really. How do you know it's my mother's ring?"

"I gave it to her."

I felt dizzy again. That feeling of vertigo. What's up is down. Left is right. North is south. I was plummeting, eyes shut.

Before she died my mother told me the story of the ring with the two tiny diamonds and two tiny pearls. The woman at the orphanage, my mother revealed, had given it to her, saying it came as a gift to accompany the child.

"At the orphanage? You met my mother there?"

"Before then."

"And you recognize the ring?" I asked K.

"How can one not? With its two tiny diamonds and two tiny pearls. Why, it's a marker. Like in folktales. The birthmark."

ENDING 3, CONTINUED

"How did I do it, you want to know?"

"Yes," K said.

"Like this."

I opened my mouth.

I lifted my tongue.

I brought my fingers to my lips.

I brought my fingers past my lips.

My fingers touched my tongue.

From under my tongue I removed the *shem*.

ENDING 7

I pointed to the pile of pages. Pages scribed by hand. In varicolored inks, crossed out and re-corrected. Pages bent. Pages brittle. Pages hard. Pages filled. Translucent pages. Transparent pages. Pages scribbled. Pages neat. Pages worn. Pages torn from my fervid mind, the wounds still fresh, the scars not formed. Pages one could walk through, the letters so large, come swing on the bars of the T, hop through the hoop of the O. O, the ecstasy of imagination! The agony of it pulsing from brain to hand, from hand to pen and paper. I peeked at him from the crook of the K.

"See these pages? All of them?"

K looked. I riffled the manuscript. Pointed to the title page.

"See?" I said. "I created you."

K jumped up. Again he impressed me—when would he cease to impress me?—with his alacrity, his youthfulness. He took the manuscript out of my hand, placed it on the desk. He stood next to me. Towered over me, it seemed, bent slightly, and put his left hand behind my back, his right hand behind and under my knees and lifted me up with ease. He held me like a baby. I became a feather in his arms.

"No, my boy," K said. His voice soft and loving, lilting like a lullaby. His blue eyes shone. "No, no, you're dreaming." He drew nearer and nearer, his face almost touching mine. "You always have been a dreamer and you always will be."

As I opened my mouth to speak—what I wanted to say I don't recall; perhaps that I love him—K said:

"Oh, the joy of creation, my little Amschl."

We went to his table. With his right hand he swept the pages, my pages, from his desk. They flew and floated in the room. His room was filled with sailing pages, hardly moving, frozen in a still photograph. Like the tiny snowflakes settling oh so slowly in a winter scene ensconced in a small round glass ball.

Pages floating. Like paper planes. Pages scribed by hand. Pages bent. Pages fixed. Pages brittle. Pages hard. Pages filled. Pages scribbled. Pages worn. Pages torn. Pages guided by the lifeblood of my soul.

K cradled me like a baby, gazing at me lovingly with his deep blue eyes like a mother at her infant child. I was like a newborn, weightless in his arms.

"Ah, the joy of creation, my little Amschl. So you created all of this?"

K pointed to the pages floating, frozen, sailing, filling the room. Pages so many we could not see his model aeroplanes; we could not see his walls, his books.

"Yes," I said.

"With your art, your magic, your glamour, your grammar, the last two words, which as you know, are etymologically related."

"Yes," I said. "And I created you too."

"Ahh," K said, as if understanding. "You said that before. On the previous page.... Now you say, Aahh!"

"Ahh," I said.

"Wider! Louder!" he commanded, his tone sharper.

"Aaahhh!" I said, my mouth open as wide as it could go.

Holding me with his left hand, with his right he plucked the *shem* from under my tongue.

"No no no," he said.

K caught me as I fell, limp.

"No no, my boy, I created you."

THE JOURNALS OF K

A SELECTION OF ENTRIES, 1924–1993
EDITED AND TRANSLATED
FROM THE CZECH
BY
KATYA LANGBROT *
(INCLUDING A CHAPTER FROM *K'S SON* LONG THOUGHT LOST)

* with editorial assistance by the author of *K's Son*

PREFACE

These journals are not diary entries. K felt that his daily life was too ordinary to jot down every mundane activity. In any case, he was not an obsessive diarist who keeps a minute record from one day to the next. Rather, one should designate his journals a memoir. From time to time, K recalls an important event from his fascinating past, revealing aspects of his life not heretofore known. However, on occasion he does depict in detail what he thought, felt, or experienced on a given day. For the most part K recalls salient events of what he has labeled his "miraculous rebirth."

Although K has approved these selections, he declined explanations or commentary.

Not every entry in K's journals is included. For reasons of privacy or confidentiality, some entries, in accordance with the writer's wishes, will not be made public.

The journals were written on 8.5" x 11" lined spiral school notebooks, in German through 1930, and in Czech thereafter, in K's easily recognizable, slanty calligraphy, handwriting that has, remarkably, changed little over the decades. Where on rare occasion it is not quite legible, I have noted it, and when a comment is warranted I have included a note at the end of K's entry.

For safekeeping the notebooks were hidden in the Holy Ark of one of Prague's synagogues. No one, not even close members of K's family, was aware of these journals, whose existence was only recently revealed to us.

This is the first volume of a projected two-volume set.

—KATYA LANGBROT

MAY 11, 1924

THE SHEM

When I had the *shem* under my tongue, I was in a different universe. Music was not the same. It was condensed. If spread on water, it would float. On the water, the notes were a raft. Numbers too were altered. They were in a different cosmos, scattered far apart, like stars, as if light years away.

Later, I got used to the *shem*. And it no longer felt like an excess of wine, but rather a kind of divine dizziness.

June 1924

The Plan

Dr. Klopstock told me there was a man dying in the next room. The idea came to me suddenly, like a curtain of light. I shared it with him. He looked at me as if a momentary madness had come over me. D had returned to Poland while I was away, and I was angry and depressed. I decided events would have to unfold the way they were destined to before I touched the Holy Ark of the Altneushul. Everyone knew I was dying. And so I would die. I gazed back at Klopstock's eyes fixedly, as though I were hypnotizing him. In a slow, soft voice, hollow as if speaking from a tomb, he said it was possible—but complicated. No one must know, he said. I told him I want to tell my dearest friend, Brod. Klopstock replied, If you tell one you tell the world. I trust Brod, I said. Klopstock repeated his previous remark. Then I said, I must tell my parents and sisters; I can't let them suffer. Of course, Klopstock replied. Absolutely. I wouldn't have it any other way. I will swear them to secrecy, I said. They will be so happy with my miraculous cure, they will do anything.

On Tuesday I will return to Prague and let them know. And then I turned to him and begged, Please, Brod is my best friend, my other self. I can't do this to him.

The doctor was silent. Then he said, If you want me to cooperate, this is my condition. I am taking a great risk. You know that.

I do, I answered.

January 1925

The Arrangement

Was it not complicated, perhaps even bureaucratically impossible, to make the arrangements? I am sure it was, but Klopstock, a true friend, never gave me the details.

The man who died, a slightly retarded fellow named Johann Eck, had been under the care of an old housekeeper, who herself was ailing and had to return to her village in Slovakia where she died. Johann had no parents; in their will they provided money for his lifelong care. With the old woman gone, Johann was all alone in the world. I don't know exactly how Klopstock did it. Perhaps he sent out word when Johann died that the man had run away. But with Johann's death, he became me and I was born again.

Now I had to prepare my parents for my "funeral"—which my father tartly called another of my fictions. But they were so glad to have me back alive they participated in the charade. Meanwhile, I had grown my Van Dyke beard and mustache and was quite transformed…*

I told them my plan and, as best I could, why I was doing it. As time passed the why became murky. But the deed was done and there was no undoing it. Once the process began it was like a stone

* Rest of line illegible. (K.L.)

rolling downhill. There was no turning back. I told my parents I would continue to live with them as a visiting second cousin from, let's say, Hamburg, and work in my father's business. They reluctantly agreed. I don't know why they did it, but they did. They could have refused outright and the plan would have crumbled then and there.

At the cemetery during my funeral I saw a bonfire beyond the edge of the mourners. At first I thought it a memorial candle for me, then realized it was simply a banal bonfire. But the more I considered that little fire on that chill June day, the more it seemed to me, maybe—but no, it could not be. He would not do that on the day of the funeral. Brod had more sense than that. Then, gradually, the scene faded from my mind.

March 1925

Word Play

Since English was not my native language, I looked at it with detachment and amusement, even frivolity, enabling me to see things a native English speaker might not see.

I once thought of a word, "contraditional," and mentioned it to a professor of English at Prague University. Never heard of it, he said. I know, I replied, I made it up.

It's a word that bears within itself its own opposite, like one of those unicum fish that is both male and female at the same time.

"Contraditional" could be read as "con tradition," meaning, as in Spanish and Italian, "with tradition." Or, it could mean its exact opposite: "against tradition," as in "pro and con." It could also be broken up into two words, "contra" and "ditional," which makes it even more problematic, because it's a word whose meaning I don't quite know yet, but which hints at being against something, maybe against having more of something: "contra additional," people who are satisfied with what they have and don't want more. There you have it. One new word, many possible meanings.

I wasn't known for word coinage or wordplay in my writing. But in conversation with Max, I liked to play dress-up with words. A root, for instance, would be the doll, and prefixes, suffixes, and bits of other words would be the clothing. Once you get into it, it's hard to extricate yourself. One wordplay leads to another. There's no end of games. Take the word above. By adding just one letter, "c," you go from contradition to contradiction. In its stripped-down, basic form, "contradiction" means "against diction." And this leads readily to "contradictionary," an entirely new, ambiguous word, which has lots of meanings. "Contradictionary" can mean "anti-dictionary," a book where you look up the meaning of a word and only then find the word. Or you look up a word and do not find any meaning. A contradictionary could also be a word book that specializes in giving you the wrong meaning of a word, like a clock that has stopped is still a clock, but it gives you the wrong time. There's no end to wordplay.

The words one writes are like puppets without the puppeteer. They speak by themselves. I set them free. Once they go, like the stories and novels I wrote, they don't need me anymore. Like grown children that you send out into the world. Like the dove that Noah sent out of the ark, that dove, like words that speak by themselves, that didn't need Noah anymore.

April 1926

Dora Saved Me

(revised, with additions, July 1951)

Dora Diamant saved me. She was my miracle. She was the irrational force that went beyond medicine, treatments, fresh mountain air. It was love. Yes, love can heal, just as hatred, tension, ill feeling can cause malaise. Only lately have scientists found that many cases of breast cancer can be traced to unhappiness. Unhappiness does something to the body. It raises blood pressure, constricts the arteries, impedes blood flow, knots your stomach, blocks vitamins, diminishes antioxidants, causes deleterious chemical changes and lets wild cells grow and unhappiness cells spread. But love? Love is the best vitamin. It cheers the spirit and creates beneficent chemical bonds in the body. It was Dora Diamant's love that cured me.

Then why didn't I stay with her? Because I couldn't stay with any one woman too long. It had nothing to do with sickness or health. It was programmed into my personality, a flaw in my character. And, anyway, a woman changes when a man changes. She loved me when I was ill, then went back home to Poland at her father's behest. And departed for good when my condition was hopeless.

Dora left everything behind, family, tradition, to stay with me. Earlier, when Milena wanted to come and live with me for a while at the sanatorium, it wasn't enough for me. She wanted to stay only two or three weeks. She claimed she couldn't leave her husband, could not extricate herself from a miserable marriage to a husband who betrayed her three times a week with the three or four mistresses that he had and which she knew about. But, you see, that wasn't enough for me, those two-three weeks. I wanted marriage with her and children. Oh, how I wanted children—but only in marriage. Those were my views, and that's why I wrote to Milena not to write to me anymore. This drove poor Milena crazy, as may be seen by the frantic, hysterical letters she wrote to Max, asking for his advice. I told Milena not to write, not to come to see me, for it would destroy me, that unhappiness would worsen my condition, devastate my ravaged lungs, and kill me.

But then came Dora, lovely Dora Diamant, my gemstone, my jewel, the diamond of my life, with the thick dusky blond hair and thick kissable lips, whose selfless love slowly caused a reversal of my almost hopeless consumption, whose love brought me back to life, for—how wrong was Milena—I had never lost my capacity for living, not then, not today, not even during those years I was in hiding. Dora rose above herself. She cast aside ordinariness, the instinctual fear women have of the unconventional. She left her ultra-Orthodox home to be with me. And in understanding me, in loving me, she cured me. But then she heeded the call of her fanatic father and, afraid to face my approaching death, betrayed me.

Years later, before my tombstone, which I would visit once a year on my yorzeit to pay my respects to the poor man, Johann Eck, buried in my grave, a miracle happened to me, to whom so many miracles happened. But I must say that as I stood there I felt completely detached. I mean there was no one in that grave that I knew or could mourn over. Let's face it, it wasn't me. But that visit, on my yorzeit, was another way of assuring myself I am really alive. And I especially appreciated it after 1945, when the Germans were defeated, *yimakh sh'mam*...may all trace of them be wiped away from human memory. Which of course will never happen because Jews also have the Hebrew motto, "*Zekhor!*" Remember! Do not forget! Like the Torah says, "Do not forget what Amalek did to you!"

Typical Jewish schizophrenia. On the one hand, blot out; on the other, "Remember!"

I looked at my gravesite with a mixture of solemnity and amusement, and then turned away, assured I was alive, delighted with the trick I had been playing on the world.

And now I also think of my sisters and other relatives and friends whose ashes are scattered in the winds above the Auschwitz crematoria, Jews who had no tombstones of their own.

NOTE: K does not mention here kissing the curtain of the Holy Ark of the Altneushul, which he has claimed sent an electrical jolt of cure through him. Perhaps Dora's curing K is just a metaphor. But, then again, who can penetrate the mystical powers of love? (K.L.)

SEPTEMBER 1926

COSMOS OF IDEAS

I had a tremendous world in my head, a cosmos of ideas, that tumbled over one another like circus clowns, and I tried to pay attention to all of them, to catch them before they vanished. I had so little time. And when I made time to write, I couldn't write quickly enough. No matter how quickly I wrote I still couldn't jot down everything surging in my mind. The ideas came like a tidal wave, a gigantic crest of water. But how could I write down a tidal wave? I only had a thimble in my hand. And I could catch no more than a thimbleful of that enormous tidal wave of water. All the rest was lost. As if there were dozens of stages around me, and on each stage someone was singing a beautiful song, a memorable song, and I could not focus on those dozen stages, those dozen songs. I could only focus on one. Because for me writing was a form of prayer and I wanted to keep this form of secular prayer alive. I had a dreamlike inner life full of dozens of songs that was always out of reach because of the dull, vapid prose of my insurance company responsibilities. It was as if a wicked man stood at a gate and with his constant chatter of unsmiling words tried to keep me from entering the gate of song.

There was a time when that legal work at the insurance company plus the extra job at my father's factory that he thrust upon me drove me to distraction. I pressed my face to the window there and gave serious thought to jumping out.

But ever since my own life was renewed I have greater connection to life, its sanctity, and no matter how depressed I am I will not press my face to the windowpane and give serious thought to ending my life. But, on the other hand, who knows, that limited time I had before 1924 may have unconsciously compressed my creative energies and powers, in a kind of elastic tension. The words of The Ethics of the Fathers, the Pirkei Avot, where Rabbi Tarfon says, "It is not granted you to complete the task—but yet you may not give it up," became a motto for me.

That phrase, by the way, "elastic tension," a particularly apt one, is Brod's, not mine.

January 1927

My Father in Shul

My father went to shul four days a year, the two days of Rosh Hashana, Yom Kippur, and the first day of Pesach, and I went with him. My attention was riveted to the Holy Ark, and when it was opened, revealing dolls without heads, it always terrified me, as did the crowds of people. My father told me I might be called upon to read from the Torah and this terrified me too. It made me literally tremble with fear. Later on, I discovered an unknown shul at the other side of town whose Ark terrified me not so much by what was in it as by what was on it. I will write about it some*

NOTE: K apparently forgot about this synagogue, for it is never again mentioned in his journals. It is likely that this "unknown" shul is the one with the lions atop the Aron Kodesh, depicted in *K's Son*. (K.L.)

---

* Thought not completed.

December 1927

Burning K's Manuscripts

On his deathbed Virgil wanted his mss of *The Aeneid* destroyed. That did not influence me at all in my decision, for I just read about it recently. It just shows that I wasn't alone.

March 1928

Source of the Great Wall

How I came across a Chinese women in Prague I'll never know. Maybe she was connected with the Chinese Embassy. She never told me. Quite a beautiful woman, small, petite, translucent porcelain skin, but I forgot the color of her eyes. They surely could not have been blue like mine. I have never met anyone from China, although in a circus, once, I saw Chinese acrobats and tumblers.

I left my apartment building one morning and she crossed my path slowly and smiled at me. She held a shopping bag in one hand and looked down at a piece of paper she had in the other. I assumed she was looking for a certain address. Perhaps she was delivering something.

With a polite preface, I asked if she needed help, hoping that she understood German. She nodded quickly. House, she said. Visit? I asked. No. She pointed to herself. House. I gathered she had recently moved in and was still having difficulty finding her building, many of which looked alike in Prague. Near here, she said, and made a little circle with her index finger. We spoke in abortive phrases. She had just moved here, and she giggled softly, helplessly, and still needed assistance with finding her own address. I know house, I said. She made a little motion with her hand that said, Come with me. I gestured to her bag, then pointed to myself and made a lifting motion. I took the bag from her. It was rather heavy. Not bricks but probably five kilo of flour. I show you way. She walked alongside me. Two turns and three streets later we stood before her building. Ahh, yes, building, she said, recognizing it. You want to come up? I make tea. Chinese tea. Thank you. I followed her up to the third floor. The flour got heavier with each landing. From her jacket pocket she took out the key and opened the door.

I stepped into the small apartment. A fragrance of jasmine hung in the air. A pleasant warmth surged in me. You like Chinese music? Of course, I said, thinking: I love music I have never heard before; it's just music I've heard that I don't like. She put on a record. The Chinese sounds, a high-pitched woman vocalist, and the perfumed air made my head spin. She began moving her head and hands ever so subtly, a happy, innocent expression on her face. Then her gestures became more elaborate, ballet-like. She may have beckoned me to dance with her, I don't know. It just seemed her fingers called to me and, my head still whirling slowly, I danced with her, and she looked up at me and said, Soon I make Chinese tea. I held her slim waist and moved as best I could to the Oriental sounds. Then she suddenly slipped away and said, Wait, I put on Chinese costume. I looked about the room. A small sofa. Some Chinese prints on the wall. A little table for the phonograph and radio.

Five minutes later she appeared wearing a traditional Chinese green silk skirt and matching jacket, decorated with gold appliquéd dragons, that revealed her fine neck and throat. The music had stopped. She put it on again and continued dancing and moved closer to me. I bent down and kissed her neck and then her ear. She looked at me but did not say a word. Take jacket off, I said, and I helped her. She wore a white brassiere. I made a motion, Take it off. She had small breasts, but her nipples astounded me. They looked like shiny deep red cherries that had been pasted on her breasts. I had never seen a Chinese woman naked before, so I couldn't tell if this was unique to her body or if all Chinese women were like that.

You have family? I asked. Son, fifteen, in school. In Prague? No, Shanghai. Her face was young, but her hands—one can always tell a woman's age by her hands—showed she must have been in her late thirties. But she said, Me, forty-four. I took her hand and walked to the phonograph, lifted the arm, then walked with her to the bedroom.

Who was this woman, I wondered, and what kind of dream-world had I fallen into? I felt I was in one of Boccaccio's tales. Every adolescent boy's dream was happening to me. I knew nothing of her language; she knew only a bit of mine. But still we spoke the same language.

Although she did not resist, her face remained impassive. Not a shred of excitement or emotion, as though her body wanted one thing but her will, her mind, were fixed on another plane; as if she wanted loving but refused intimacy. As if by seeming passive and not enjoying it, or, at least, giving the impression she wasn't enjoying it, or sending a signal to me by her stoic-faced, inscrutably Oriental, absolutely unfeeling demeanor that she was so totally removed, she wasn't actually betraying her husband.

You sick, she said, not as a question but as a declarative. How did she know that I once had tuberculosis? There was no sign of it on me. No sick, I said. Healthy. Sex sick, she said and pointed. Did she mean syphilis? I laughed. No no, I said, and laughed at the absurdity of it. Not that sickness. Yes yes, you sick, she said, as if by saying that she could excuse to herself her lack of enjoyment, or maybe explain to me her passivity by saying she was anxious about getting sick, catching something from me. Her quick concupiscence had a strange turn for me. Was she assuaging her guilt somewhat by accenting illness? She wouldn't kiss me. Her lips clamped shut tightly. Maybe you sick, I said. And I afraid. She shook her head. You first man who not my husband. Ahh, I said, so you're married. He works? Where? But she either didn't understand me or didn't want to answer. She nodded, said, Works where. I asked, What time he home? She held up seven fingers. It was only 4:30 but I felt it was time to go. She was warm and cold. Porcelain. A wall. The Great Wall of China. Several entrances. But still a wall. Me come tomorrow. You make Chinese tea. Tea, she said. You sick. I know.

NOTE: There is some puzzlement here. The entry, dated March 1928, has two contradictory statements. (Also, remember that often in K's journals he is writing about an event that may have taken place years ago.) In any case, K indicates that he no longer has tuberculosis, which would place the encounter sometime after late spring 1924, when he was cured. (On the other hand, he could have been fibbing to the Chinese woman.) At the same time, K states that this encounter inspired his story, "The Great Wall of China," which was written in 1917, the actual year he was diagnosed with tuberculosis. Yes, a contradiction. (See K's entry, March 1925, where he discusses word coinage, "contradictionary.") But, as usual, K will not comment on his journal entries. (K.L.)

January 1930

How Brod Made Me a Writer

Max made me a writer before I was a published author, mentioning my name along with Thomas Mann, Meyrink, and Wedekind in 1907. Brod had read some of my stories but I had not been published yet.

I liked Max's novel, *The Kingdom of Love*; it's rather hard to read a novel in which one appears supposedly after one is dead. But it is both an imaginative and accurate work. Still, I always felt that Max was a better composer than writer.

December 1930

How to Interpret My Works

Some books read from left to right, some right to left, some up and down. My books read inside out, backwards, in mirror language. That's the secret of interpreting my work that no one has discovered yet.

September 1932

Creativity Passing through This World

Someone once wrote that I couldn't wait for my daily grind of work at the office to end so I could find time to be at peace and write. Most people pass through this world only once. I passed through twice. Can you think of anything more creative than that? I know this is specious reasoning, playing with words. But don't we writers always do just that? It is our stock in trade. And, anyway, this so-called drive of mine to write is a gross exaggeration. I didn't spend all my free time writing. I loved to go to cafés, sit with friends, travel, play billiards, go for walks in the country, attend theater, study Hebrew and Yiddish, watch aeroplanes. The two in my room I called my flying prayer shawls, my gliding *taleisim*. I wasn't always driven. Rarely, in fact. For if I were, I would have written more.

When Brod began publishing my works, I realized that the little bonfire I had seen at the cemetery could not have been Brod's doing.

APRIL 1933

TWO WORLDS EXIST

I have come to the conclusion that there are two worlds. One is ours over which we have no control. The other God is in, in a parallel world, and He closes His eyes and spins a wheel of fortune, which determines what happens here.

NOTE: It is quite likely that this is K's veiled comment about Hitler's rise to power in Germany. (K.L.)

July 1933

A Fiftieth Anniversary K Symposium

At the K fiftieth-birthday celebration in Prague in 1933, I had an interesting encounter. The girl who showed me to my seat was a Jewish graduate student in Prague University. She said she was writing a dissertation on K. Because she was quite attractive I told her I knew intimately a number of the people in K's circle, including Max Brod and others. Will you have time to talk to me? she wanted to know. (The very question I was hoping for.) I took her to a café and as I spoke about K and Brod, she reveling in anecdotes she had never heard, I looked into the girl's eyes and saw she was falling in love with me. Her name was Sara.

It was my last affair. The one that followed, many years later, was not an affair. That was destiny.

But even destiny has its quirks and ironies. When we parted, I asked Sara her family name. She said Diamant. My heart fell. "From the family of the girl who was K's love?" I asked, my words quaking. I wavered in and out of consciousness. "I'm her much younger cousin. I had to leave Poland because the religious life there was too oppressive for me." I asked about Dora. Married? Children? Well? "No, not married, never married. And how do you know so much about K and his circle?" Sara asked. "I'm Philippe Klein, K's second cousin," I said. "K told me everything."

"We live in a mirror world, don't we?" were Sara's parting words. "Another K and another Diamant together again."

June 1938

[Untitled]

In his biography of me, Max says that my "childhood must have been lonely." He was right. It was. Despite parents and sisters.

I had a Dickensian imagination even in my twenties, before I began to write. I dreamt of becoming a rich man and driving into the ghetto on a horse-drawn coach and rescuing a beautiful girl whom someone was beating.

I look at old photos of myself now and see a handsome man. But then I thought of myself as ugly, poorly dressed, hunched over despite my height. I was thoroughly dissatisfied with myself. If you think of yourself as a lowly worm, it's not too great an imaginative leap to imagine yourself waking up one morning as a long worm or insect. I once mentioned this to a fellow writer, who asked if this might be a direct influence on my famous story. I told him: in writing the only direct influence is plagiarism.

I was a rather good student except in mathematics. I passed only because I cried during the exams. Yes. Literally. I cried. And the boy who sat next to me, I still remember his name, Hugo, let me copy his answers. Once, in the seventh grade, our teacher told us to make up a history exam. There were twelve boys in the class and each one would have to submit a question by the next day. Of course, all the students got together that day in my house while my parents were away working and we exchanged questions. But we did it cleverly. If everyone was to get one hundred the teacher would suspect collusion. So we assigned grades. Our two class dummies, Mordecai Sahn and Samuel Dankhalter, who usually failed, were allowed to get seventy, and not a drop more. We forced them to give some wrong answers. And those who usually got C's got B's and so on.

January 1939

With Max Brod to a Hasidic Shaleshudess

With my Prague friends, Felix Weltsch and Franz Werfel, we discussed literature and, of course, Zionism. In addition to those topics, with Brod I also had religious encounters. Once Max took me, on a Saturday evening, just before the Sabbath was departing, to the home of a Hasidic rebbe. He was a refugee from Poland, now living in a suburb of Prague. The rebbe had an open house for the *shaleshudess* meal, which is a redundancy, for the word "meal" is contained in that Hebrew/Yiddish word.

In the dining room, the Jews, all wearing the round fur hats known as *shtreiml*, sat around the table singing sad songs, trying to extend the Sabbath, trying to hold on for just a bit longer to its mystic power. These Sabbath songs, these *zemiros*, replete with sadness—not gloom, mind you, not depression, not unhappiness or despair—just sadness at the departure of the Sabbath, which relieved the Jews of their earthly woes, and for the love of which they expressed with their lively but minor-key melodies, made an impression on me.

Impression, yes. But they didn't snare me. I did not become a participant. It was as if I were attending a theater, as if watching one of Chekhov's plays. Fascinated. Intrigued. But not moved to the point where I would ascend to the stage and sit with the characters. I was just an observer. The only difference was that this Hasidic *shtibl*, as I watched the Hasidism singing their *shaleshudess zemiros*, this was my theater, my stage. Nevertheless, it didn't move me enough to join. Yet I admired the devotion of the participants.

Years later, just before the Great War, I went to another such evening when I was traveling in Munkatch in northern Hungary. In Roman Vishniac's wonderful collection of photos from Eastern Europe there is one he secretly took from the women's gallery without the rebbe or the Hasidim realizing it. A Hasidic friend of Vishniac's had helped him get into the shul and hide him upstairs in the woman's gallery. Of course they were totally against letting themselves be photographed, and especially on the Sabbath. The picture was taken on a time exposure. A flash would have been too obvious. If one looks carefully at the photograph one can see Max and me, the only men without a *shtreiml*, sitting at the table, the sixth and seventh men to the left of the white-bearded Munkatcher rebbe.

AUGUST 1939

A DREAM

I once had a dream that I was traveling to the USA, which I have never visited, and put my belongings in a room with a false front so that the enemy wouldn't get them. Then, in a hotel in Alabama, the clerk says to me, while I'm registering, How come you're not wearing your yellow star if you're…*

* Rest of line illegible.

September 2, 1939

The Penal Machine

Yesterday the Penal Machine took over Europe. What device can counteract it?

1942 [NO MONTH GIVEN]

THE GERMANS

They went upstairs even though there was no upstairs. They were everywhere. In attics. In cellars. In wood they were termites. In air, microbes. Under water they were sharks. On land they were power, terror, the ubiquitous evil beast in ancient fables.

NOTE: These are K's only journal entries during the war. (K.L.)

June 1945

Eating in the Attic

Behold, truly the eye of the Lord is on those who stand in awe of Him and await His lovingkindness to deliver them from death and sustain them in famine.

You ask about food? Do you remember the scene in Noah's Ark where the dove brings back a twig? I have mentioned that dove before. The same dove that fed me. There was a window in the attic of the Altneushul and I opened it one morning and the dove flew in, bringing food. Reread the quote from Psalm 33 above. Yes, He sustained me in hunger and delivered me from death. And, of course, the g…

NOTE: K doesn't finish the word or the sentence. (K.L.)

??? September 1945

Milena

(handwriting unclear as to date)

My darling Milena once wrote that I do not have the capacity for living. She was as worldly as dear Dora was innocent. Poor Milena—though not Jewish, she too, like my sisters, was taken by the Germans and murdered by them in a concentration camp. Milena said of me that I am not of this world. Things like typewriters mystified me, she said. When she remarked that I did not have the capacity for living, she did not mean living the good life, living it up, as the American slang expression has it. She meant living, period. Not having the capacity for living meant I would never get well. That I will die soon.

In my imagination I visited her, let's say in the mid-thirties, and revealed myself to her, proving her wrong, showing her that not only did I have a capacity for living but for defeating my nemesis, my illness. That I indeed improved. That I would not die, but live, as the Bible declares.

But, of course, although I could have, I did not act out my fantasy. The surprise, the shock, would have killed her. I couldn't, wouldn't, do anything like that.

You could have written to her, I hear someone suggest.

Yes.

That "Yes" contains many resonances, like an empty barrel. Yes, I could have. Yes, it was over between us. Yes, but what good would it have accomplished?

My life was my secret and I kept it well.

April 1947

On Girls' Legs

In his novel, where I appear briefly, Max Brod has a rather modern view on women's legs. He says, Nowadays, girls have legs up to their necks. I never thought Brod capable of such an observation, of such an image.

May 15, 1948

Jewish Dreams

Today, the two-thousand-year-old Jewish dream of return to Zion has been accomplished. Thank God, the State of Israel has been founded. The Jews have a homeland.

But do I?

MAY 1950

WITH S.Y. AGNON IN JERSUSALEM

When I visited Israel for the first time in 1950, I went to Jerusalem to see S. Y. Agnon, the great Hebrew writer with whom I have often been compared. Born in 1888, he was a few years younger than I. At once we had a commonality of spirit. Agnon, a man of imagination with a penchant for the metaphysical and the surreal (read his great novella, *'Iddo* and *'Eynam*), at once believed who I claimed to be. We embraced and he welcomed me as long-lost kin and told me to call him Shmuel Yosef. I liked at once this friendly, witty, and traditional man with the black velvet yarmulke on his head.

And Agnon made sure to put me at my ease by telling me that a K-esque story of his was published in 1908, when he was twenty, and before I ever saw any of my work in print. We spoke the language we both knew, German, with a bit of Yiddish. He marveled how a Central European Jew like me, with no familial tradition of Yiddish, could even speak it haltingly. I told him my Yiddish is basically self-taught and described how I brought a famous Polish Yiddish theater group to Prague.

But when I began to speak Hebrew I really stunned him. I explained that I had had private tutoring in Germany, and added classes as well in an institute for higher Jewish learning. He did not know we had both been in Germany in the early 1920s and remarked, "Too bad I did not know you then." After discussing writers we had read, I began speaking about music. Agnon said: "Music? Don't talk to me about music."

In his novel about Agnon, *The Yemenite Girl*, which I read in the Crypto-Slovenian translation, author Curt Leviant gets it right on the mark when he has Agnon say, "God gave man eight notes, and look how many noises he can make with them." Agnon feels music sets a wall around us, almost imprisons us. Separates us from the real world. I said that Freud shared his view, and Nabokov too. Neither had any appreciation nor ear for music. I admitted that despite my love for classical music my skill with tonalities was so bad that, according to Max Brod, I couldn't tell the difference between the *Merry Widow* and Papagena, even though music, like language, flows sequentially, not like a painting where there is no sequentiality, where you see everything at once. Then I mentioned the glory of *The Magic Flute*, which Agnon claimed he had never heard of. But I am sure he was shamming, for right away he asked me, with a twinkle in his surprisingly light blue eyes, if I could tell the difference between Papagena and Papageno.

Agnon was a shrewd, good-humored man, very engaging and hospitable. As he served me cognac and home-baked cookies his wife had made, he told he had read all my works. He would keep my secret, he promised, and added that my miraculous story just confirms the reality of all my fiction and all of his.

But before I ate and drank, he offered me a yarmulke and suggested I make the proper blessing. "This will give me the mitzva," he said, "of answering Amen."

NOTE: S.Y. Agnon won the Nobel Prize in Literature in 1966, sharing it with another Jewish writer, the poet Nelly Sachs. It should also be noted that, contrary to their assumption, K and Agnon were not in Germany at the same time, for Agnon returned to Palestine in 1921, while K was there only in 1923. (K.L.)

June 8, 1950

Visit to Brod

I stood at Brod's door, the second-floor apartment on Zamenhof Street, one of the quiet streets of old Tel Aviv. I heard music. Brod was playing the piano, perhaps composing. My heart was racing. I looked at the little brass plate on the door: Dr. Max Brod, underneath which was another metal sign: PLEASE DO NOT KNOCK OR RING BETWEEN 2 AND 4 P.M. I looked at my watch. Four thirty.

I rang. He opened the door; I recognized him at once. Short, slight, oval face, with the intelligent, good-humored mien I remembered from decades ago. Brod has all his hair, no longer black but silver grey.

"Shalom," said Brod. He said some more words in Hebrew.

"Shalom, I'm from Prague, Dr. Brod," I said in German. "To quote Shakespeare, I have little Yiddish, less Hebrew."

Brod's eyes lit up as he laughed. "Ah, please, please come in. From Prague. And you survived. Who are you?"

I hesitated. Bit my lip. I didn't realize I was biting my lip until I sensed the pain. A difficult moment in my life. One I had not rehearsed, not thought through. I was so excited about the possibility of seeing Max, how I would negotiate the details of the encounter never entered my mind. I knew it would be difficult but I had no prepared script. Aside from my parents and sisters (and Agnon), I had not revealed my identity to anyone.

I gazed down at Brod.

In retrospect, I should have spoken differently.

"Don't you recognize me?"

"No. I can't say I do. I might say there is a vague familiarity in those piercing blue eyes, as if I've seen you before, but no, I can't say I do. Please tell me. Come in. Sit down, please."

I should have prepared him. I should have gone about it more delicately.

"I'm…it's me."

I thought he would rush to embrace me with a cry of joy.

But my words, as if propelled from a wind tunnel, made Brod move back. They seemed to push him toward the wall. His eyes widened and his mouth dropped. I had never seen my friend's gentle face so white.

"Impossible," he cried out. "But…but…this is utter nonsense. Do you expect me to believe this? Who are you? I, we, his family and friends attended his funeral."

"I know," I said softly. "You tried to speak but you broke down, my poor Maxie. And I had to step in and say a few kind words about myself."

"Please stop—or leave."

"Don't you believe it's me?"

Brod sat down. "No." He sighed. "I do not.… Why are you doing this?"

"Am I so unrecognizable? Can't you see past my white beard and mustache?"

"It has nothing to do with recognizability. Human beings do not return from the dead. Nor do normal people create painful theater for strangers."

I asked for five more minutes to explain. Brod consented. I told him the entire story from beginning to end, including most of the speech my "cousin" delivered that day. It probably took fifteen minutes but Brod did not interrupt.

Max looked me over. His tone changed. "Well, the height matches my friend's. And that eulogy—most extraordinary. But that is all. I am sorry."

"And I, Maxie, am even more sorry…and the voice? Has my voice changed that much, Brod of the fine musical ear?"

He did not reply.

"I liked your biography." It was a little thick in the prose, I thought, but I did not tell him this. But I did say, "You remember the long passage in your book where you quote an article of mine in a professional insurance magazine outlining the danger to workers from cutting machines? You miss pointing out how similar in style is my precise, analytical, bureaucratic description of the saws to my detailed description of the horrendous machine in 'The Penal Colony.'"

"You never intended that I totally burn all the manuscripts, right?" Brod said suddenly.

He brought it up, not I. I didn't want to make him feel uncomfortable.

Nevertheless, I said, "It was in my will."

"But I did destroy them," was Brod's response.

"But you didn't."

"But I did. You commanded that I destroy your unpublished works."

"But you didn't, Max. Why do you keep saying you did?"

"But, as you will soon see, I followed the letter of your instructions if not their intent."

"But how?"

"As soon as I heard you died, I copied out the first page of some of your works into a bundle and at a clearing not far from the gravesite I burned them…"

"The bonfire—"

"…thereby fulfilling…"

"—at the cemetery that day."

"…your wish."

"So I was right. I always wondered about that fire. For a while I thought it was indeed you burning my manuscripts."

"And you wanted to stop me."

"But I couldn't...it would have ruined everything."

"Aha! You see?"

"I couldn't undo my pose."

"Just as I thought. You never really wanted me to destroy your work. Otherwise, you would have chosen someone else."

"Max, you can't question me as K and yet not believe it's me. But even if you don't believe me, and I can understand why you don't, please don't tell anyone about this visit. Aside from my parents and sisters, the former long gone, the latter killed by the Germans, no one knows I'm alive."

But as I got to the door, Brod invited me to visit him again next time I came to Israel.

June 12, 1950

Thoughts on Brod

That was another of my regrets—betraying dear Brod. We used to write to each other two or three times a week even though we lived in Prague, in the same neighborhood. And I never shared with him my most intimate secret. I had made my decision and adamantly kept it. No one else must know. Not even my friend, my other self. That is why it took courage to visit him when I was in Israel in 1950.

I can't get Max Brod out of my mind.

I knocked. He opened the door and, as in a magic show, my friend appeared. It took all the strength I had to restrain myself from embracing him and kissing his cheeks. How I imagined—how powerful is fantasy—that we would at once recognize each other and fall into each other's embrace, weeping with joy. I told him I have regards from someone he wouldn't believe is alive, one of his dearest friends. He took me into his book-lined living room. While at sixty-nine my hair was already all white, his was a mixture of black and grey. Brod, same age as I, had remained slim, and from the back he still looked like a little boy.

Then I told him who I was. He didn't believe me. I understood his incredulity. If the reverse had held true and he were me and I were him, I wouldn't have believed him either. When I sounded out my family name, I saw a shadow of fright cross his face. Never had I seen Brod's gentle, good-humored face so pale. He thought I had come back from the dead to haunt him, to punish him, to wreak vengeance on him for not obeying my will, for not burning, destroying my manuscripts as I had specifically wished. For not executing a dead man's will is a serious violation of trust.

"I came to greet you, Maxie, not berate you. It was you who made me famous."

He denied it, saying, "No, it was your genius. But if you really intended for me to burn your manuscripts, you could easily have chosen someone else, someone who didn't appreciate your talent, some hack who would have been willing to be the executor of your estate and dumbly do what was ordered. You wouldn't have chosen someone who loved you like a brother the way I did. By choosing me you knew beyond a shadow of a doubt that I would not obey your last will and testament."

"But you waited about ten years after my death, until the early 1930s, to begin publishing my works."

"Now you're complaining about that too? You can't have it both ways."

"Neither can you, Maxie. You can't criticize me as K and not believe it's me."

"And if you wanted to protest my publication, you could have asked your father or your sisters, to whom the royalties were being paid, to stop the publication."

"Do you or do you not believe it's me?"

Brod still didn't believe it was me. He said it was impossible that I had come back from the dead and was now here in Israel. And why did I wait so long to contact him?

"You could have found me earlier," he said in a plaintive tone.

In this strange manner, he both accepted and denied the fact that I was K.

As I think of that scene now that I'm writing it in my room in Prague, I recall how frustrating it was for me that my best friend did not believe me, how sad I wasn't able to convince him.

With pen in hand, I sense that I frown, tilt my head, and even now I move my lips in a little moue of not quite disappointment, but rather as an expression of someone who shrugs and declares: That's life. What can you do?

June 20, 1950

With Brod

I knocked on the door. The piano sounds stopped. I heard brisk footsteps. My heart was pounding. He opened the door without asking who was there.

"Hello, Max," I said. "Shalom."

I could see he was puzzled.

"Shalom. With whom do I have the pleasure of speaking?"

"My spoken Hebrew is still weak. I would prefer speaking the language we used to speak: German."

"But who are you?"

"K."

Brod stepped back. "Impossible."

"Stanley K," I said. "Ks' cousin." By now I had moved from the small hallway into his living room. As I expected, books everywhere. "You never really met K's cousin, except very briefly at the funeral. I was very moved by how you choked up and could not speak."

"What funeral?"

"*The* funeral. K's funeral. And when you could not speak, I stepped in and said a few words in honor of my beloved cousin."

"The funeral," Max said. He looked stunned. He looked as if he were holding on to that word to get his bearings.

"Yes."

"I looked for you. I sought you out at the shiva. But you were gone."

"I had to go back to Hamburg or wherever I claimed I was from."

I saw the crease forming on Maxie's brow. The ambiguity, the veiled hint at deception, he caught it. But it confused him.

"Stanley?" Brod wisely accented, questioned, the very un-Pragueish name.

"Yes, Maxie. Actually, no, Maxie."

My use of the diminutive, the endearing name I always called him, gave him another shock.

"You look wonderful," I said. "It doesn't seem like twenty-six years have passed."

But he disregarded that. "What kind of name is Stanley? That's an American name." He looked me up and down, measuring my height with his gaze.

Did Brod recognize me, or was it my wishful thinking? I had a question for him. At first I restrained myself—thought of asking, should have asked, it would only have been courteous, decent, *mentshlikh*, to ask, How have you been? But instead I blurted out:

"Why didn't you destroy all of my manuscripts? I asked you to. My will specified it. It was a legal document. No one, absolutely no one, could claim it wasn't a valid legal document. Drawn up by a lawyer. Me. Your best friend. Why couldn't you honor it?"

"But you are..." and Brod didn't finish the sentence, didn't begin the word. His face was pinched, pale. In his voice a tremor palpitated.

I took a deep breath.

"Dead men don't breathe. Argue. Question. It's me, Maxie. I didn't die...I was cured. Remember? From the sanatorium I wanted to go home for a week."

"Yes. I was away in Slovakia. Your mother told me that Doctor Klopstock had consented to your trip."

"The day I left Prague to return to Vienna, on my way back to the train station, I went in first to say goodbye to the Altneushul. Since it was noontime it was empty. I went up to the Aron Kodesh, touched the curtain, kissed it. An electric shock of ecstasy went through me."

And then I told him the rest of the story, including the *faux* funeral. I apologized to him for deserting him, for not telling him, for not contacting him again. "Only my parents and sisters knew, and everyone was sworn to silence.... Do you believe me, Maxie?"

He didn't reply. Again he looked me over from head to toe. I saw him staring at my white Van Dyke. I sensed the thoughts going through his head. He's as tall as K, somewhat resembles him. But he could be an imposter.

Brod shook his head, thinking: Impossible. He's playing a strange game.

"Why didn't you obey the terms of my will?" I asked again.

Brod was apparently too overcome by my initial challenge a few moments earlier. But now that I asked the question a second time, he perked up. No doubt this matter must have distressed him for years. He shot back with an answer, parts of which were surely prepared ages ago for a question addressed to him no doubt many times. But never by the author himself.

"Then why did you choose me? You knew, deep down you knew I would not, could not possibly, obey your ridiculous, immature, childishly willful instructions. If you really wanted your writing destroyed, you could have done the job yourself when you were back home in Prague for those few days, or you would have, could have, chosen someone else. You knew, don't tell me you didn't know, that I wouldn't do it. As it is forbidden to take a life, so it is forbidden to take a life's work."

"Do you believe me that I am K?"

"Frankly, no."

"Then how can you talk to me, argue with me, as though K stands before you and at the same time not believe me?"

I laughed. I laughed at the absurdity of it. I laughed at the absurdity of K standing before Brod in Tel Aviv in 1950.

Brod laughed too..

"Man is a complex, contradictory creature," he said.

On my way to the door I imagined I was on stage, in a play, and I stopped dramatically. I addressed the first three words to the door, speaking loudly:

"And another thing…" And then I wheeled and faced him. "About the sex passages."

"What sex passages?"

"Exactly. What sex passages? You took the words right out of my mouth. And out of my books. I've looked and looked and couldn't find them. Why did you delete? Why did you act as a censor? Who gave you permission to impose your prudery on my works? Who gave you permission to be holier than me?"

As I spoke I saw him turn white. And then a wave of rose, reddening to scarlet, filled his face. My God, my Maxie blushed like a sixteen-year-old girl caught by her parents kissing a boy. Like a sky flaming at sunset the flush came over his cheeks, to his ears, to the bridge of his nose, red even up to his eyelids. And I immediately regretted hurting him, embarrassing him. The Ethics of the Fathers in the Talmud states, "He who makes his friend's face turn white in public loses his share in the World to Come." But it was just the two of us. No one else was in the room. Still, I felt bad for him. I hadn't anticipated such an emotion.

"As if 'The Metamorphosis' has a lot of sex," Brod said.

"You know as well as I do it's not there, so why are you saying that? It's from *The Trial* and *The Castle* and *Amerika* and other works, works that you recast to your standards."

"I wanted your works to be acceptable. And accepted. I didn't want to take a chance of having them rejected just because of those passages."

"Whose works?" I said slyly.

"Yours." But Brod choked on the word.

"Aha," I muttered through barely parted lips. "But you still don't believe I'm K, do you?"

"No."

"Then how can you defend yourself so vigorously? And if I were not K, how would I know about the deleted passages, Maxie? You can't have it both ways."

Brod did not—could not—reply.

"All right! Then I don't believe you're Brod. Why did you put that *faux* Dr. Brod sign on your door?"

But Max saw the twinkle in my eye. He understood, even after all these years; he got the nuance of my voice, its special comic timbre, and he smiled, then began to laugh.

"If I'm not Brod, and you may very well be right," and now the laughter faded from his voice and face, "because Brod died that day along with you in the cemetery—if I'm not Brod how can you complain about what I did? You can't complain about me not adhering to your will, and then complain about censorship. The two are mutually contradictory.... You can't have it both ways."

We looked at, we stared at each other. At an impasse. Which way would it turn?

"Then we must conclude," I said, "that we're living in a K-esque world where illogic prevails and contradiction is king."

I think I saw a slight nod. Brod barely, but just barely, ticked his head up a millimeter, down a millimeter.

"Sex maniac," he said, giggling like he used to.

"Censor."

"Skirt-chaser."

"Jesuit. Fanatic. Deleter of holy writ." I could barely speak for the laughter interlaced my words.

And soon we were both giggling together like we used to years ago in our youth in Prague.

"But one thing is sure," I said.

"What's that?"

"Maybe I'm not K and you're not Brod, but the love between these two idiots staring at each other in consternation and laughter and disbelief, both of us miraculously alive, is as strong as ever."

And we took one, two steps toward each other and embraced like David and Jonathan.

I don't know whose tears ran down my cheeks onto my neck, mine or Maxie's.

NOTE: There are noticeable differences between K's first journal entry pertaining to his visit with Brod in Tel Aviv and the two others. Perhaps the second or third one is, to use K's phrase in the above entry, "wishful thinking" on his part, words K wanted to say but didn't. On the other hand, it is possible that all three took place. But for the sake of accuracy and completion all are included. K refuses to comment. "My journals are what they are. I don't provide Rashi commentary," he says. (K.L.)

January 1952

Clothing

I always wore white shirts, winter and summer. I couldn't imagine myself wearing any other color. Years back the collars were round, as were the brim and shape of my black derbies. With the passing of time the collars became less round and more and more pointy. Colored shirts came into fashion, checked and dotted and striped ones, like the sheep that Jacob bred on Laban's farm. But these I would never wear; although I tolerated them on others.

And jeans? Never, nevah, nepa.

Jeans were for peasants.

1952 [NO MONTH GIVEN]

Dora

In 1951, D returned for two weeks and then, surprisingly, three months later to inform me she's pregnant. But she says she wants an abortion. She says she cannot care for the baby. I refuse. Our child, I explained to her, the family I longed for with her decades ago. Another miracle. An unending series of miracles. And you want this miracle scraped with a surgeon's knife? No. Not. Never. I'll find a Jewish couple who will adopt the baby.

I want the child to live.

I don't accept her flimsy excuse that she's too old to be a mother and care for a baby. That she's unsuited.

I will not elaborate on our many exchanges, on my feelings and D's feelings. Suffice to say that through the shamesh at the Altneushul we found a childless couple, now working in Prague, to adopt the baby. I deliberately did not meet the couple, nor did I want to learn their name. The final arrangements were made by the Jewish Children's Home, Prague's famous caring Jewish orphanage.

Now all we had to do was wait.

I can't speak of the tragedy. Maybe it was my fault. Had I listened to her she would still be with us, with me. But like Rachel she gave life while giving up her own.

Eight days later we had a sad, subdued bris for the little boy. Before the baby was born I spoke of a possible name if it would be a boy. D protested, saying that Ashkenazi Jews do not name children after living relatives and certainly not after a father. I told her it wasn't after me but after my great-grandfather. We then spoke again about the adoption. She said she didn't want to be present when the baby was given away—and how prophetic, alas, were her words.

Yes, there was a little tweak in my heart as our baby, D's and mine, was given away. The Jewish Children's Home did not tell the couple that the mother had died in childbirth. Why spoil their joy? The shamesh and the officials at the Home liked the couple—bright, intelligent, sensitive—and I knew they would make good parents to the infant.

It was good I didn't have a child with D in the 1920s. I have often stated that I wanted a child with her under normal family circumstances. And anyway, they, them, the evil ones, would have killed the child. But when I met her after the war I was a different man and it was a different world. True, I was old, but after my so-called death I never looked at myself in a mirror again and so in my mind's eye I was a young man and I felt good. In fact, the older I got the better I felt. My insomnia was gone, I was vital, strong, healthy. I never felt older than mid-thirties. Only one's outside changes. Within, one is always young.

April 1962

Max Brod, Again

Twelve years passed since I was in Israel, since I saw Brod. Now I visited him again. This time I brought all the letters he had written to me that I had saved.

His eyes gleamed. He smiled. He hugged me, pressed me close to him. Tears stood in his eyes.

"Fear not, doubt not," I told him. "It is indeed I."

"So you lived," Brod said. "And you let your friend, your brother, mourn for you. You let me suffer that day. I had no tears left."

"Yes," I said, and I could not look him in the eye. "And for that inexplicable decision I have not been able to forgive myself. From the bottom of my heart I beg for your forgiveness. I know I betrayed you."

Brod nodded, closed his eyes as if understanding. But he did not say he forgave me.

"So you died and didn't die."

"Yes. Exactly. I died and didn't die. I died because I never wrote again. Never wanted to. Never, never, never ever had an urge to. Once, I had a passing fancy of writing a memoir that I would call *Davka K.* But I never got beyond the title. The name of the book, with its delightful rhyme, was so brilliant no text could surpass it. So I stopped while I was ahead. True, I never interfered with you publishing my works. And each time one book came out I had the feeling that I had just written it. But then again, you thought, and so did everyone else, that I was dead. And I did not press my parents or sisters to stop you."

"A staged death," Brod said in bewonderment.

"Without Klopstock it would not have been possible. You see this Van Dyke beard? Same one I grew then. A beard, a slight stoop, a limp for a while at the funeral, a French beret and a walking stick—those were the props. The plan was, as discussed with Klopstock, that I would be a deaf, mute cousin. I would be reborn as Ignatz K and work in my father's warehouse. But I rejected that idea. Suppose I slipped up. Suppose I hurt myself and yelled, 'Ouch!' Divesting myself of being K was bad enough. But not being able to talk? An impossible task.

"And besides Klopstock, Nora lifted my spirits. Why did I say Nora? Nora is from *A Doll's House*. Of course, I mean Dora. My love. Do you know what a medicine love can be? And what a fateful virus scorn, hate, unlove, neglect can be? Only now, in the middle of the twentieth century, are scientists, doctors, oncologists finally conceding the power of the invisible atoms in love and hope, optimism and faith."

"Do you have family?" Brod asked very gingerly. "Children?"

"I do."

And a happy beam of light spread across Brod's countenance as I told him about my children.

I looked at my friend. Who would believe that Brod and K would be embracing in Tel Aviv, renewing their decades-old friendship? Max Brod: my genius, my savior. It was Brod's devotion that made K immortal. It was he who brought me worldwide fame. In 1950, when I left him, despite his remarks that he did not believe me, I sensed a modicum of doubt, even regret for his incredulity. Perhaps that is why he asked me to visit him again next time I came to Israel. Perhaps he realized that no impostor would want to play a trick like that on an innocent, decent man—or seek to impersonate his long-dead best friend.

I did not write to Brod between 1950 and 1962, although I later regretted this too. But we did correspond after my second visit, when we parted like brothers. All the love that had flowed between us during our youth was expressed in that parting embrace and exchange of kisses. We loved each other like David and Jonathan. Yet I never thought of moving from Prague and living in Tel Aviv next to Max, even though I was a Zionist, an early supporter of Zionism.

Like a true Zionist, I preferred my own homeland.

NOTE: While the June 1924 entry tells us that Dr. Klopstock asked, rather, obliged K not to reveal his secret to anyone outside the immediate family, in the above entry K apologizes to Brod for betraying him. He doesn't tell his friend that his silence was one of the conditions that Dr. Klopstock had imposed as the price of his cooperation. Given this, Brod could have assumed that it was K's choice to exclude Brod from his plan. (K.L.)

July 3, 1963

Eightieth Anniversary K Symposium

To celebrate my eightieth birthday, I attended a K symposium held in Prague to which scholars from all over the world came. In honor of the symposium, the communist authorities removed travel restrictions. People breathed easier for a few days. I would attend these conferences once in a while for my own amusement. Sometimes I would register with a shadow anagram of my name, like Malma or Tarta. Once I signed in as Gregor Samsa. The receptionist smiled at my little joke but said nothing, perhaps because she had nothing to say. But for my eightieth birthday, I registered as K. No first name, just K.

NOTE: K says nothing about the papers presented. Perhaps they did not impress him. See March 1965 entry. (K.L.)

SEPTEMBER 1964

RESEMBLANCE

After K's death forty years ago, people occasionally gazed at me and said how much I resembled K. I'd smile and say, The men in our family have a tendency to resemble one another. Of course, no one said this to me immediately at K's death because they were discreet and thought it might upset me, even though I was a distant cousin...* But of course later on, when my hair turned grey, then white, as did my Van Dyke beard, the longer the time passed from 1924, the less people mentioned any resemblance between me, Philippe Klein, and K.

---

* Rest of line illegible.

MARCH 1965

BEING K

I ask myself sometimes: Do I miss being K? The answer I give is No. For I am still K and will be. I had the pleasure of reading my obituaries, which few experience. We all would like to do this; it's a natural, universal phenomenon, something like the dream we all have of falling. Having a split personality was rather amusing. Divorcing myself from myself and being an observer. Here and not here. There and not there. The K conferences are the most amusing. Occasionally, I even make an abrasive, challenging, or absurd comment from the floor. They know me as a nudnick, but a knowledgeable nudnick. I chuckle at the stupidities I hear and those I read in the *International K Newsletter*, where people pontificate with absolute authority and even are professors of K studies. But they haven't the slightest idea of the Jewish, Hebrew, or Biblical content or allusions in my writing. They substitute guesswork, gall, arrogance, and bluff for true understanding. Main thing is that they have PhDs, are called professor, and attend conferences.

Do I miss writing? Publishing? I was always of two minds on this. And that is no contradiction, no post-mortem,* forgive the pun, change of heart. Even Max will aver that early on I refused to show

* K writes this word in Latin in his Czech text. (K.L.)

what I had written. It took lots of cajoling and pleading just to get me to show him a manuscript. When I did show it to Max, it was done with such trepidation, with such fear of inadequacy, that it put my stomach in knots and gave me a splitting headache. And I mean splitting. It was as if I was cleaved in two. Like the feeling a pane of glass must have in the spot where it cracks. But then, when Brod praised my piece, I didn't mind reading it aloud to my coterie of friends.

I was never absolutely driven. Some people are driven to create. I wasn't. And when I did write it was not necessarily to be published. And I didn't spend the little free time I had at the writing desk.

On occasion, I was proud of my work, delighted with it. But most of the time I would be in bad humour, a pessimist about my abilities. Then I would think of creation as one of God's mistakes, saying that the day God made man was one of His bad days. But now, at my age, despite the Holocaust, despite the German beasts—God, I can't believe I wrote in German; I'm considered a *German* writer and have a reputation of being a great stylist in that accursed tongue; I should have written in Czech—despite all this I have become less cynical, more hopeful. My illness brought me to the realm where nightmare becomes real, and yet I survived and kept on surviving. My return home from the bourne from which no traveler returns was transformative.* Before my rebirth I always had difficulty falling asleep. Ever since then I sleep like a baby. And noise doesn't bother me so much anymore.

* Written in English. (K.L.)

February 1976

Reading

I do lots of reading. *The International Herald Tribune* in the library, and in my house a couple of Czech newspapers, a Hebrew vocalized weekly from Tel Aviv, a Yiddish paper published in Paris and the *Prager Tagblatt*. My bookshelves are full of my books, translated into various languages, and some large dictionaries: French, Italian, Hebrew, English, Yiddish, German, and Czech.

My books have been translated into more than thirty languages but I am most proud of Melech Ravitch's translation into Yiddish of my novel, *The Trial*.

NOTE: The reader will observe that there is a great hiatus between March 1965 and February 1976, and then a leap to July 1983. It is possible that under the stress of Czech communism K did not want to record any entries. There are just a few scattered during those years, but we did not think they were significant enough to include them in this collection. (K.L.)

July 3, 1983

Centennial

I vowed that if I reached this date I would make nothing special of it. But as the date grew closer and closer I marveled at my blessed life and gave humble thanks for it. Today, my little family celebrated with me.

Perhaps I am too old for the following anecdote, but on second thought no one is too old for anything.

People always thought only books interested me. Everyone knows by now how much more multifaceted I am/was. Once a rabbi came up to me after services on the Sabbath between Rosh Hashana and Yom Kippur with the latest news. He said, Do you realize that when the Messiah comes there will be no need for desire?

I think I was eighty when he told me this.

No desire? I said, astonished, and added, I thought the Messiah is supposed to bring heaven down to earth, not hell.

That's right, he said, paying no heed to my blasphemous remark. He sounded positively delighted with his glad tidings.

No sex? I said.

No sex, he exalted, bubbling with joy, as if the Messiah had already come.

Do me a favor, I said.

Yes, of course, Mr. Klein, anything.

Next time you speak to God, ask him to keep the Messiah bound a bit longer. He has waited a long time to be unbound. Let him wait a little longer.

Do I still feel that way, on my hundredth birthday? I can sense a little devilish smirk on my lips.

Yes, up till last year.

July 1985

Dark Energy

I'm just a speck in the universe. Consider mysteries like dark energy, phantom energy, anti-gravity. These are forces, astrophysicists declare, that are defying the orderly, predictable cosmos and are turning the study of physics upside down. Scientists cannot understand it, but telescopes and calculations are confirming the mysteries. These forces may reverse creation and doom the cosmos in billions of years. The universe may explode or implode. Put that mystery, put dark energy or anti-gravity in the same basket as the mystery of K, and one can conclude how believable, real, not weird at all, is the so-called mystery of the death and life of K.

September 1989

Love of Learning

Max and I, Felix and I, our entire circle, we had an aesthetic. We would read to each other passages from books we liked and analyze them. What can I compare it to? The closest I can come to explaining love of learning is the love of woman. It was exciting, stimulating, satisfying—and it made us yearn for more. We looked forward to reading and discussing like a workman looks forward to a day of rest, like a Jew yearns for the Messiah. Our universities were saturated with people who loved books, ideas, not like students at American universities today, which are a parody of learning, places where great books are no longer important. And how limited are some of the professors who teach there. I read about a big scandal reported in the *International Herald Tribune*: about a professor in Sydney, Australia, with the improbable name Kaspar Kugel, who specialized in the history of art at Outback College. His wife wrote all his books because he couldn't put two sentences together without using adhesive tape or glue. And when his school created an Institute for Judaic Studies, this intellectual midget was invited to teach a course called Judaism in Art. Their reasoning: since Kugel was a Jew, he had to know about Jewish art. He didn't know Hebrew, so he couldn't discuss Biblical themes; he didn't know Yiddish or Yiddish folklore, so Chagall and other East European Jewish artists were a mystery to him. Since he didn't know Judaism, he was the perfect candidate for the job. With no knowledge of the subject he could be perfectly objective. Kugel's wife would have lectured for him but she couldn't ventriloquize.

But our universities here are no better. I recently met a professor of the philosophy of gargling. I am not joking. Here in Prague. He has been on many European television shows and even on our own National Comedy Hour, where he was sandwiched in between a talking dog and the Eskimo Sealskin Quartet. His name is Professor Geldman and he is proud of his two first names, Gyorgy Gilbert, which he proudly uses in the articles he never writes. He is a full professor of gargling at the Medical University. You think gargling is simple? he is quoted as saying. There are different types of gargling, with melodies or without. Research has shown you can gargle up and down the scale. There is silent gargling and melody sans sound. Only Geldman knows the difference. He can gargle in Czech, Slovak, Russian, and several Gypsy dialects. He is working on English, which because of its many sibilant sounds is quite difficult, and French, or silent gargling, which is the most difficult of all.

In order to get a professorship Gargles Geldman had to publish a book, with a small demo record of how to gargle in tune. During his thirty-three years of teaching he could only gargle up one book, but it's the standard in the field: *The Philosophy of Gargling.* He is now working on a related topic: *The History of Hiccups.*

NOTE: This must be a joke for there is no such book and no such professor at the Prague Medical University. With a twinkle in his eye, K refuses to comment. It is no doubt a parody on a stupid teacher he once met. (K.L.)

November 1990

My Likeness

When the Soviets and their Czech communist henchmen had the country in their iron grip, reading and selling my works was forbidden.

Today, my likeness, with my blue, brooding eyes and intent stare, appears on mass-produced T-shirts sold by street vendors and tourist shops in Prague, especially during the summer in Old Town Square. I see young men and women wearing them everywhere, almost as if my face has become a national banner.

And how I wish I could show my parents and my sisters the quaint Café K. And my face on coffee mugs. Brod too would have smiled.

December 1991

A Dream of Old Age

I once dreamt that a young angel asked me if I have any problems with old age. A talkative little angel was he. He hadn't yet learned reticence. Seeing me hesitate to answer quickly, he jumped in with:

It's probably digestion. Or insomnia. All old people have that. You probably can't fall asleep for hours. True, I said, that had been a problem of mine during my twenties. Then surely it must be the prostate, said the angel. You have to get up three or four times a night to pee, excuse me, I mean urinate, and then you have to wait for what seems like minutes for the flow to begin.

I shook my head.

Maybe it's cravings you have, the young angel continued. For sweets. Old men like chocolate.

I nodded. I'm famous for my chocomania. I love especially the European liquor-filled chocolates which I skillfully penetrate ever so slightly with an incisor and then slowly suck out the liquor and then crunch the chocolate and the sugar lace that still has the essence of the brandy, the cherry kirsch or the cognac.

But you can't enjoy those, alas, said the young angel, because you have diabetes.

Dead wrong.

Do you have *any* problems with old age?

Yes. Sometimes when I put on my trousers I put my left leg into the right trouser leg.

Then you pull it out?

Pull what out?

Your leg.

Which is where?

In the wrong trouser leg, the angel said, exasperated.

No, I said.

No?

No, I said.

You stay that way?

No.

But it has to be one or the other. Either in or out.

No. I just turn around.

Although it was just a dream, I should have laughed but I didn't. I kept a straight face. Not a hair moved on my white mustache; no wind of movement disturbed the hairs of my Van Dyke. If "Metamorphosis" was funny, *a fortiori* that slipping the left leg into the right trouser leg and turning around was hilarious. That was the punch line to the absurdity. But I didn't even smile.

Then I added: And sometimes I turn the pants around.

But angels do not weep. And they cannot laugh.

April 1992

Einstein

No one knows about this picture. You will not find it in the countless albums on Prague, K in Prague, K here, K there. But in one of my albums is a precious photograph taken many, many years ago where Einstein and I stand next to each other. I with serious mien, in jacket, high collar, shirt and tie, unsmiling, as in all my photos, as in all photos of Europeans at the time. And Albert, in sweater, mustache as usual, a wise Mona Lisa smile hovering in his eyes,

I can hear someone saying, I didn't know there was a picture of you and Einstein. I didn't know you met him.

I could say, There's a lot you don't know. But the words hang there, unsaid, unread, a white shade drawn over them. All one has to do is pull up the shade or part the curtains if the shade isn't there. Does this make sense? No? Good. I didn't want it to.

Before I left, I told Einstein: I admire you for your knowledge of the universe. Then he said something I'll never forget: And I admire you even more for your use of imagination. For imagination, Einstein said, is more important than knowledge. With it you can travel even farther than the most distant star. I can calculate the speed of the light from the stars, said Albert, but you, K, you calculate the stars themselves. I can observe the laws of gravity, but your imagination bends gravity and creates a rainbow out of light.

October 1993

Another K

Did you ever hear of Danny K? my young American friend asked.

Of course. I got to know his films after the war. I loved every one of them. Did you know he had a serious side?

No.

Danny K also starred in a film, *Me and the Colonel*, based on my friend Franz Werfel's *Jacobowsky and the Colonel*. When I saw that Danny K could be both funny and serious, I immediately thought he would be perfect if they ever made a film of "Metamorphosis." Not the dreary sadness of *The Trial*, although that has its comic moments too, but a true comedy—why are you sitting there with an open mouth all of a sudden, my boy?

My young friend jumped up. You won't believe this, he said. This is incredible! Danny and you, the two K's, were my two heroes. I just met him at a dinner in New York a couple of months ago. I asked him if he read K and Danny said yes. When I asked him his favorite K work, he said, "The Metamorphosis." Moreover, Danny said he once proposed a film of the story to his studio, starring him, in a comedy.

How brilliant, I replied. With Danny K. A comedy. Just as it should be.

But the studio turned him down, my American friend continued. And then, just as I was making preparations for my Prague trip, poor Danny K died.

I am so sorry to hear this. What a wonderful actor and wonderful man.

I would have wanted to see him in that film. But it didn't happen.

Lots of things we want in this world do not happen, I said.

I was supposed to make a documentary of him, but that didn't happen either.

We sat in silence for a while.

Then the young American asked me, Have you written anything over the years?

Aha! Oho! So that's it! I said with a rather sarcastic edge to my voice. So it's manuscripts you want. The discovery of the century. The literary find of the millennium. A new work by K.

But my young friend shook his head and said softly, No, it's just curiosity. I have no intention of seeking gain from your manuscripts or from what you've written that hasn't been published.

He said this so gently and so sincerely I immediately regretted my sarcasm. He does not look like the sort that would seek illicit gain from knowing who I was.

To brighten the mood in the room I told my American friend, Did you know that Thomas Mann called me a "religious humorist"?

Yes, he replied. In his "Homage," his introduction to the English translation of *The Castle*.

I said I don't agree with Mann's adjective, although the search for God is indeed in my works. But with his noun, "humorist," I heartily concur.

The young American nodded. He said, I remember that hilarious scene at the beginning of *The Castle* with Frieda at the bar. And later, when K throws out his two assistants, they pop in through the window. Just like something out of the Marx Brothers. I can just see Harpo and Chico doing that. Of course, they came later.

I know, I said. But you have to remember: I am the Marx Brothers. All three...rather, to be accurate, all five of them.

We both smiled. Then I added: Thomas Mann, by the way, is one of the few who noted that I am basically a humorist, which most people are blind to. Yes, I know, except you. He also quotes Brod that when I read from *The Trial*, Brod and Werfel and all the others laughed till they cried, as I did too.

NOTE: With the foregoing entry we come to the end of this volume of K's Journals. The following pages are *not* from K's writings. They are by K's young American friend, the documentary filmmaker, and were forgotten in K's room. K very likely slipped them into his journal book inadvertently and they surfaced just recently. They shed light on K and are used here with the permission of both K and the author. (K.L.)

(Please remember, the first person "I" here is not K, but the American documentary filmmaker speaking.)

I couldn't wait to get back to see Eva. The other day she had wanted to tell me something but was called to the Jewish Old Age Home and she said she'd tell me next time. Now we began chatting in our usually amiable manner. Mr. Klein was out walking, she said. Again she said she wanted to tell me something.

Eva put her hand on mine. The five fingers of her right hand crisscrossed my five fingers. I couldn't help comparing the touch of hands. Just the other day K had held my face. Now another member of his household, his landlady, Eva, was holding my fingers. The touch felt the same; soft, warm, loving. But maybe that's the link, expressed in touch, palpable, non-metaphysical, of the instant contact Jews have with one another.

"What I wanted to tell you..."

My ears, my hearing, all my auditory faculties went out to the quiet street, to the entrance to the house, to the little garden in front, waiting for footfalls, a bell to ring, key in lock, a door slamming that would interrupt and perhaps postpone again what Eva Langbrot wanted to tell me. But no, there was silence. Total stillness.

The door was open, I mean metaphorically, for her to continue.

"You see, it's like this..."

And she smiled.

So did I. Still, I silently urged her to speed up her revelation.

Eva's look seemed to say, You're clever enough to know what's coming.

But no, I didn't. I may have been clever enough, but I did not know what was coming. I was curious, in suspense, yes, ever since last time, when she started telling me but was called away. I could have phoned her and I suppose she would have told me. Then again, maybe not. But I wanted to hear it from her in person.

"Only people within our little family know this. No one else."

And Eva smiled again.

I smiled too.

Eva held my hand, as if by touch her thoughts would osmose into mine and I would know what she was going to say before she said it.

That Mr. Klein, I imagined her telling me, although he likes to claim he's nearly 111 years old, is really 82 and her slightly older brother, and not a boarder at all in the house but a member of the family who has an idée fixe, quite a harmless one, that he is K, a fact that he rarely reveals and only to members of the family or very dear friends, which I am, given my close relationship to him, and thank God Mr. Klein doesn't do this publicly like other madmen in Prague, of whom there is no shortage, like those who think they are K's son, or the Good Soldier Schweik, or Tomáš Masaryk, or Antonín Dvořák, making fools of themselves and embarrassing their families to their eternal shame, but oh no, not Mr. Klein, he keeps his idée fixe to himself, thank God.

And then she said, "Ah, here he is. Here comes Mr. Klein." He entered, nodded to each of us.

"Good morning, Papa," Eva said. And she smiled at me. "Did you have a pleasant walk, Papa?" She kissed him on the cheek.

"Wonderful. As usual.... And how are you, my boy?"

"Quite well. Astounded. As I usually am in this house."

And then I said something totally redundant. Still, I had to say it. "What did you want to tell me, Eva?"

But she only said, "Now you know," and again she clasped her hands, the hands that played the piano so magically, over mine.

ABOUT THE TRANSLATOR OF THE JOURNALS OF K

The English version of *Journals of K*, translated from the Czech, is Katya Langbrot's first book. She lives in Prague with her husband, a documentary filmmaker, and their son Jiri-Diamant, a grandson of K on his father's side and, on his mother's side, a great-great-grandson of the famous writer. The journals, unknown for decades and hidden by the writer, were presented to Katya as a wedding gift by her great-grandfather, who, after the ceremony in the Altneushul, walked over to the Holy Ark and, from a secret panel, removed the notebooks. Katya is now working on Volume Two.

The English version of *Journals*
is dedicated
to
the memory of
my grand-uncle
Jiri Krupka-Weisz
and
my mother-in-law
Dora Diamant

ABOUT CURT LEVIANT

Curt Leviant is author of nine critically acclaimed works of fiction. He has won the Edward Lewis Wallant Award and writing fellowships from the National Endowment for the Arts, the Rockefeller Foundation, the Jerusalem Foundation, the Emily Harvey Foundation in Venice, and the New Jersey Arts Council. His work has been included in *Best American Short Stories, Prize Stories: The O. Henry Awards,* and other anthologies, and praised by Nobel laureates Saul Bellow and Elie Wiesel.

Leviant's novels have been translated into French, Italian, Spanish, Greek, Romanian, and other languages, and some of these works in translation have become international bestsellers. *Kafka's Son* was published in French in 2009 to considerable acclaim.